CHRONICLES OF A CURSED GODDESS
VOLUME I

SILLA'S AWAKENING

J.M. Durham

SILLA'S AWAKENING

Addison & Highsmith

Addison & Highsmith Publishers

Las Vegas ◊ Chicago ◊ Palm Beach

Published in the United States of America by

Histria Books
7181 N. Hualapai Way, Ste. 130-86
Las Vegas, NV 89166 USA
HistriaBooks.com

Addison & Highsmith is an imprint of Histria Books dedicated to outstanding works of fiction. Titles published under the imprints of Histria Books are distributed worldwide.

Library of Congress Control Number: 2024931034

ISBN 978-1-59211-433-7 (softbound)
ISBN 978-1-59211-446-7 (eBook)

I

"Okay, we are ready for the soul-binding to commence," said Dr. Octavius Gladen.

Dr. Gladen was a man of forty-seven years and the father of Silla Gladen. Octavius was of average height, and slim. He had traveled and worked nonstop for the last twenty years. There was a clear haggardness that always showed on his face. He had short, graying hair and brown eyes.

"Father, what is the actual process for this binding to happen?" asked Silla inquisitively, but also in a smaller than usual tone.

"Not to worry, honey. You and Omega will not feel any pain, and the entire process will be over almost instantaneously!" exclaimed Dr. Gladen with a gentle smile.

Dr. Gladen loved magic, which was all but forgotten in much of the land of Arrdus.

Of all the kingdoms in Arrdus, small or big, only Irkdale, far to the northeast, didn't treat magic as some unspeakable taboo. Some five hundred years ago, magic, once used freely by all, was lost to almost everyone, although few today knew why.

Dr. Gladen studied magic in Irkdale for much of his life, spending more time there than even his home in the Kingdom of Rahm.

"There is something significant that I must implore before starting this binding," said Dr. Gladen, no longer smiling.

"After I finish this binding curse magic... I will die."

Before they could interrupt, he continued his explanation. "For two souls to be bound for all eternity, another soul must be willingly sacrificed and lost for all eternity. I cannot ask anyone else to sacrifice their everlasting soul."

Silla had a knack for remaining level-headed, but her anxiety was nothing to be ashamed of in such an unusual situation. For those who didn't know her, Silla could come off as spoiled and demanding, but she was also wholesome and sincere. She had a sharp nose, long brown hair, and distinct, bright green eyes.

"Silla, after this business is finished, I need you and Omega to go to my study where you will find a rather peculiar chest. I will not detail what is inside but suffice it to say that questions will be both answered and created. Both you and Omega will become one soul. With enough practice, or in times of emotional stress or bliss, you will be able to not only understand one another's thoughts but also see what the other sees and experience all of each other's senses."

Omega wondered how the doctor knew these fantastical truths. Octavius spoke as one with excellent tacit knowledge of a subject.

"Dr. Gladen," spoke Omega… a man of unknown age, but in his late twenties, one would assume, in his usual soft voice, "if you die after binding us, what are we supposed to do next?"

"Ah… my dear boy. You have experienced so much darkness, but I promise you that there is light out there. Hopefully, after today, you can begin to see it," explained Dr. Gladen, sincerely.

Omega and Silla looked at each other, nodded, and let the doctor continue leaving his final instructions.

"After I die, all of the information that you will need to begin the first phase of your world-traversing adventure can be found in the chest I mentioned earlier. As for my body …"

The sudden realization of impending death must have hit him because he grew silent for what seemed an eternity, when, in fact, it was only mere seconds.

"Sorry… as for my body, please dispose of it in a way that only Omega is capable of. Keeping my death secret for as long as possible will only aid your struggles."

Omega felt there was much that the doc was not relaying as his words were heavy with underlined meaning.

Dr. Gladen, not wanting to waste any more time and readily feeling his imminent demise, decided it was time to end his life.

"Please do not worry, Father. Omega and I will live on and do our utmost to fulfill the stakes of whatever is in that chest."

"I cannot go into detail now, Silla, but you will soon be capable of changing everything. I hope that the two of you can remain aligned in all of your choices... even when you discover the truth." Octavius's eyes froze on Omega, giving him a small smile, eyes full of deep regret.

Curse magic was mainly performed via incantation and blood. Depending on the curse, sometimes an entire soul was needed. Omega and Silla were now laying on a long wooden table, head-to-head, in a dimly candlelit room with no windows and only one door. As magic of any kind was taboo in Arrdus, there was no need to take chances of any passerby stumbling upon a glimpse.

"Now it is time to draw the blood of both parties," said Octavius. "I must form a circle with Omega's blood on Silla's body and finish it on Omega's body with Silla's blood. I am sorry, Silla, but please put out your hand."

Grabbing Silla's hand, Octavius used his knife to cut her palm and collected enough blood to draw a half-circle. This line had to go all the way under the table, as the connection could not be broken.

After receiving Silla's blood and wrapping up her hand, Dr. Gladen switched to Omega.

"I'll have to use your forearm, Omega. Even as a magic expert... what you can do astonishes even me. I will miss not being able to see it in action."

After obtaining enough blood from Omega and bandaging his forearm, the magic-loving doctor began to draw the circle with Omega's blood on Silla's forehead. The blood traveled all the way down her body until it met the table, cascading down her foot.

After getting halfway under the table, it was time for the blood to change over to Silla's. The same process went up and around the table, and up Omega's body until the blood ended at Omega's forehead.

There was now only a little spot missing to complete the circle, a spot about the size of a grown man's palm.

"Okay, it is time for the *soul* part of the curse, which is where my blood comes into play."

Cutting his hand, he made a line of blood that would connect and finish the circle.

"Silla, Omega… after I place my hand, finishing the connection, my soul will be extinguished, and your two souls will be forever connected. I wish both of you the best of luck, and remember, no matter what happens and what you discover, please endure it for the greater good of the world."

"Is the incantation complicated and long, Father?"

"Actually, that is the easiest part," boasted the doctor.

"Goodbye, my daughter. Omega, make sure no matter what happens in the future, you must always protect Silla."

In a loud, clear, booming voice, Doctor Octavius Gladen spoke the final word of his life: "BIND!" as he slapped down his palm, completing the circle. Much like he had told them earlier, instantly after saying the incantation and completing the connection, Dr. Gladen dropped to the ground with lifeless, colorless, soulless eyes.

At that exact moment, a man somewhere far away opened his eyes. In a cacophony of laughter, he exclaimed, "Octavius, you have made your choice and left this world! You have done well to block me out for the past year."

At that same time, another man was entering. The first man said, "Now is the time to return to Braske and find those we are looking for."

"I understand, Father. I will take my leave," said the tall man wearing a confident smile.

Now back in the room in Rahm.

"Did you hear that, Omega? I could swear that I heard some distant, disparaging laughter and garbled speech."

Meanwhile, Omega was looking around in disbelief. "It can't be …"

Silla couldn't make heads or tails of what she thought she heard and then noticed her father.

"It must have worked," said Silla as she got up from the table and looked at her father on the ground, a single tear rolling solemnly.

"Even though I did not spend as much time with him as a normal daughter spends with her father, I will miss his never-ending thirst for knowledge and his ability to make me smile."

"So, I guess I should do what he asked of me, with his body," stated Omega in his soft voice.

Omega took off one of the two gloves he was wearing, revealing a very normal-looking right hand. What his hands were capable of, however, was anything but ordinary. Omega was one of the few people on the continent of Arrdus, outside the Irkdale Kingdom and the Church of Seven, that possessed magic. Omega was tall and strong, and he had hazel eyes and a powerful nose. He had black, unkempt hair that went to his shoulders.

"Are you ready to say goodbye?"

Silla smiled. "No need. Father lived his life doing what he loved and died doing what he loved, so there is little need for sadness and farewells."

Omega, unsure if she truly meant those feelings, reached out and touched Octavian on the arm, causing his entire body to vanish into nothingness.

"I have to say, no matter how many times I see that, it's still foreign and frightening."

"For me, as well."

"I guess it is time for us to go take a look at the contents of that chest and start planning our departure from the safe confines of Rahm Kingdom," stated Silla in a somewhat excited voice.

Omega could tell that she was Dr. Gladen's daughter, as they both had that knack for saying what is on their mind without being able to hide or mask their inner emotions.

II

"The chest should be easy to spot, right?" questioned Omega.

"Yes, it should be; if I know my father, it is going to be an auspicious chest that doesn't belong with its surroundings."

Upon entering the study, which was just a couple of doors down the hall from the soul-binding room, Silla and Omega almost immediately noticed the chest they were looking for. The room itself was relatively small, closer to a closet than a full-fledged room, and the overly long chest touched both walls at the back of the room, some six feet across.

"This is it, I have no doubt, and look at the lock, if we can even call it that," explained Silla.

The lock that had Silla perplexed was a piece of an iron bar that was twisted and turned upon itself in a way that seemed impossible for someone of less than godlike strength. She understood why such vital things were left in there, without any guards.

There were not many ways to get in the chest that would not damage the contents, such as dropping from a cliff or trying to blow off the iron.

"I guess it's my turn," said Omega as he was approaching the iron bar.

He now took off his left glove. With both hands bared, he grabbed each end of the pretzel-like iron bar, and it disappeared.

"Now, let's peruse the contents of this oddly shaped chest," stated Silla in a firm voice full of determination and some glee.

After opening the chest, the two noticed an extraordinary crown. It looked like it might be made of pure ruby, with gold somehow woven through it, and it gave off a tremendous aura, radiating with energy.

They could tell that this crown was both prestigious and ancient. After taking the crown and putting it to the side, Omega and Silla noticed nothing but documents in there.

There were scrolls, parchment, tiny notes, three-foot-long sheets of lambskin, and many other types of materials. Many of them were in different languages and seemingly from different eras in history. They could tell that the doctor had been searching for and collecting these essential histories for most of his life.

Directly underneath the crown was a piece of ordinary-looking paper that said "Silla" on it, so they first took that one.

Silla and Omega, please read this document, commit it to memory, and then destroy it. The rest of the documents, most of which you will be unable to read as of yet, you can leave, as many of them were little more than my musings. In the future, Silla, you will be able to read all of these, and you might find some intriguing notes on many different subjects and lore. Silla, I will now tell you your birthright, and I will tell you about your mother. You don't know this, but you have magic in you that the world has not seen in five hundred years. After you were born and showed the first signs of your magic as a baby, your mother and I decided that it was best to seal that magic. At the time, we could not help you harness it or protect you from those who would want to exploit it. I know that you have had questions about what happened to your mother and why you have no memories of her. I never dared to sit down with you and have that talk, and you also know that I was not around a lot for much of your youth... another regret, but I digress. Your mother was a member of a secret and ancient group known as the Velantosse.

These Velantosse have been the protectors of the girl born with the power of creation for some fifteen thousand years. To seal your magic, both your mother and I had to put a sealing curse on you, which, as you know by now, curses almost always cost some-thing severe as payment. Your mother gave up her life to protect yours, as you are destined to be a Goddess of Creation. Many examples in history show when a Goddess comes into the world, there is always war, betrayal, and death from those that want the power for themselves and their own ends. There are some fascinating stories from your predecessors that you will likely come across in your journey. If you are wondering, yes, the curse is still in effect, but it will break exactly one year from when I die, as that was another detail of the incantation. I believe that it will weaken gradually throughout the year, but having never performed such a seal, it is only my guess. As far as what you will need to do moving forward, your own destiny will play out as it will, but what you need from this chest is the Goddess Crown, as it was named by the original Crea-tionist, Glyndyl Espacius, some fifteen thousand years ago. The crown is part of a set of armaments, as you like. Although the exact location and even descriptions of the other pieces are kept secret, each Velantosse charged with a piece's protection will always exist. Your mother was charged with protecting the crown as a Guardian, so it is now yours. I know that there is a separate piece in each of the six main kingdoms of Arrdus. You will have to obtain five remaining pieces before the one year is up, and your powers altogether show themselves to the world.

As you progress in your travels, you will undoubtedly learn more about the Goddess armament, the Velantosse, the evil that lies in wait for the next iteration of the Creationist, and yourself. So, for the last part of my last words to you, I would suggest going to Culver first, as it is the closest kingdom to Rahm. I have a friend there, Rose, who you know, and she will surely help you and Omega in your travels. She said that she spends much of her time at the "New Attic," an inn at the capital center. She has helped me study the Velantosse and the past Creationists and will prove a valuable ally. Also, make sure to keep the crown safe and hidden, and I suggest not wearing it until you have them all, but if curiosity cannot be squelched, make sure Omega is near you.

Each piece has been infused with the blood and soul of every successor in the line, and you surely noticed the power emanating from the crown. There are those out there that may have ways of locating the armament once worn. Saying he has a connection to them is fitting. These shadows, however, have far more sinister plans than I could discover. The Sacred Seven worshipers will likely give you a hard time because of what you will become, so try to avoid them. There are more of them than you realize, and they are all overzealous when given an opportunity. You must be especially careful of Piatous. His magic is no less impressive or rare than that of Omega.

You are probably inundated with questions, but the most pressing is how to find the other pieces and who to ask. For this, I can only say that you will have to be creative and inquisitive, which, luckily, you take after your father in those two qualities. One thing that should help you is knowing your mother's pre-marriage name, which was Iris Darcius. Other Velantosse likely know this name, which might aid you in your quest. There are other essential facts, but I cannot risk putting them in this letter. You will learn why in the future. Even now, it takes all of my concentration to block him out. Goodbye, Silla. No matter what happens and what you find in your journey, remember that your mother and I always loved you more than life itself.

"Well, that was a lot of stuff to take in," said Omega.

Omega looked at Silla. To his surprise, she was re-reading the letter, with a small smile on her face, as if she was getting validation for some thought that she had been having for a very long time.

"You look like you were expecting this to be what was in the chest."

"For some reason, I have always felt like something was inside of me. Something that I could not explain. I dared not speak about it to anyone due to the magic taboo throughout Arrdus, and this gives credence to that lifelong feeling."

As Silla was contemplating her fate, Omega found his focus on one specific area of the doctor's letter.

"Who is the *he* that your father referred to?"

"I also found the context strange... but I haven't the foggiest clue what it means," stated Silla.

Silla was now standing, crown in hand. She reached for her backpack, put the crown inside, and put it on, ready to get on their way.

"Since we have no further need to be in Rahm, we should begin preparing to head to Culver. As far as I remember, the capital is less than one hundred miles southeast of here."

Omega interjected, "Did your father happen to leave any money in the chest? I've seen you use it over the last year. It must be important."

"Getting a couple of horses and supplies for the trip shouldn't cost more than a few silver pieces, but I see nothing in the chest, nor anything that I could even tell the value of," said a slightly dejected Silla.

"Also, aren't we going to destroy that letter?" asked Omega as he reached out his hand.

"No. For now, I will hold onto it, as I think it will do us better if it still exists."

Omega was feeling antsy. "Okay, can we go outside now? I am starting to get anxious, having been inside for so long."

Omega did not like being inside walls for very long and never slept inside, but always somewhere outside near the house.

"Okay," stated Silla. "I know your anxieties well; let's go outside and see if we can find some way to make money. Quicker is preferable as we now have a deadline."

After staring at the crown only a moment, but lost in deep thought, Silla led Omega outside the Gladen household and into Rahm's castle town.

Rahm was the second smallest kingdom in Arrdus, only larger in total landmass than the Gradon Archipelago. Its capital, however, was one of the most advanced domains with its high, sturdy walls and a reliable economic system. Rahm's current leader was King Marxus IX, who was still young for a king at thirty-nine years. He took over for his father who passed away from sickness the year prior.

Marxus had long black hair and black eyes. Well built and formidable to look at.

Much of Rahm's capital was stone and wood, and it had three different levels, tiers, that scaled upward. The bottom tier was for those of no special status, basic workers, and the impoverished. The second level was where most of the markets and businesses existed and had some housing in each of the four corners. The highest level was reserved for the court members, the royal family, the wealthiest citizens, or those who had given substantial service to the realm.

Although there was a clear hierarchy in the architecture, there were few grumblings from the lowest level. Rahm had a system of jobs and responsibilities for all citizens. Keeping people busy and giving them purpose kept idealistic thoughts like rebellion away. This was what Marxus's father believed. The upper tier was also the home of Rahm's Tower of the Sacred Seven, which referred to the seven gods and goddesses acceptable for worship.

Each of the six powerful kingdoms in Arrdus had a tower, but there were also towers on other continents. A large portion of the world accepted The Sacred Seven's scriptures as fact.

The seven gods and goddesses were the God of War, Melchior: Brave and Strong. The God of Death and Reincarnation, Sulce: Formless and Feared. The God of Harvest and Famine, Juniper: Merciful yet Steadfast. The Goddess of Creation, Hespa: The first and above all others. The Goddess of Love, Marse: Benevolent and a hopeless romantic. The Goddess of Fate, Desitine: Tireless and Unyielding. And the Goddess of Healing and Sickness, Viscidia: Humble and Devout. Although all seven were worshipped at each tower, each kingdom had a patron or matron deity. Rahm's patron deity was Juniper, the God of Harvest and Famine.

"Let's go to the nearest tavern, Old John's, and see if there are any job postings that we could do quickly," said Silla in her usual, slightly bossy tone.

Old John's, a small tavern, was only about 500 feet from Silla's house, so it did not take long for the two to get there. The inn smelled of wine and meat, and it made Omega's nose perk up when they got within the smelling range. Before they could go inside to talk to Old John, Omega noticed a bulletin post on the wall that drove out the scents of meat and ale.

"Look at this," pointed an intrigued Omega, "there is an open call for participants in the arena on the lowest level, and it is today!"

The bulletin post stated that the first thirty people that signed up got to participate in the arena event. The arena was a battle-to-the-death-style stage. Still, it was wholly voluntary, and forced participation was outlawed many years ago by the previous king.

Now those down on their luck, or even those that wanted to prove their valor in combat, had an avenue to participate and make some good money.

"The winner gets a portion of all of the money that is wagered on all the other contestants, and it's free to enter! Let's go right now, and I'll sign up before they hit the maximum number of participants."

Silla wasn't too sure about this idea, as their journey was just beginning, and what would she do if Omega got himself killed, but she knew that once he said he would do something, he would never go back on his word.

The arena was located about a quarter mile east of the southern gate, on the lowest level. There were often people battling, whether it be early or late. Many of the showcases were not to-the-death but more tournament-style, with losers either yielding or being knocked unconscious. It took about an hour to get from the second level where Old John's was to the arena.

Their trip wasn't the most talkative, as Omega seamlessly got into the mood for fighting. Silla didn't want to break his concentration, but she was always interested in shopping at the stalls throughout the market.

The arena was an enclosed, domed structure. It was large and well-built. One could tell by looking that the arena made a fair amount of money. It had raised walls around the fighting area and staggering stands so everyone could see the show. Upon entering the site, the sign-up for that day's contest was to the right of the entrance.

A short lady, with reddish-brown hair matted to the side of her face, was behind the enclosed area and asked Omega's and Silla's business in the arena.

"Are there any spots left open for the winner-take-all-battle?" implored Omega.

"Why yes, there are three spots left to fill before we can start the contest," explained the attendant.

"Would you like to put down your name and enter the contest as a willing participant, knowing fully that although death is not a requirement, it is also not outlawed for this match?"

"Yes, my name is Omega, and I am ready to win some gold." Omega hastily scribbled his name down on the ledger. His penmanship was similar to that of a child.

"Okay, I must ask that you also place a blot of blood next to your signature." After grabbing Omega's arm, him not letting her pull off his glove, she poked him and placed the blood on the list.

Omega and Silla could see many spots of blood that belonged to the other participants.

"The blood is for The Organization. If you are worthy, they will make contact in the future. Please head towards the area over there," explained the attendant, as she pointed towards a forked hall. One side went to the seating area and the other to the participant's staging area. Some tapestries and paintings depicted some of the more loyal, generous patrons, and also that of previous grand champions, but Omega had tunnel vision.

Omega started off towards the right side without saying a word, but he was stopped by Silla.

"Please be careful out there, and even though we do need money, if you find yourself in too much danger, just surrender and leave. We can find another way."

Omega, for all his shortcomings, was always confident.

"I'll win, with ease."

"I'm sure I don't have to tell you this, but you cannot take off your gloves and use your magic. No matter what situation you find yourself in, magic is not acceptable."

Omega was already halfway to the fork before an annoyed Silla even finished speaking.

III

As Omega was making his way to the back, Silla made her way to the wagering counter to place the two silvers she had found in her house on Omega to win. She figured if he was going to do it, she might as well believe in him. Also, as an unknown fighter, his odds would be in her favor.

Omega was now waiting in the staging area for the remaining contestants to sign up, and he could see quite a few warriors in the room.

There was an attendant that spotted Omega. "Hello, my name is Fondus. Which weapon would you like to bring with you into the fight?"

There were long spears, halberds, swords of many different lengths and sizes, nets, tridents, and hammers, both small and enormous.

Omega looked at him. "I will not be taking any weapons into the arena. I will win using only these." He showed Fondus his gloved hands.

Fondus looked at him. *I wonder if he has a death wish, or maybe he's some kind of foreign martial artist champion,* he thought but decided to move onto the next warrior.

Some of the other warriors heard the encounter and were not impressed.

"You will be the first to die out there," said one of the participants, although Omega wasn't listening.

Finally, the last entry came in, after Omega had waited twenty minutes. After the final entrant chose his weapon, they were instructed on the rules. There was one—the last man standing wins. Even though participants could ask for a yield, others were not disqualified if they ignored it.

Now, Omega was walking through the tight tunnel that led to the arena fighting area. There was a palpable level of anticipation of what was about to occur. Any light conversations had stopped, as they all knew that they would be arch-enemies soon—the tunnel smelled of dried blood and sweat. No light from outside showed in that tunnel. Only two torches in their sconces lit the way.

Now in the fighting area, there was an announcer near the center of the fighting pit on a twenty-foot, raised pillar with a megaphone made from what looked to be a carved-out horn from some humongous beast. The man was dressed loudly, wearing a red top hat and a black and sky-blue coat.

"Okay, patrons, thank you for your patience! It is time for the main event, free-fighting, Battle Royale between these thirty brave, valorous souls! Only one warrior will win in the end, and it will be a glorious day!"

The participants spread out before it started. No lots drawn or assigned areas, a complete free-for-all. As the beginning bell rang, Omega looked around him, and the nearest person was about ten feet away, looking right back at him.

Omega began to take off one of his gloves, and right at that time, Silla noticed this and started shouting, "Omega, you can't use that in here! You can't! We are not prepared for the consequences!"

Omega heard her but started walking towards his first enemy, sliding the glove farther down, and right then, Silla shouted louder than ever before, "I FORBID YOU!!"

Just then, Omega felt a sharp pierce in his chest, and it felt like his very blood was on fire. He dropped to his knees, grabbing his chest, and fell face-first, out of consciousness, onto the ground.

At that time, Omega was drifting somewhere between alive and dead, and some of his childhood was playing through his mind…

"We have a new experimental subject," said a researcher, looking at a small child, probably around five years old.

"This is experimental charge number 54, here to be a magic slave. He of course has no showings of magic, but as with the rest of the charges, we will go through the standard procedures of drawing out latent magic potential," said the head researcher.

"I have to say, you have not been here long, but you are quite adept at bringing in new test subjects," said the head researcher, talking to a young man next to him, who brought Omega to the lab.

Now number 54, a young Omega was scared and crying, and right then was grabbed by the neck, picked up, and thrown into a cell, not much bigger than the closet at Dr. Gladen's house.

"This is your new home, and you will one day be our magic slave. No matter what it takes, you will do what we want," said the head researcher.

"He is too young for the pain stage of experiments, so we will make sure to feed him well so he can grow, but until then, we will use fear. Okay, proceed with the first round."

Number 54 was in the corner of his cell. The researchers brought in two rabid dogs, attaching them to the wall with chains that allowed them to cover the entire cell, except for the corner that 54 was in.

The dogs tried with all their might to get to a terrified 54. The dogs were able to get close enough that their snarling spit could splatter 54's face. They did not stop until they died from exhaustion, which took about six hours.

The researchers watched and took notes during the entire process, hopeful that 54's magic would show itself, out of his fear.

The belief of the researchers in Irkdale was that magic was best brought out by necessity, and in their minds, the need that came from fear, pain, wrath, rage, and lost love brought a more robust and powerful chance of magic release.

The experiments usually led to complete emotional destruction, which helped those that developed magic into not rebelling but faithfully serving their roles as magic slaves. What the magic slaves were for was part of a much grander plan.

After many waves of different animals came, some people were captured and put in the cell with 54. They were also chained up and were told that if they could reach and kill this child, now six years old, they would not only be set free but given a large sum of money. All the people that failed to get loose of their chains or failed to cause 54's magic to release were killed in front of him.

Another image was done. These flashbacks were coming and going, incomplete and short, but very traumatic.

Fifty-four was sleeping in his small confinement. It had been a couple of days with no visitors, but then he heard someone calling to him. A nice, soft-spoken lady.

"Hello, child. I am here to help you get out of this horrible place. I broke in to break you and others out… Let's go."

Fifty-four, who was all but mentally broken at that point, looked at the lady with hope, and as he reached out to grab her hand, he noticed a sheen.

At that moment, a flash of heat hit his forehead, for it was the sheen of a blade that slashed him just below his scalp. That specific event had the most lasting effects on what little hope young 54 had for humanity.

After another three years of various creatures, humans, and even animal experiments that the Irkdaleons had made, 54 was finally big enough to move to the pain stage. The fear stage had not produced any tangible results other than the beginning of the destruction of Omega's emotional stability.

Back in the arena, Omega's eyes popped open as he lay where he fell, now having thought about experiences that he had been trying to erase from his mind for years. Omega got up, looked around, then slid the glove firmly back on his hand.

He saw that he had been out of consciousness for what seemed a while, as there were only five remaining warriors other than himself, with many corpses around the arena. He saw some of the contestants that had yielded had headed back to the staging area.

Just then, the announcer noticed Omega get up. "Wow! This contestant, who looked like he dropped dead from fear earlier, may have been playing opossum, which looks to be quite the strategic move!"

At that time, Silla, who had been very afraid after seeing Omega collapse, was relieved that he was up but noticed that he had a different aura about him.

Omega started walking, almost in a trance, towards the nearest contestant. It was a man with a trident and a net.

The man threw the net towards Omega, who jumped backward out of the way. At that time, the trident-man thrust his weapon at Omega's chest, and he turned sideways with the trident catching his shirt, ripping it. As Omega slid past the trident, he grabbed the man's throat.

He then proceeded to smash his head into the man's nose, crumbling the cartilage. The man, screaming in pain, fell over backward. Omega dropped down, sitting on the man's chest. He reached both hands down, ripping out the man's eyes. He was now Omega's first victim of the contest.

Now beside herself with disbelief at what she was seeing, Silla could only think that something was wrong with Omega, almost like he was a different person, but all she could do was watch.

He then went on to rip off the now shredded shirt he was wearing, revealing an upper body that was harder than most but also filled with scars. There were small scars and large ones. There were wounds from burns, blades, whips, staves, and many other instruments. The most extensive went from his left shoulder blade down to his right kidney, about an inch wide all the way down… flayed.

After handling his own opponent, the contestant closest to Omega started coming over. This warrior had a sword and shield combo, which had proven very effective against his previous foes.

Omega, with that same trance-like walk, swaying left and back right, made his way within range of his opponent. The warrior proceeded to swing his sword, barely missing Omega, who slipped around the shield, with almost animal-like quickness.

Omega quickly grabbed the warrior's long hair, yanking it back, revealing the man's neck. He bit down with all his might on the jugular vein, tearing at the man's neck like a wolf.

Blood exploded from the man, completely enveloping Omega; as the man dropped dead, the entire crowd fell silent, looking at this monster in the arena.

Silla could hear the woman close to her whisper, "Sacred Seven, save his soul."

The last contestant, who had previously killed ten others, was now in direct eye contact with Omega, who was about thirty feet away. This man wielded a giant maul.

The man shouted, "I don't know who you are, but I am the great gladiator, Jaxius, winner of countless deathmatches, earning more winnings than anyone in the history of the arena! I am also currently ranked as the fourth-strongest warrior in all of Arrdus."

Omega, completely covered in his previous victim's blood, not saying a word, walked towards Jaxius. Omega's most frightening aspect was his lifeless, empty eyes… Eyes that appeared to have never known hope, love, light, or preciousness. Eyes that had only known despair.

Jaxius, now in range, started to swing his giant maul in a swooping motion. Omega buckled his own knees, dropping underneath the swing, just in time.

Omega then leaped up with all his strength, slamming his head into the jaw of Jaxius, whose teeth shattered from the impact. As Jaxius started to fall backward, dropping his maul, Omega reached out and grabbed his opponent's drooping jaw, propping up Jaxius's faltering body.

At that moment, Silla looked away in anguish. Omega completed his victory by ripping off the entire mandible of Jaxius, who lifelessly fell to the ground.

The Battle Royale was officially over.

"Umm, please proceed to the front counter," said a shaken-up, less boisterous announcer.

Now making her way to the exit of the arena, Silla saw Omega coming from the staging area, heading towards the counter to pick up their winnings. Silla was still somewhat stunned by what she just witnessed, but there were even more intense concerns on her mind.

"Omega, how are you feeling?" asked Silla in an unusually small voice.

Omega turned to meet Silla's eyes with his usual small smile. "I'm fine. I lost my humanity for a moment, is all. After you bellowed, something happened... inside me, and I collapsed. Then all of these memories that I thought I was free of bubbled to the surface ..."

"I think that I just experienced what Father was talking about when he said that we would be able to experience each other's minds. Whatever those thoughts and memories were, I was able to experience them from your point of view. I am so sorry that you had to go through that."

As Silla was reaching her hand to embrace Omega's shoulder, he grabbed her wrist with some force.

"Silla, listen very closely to what I am about to say. You seem to have some ability to control me when you put your mind to it. I think that happened when I was taking my glove off. After being controlled most of my entire life, I would ask that you not do that again."

Silla pulled away from Omega, their eyes locking together.

"I did that for your own good. We are not in a place where magic is allowed or tolerated. Even talking openly about magic is not a good idea in most Arrdus... I did not know that I could control you. I do apologize if that made you feel anxious or small, but I cannot promise that if I need to stop you from bringing ruin to yourself or me, that I won't do it again."

"You did those people a disservice, making them feel terrible pain before they died… I can only assume that disappearing is more peaceful. But I'll leave it at that for now," said Omega, walking away.

Omega and Silla walked out of the arena with not only a new understanding of each other, for better or worse, but also with enough money to get the horses and supplies they would need to get to Culver, and hopefully one step closer to the next piece of Goddess treasure.

For the time being, having put their disagreements and concerns to the side, Omega and Silla made their way to the nearest stable.

"Look there, Omega. This stable should be able to sell us two horses as they appear to have quite a few on hand," explained Silla, who was again focused on the bigger picture.

"Excuse me, can someone help me with purchasing two of these horses? We want to travel to Culver as soon as possible."

A middle-aged man, short and plump, popped around the corner with a big smile. "Yes, ma'am. I would be happy to sell you two of my fine mares. Right now, I can let these two," he pointed to one brown and one black mare, "go for two gold pieces each, and I will throw in the saddles, reigns, and all that is needed for a journey to Culver."

Silla and Omega, neither having any idea what a horse fetches, said, "Okay, that sounds fair to us. How long until they are both saddled up and ready to depart?" asked Silla, noticing that it was getting late in the afternoon.

The stable owner made them aware that the mares would be ready to depart in the morning. Silla and Omega made their way to the nearest inn, where they could stay the night and gather some supplies they might need.

Culver's capital was only about a two-day ride at a moderate pace. The two did not need much to take with them and could worry about supplies for their journey once in Culver.

IV

At a tavern called The Silver's Grace, about ten leagues north of Culver's capital, a woman walked in and headed to the counter. She was in her mid-twenties, with vibrant red hair that usually ran past her butt, except now it was in a tight, drooping bun atop her head. She wore a veil covering most of her face underneath her amazingly blue eyes.

"Hello, Pr—" Being waved at by the woman, the owner of the tavern, Beatrice, stopped, smiling. "Okay, Kita, are you here to work again tonight? You really don't have to do this so often. If your father were to find out, he would be quite upset with me."

"Don't worry about him. I am very good at sneaking away, and I always enjoy my time here. I still need to pay you back for all the free breakfasts throughout the years. Besides, my father has five other children to occupy his mind," said Kita.

"Pish-posh. They were free because I wanted them to be. Still, I do enjoy your company, and the patrons enjoy your exuberance," stated Beatrice, now hugging Kita.

The tavern was in Briaridge, which was very near the Nugle river. The Nugle was the longest river in Arrdus, running from the Irkdale mountain range down to Braske bay, spanning almost 1500 miles.

The Nugle was a river that the citizens of Braske, Rahm, Culver, and Faruqh all traveled regularly, and it stretched diagonally throughout almost the entire continent. Briaridge was an average town by Culver-Kingdom standards, with some five hundred residents calling it home.

Kita grew up in the Culver castle-town to the south of Briaridge. Recently she had been traveling back and forth to the inn, as The Silver's Grace's owner was also her aunt.

"So, I haven't seen you in a couple of months, Kita. How's the world turning outside Briaridge?"

As Kita was serving patrons flagons of mead, smiling her huge smile, even noticeable under the veil, she answered, "Much the same, although my youngest brother, Thomo, got a new pet if you can call it so… It's a large black bear that they captured and put in the yard outside the castle. He can't really play with it, of course, but he does feed it, and he even put some different animals and fruit trees for the bear to find its own food."

"Thomo has always been rather spoiled, but he always seems to have a good head on his shoulders, even if his interests are peculiar."

Patrons were coming and going for the next couple of hours, as it was now nighttime, and the various workers doing various jobs were done for the day.

Now almost closing time, a man that Kita did not want to see but knew would find her as she was usually in the same spot, entered the tavern.

"Hello, Ms. Beatrice. Is she here?" said the tall man, with his slick hair and a bushy mustache. "Ah, hi there, Joe. Yeah, she is in the back, taking out some of the trash. Did my brother send you?"

"Actually, I took the initiative to come get her myself. There are some duties that she must attend to in the afternoon tomorrow. You know, official matters."

At this time, Kita was coming in through the back door and spotted Joe standing next to her aunt. "Damn," was all that Kita had to say, and bid her aunt farewell, taking a box of fresh bread, which was her younger sister, Kapril's, favorite.

As the two made their way toward the wagon that Joe brought, a couple of armed guards were there to accompany them home.

"You know that your father is very lenient with you, letting you come to your aunt's whenever you want, but you should bring me, your personal guard, or at the least tell someone when you are going somewhere. You have responsibilities back in the castle, and you never know what enemies might be hiding and waiting to attack you."

"Enemies in Briaridge?" remarked Kita as she started to laugh, removing her veil, showing possibly the brightest and biggest smile in all Arrdus. A smile that might one day change the world.

It took about twelve hours to get from Briaridge to Culver, at a moderate pace, and Kita was as chatty as ever, even if disappointed in getting caught so quick.

As the carriage pulled into the inner-castle area, a young girl, of fourteen years, with the same blood-red hair as Kita, was sitting near a fountain.

"Hey, sis, you're back. Did you bring me anything?" asked Kita's youngest sibling, Kansel.

Kita jumped down from the carriage, looking anxious at first, showing Kansel that perhaps she forgot to bring anything, which showed immediately on Kansel's face. Just then, Kita smiled brightly and gave her a hug, pulling out from behind her back a large flagon of root beer, Kansel's favorite.

"Aunt's root beer!" exclaimed a now overly excited Kansel, as she grabbed it, removed the top, and proceeded to drink half of it in one gulp.

"Have you seen Kapril this morning? I brought her favorite bread."

As Kansel wiped her mouth and began to answer, she stopped at another's voice.

"Kitannica, I have been waiting for you."

Kita turned to see her father, King Thomascus Deckler, the ruling monarch of Culver Kingdom.

"Please, Father, I have told you I prefer to go by Kita. What could be so important that I got dragged back here not long after getting to The Silver's Grace?"

King Thomascus Deckler was forty-nine years old, and he and his sons all had hair as black as the darkest night and eyes a stunning honey color. He had been ruling Culver for the last nine years, after his uncle, Brian, the previous king, died with no direct heir.

King Thomascus Deckler's own father died not long after Thomascus was born in a skirmish with Rahm. Some distant relatives had their own claims to Brian's throne, unfortunately, but Thomascus was the number one ranked fighter in Arrdus. He dealt with those claims swiftly, and everyone else fell in line.

Due in no small part to the fear and respect that King Thomascus Deckler demanded, Culver operated peacefully.

"Come, Kitannica, we have a few things to discuss before I meet with the officials and ministers."

Kita looked at Kansel and flicked her forehead. "Give Kapril the bread if she comes around before I finish with Father."

Kita followed her father to the inner throne room, which was quite extravagant and wide. Many huge braziers splayed the middle aisle where her elder brother was standing, seemingly also waiting for her to return.

"Hey Thompsel, how's Jennifer and the baby doing?"

Thompsel, who was Kita's only elder sibling, was very tall and stout, more so than his father. He had the same black hair and honey eyes, and he was always kindhearted but could be stern when necessary.

"Hello, Kitannica. My family is in good health. Jennifer wants you to visit when you have time. We are currently here for more important matters, though, so let us get down to business."

The king chimed in, "Right you are, son. Kitannica, there will be some huge changes coming to Arrdus soon. Changes for the better, your brother and I hope, but when that time comes, I will need you and your siblings to all give your best for Culver and for your father."

Kita really had no idea what they were talking about. She had no interest in politics, but as the oldest daughter, she often had unwanted responsibilities. After a couple of hours, she came out from the main hall to the courtyard, still pondering what she had heard, and spotted Kapril eating the bread by one of the fountains.

Kita tapped on her shoulder and quickly slid over to the opposite side. Unfortunately, Kapril was used to this joke and met Kita on that side.

"Boo, that joke is no fun if you don't play along, sis," said Kita, sitting next to her favorite sister and best friend.

They were only one year apart in age and have no memory of not spending their entire lives together, playing, learning, and experiencing Culver life.

"This bread is as good as ever, sis. Auntie sure is good at cooking, but I shouldn't eat all of this and get fat. I don't want to get married yet, but being fat won't help either."

Kita looked at Kapril as she said this and thought that Kapril was the most beautiful woman in the family and probably the whole world.

Kapril was shorter than Kita by a half-head, and she had much shorter hair. However, it was just as red as Kita's, and it was always parted to the left side. Kita thought Kapril had a better figure. Kapril liked wearing accessories such as earrings, necklaces, and bracelets that usually matched her clear-blue, aquamarine eyes.

"You're crazy if you think that every guy in the world wouldn't knock down father's door to ask for your hand in marriage. I just hope that we don't fall in love with the same guy one day, as I don't think I would have much hope of winning."

Kapril was amused by that and wanted to hang out some more with her sister.

"Hey, Kita, how about we go out to the market area and do some shopping? What do you think?" Kapril was less outgoing than Kita, so she usually stayed in the main castle area. She usually studied or helped her mother and siblings, and she envied Kita's free-spirited nature. However, she would never admit that to anyone.

"Okay, that sounds great, but let's buy something for Jennifer while we are out."

Outside the gates, they started to move from place to place. Although it was only for a moment, Kita noticed someone that garnered her attention walk past her. There was a tall, well-built man with strange, possibly bloodstained gloves and a scar across the top of his forehead.

V

"So, the Nugle is about the halfway point from Rahm to Culver," said Silla, pointing at the approaching river. The two of them decided to stop and set up camp for the night, right next to the calm waters.

As the two of them gathered some nearby wood to make a fire, Omega turned to Silla. "What is the plan after we get to Culver? I wonder if there is a sure way to locate the next piece of the armament, or if we will simply be grasping at straws."

"Father said that Rose was waiting for us. You will like Rose, she's probably as smart as my father, and very nice. She used to do all kinds of research with my father, so I am hoping that she is in the know about anything Velantosse-related in Culver."

Omega was relieved to hear that Rose was also a researcher and might have insights.

"This is off-topic, but do you have any ideas as to why doc wanted to bind our souls in the first place? I was fine with doing it because he saved me, named me, gave me hope, and brought me to Rahm. I owed him my life, but why did you agree? You don't really seem the type to do something on a whim, being as calculating as the doc."

"To answer the first question, he never gave a reason why he wanted us bound. Father just told me to trust him and that it was something he felt obligated to do, for both our sakes. As you can guess, this answer did not satisfy me, but he was reluctant to even broach the subject again as if he was trying to hide something. To answer your second question, I would ask you if you remember the first time we met?"

Now it was evening time near the river, with a gentle fire crackling and the smooth sound of the waters calmly going their way.

Omega thought about her question. "Yes, it was about one year ago, after he helped me escape Irkdale, and we made our way down the Nugle all the way to Rahm. When we got to his house, you were there, sleeping in your bed. It seemed like you two had not seen each other in a long time because both of you were very happy to embrace."

"Actually, I think it had been about two years since we last met before that night, but my first thought was, who is this big guy with the stern look and scars all over his arms? You were not the easiest thing to look at, but you seemed quiet enough, and father told me about rescuing you from Irkdale and wanting you to stay with us for the time being. From the time he brought you back until the day he died, I saw him almost every day, so I was also thankful to you, even if you didn't know it." Silla was now lying comfortably next to the fire.

Silla began reminiscing about one night a couple of weeks after Omega moved into the house.

"Father, why does Omega sleep outside every night, and what are those strange cages he has on each hand?"

Dr. Gladen, who was eating a late snack, said, mouth half full, "From what I gather, Omega spent most of his life in a tiny cell, where various experimentations were performed on him. Now that he has his freedom, either he does not trust walls and doors, or he simply can't get enough fresh air; only time will tell. As for those cages, for the moment, they are a necessity. Omega possesses dangerous, unpredictable magic."

Silla became even more interested after hearing that. "What kind of magic needs one's hands to be in cages?"

"Omega has destruction magic. One that I have never seen before and have never come across, even in ancient texts. Omega simply can disintegrate anything that he touches. As of yet, he cannot freely control this power, so anything that touches the inside of his hand, be it his palm or any of his fingers, that something will cease to exist, in a tangible way."

Silla was amazed that something like that existed in this world but was also skeptical.

"Have you seen him use this power firsthand, Father?"

After being silent for a moment, Dr. Gladen continued, "No, I haven't, but he did tell me about it, and I figure he has no reason to lie. Also, I have heard of the experiments that go on in Irkdale, and it is likely that many before Omega also had some form of magic *unlocked* via different treatments."

Later that night, Silla would make a choice that could have shaped many people's lives in a very different way.

As Omega lay sleeping outside the window to one of the house's bedrooms, Silla came around the corner very late at night and looked down at him and the cages on his hands.

"I wonder if you made up the story about your magic to get my father to take you back to Rahm for some unknown reason. How about I just touch that palm of yours and see what happens."

Silla reached down and slid her hand in the cage. It was a cube-shaped wireframe with a wrist attachment in the center. It was just big enough that Omega could not touch the wrist holder or any of the frames. Its original intention was to keep the scientists safe while they prodded Omega.

Just as Silla made contact with Omega's palm, he woke up with a jolt. "Don't!" But it was too late, and the connection was made, but to Omega's extreme surprise, nothing happened to Silla.

Now, her hand in the cage, she was slapping his palm. "Were you making up your magic and lying to my father?"

Omega, now taken aback, said, "Could you take your hand out, so I can stand up, please?"

Dr. Gladen had heard Omega when he shouted and was now outside.

"What's going on out here, so late?" he demanded, looking at the two of them staring at each other, Omega confused, and Silla somewhat angry.

"I just touched his palm while he was sleeping, and nothing happened to me, Father. I did not cease to exist."

Dr. Gladen, himself perplexed, asked Omega to walk to the nearby sunflower and touch it. The doc wanted to see if Omega had learned how to control his powers, even in his sleep.

Omega reached down and touched the flower, and instantly, poof, no more flower. At that moment, Silla shrieked, "I could have died!" She said this with a slight smile that Omega found interesting, almost like the magic was more interesting than her near-death experience.

"As I suspected. Omega does have destruction magic. When you become more comfortable with it, you can name it. I can confidently say you are the first wielder.

Now, this may be the biggest mistake I have ever made, but Silla, would you touch Omega's palm again?"

Omega had waited, and Dr. Gladen had finished removing both cages from Omega's hands carefully.

Without any hesitation, Silla walked up to Omega and put her hand flat into his hand, palm to palm, and there was no reaction from Omega's magic.

An even more excited Dr. Gladen said, "This is beyond imaginable, that you, my daughter, might be the only person in the world that Omega's magic does not affect. In fact, because of what we just witnessed, I have an idea of how I can get rid of those cages. Omega, you will be able to still protect the world from your magic until you can control it, but no more cages."

At this time, Dr. Gladen, without finishing voicing his new idea, ran into the house, leaving Omega and Silla hand to hand.

"It's probably okay to disconnect now, Silla."

At that, Silla, who seemed to be deep in her own thoughts, noticed her hand on his and that her father was nowhere around.

"Where did my father go? I thought I heard him speaking about ridding you of the cages, but my mind was wandering in and out of my current surroundings."

Omega, having removed his hand from Silla's but being careful to have his palms up at all times, replied, "He went inside because he had what appeared to be an epiphany about my cages. Let's go see what he's up to in there. I can smell Irkdale on those things."

Upon entering the main room from the backyard, a couple of hallways led in opposite directions. One went towards the kitchen and the bedrooms. The other, where they could hear Dr. Gladen rummaging and making some loud ruckus, led to the study, the library, and the laboratory.

Dr. Gladen was in the laboratory with some empty vials on the table, and some leather and thread, and some other materials for his creation.

"Ah, I have an idea that will utilize Silla's immunity to your magic, Omega. It will give you something to cover those hands that is much more stylish and far less traumatic than those ghoulish cages that you have been forced to wear."

Dr. Gladen had a large sheet of very dark leather sprawled out on the desk, and he then turned towards Silla. "Could you be a dear and let me draw some blood from you? About four vials should be enough for both."

Silla was beginning to understand her father's idea, so she let her father cut her palm and let the blood flow into a beaker until it was almost full, and then she bandaged up her hand.

While this was happening, Omega had found himself perusing the laboratory contents. It was the first time he had entered this part of the house.

The sheer number of documents was overwhelming. They were on top of shelves and tables and on the floor, glued to some of the walls, and some had foreign diagrams with strange symbols. The laboratory was more prominent than it seemed.

There were shelves, resembling a library, with books. Still, there were also tools on them, jars of various creatures' entrails and brains, and a score of what appeared to be different blood types. None of these had labels or any noticeable cataloging system, and Omega wondered how anyone would know what was in the hundreds of seemingly randomly placed vials and jars.

Dr. Gladen had noticed that Omega had stepped away from him and Silla, enthralled by the wonderment of the lab.

As if he could read Omega's thoughts, he explained, "You probably are wondering why nothing is labeled, and how I stay organized. I have never been a compulsively organized person, but I do have an absolutely absurd memory. You see that vial of dark blue liquid there? That is the blood of an extremely rare creature. I traded information for some of its blood. It was a vamprine," said Dr. Gladen, still pointing at the vial, with a very proud look on his face.

Omega had never heard of a vamprine, but having spent every waking memory in a cage, there were many creatures that Omega had no knowledge of.

"I traded some of my precious translations on an ancient civilization to the vamprine, as he was certain that that group of people was where his original creator was from. He is likely still out in the world, searching for his answers."

Dr. Gladen was clearly happy to reminisce about the vamprine. It was a good experience.

Now, Omega made his way back to the workstation that Dr. Gladen and Silla had been at; they were ready to measure his hands.

"I soaked this leather with Silla's blood, and after letting it dry, if my theory pans out, when you put your hands on here and let me measure, the leather should not disappear."

Omega placed his hands down, and nothing happened. He had begun to understand what was going on. He was finding a rare appearance of a specific emotion; joy.

"Okay, now that we have the measurements, you and Silla should go to the kitchen and get something to eat. I will be done with these within the hour."

After about forty-five minutes, Silla and Omega were eating some soup in the kitchen, Omega with a straw, of course. At the perfect time, Dr. Gladen came in with the finished product.

"Ah, great timing, Omega. Are you ready to hold a spoon and eat dinner without a straw?" Omega reached out and grabbed the first glove, being careful not to touch Dr. Gladen's hand, and put it on. He then grabbed the second glove and put it on, neither of which was destroyed.

Almost overcome with emotion, he shakily grabbed the spoon on the table, scooped some soup, and took a big bite. He dropped the spoon and reached over and gave Dr. Gladen a hug. "Thank you, doc, for this small piece of normalcy."

Now, back at the fire, which was now almost only embers, Silla had finished her story. "I chose to accept our souls being bound because it seemed like we were already connected. Your destruction magic does not work on me, and my blood-created gloves that give you hope, so it was an easy choice to get on board with."

At this time, Silla looked over, and it seemed as if Omega had fallen asleep, and even though it was dark, he appeared to have the ever-smallest smile on his face.

VI

Omega and Silla were now in sight of Culver castle-town, which was otherwise known as the capital. Culver itself was the largest of all the sovereign states in Arrdus, having slightly more land than its neighbor to the east, Faruqh. Culver was also in the center of Arrdus, so it was a hub for all travel throughout the continent.

Culver was bordered by Rahm on its northwest, by Faruqh on its east, by Braske on its southwest, by the Ardian Sea to the south, and by Ruseberg to the north. Culver also contained Lake Arrdus, the largest lake on the continent. It was located some seventy miles south of Culver's capital.

The Culver mountain range was located west of Lake Arrdus, and it included the highest peak in Arrdus, *Bellinda's Spike*. There was not much known on how this mountain peak got its name. Still, folklore had it that a powerful magician created the peak out of vanity.

Though the masses told this story to their children, few actually believed its origins. Culver was a fair-weathered state, not getting too cold in the winter or too hot in the summer, and was always a popular place to visit for many travelers.

Now getting close to the western gate, Silla and Omega marveled at the size of Culver castle, which had to be twice the size of Rahm's.

"I have been here once before, but it was many years ago, and I forgot how humungous the castle was," said Silla as she stretched her neck to look up at the approaching castle.

"The capital is so vast, it seems like there has to be some valuable information in its walls, to help us on our quest," interjected Omega, now looking around.

"I guess we should head straight for the New Attic and see what Rose has to say and what information she might have gathered on the Velantosse," said Silla in a voice that was mixed with hope and excitement.

As the two approached the gate, they noticed that the town guards stopped people trying to go into the capital.

"What do you think they are looking for? I hope that they let us in," said Silla anxiously.

"One way or another, we will get into Culver," said a stone-faced Omega as they approached the guards.

Silla did not know what his last comment meant, but she glanced at his hands to make sure the gloves were still on, and perhaps Omega noticed her glance because he smirked.

"Okay, you two, please tell us where you are coming from and what business you have in Culver's capital?" demanded the town guard.

"Ah… we are coming from Rahm, and we have plans to go to the New Attic, to meet our friend, and then go and visit Lake Arrdus tomorrow," replied Silla, trying to give her most cheeky smile.

"Oh, Lake Arrdus! It is beautiful this time of year, so please enjoy your time here and at the lake. The New Attic is in the center of town. Still, there is some military training going on near the Hawk River east of the capital, so make sure you use the main road to the south of Culver when heading to the lake."

Silla was somewhat surprised that her girlish charm worked. "Thank you very much, and don't work too hard," she said, giving one last big smile.

"I rarely see you smile like that," said Omega in a somewhat joking manner.

"So, you didn't like it?" she wondered as she glanced at Omega.

"Just the opposite, I'd like to see it more often," answered Omega, not looking at her.

Silla was glad that Omega wasn't looking because she knew that she was blushing.

"We know that our destination is in the center of town, but this place is huge, so we should try to find the quickest route," said Omega in wonderment.

Now inside the gates, the town was extremely busy with thousands of people going their way and going about their daily activities. The roads were all cobbled, which gave that relaxing sound from the people, carts, and horse-hooves. Unlike Rahm, which was built in tiers, Culver was very flat. The dead center of the capital was where the castle could be found. The guards' quarters and officers' homes surrounded the castle on all sides. It felt like the royalty had no fear of revolution or rebellion from the citizens. It would be relatively easy for an attack to reach the royal family. Omega and Silla found themselves in the middle of a bazaar, so they decided to look as they worked towards the New Attic, just west of the castle.

"Ohhhh, look at this! And that over there," exclaimed a very excited and more childish than normal Silla. She looked at some beautiful shoes and hats that one very tall lady was selling at a stall.

"You have excellent taste, young lady. These shoes would look absolutely fantastic on your dainty feet. Would you like to try them on, and your husband there could buy them for you?"

At that last comment, Silla dropped the shoes. "We are not together in that way… We are traveling together to meet my friend at the New Attic. By the way, can you point me in the right direction of the tavern?"

The tall saleswoman chuckled at Silla.

"I would be happy to. It will be along the main road until you see the Library of Culver History, and once you see that, take a left and just keep going until you get to the Attic. You can't miss it."

Silla waved to the tall lady as she and Omega started going down the main road. They darted from one stall to the other as they made their way.

Without even realizing it, they had been walking for about an hour and a half, perusing wears. Although Silla did most of the talking, Omega seemed to be having a good time also. They now found themselves in front of the library, and Silla looked at it longingly.

"I am sure that Rose is expecting us, so we shouldn't dally, but my inquisitive spirit really wants to go inside the library of history."

Omega looked at the library, which was not very large. Still, he could tell that they took outstanding care of it because the landscaping in front was immaculate, and there was no damage on the walls, doors, windows, and roof.

"If we go in there now, we would likely be in there for hours. Perhaps we go meet Rose, get something to eat, rest for tonight, and then come and do some research here tomorrow? It is probably unlikely for any information of a super ancient and secret society like Velantosse to be in there. Still, it's worth chancing, right?"

"That is such an astute idea that I am a little disappointed in myself that I didn't think of it first," said Silla as she playfully bumped into Omega with her hip.

Being caught off guard, Omega grabbed Silla by the shoulders, his face quite close to hers. "Are you okay?"

Silla, not expecting that reaction, pulled away from him quickly and a little awkwardly.

"Sorry, I stepped on the edge of the stone and lost my balance." Silla now had a very red face. "Let's follow your idea and go and find Rose at the New Attic," she said as she walked away very quickly.

Omega looked down and saw only smooth cobbled stone. It was the first time that Silla had playfully made contact with Omega.

VII

"Ah, there is the New Attic." Silla pointed towards a rather luxurious inn that had seating outside. It also had a large stable, and from the outside's looks, at least a dozen rooms for rent.

"Here's hoping that Rose is in there."

At that moment, Silla noticed that Omega's attention was not on her but on two women with the reddest hair she had ever seen. They were walking away from them towards an intersection and then out of sight.

"See something you like?" asked Silla in a casual manner.

However, Omega didn't realize she had asked him anything. After a few seconds of looking where the two women had been, he caught Silla's gaze.

"Oh, sorry, for some reason, I could not look away… Let's go inside and hopefully meet your friend."

Upon entering the New Attic, the two were met with a bustling gaggle of people, some coming, some going, but all enjoying themselves. The inside of the Attic had high ceilings, long tables, short tables, round tables, and square tables. A musician took requests for popular Culver songs on his flute, and even a few dogs and cats were rummaging the floors for scraps. Although it was lively, Omega and Silla's spaciousness did not feel crowded, and overall, the place felt welcoming and homely.

Omega was now following Silla, as he had no idea what Rose looked like, and at that moment, he heard a voice call out, "Silla! Hey Silla, over here! It's me, Rose."

Silla looked and then ran over and greeted Rose with a big hug.

"Rose, I haven't seen you in ages." Silla was quite excited and almost forgot to introduce Omega as he ambled up behind her.

"Right," said Silla as she gestured towards him, "this is Omega, the one that Father told you about in your correspondence."

Rose was thirty-one years old, and she was taller than Silla by almost a full head. She had long brown hair that went halfway down her back, and although she was slim-waisted, she was very shapely in both the bosom and butt.

Silla, who had always been jealous of Rose's figure, looked at Omega, who she figured would be gawking. To her astonishment, he was seemingly deep in thought, with a blank look on his face as he stared into thin air.

"Oy! You're Omega, right?"

Omega, snapping out of whatever was entrancing his attention, finally noticed Rose, and after a quick peruse, shook her hand. "Yes, I am Omega."

"Okay, how about we go upstairs for now. I have a room with three beds already paid for, for the evening, so we can chat and hopefully get this adventure off on in a reliable manner," said Rose. She gave off a confidence that few could match. However, it did not come over as cockiness but was very endearing and hope-inducing.

After making their way to the room, they sat at a table in the center of the room. Rose unrolled a large map on the corner table. It was about five feet tall and seven feet wide. It showed in very much detail all of Arrdus, from Braske Bay to Irkdale mountains, and Blackbow's hold to the Gradon Archipelago.

"So, I'm sure both of you are hopeful that I have a plethora of knowledge regarding the Velantosse and the different pieces of the Goddess armament. I have good news and bad news regarding these two queries, so my usual style is to give the bad news first and then end on a high note."

Silla looked at Omega to see if he was as nervous and excited as her, only to notice that he was sitting there with his eyes closed.

Rose noticed it also. "Oy, Omega," started Rose, as she flicked a piece of wood at his chest.

"Hmm, sorry; I'm listening. Please continue," said Omega, who had opened his eyes to see a pencil in his lap.

"Okay, so the bad news on the Velantosse front is that I have zero ideas on who the Culver Guardian is, and I also have not a clue of how to go about searching for the person. Also, on a related note, I have never noticed anyone talk about or caught any useful rumors regarding the piece of armament, nor do I even know which piece is supposed to be in Culver."

After Rose finished that sentence, she gave a broad smile, which made Omega smile and Silla frown.

"Why are you smiling after giving such a terrible admission of ignorance on these important subjects?" Silla asked this, knowing full well how aggressive it sounded.

Rose laughed for a couple of seconds and simply said, "Now it's time for the good news. From what I have noticed throughout my research on relevant topics from this era and in historical texts, there is a specific location in Arrdus that appears far too often in the literature to be a mere coincidence. Have either of you heard of the Freewoods far to the north of Arrdus? The Freewoods actually run into the mysterious deadlands north of the Arrdussian border."

Omega, of course, had little knowledge of anything, geographically speaking, other than his cell in Irkdale and Dr. Gladen's house in Rahm.

Silla, on the other hand, had read about them a little in some books that her father had in his library.

"I have read about the Freewoods a few times, but I admittedly do not know much about what is inside that forest."

Rose proceeded to point at the map, north of Rahm's northern border, and northeast of the fertile communal farming lands that Rahm, Culver, Faruqh, Braske, and Gradon share, and there was the Freewoods.

"In the literature that I have been studying, quite often there is mention of some of your predecessors either visiting or remaining in the Freewoods for long periods, even though there isn't much mentioned about what they did there. I think that something related to the Velantosse is in that forest, and I think that should be our first destination."

Silla thought that it was great that they finally had at least a semblance of a lead, and she proceeded to calculate how long it would take to get there.

Rose noticed her and pointed out that the main road that runs north out of Culver would take them almost all the way to the Freewoods, which would greatly aid travel time. It was a well-maintained, valuable road.

After making their plans, the three went downstairs to grab dinner.

Omega was always ready for mealtimes. He had to eat in dungeons and other terrible places that did not do much for his appetite for most of his life.

"Okay, how about we get a good night's sleep and make our arrangements early tomorrow and set off in the afternoon?" asked Rose, who had finished her third cup of wine.

"That sounds good. Omega, please be careful out there, and try to find somewhere out of the way to sleep. Many guests might find your sleeping habits queer."

This was the first time Rose had experienced one of Omega's proclivities, and she was very interested.

"Oy, Omega. It's okay to sleep in the same room, even though it is just us women."

"Sorry, I prefer to not be inside walls and doors for too long, and I only sleep outside. Excuse me."

After finishing his meal, Omega headed outside and looked around, finding a nice spot near the stables. It had covering but was also away from foot traffic and should work for sleeping without bothering anybody.

Silla began explaining what little she knew of Omega's upbringing and life. However, she did not talk about what she saw of Omega's memories during that time in the arena.

"I guess it makes sense after experiencing such unimaginable surroundings for over twenty years, and the number of inner-scars that would leave on a person. He seems to have a good head on his shoulders for having gone through so much, and he doesn't seem the least bit aggressive.

VIII

After waking and getting ready, Silla and Rose went outside and looked around, searching for Omega.

"Oy, there he is over there," said Rose, pointing towards the opposite side of the entrance near the stables, where she saw Omega in a heavy sleep.

"Omega, it is time to get going. We have a long journey to take us to the Freewoods," said Silla in a gentle yet firm voice as she grabbed his arm.

Omega opened his eyes, meeting hers for a second before getting up and brushing the dirt off his backside.

"It got a little chilly last night. Omega, did you get cold out here?" asked Rose, who had used an extra blanket last night.

"I didn't notice it getting cold last night, but if there is one positive to how I was raised, it is that I have a very resilient body. I don't notice cold or pain very often."

"Has anyone ever told you that you have very gentle eyes, Omega?" asked Rose as she stared at Omega while he was getting ready to depart.

"I think Silla's father mentioned it before, and sometimes I wonder if that is why he saved me. Perhaps he had the thinking that I had the potential for not being completely ruined as a person." Omega said this half-kidding.

Rose, Omega, and Silla made their way towards the town's northern gate after spending most of the morning gathering what they would need for their travels. It was approximately 300 miles from Culver's north gate exit to the beginning of the Freewoods. On some good horses, traveling most of the day and resting at night, it would take about two weeks to get there, so they decided to get enough provisions to get them to a town somewhere in the middle, where they would restock.

"As far as I know, there is a small town named Briaridge right near the Nugle River, where we will be able to restock for the larger part of the trip. We will hopefully also be able to get some good information on the Freewoods," said Rose as they exited the north gate of Culver on their horses with full saddlebags.

Outside of Culver's northern gate, many soldiers were going about their business, either shouting orders or training their swordsmanship and archery.

They didn't bother the three, and they appeared to be doing intense training, but there were no wars that Silla knew about.

"Hey, Rose, what's with all of the soldiers? We also heard about soldiers on the east side of Culver being in formation."

"I have heard some rumors recently that Culver might be planning to try and extend their borders. I don't know its extent, but an all-out empire seems to be the odds-on favorite. I don't know why or how they would plan to capture Rahm and Faruqh."

"They want to invade their neighbors, but for what purpose, I wonder? I had always thought that there was a lasting peace between all of the surrounding states, and little was to be gained from fighting each other."

After making her point, Silla was quiet for a while until Omega brought up the fact that Rose was also considering.

"Are you concerned about Rahm? It is your home, after all."

Silla looked at both of them and shrugged. "It is my home, but I am not a soldier, nor a noble, and I have my own concerns that will definitely need all of my attention. I won't let these rumors distract me for too long."

It was about twelve hours from Culver to Briaridge at a steady pace. Hence, the three of them showed up in the village at dawn, having rode all day and night, and they were exhausted, leading them to stop at the nearest inn.

"There is an inn right up here called The Silver's Grace. I think we should get a room booked for today and tomorrow and try to see if there are locals that can help us understand the layout of the Freewoods. I'm certain that at least one person has traveled to those woods," said Rose in a way that sounded like she was convincing herself.

At dawn, the denizens of Briaridge were starting to make their way to their respective responsibilities, with quite a few working at the mills and blacksmith shops that did a lot of work for Culver Castle-town. It seemed busier than expected. Even at this time, most of the shops were in full swing. The three travelers noticed that the blacksmith shops were closed to ordinary customers, showing they were currently only outsourcing for the greater Culver kingdom.

As the three made their way towards one of the three blacksmith shops in Briaridge, Rose spoke up.

"Oy, mister blacksmith. I noticed that you are not open to the public. Are you only doing work for the king, currently?"

"Yes, ma'am, all of the master craftsmen of Briaridge have been commissioned by the king to fulfill our duties as Culver workers and citizens. We were not given much information on what all these weapons and armors are for, but it is not hard to guess that war is coming. Sorry, I have to get back to work to fill my quota by the end of the day."

"Hmm, I guess those rumors that you heard about have some credibility," said Silla as they continued to walk towards The Silver's Grace.

"I hope that the inns have vacancies for normal people like us, and not only the craftsman and all the extra helpers that I'm sure they had to hire," said Rose.

The three came upon The Silver's Grace, and the proprietor happened to open the door simultaneously. "Oh, hello there! Are you three here looking for lodging?"

"Hopefully. Are you currently taking non-commissioned people like us?" asked Silla with a clearly hopeful tone in her voice.

The proprietor laughed out loud. "Ha, yes, ma'am, we have some rooms available. Why don't you come in and fill out the ledger, and we can get you set up."

As the three walked up to the front counter, they noticed that it was very empty, unlike the rest of the early-morning-bustling town…

"Oh, I forgot to introduce myself. I am Beatrice, the owner of The Silver's Grace. I am also the older sister of the King of Culver, little Thomy."

"Hello, I am Silla, a citizen of Rahm, and this is Rose and Omega. We hope to get a room for tonight and tomorrow, and then we will be on our way the next day. Also, we would like to ask around for anyone that might have first-hand knowledge of the Freewoods."

"Hmm, the Freewoods, huh? If my niece were here, she would be perfect for helping you since she has been to the Freewoods probably a dozen times for hunting and adventuring. She is a very free-spirited lady, even though she is a princess of Culver. She acts oppositely of how most people would perceive."

"Have you heard from this niece or know if she plans to come here soon?" asked Rose while Omega was looking around the inn.

"She never tells me when she is coming. Even though it takes half a day to get here, she comes often enough to assume that she might be here within a few days."

Beatrice had a welcoming smile, perfect for someone that ran an inn.

After signing the ledger, Rose decided to nap in the room, so Silla and Omega made their way outside to go around town for a while.

"Excuse me," said Silla to a nearby old lady sitting on a wooden bench near a general store.

"I am Silla, and this is Omega. We are new to Briaridge and plan to head to the Freewoods in a couple of days. I was wondering if you know anyone that has some knowledge of the area, or even a guide would be great."

The lady was nice enough and chatted them up for a few minutes, but ultimately, she did not know much about the forest. Still, she did suggest that the two go to Oliver's Goods and Feed because the proprietor had been to the Freewoods at least a half dozen times over the last few years.

Oliver's, luckily, was just behind where the old lady was sitting, so the two of them made their way inside to chat with the proprietor. As the two walked up, there were two large signs on either side of the main double doors reading, "Oliver's" and "Goods & Feed," respectively, and the place looked like it was oft frequented.

"This is a nice shop, Omega. Hopefully, Mr. Oliver can give us some clues about the Freewoods."

The store had fewer patrons than Silla figured it would.

She thought it was a prosperous sign, as she could get her answers sooner than later in the current setting.

The two walked up to the counter and saw an elderly gentleman with a stern face and many wrinkles. He had an intriguing look mixed with both approachability and austerity.

"Excuse me, are you, Mr. Oliver, the proprietor?" asked Silla.

"Ah, yes, I am Oliver Greenwood, the owner of this fine shop. I have actually owned and operated this place for some fifty years if you can believe it from my youthful appearance."

Silla was taken aback by the joke, which made Mr. Greenwood laugh out loud.

"You seem like a girl that has some query in mind."

As she wondered why he didn't reference Omega, she noticed that he was down one of the aisles looking at some of the display cases, seemingly uninterested in the conversation. Silla thought about dragging him back up but decided against it.

"Yessir, I was told by a nice old lady outside that you have made quite a few trips into the Freewoods, and we were," she now pointed at Omega to include him, "hoping that you could give us some information that would help our voyage go smoother."

"Ah, must be Mrs. Greenwood that told you to seek me out." Oliver pointed outside the glass doors at the lady on the bench.

"My wife loves to sit in front of the shop and chat up potential customers and offer help where it's needed. It is one of the many reasons why I fell in love with her almost fifty years ago. Might I ask you why you want to go to the Freewoods? It is not a place of Culver or any other kingdom, and although it is not populated with many people, there are quite a few beasts that call its borders home."

Silla had planned to not reveal herself to anyone not directly related to the struggle until she had no other choice.

"I am sorry, but our reasons for going are our own, and I can't casually reveal them."

Silla noticed the silence that ensued and realized that it was unlikely he could offer specific help without knowing specific details, so she decided to change tactics.

"Also, I know it is a long trip from Briaridge to the Freewoods, so do you recommend another stop between here and the end-goal?"

"Sure. What I would normally do on my trips is to stop at Broken Bridge. It's the last settlement inside the Rahminian border. Briaridge, you see, is not far from the Culver-Rahm border. After Broken Bridge, there are no more suitable villages. After making it out of Rahm's territory, you will find yourselves in some of the freelands, which are not usually dangerous. However, you should always remember that the people in the freelands do not adhere to the laws and customs of the bigger and smaller sovereign kingdoms splayed through Arrdus."

Silla made a note of Broken Bridge on her tablet with her charcoal pencil. Oliver noticed and pointed her to the isle that Omega was at. It had a large selection of writing apparatuses and papers.

"If you want to, we can chat some more after you peruse my goods, and if you have horses, I have some excellent feed options that can give great energy to your stallions and mares."

Silla nodded to Mr. Greenwood and made her way towards Omega, who had walked up and down almost every aisle while she was chatting.

"Why did you wander off on your own as soon as we came in?" asked Silla in a tone that wasn't too stern.

Omega, noticing she was walking towards him, grabbed an expensive-looking graphite pencil and showed it to her instead of answering her question.

"This looks like a suitable replacement for your charcoal pencil."

Silla was distracted for a second at his thoughtfulness and forgot to continue scolding him.

The two decided to get some feed for the horses and the graphite pencil and some more paper for Silla, and then bid farewell to Mr. Greenwood. They decided to head back to The Silver's Grace, as they were tired from traveling and wandering the town, and it was also getting late in the afternoon.

Upon returning and going into the room they had rented, Rose was still fast asleep on the bed, so Silla decided to join her in taking a nap. In contrast, Omega went downstairs to get something to eat.

After heading downstairs and taking a seat at the bar, Beatrice noticed him and came over. "Where are your friends, Omega?"

"You remembered my name from early this morning. I don't usually give off a lasting impression."

Beatrice smiled at him.

"You are a very unique-looking lad, so I think I'd be hard-pressed to find someone that didn't remember you. So, are you hungry, thirsty, or just enjoying the ambiance?"

"I'm starving, actually. When we first arrived, it smelled so amazing in here that my mouth was watering. I've been thinking about it all day long."

This comment made Beatrice, as the proprietor, extremely grateful.

"Okay then, since it's late in the afternoon, how about some braised rabbit with potatoes and carrots? If I do say so myself, it is delicious, and you won't be disappointed."

Omega could only nod his head and then he made his way to a nearby table. He ordered a mug of ale and ate his meal, which was even better than the owner described, and then he made his way outside to find a place to take a much-needed nap.

IX

It was about eleven in the evening, and Omega had been asleep outside The Silver's Grace for maybe four or five hours.

Hearing the late-night bustling crowd of the inn, Omega woke up from his deep slumber. He was far enough away from the noise, having been sleeping closer to the back entrance. He found another noise, a humming, much more enjoyable.

Omega found the tone and pitch of the song very appealing and got up to make his way towards the sound's origin.

It was fully dark outside, behind the inn, so when Omega made his way around the corner and towards the little shed that was behind The Silver's Grace, he could barely make out the person that he assumed was doing the humming.

Just then, another person made their way, coming from the inn's back door, moving towards the woman.

As the lady melodically sang her tune, she was busy putting the old empty jars and bottles into the shed and grabbing new wine and ale.

"Oy, miss. You ab susch a beautiful voice. I'b noticed you working here in the past," said a fat man who had more than a few too many ales.

Not having turned around, the lady stopped humming to answer the man with her cheerful voice.

"Thank you, I just got here a few minutes ago, and I try to come as often as I can from the capital. I appreciate it when patrons have a good time here at the Grace, and I think my singing brings some enjoyment to the atmosphere."

The man had stepped up right behind her at this point, as he whispered in her ear, "There is something else you can do to help me have a good time."

Just then, the man grabbed the barmaid from behind, covering her mouth to prevent her from making others aware and ruining his fun.

He then began to fondle her through her shirt. He used his weight to push her body up against the sidewall of the shed, leaving her with little opportunity to struggle or get free.

There were muffled screams and wild kicking motions from the barmaid, but it was to no avail. After being kicked in the shin, the fat man pulled her off the wall and slammed her to the ground, using his size to keep her from moving an inch. He proceeded to rip open her top and started making his way with his hands down her stomach to her skirt.

As the fat man was getting close to the climax of his fun, hand inching downward, another hand, coming from behind, found his neck.

Much to his surprise, he was lifted as if he were a child. As he tried to wrestle free, his head was slammed into the wall of the shed, with a loud crack, which could have come from the wall splitting or from the rapist's head.

After the body fell, it turned out to be Omega that foiled the fat man's fun.

After taking care of the rapist, Omega looked down at the collapsed barmaid, noticing her exposed chest. Even with his lack of experience in societal norms, even he could tell that she should be covered.

He took off his shirt, exposing all his scars. He wrapped up the lady with his shirt, picked her up in his arms, and carried her to the inn's back door, which led first into the storage area, then the kitchen, and then into the seating area. Omega opened the door, checking that nobody was around, carrying her to a nearby space where some sacks of potatoes lay and leaned her up against them.

As her face came into the dim light, Omega noticed that she had the reddest hair that he had ever seen, and he thought she looked familiar.

Just then, Beatrice made her way into the storage room to grab some carrots. She spotted Omega standing next to the potatoes.

"Hello, Omega, what are you doing back here?"

As she asked, she noticed he was shirtless, and she caught the unforgettable sight of scars that blanketed his arms and torso.

"Sorry, your barmaid was attacked outside, and I thought this was the best place for her."

"What barmaid?" wondered Beatrice aloud, and it then dawned on her who he referenced.

She noticed the hunched-over body of the attacked barmaid. She rushed over, pushing Omega aside, and saw that she was wrapped up in Omega's shirt.

"How far did it go? Did you stop it in time?!" asked a worried Beatrice.

"The way my body looks... you didn't even assume it was me that attacked her?"

She looked at him. "The way she is so tightly wrapped in your shirt, I can tell that it was not you. Although one has nothing to do with the other, someone with eyes like those, you wouldn't do this to a lady."

Omega gave a small smile of appreciation.

"I smashed his head into your shed after he ripped her top before anything else could happen. I think she passed out when he slammed her down... sorry," said a very calm Omega.

"Thank you very much. Hopefully, he is still alive, so I can exact my own revenge in a much more painful way. But, for now, I will clear out the bar early and take care of her. Feel free to help yourself to some wine or ale, and tomorrow I will thank you properly."

As Beatrice made her way into the kitchen area to clear out the patrons and get some help to take the collapsed woman to her room, Omega grabbed a bottle of ale from the counter. Before heading out the back door, he gave another look to the lady. He thought again that she seemed so familiar.

After having his bottle of ale, Omega made his way back to his spot, feeling sluggish from the ale and a bit tired from the stress of what just happened. After taking a seat up against the wall, it wasn't twenty seconds before he was sound asleep.

Back in the Grace, Beatrice had placed the barmaid into her room and gave her a couple of shakes when the woman finally woke up.

"Ah, finally, my precious niece!" said an excited and stressed-out Beatrice. "Kita, are you okay?"

Kita looked at her aunt and then realized where she was, looked at her chest, and noticed the shirt wrapped around her.

"I tried to take that shirt off and put you into one of my blouses, but you kept clinging to it, even though you were unconscious."

Kita started to sit up on the bed. "Whose shirt is this that's wrapped around me?"

"That is Omega's shirt. He is a patron that showed up yesterday morning, and he happened upon you being attacked. From what I can gather, he stopped the attacker right after you passed out, and then he wrapped you up and carried you inside."

Kita, now getting up from the bed, was beside herself. "Where is he now? I have to thank him." Beatrice was a little confused by the urgency, but she knew better than to hinder a determined Kita.

"I let him have some free ale, so I figure he is either at the bar or made his way up to his room, number three, for the night."

Almost before she stopped speaking, Kita adjusted Omega's shirt to wear it properly buttoned and made her way out of the door and to the bar.

Kita did not know what Omega looked like, but there were only two of the fellow staff at the bar, so she made her way up the stairs to room number three. After knocking on the door a couple of times, it opened.

"Hmm, what's the ruckus so late at night?" asked a groggy Rose.

It seemed that Kita was not expecting a woman to open the door. She was taken aback for a moment—a beautiful woman in a loose top and panties.

"Is there someone named Omega in this room?"

Rose looked at her, her eyes now cleared, and realized that this lady was gorgeous. Almost fairytale beautiful.

"We are his companions," she said as she pointed to a sprawled-out, snoring Silla, still fast asleep, "but he doesn't like to sleep indoors, so I would venture that he is outside sleeping nearby."

"Okay, thank you, and sorry to disturb your sleep," said Kita as she hurriedly made her way back down the stairs.

"Am I really sleepy, or was she wearing Omega's shirt?" As soon as Rose made it back to the bed, she shoved Silla off her side and went back to sleep. Even with two beds, they always shared.

Kita made her way outside and searched around the inn, and she finally spotted a figure leaning up against the wall not far from the stables.

As Kita approached, she noticed that the man had no shirt on, which all but guaranteed that she had finally found Omega.

Kita was now standing directly in front of Omega, only a couple of feet away. With the now cloudless sky, the moonlight showed Kita all of the scars that ensconced Omega's chest, stomach, and arms.

"I wonder what kind of life you have led to having so many scars, but to still have the courage and desire to save a complete stranger in need," whispered Kita.

At that time, Kita noticed the solitary scar on Omega's head, just under his hairline. She reached her hand out to touch that scar. When she was an inch away, a hand grabbed her wrist.

Omega had opened his eyes and realized who it was, almost immediately. His shirt, her red hair, and distinct smell. It was the lady that he had saved earlier that night.

Her hand and face were really close to his, and he was unsure how to handle such a situation. At that time, Kita smiled the brightest smile that Omega had ever seen. Omega noticed that she added a little noise when she smiled, like an exclamation or very short chuckle.

"Hi, you must be Omega, the one who saved me earlier. My name is Kita."

"Kita... I like it," said Omega, unable to take his eyes out of that blue ocean.

This back-and-forth was happening while Omega was still clutching Kita's wrist. He looked at her hand and noticed what she was planning when she asked, "Can I have my hand back, please? I was interested in your scar but didn't realize it might be rude to touch it."

Omega pressed her palm against his scar and then let go of her wrist, which Kita was not expecting, which made her smile again.

"Even though we just met, I can tell that you are a very unique person, Omega. Oh, by the way, what is your surname?"

"I'm not sure what my birth name is or who my parents were, but the one that saved me named me Omega, so I have simply been using that given name."

"You become more intriguing every few seconds, Omega. I'd love to get to know you more once we've had some good rest. If you don't mind, I'd like to sleep next to you. After what happened, I feel more comfortable and safer next to the person that saved me."

If anybody were listening, her tone was coquettish, to say the least.

Omega was unsure how to handle most mundane social situations, and this one topped the list.

"It might not be comfortable," was all he could muster.

As Kita sat down next to Omega and leaned against the wall, close enough that he could feel her body heat, she laid the side of her head on his shoulder and said, "Feels comfortable enough to me."

Even though he couldn't see her face, he could hear her small chuckle that accompanied her smile.

Now fully rested, Silla and Rose both got up with the sun and prepared to venture out for their last day in Briaridge. "Okay, let's go out and find Omega, and then we can gather anything we need and explore the town a little bit before leaving," said an upbeat Silla.

"Oh yeah, that reminds me. Something strange happened last night. Some lovely lady came knocking, looking for Omega."

Silla had no idea what was going on, but she didn't like the sound of it. They both went downstairs. Beatrice had just brewed some tea, still piping hot, and offered it to them.

"Here's some fresh tea to wake you up, and a small thank you for what happened last night," said Beatrice, who you could tell did not get much sleep. Perhaps there was a speck of blood on her neck.

"What happened last night?" asked both Rose and Silla.

"I guess I should let Omega and Kita explain. I was not actually there when it all happened."

Silla took a cup of tea, which she was going to give to Omega, but as they made their way around the corner towards the stables, Silla saw a sight that made her drop the cup of tea and give a shout.

Now in the bright daylight, anyone who happened by could see that Omega was sleeping deeply against the wall. At some time during the night, Kita's head had slid off his shoulder, and she was asleep in his lap.

At the sound of Silla's shout, Omega woke with a catch of the throat. Omega's sudden shake also woke up Kita.

As Kita stretched, she looked forward and saw Silla, looking directly into Kita's eyes, with a glare of incredulity. At that moment, Omega stood up and offered Kita his hand to help her up, which she graciously took.

Silla then noticed that Kita was wearing Omega's shirt and took a step back.

"How could so many things change in one night?" asked Silla almost to herself, although it was out loud.

"Oy, you're the lady that came last night looking for Omega. Clearly, you found him," said Rose as she approached Kita with her hand out.

"I'm Rose, and this is Silla."

Rose grabbed Silla's hand and pulled her towards the fray.

"Hi, my name is Kita."

Kita noticed Silla looking at her shirt. As she looked down and then looked at Omega, who was still shirtless, she perceived the reason for the incredulous look earlier.

"Oh, not to worry, Silla. Nothing like that happened between us last night."

Omega was clueless about what they were referencing. He was stretching, yawning, and scratching his head simultaneously, which made Kita smile.

"I'm going to go in and change out of your shirt, Omega. I'll bring it back lat—"

Omega cut in, "No rush, I have other shirts," as he wiped away the yawn-produced tears from his eyes.

"Okay, I'll keep it then," said Kita as she made her way towards the entrance of the Grace.

"That was the best sleep I've ever had in my life!" exclaimed Omega with one more big stretch.

Rose was experienced enough to understand most of Silla's silence. She tried her best to alleviate any unease and tension.

"Okay, let's go get you a shirt, Omega, and then you can tell us what happened last night."

After some time, Omega explained what happened between him and Kita the night before, making Silla feel much better, as she was no longer in the dark.

"So, you heard her singing, which led you to her, and you happened upon her being attacked and saved both her innocence and possibly her life. Then she sought you out to thank you."

"It must be Desitine that brought you two together," said Rose, who was pouring everyone a cup of tea.

"For now, let's get ourselves ready for departure. We have a long journey to the Freewoods ahead of us, and we should be clearheaded," said Silla in a somewhat annoyed tone, which made Rose chuckle.

"Honestly, for a moment, I completely forgot about your mission, Silla, I'm sorry," stated Omega, now looking at Silla.

"Our mission, Omega."

"Right."

About the time that Silla, Rose, and Omega had finished packing their horses, readying themselves for the next leg of their journey, someone came around the side of the inn, where the stables were located.

"Omega! Are you leaving without even saying goodbye?" asked Kita as she walked up to the three.

Omega turned and looked at Kita, who was now wearing a knee-length purple dress with all of her hair lying flat, all the way past her butt.

"Ah, sorry, I could stay if you want—" Before he could finish, Silla cut him off.

"We have important things to do, Omega; you cannot separate from me."

Omega hardly noticed that Silla said anything and then remembered that the two were bound. He *was* curious as to what extent but decided that was best left for later.

"Goodbye, Kita. Please look after yourself and try not to go out at night by yourself."

This made Kita laugh.

"Trust me, my boss let me have an earful after we woke up this morning. Maybe we don't have to separate quite yet, though. Boss lady told me that you were going to the Freewoods for your own reasons, but I think I can be of use to you since I've been to that huge forest a few times. I have hunted and explored a small portion of that forest in the past."

Before Omega or Rose could make any comments or inquiries, Silla responded resolutely.

"Thank you for the offer, but we can manage on our own."

Kita was confused by the resounding refusal, but Rose chimed in first.

"Silla. I have zero ideas about what lies in the Freewoods or where to start looking for what we seek. If Kita has explored the Freewoods, then the value of that knowledge is immeasurable."

While Rose and Silla were making valid points, back and forth, Omega walked up to Kita and held out his gloved right hand, simply saying, "You can go."

Kita jumped past his hand at hearing this and gave him a big hug, arms wrapped around his neck, and on her tiptoes. This happened to be Omega's very first hug from a woman.

Omega could only stand there, hands at his side, while Silla and Rose stopped arguing and stared at the two. Rose with a little smile, and Silla with a look of disbelief and then a scowl of anger.

"We will work on your hugging skills, Omega," said Kita as she ended the embrace and gave him a big smile.

Having made the proper arrangements with her boss, Kita, Omega, Silla, and Rose departed from Briaridge, with Broken Bridge being their next destination.

X

Inside the main palace hall of Culver castle, there was a conference of mighty people from all over Arrdus. Seating at such a meeting, even if never explicitly spoken, determined your importance and the weight of your voice.

Closer to the entrance meant you had little influence in the grand picture, and furthest from the door told your voice could move mountains.

The representatives in the conference, closest to the entrance, were the envoys from Ruseberg and Black Garden kingdoms. Left and right of the central aisle, respectively. The smallest in both influence and military strength of the Seven-Power Conference.

A little farther away from the entrance was the representative from Braske, which used a multi-leader voting system instead of an autocratic system like all the other nations.

The merchant guild master, Frontus Muckle, was one of the five leaders in Braske and the one chosen to attend the Seven-Power Conference.

Frontus was a middle-aged man with short black hair, slightly balding at the top. He was of average height and a little large in the gut area. Unlike what people thought when they pictured a merchant leader, he was very frugal and did not wear any gaudy clothing.

A little farther away from the entrance sat Queen Regent Felicia Aggrus of Faruqh. Queen Regent Felicia was in her fifties, having her second son much later than the first. Her firstborn died over twenty years ago. She was still beautiful, and she dressed well. Today she was adorned in an elegant, lilac gown.

Faruqh was a vast kingdom, both in military numbers and landmass. Still, they had recently lost their king to illness. The heir apparent, Masen Aggrus, was too young at fourteen to take on the responsibilities of running the courts, ministers, and everything that came along with the throne.

It was plain to see that the other kingdoms in Arrdus did not think much of the Queen Regent and her influence because the previous King Astile's seat was farther from the entrance.

Now getting even farther from the entrance sat the longest-reigning king, Drune Sarke of the Gradon Archipelago.

King Drune was sixty-five years old and had been the king of Gradon since he was sixteen years old. Drune's uncle, Melkus, murdered Drune's father, Drude, to usurp the throne but unexpectedly met his match at the end of Drune's sword when he tried to end the succession line.

Before he became too old to wield a sword effectively, he ranked as the number one warrior in Arrdus. A title he proudly held for some thirty years before handing it over to the king of Culver.

Drune had a full, thick head of reddish-brown hair, shoulder-length with minimal gray, and even in his advanced age, he looked quite strong and sturdy.

Now, for the last two kingdoms at the conference, Rahm and Culver. They usually sat evenly at these conferences. They were the two most powerful kingdoms, and interestingly enough, the two castles were closest to each other.

King Marxus IX of Rahm made his way to the last section on the left of the aisle. King Marxus IX was the youngest monarch, and he was well-built. However, as a kid, he had an accident while riding his horse that permanently injured his shoulder. He could not effectively wield a sword.

Everyone assumed that King Thomascus Deckler of Culver would take his usual seat on the aisle's right side.

The palace hall was typically used by King Deckler. Therefore, his throne was his regular seat, but during these conferences, which were always held in Culver due to its central location, the throne remained empty as a show of solidarity.

King Deckler made his way directly to his throne, turned around, looked around at each representative, and sat down with purpose. The hall was silent for what seemed an eternity, with each kingdom's representative waiting to see who would speak up first. To nobody's surprise, it was King Drune of Gradon.

"What do you mean by sitting on that throne, Thomascus?"

Thomascus looked at Drune, not defiantly or with anger, but with a welcoming smile. At that time, Thomascus's oldest child, Thompsel, walked in from one of the chambers behind the throne. The conference officially began.

"Excuse me, King Drune, there is much to get into today, so I'll get right down to business," Thompsel said in his deep charismatic voice.

Thompsel was usually the tallest, strongest man in any room. That, coupled with his charisma, deep black hair, and honey-colored eyes, made for an unforgettable experience.

"Today's conference is going to be different than any in the past, and it will be the last of its kind. After today, if everything goes as I have planned, the continent of Arrdus will become unified in its purpose, and my father will become the first emperor of the Arrdussian Empire."

At this comment, there were some murmurs from Black Garden and Braske, but outright laughter from King Drune.

"Boy, I might be old, but I have no plans of giving up my islands that I've fought and bled to protect for the last fifty years."

The only representative that remained silent was King Marxus IX.

"I understand dropping an outlandish statement like that will have everyone very anxious, but by the end of what I have to say, everyone here will be content. Also, nobody is being asked to give up their land or leave their homes."

"Firstly, let me ask some questions. How many of you know that about five years ago, the continent of Zarrek had a massive civil war that led to the Panser Clan coming into power and being quite destructive towards their own people?"

Everyone in the room raised their hands, some scoffing at the thought of Culver thinking them that ignorant.

"Okay, now how many of you know that within the last two years, there has been a new man coming into power in Zarrek, and this man single-handedly, systematically wiped out three entire clans, numbering some 200 high-ranking members, to usurp the throne? This man's name is Grexle, and he is said to have formidable fighting skills and a ruthlessness few have ever imagined... Even I wouldn't fight him without sufficient reason."

Only King Drune raised his hand. "I did not know the full details, as you have laid out, but I had heard that there was a usurper in Zarrek."

"As expected from the former most formidable fighter in Arrdus," said Thompsel.

"Now comes the information that I am confident zero here know about. From what my spies tell me, Grexle has been building long ships, around the clock, since he took his seat of power. He has also unified all of the remaining clans and their armies, and along with his own, their total numbers are believed to be over 200,000 soldiers."

That many soldiers were not a common talking point, so everyone except Rahm's king began to murmur and gasp.

"My spies also have reported that very soon Grexle will have completed enough long-ships to allow the entirety of their army to traverse the Ardian sea. Their plan would be to have all arrive together."

Everyone became silent and started to pick up on the idea and gravity of what Thompsel was relaying.

"Now, how many soldiers do you think all of our combined, standing armies have?"

Information such as this was not openly discussed, obviously, so nobody wanted to speak first.

"Going region by region, I can tell you," said Thompsel.

"Ruseberg and Black Garden have about 10,000 each. Correct?" Both envoys nodded.

"Faruqh has about 50,000. Correct?" The Queen Regent hesitantly nodded.

"Braske has only a small coastal guard, and the militia, totaling about 9,000. Correct?" Frontus nodded.

As this was going on, all representatives realized that Thompsel was flexing his knowledge of their inner workings. Numbers that outsiders shouldn't have easy access to.

"Next, we have Gradon Archipelago, which has about seventy-five warships and some 25,000 soldiers, with another 5,000 on the lands that Gradon controls, east of Faruqh. Correct?"

King Drune stood up. "That's too accurate for someone that has never been to my kingdom."

Thompsel could only smile.

"And now we come to Rahm. King Marxus, you have about 45,000 soldiers. Correct?"

King Marxus IX spoke for the first time. "Your spy network is vast indeed."

"Thank you. Now, for Culver, we have a total of 83,348 as of the last full count. All of our armies, combined, have close to the number that Grexle will be sending our way very soon."

"I'm sure most of you now have a grasp of the severity of us being separate nations. We need to unite, under one ruler, having one standing army. It will be too easy to pick us off one by one."

King Drune stood up and walked to the center of the aisle.

"Okay, let's say that we all decided that uniting was the only way to survive as a continent, and let's also assume that we believe Zarrek is planning to invade. Why does it have to be Culver and Thomascus that take rule over us all?"

"An excellent question. Culver will take control of power because of its central location, its trade power and flexibility, its military power, and the fact that it has the two strongest warriors in all of Arrdus: The new emperor," he said as he pointed to his father, "and the crown prince," referring to himself. At that last part, Thompsel's ever-present smile was gone.

"Before everyone gets fearful and even more anxious, I will say that I have zero desire or intention to take this power via violence. For one, there is no time for multiple civil wars. Another reason is the loss of soldiers on all sides would do us no good once Zarrek makes that voyage across the sea. I am willing to give concessions to most nations that will allow us to amicably come to the desired result."

Looking at the different representatives, there was fear in some of their eyes, hidden defiance in others, and what might be thought of as intrigue in others.

"Now for the proposed concessions. Firstly, Black Garden and Ruseberg: there will be no concessions, and Culver will absorb the two nations into itself, and they will both cease to exist. This is the best option that I can offer. The two nations have little power, even smaller influence, and are not worth giving further concession considerations."

The two smaller nations' envoys felt like they were in a scene where they did not belong.

"I have no power to make this decision, but I will relay everything that happens here to my king, and I am sure he will make the wise decision," said the envoy of Black Garden. The envoy of Ruseberg gave a similar remark.

"Excellent. Now for Braske, I have a special concession to offer. From my spies' reports, the governing system you have in Braske operates very efficiently. There is no need to make sweeping changes. All the emperor requires of Braske is a 25 percent annual tribute derived from your total revenue of all business and 25 percent of your share of the communal harvest, which is to feed the soldiers. Each nation will also provide 25 percent of their shares of the harvest, so there is no need to feel alienated. Lastly, all nations' soldiers will be controlled by the greater empire."

After listening to Thompsel make his offer, Frontus countered, "Might I ask for two further additions? First, Braske has always had issues with raiders and pirates pillaging from cargo ships. I request that you send enough soldiers and ships to form a strong shoreline and coast guard unit that makes everyone feel safe. And secondly, I would propose that someone from Braske be in charge of all the bookkeeping for the communal harvests moving forward."

Thompsel looked at Frontus and then laughed.

This made Frontus feel as if he angered the proposed crown prince.

"You will have your current coastal guard size tripled, and I will even come down and personally inspect the building of the ships. I also have some ideas for new weapons, especially optimal for boats."

"As for your second request, that is also not a problem. Do you have someone in mind for the new position of Provisions Minister?"

"Argle Brace, our fishermen guild master, has a keen eye for numbers, and I think he would be an excellent choice."

"Done. Are you now willing to swear loyalty and fealty to your new emperor?" Thompsel pointed to his father, who had not had to say a word yet.

Frontus looked at King Thomascus and bowed to him.

"I have to take this back and discuss it with the other members of the council, but if I'm honest, most of us assumed this day would come eventually, and we have made plans just in case."

"My information on Braske was indeed correct, very forward-thinking and rational."

"Okay, next up is Faruqh and the Queen Regent. After the death of your husband, King Astile, Faruqh has lost much of its influence and power. Still, I am prepared to make a very particular offer that I think will bring prosperity and peace to both your nation and your heart."

Thompsel said this with a very charismatic smile, which would make any woman's heart flutter, even a Queen Regent.

"For Faruqh, I would like the same 25 percent cut from your harvest, and all of your soldiers would be my father's. I would also want to place a few ministers in your court for oversight and to aid in making decisions, but all power, of course, would remain with Your Highness."

Before the Queen Regent could respond, Thompsel brought up his next proposal.

"Now, what I am willing to offer is a marriage proposal for your son, Masen. Your son and my youngest sister, Kansel, are very close in age. I think that these two being married would have a plethora of advantages for Faruqh."

The Queen Regent looked hesitant and distant, which Thompsel noticed right away.

"As a Queen Regent with a young son, you have to always be vigilant in keeping yourself and the future king safe. It is always most dangerous in a kingdom when a monarch dies without an heir ready to take over, fluidly."

"If I'm not mistaken, there are likely plenty of plots and possibly already attempts on both your lives. Correct?

The Queen Regent nodded. "Yes, I knew that after Astile died I would have to rely on my personal guard and loyal officials. There have been three attempts on my life, that I am aware of, in the last year alone."

"I understand that concern, and I think by accepting the protection that comes with becoming part of this empire, and the protection that comes with being a direct relative of myself and my father, nobody would dare make another attempt at usurping your son's rightful throne. Once you become the Queen Mother of my sister, who would be a direct princess of the Arrdussian empire, everybody will fall in line and become loyal subjects. I don't want to rule with fear, but when it's used properly, it is a very effective deterrent."

"So, Faruqh would have to pay tribute, in gold and provisions and, in return, receive ultimate protection and peace and be given a much better chance to come out, still free, from the Zarrekian invasion that is coming soon?" asked Queen Regent.

"Yes, that sounds about right," answered Thompsel.

"I have two conditions that I would hope you consider: Firstly, I would like to foster Kansel, from now until both she and my son come of age, in Faruqh, to get her accustomed to the palace, people, and my son."

"Secondly, I would ask for something that might offend you ..."

She looked at Thomascus on his throne when she said that. Then she turned back to Thompsel.

"I would like to request that if after one year, there is no information about Zarrek moving towards their invasion or any other news about aggressive activities, then my agreement becomes void, and Faruqh returns to its status of a sovereign nation."

Thompsel thought for perhaps one second. "Both conditions are straightforward and agreeable. Kansel going to Faruqh was in my original plan. All I require is that she retains her current servants. Her personal guard, led by Sir Fradius, goes with her. As for the second condition, the situation with Grexle and Zarrek is more dire and short-term than many of you realize, so I have no doubts that in one year we will already be at war."

Next in line were King Drune and King Marxus IX's two situations, which Thompsel assumed would be the most difficult to come to an amicable closure. In his usual, extremely straightforward style, he made this concern known.

"Next, we come to King Drune. I assume you won't make this easy for me," he said as he looked at King Drune.

Drune stood up and grabbed his sword, which was still in its scabbard. At this, some of Thompson's guards reached for their respective swords, which led Thompsel to put up his hand, signaling to stay their blades.

Drune approached Thompsel; he held up the sword at eye-level and offered it to Thompsel.

"I have one request and one concern. Which would you like to tackle first?"

Thompsel looked at Drune, and he noticed that there was indeed a concern in those old eyes.

"The concern is of more importance to me, so let's start there."

"Okay. As all of you know, I don't have any living children—both of my children died in the war with the Persius Islands to the southeast of Gradon. My son and daughter were twins and brave warriors. Unfortunately, they were betrayed by those closest to them, all of whom I later massacred.

"That was over twenty years ago, and my queen was so heartbroken that she has been in silent mourning ever since. My current heir is my late sister's only granddaughter, my grandniece, Madelin. I am not getting any younger, and I honestly don't know what will become of my family and kingdom after I am gone. I'd like to ask that Culver looks after my heir."

Everyone could tell that Drune was not accustomed to asking for help, as the words left his throat like they were quite forced.

"Your grandniece is seventeen. Correct?" asked Thompsel. Drune nodded, now used to Thompsel's knowledge of such information.

"I can offer something better than a promise of protection. My younger brother, Thomo, is two years younger than Madelin. I would be proud to offer him to marry your grandniece and become your foster grandnephew and learn the proper way to run a nation."

Those in attendance could see intrigue and hope in Drune's eyes.

"After he comes of age, the two would be married, and not only your kingdom but your lineage would be destined to survive and thrive. On a side note, my brother is very handsome, and I am sure that Maddelin will not be disappointed. If your concern is alleviated, then please continue with your request."

"I doubt this request will go over very well with Thomascus, but he has a short sword that I have admired for many years, and I request that sword, in exchange for my own," he said, holding his out, pointing towards Thomascus.

Thompsel looked at his father with a look that showed he knew how beloved that sword was.

Thomascus stood up for the first time and walked to the chamber directly behind the throne. After a few moments, he walked back in with a sword, unlike any other.

The blade of the sword was about two feet long. It appeared to be made of dark metal, almost black with a deep red sheen all the way through, perhaps being folded with ruby dust, and its hilt was a mixture of gold and ruby. The pommel appeared to be a large, molded chunk of ruby with gold weaved through it, and everyone could feel some raw energy radiating from the magnificent blade.

Thomascus approached King Drune, blade in hand.

Thompsel knew that his father would not give the sword, so he was ready to intervene when Thomascus moved to kill King Drune, where he stood.

"Are you willing to be as benevolent as your son seems to be?" asked King Drune as Thomascus approached him.

Thomascus held up the sword, which he named Death's Flame, and spoke.

"Death's Flame is not something I would ever give, freely. There is a condition that comes with this sword to show that one earned it. Just like I did when I got the sword, you have to take it from me."

Drune looked at him for a few seconds. "Okay, I accept the challenge."

At that moment, King Drune's elite guard captain spoke up.

"Your Highness, might I have the honor of winning the sword for you?"

King Drune turned around.

"Captain Arthur, are you worried that I am too old to win on my own?"

At that, Arthur bowed. "I wouldn't dare."

Thompsel had some worries on his mind, so he finally decided to speak up.

"That is not a bad idea. I would like to make a request for my father and King Drune."

Thomascus seemed taken aback by Thompsel's interruption, as he showed a hint of annoyance on his face.

"Please hear me out, Father, for the sake of the realm."

King Drune was willing.

"You have been very forthright so far today, so I am willing to listen to your request."

"Thank you. My hope is that both Captain Arthur and I could perform this task of earning the sword for our respective superiors."

Captain Arthur stepped forward with his longsword and shield held at his side.

"I accept Crown Prince Thompsel's proposal... as long as Your Highness does."

He bowed to King Thomascus. It was plain to see that Thompsel had done something his father was not expecting, and there was silence for a few seconds.

What was most important to note about Thomascus was that, above all else, he loved to fight and always wanted to find other strong people to battle. It did not begin from a place of malice; it was just his way of life.

Thompsel figured that both Drune and Thomascus had the same thoughts about fighting a strong opponent. Still, he was concerned about the consequences if and when his father killed Drune.

"As you wish, son. I'll have some words with you in private, after the conference."

Thomascus went and sat on his throne. Thompsel was relieved to save the situation, although he was admittedly not hankering for the scolding that was coming later.

Now the two contestants made their way out of the palace and down two levels of stairs. Their place of battle was near a fountain that depicted a few children playing, with water shooting out of their hands.

"Captain Arthur, this is a contest to see which opponent can disarm the other first, and I would appreciate it if neither of us died today."

Arthur nodded and brandished his longsword, which was the standard blade for elite guards in Gradon. He preferred this style, even when offered a personalized sword, as it was the type that first showed him his elite status. His shield was iron and rectangular, to his waist if it was placed on the ground. Arthur was big, albeit shorter than Thompsel. As was the norm of Gradon soldiers, he had a shaved head, and he had a scar half-visible on his collarbone.

Thompsel's sword was a two-handed behemoth. The blade was no less than five feet in length and six inches wide. When he picked it up and held it, one could see all of his arm muscles working at full capacity. At the end of the hilt was a spike that he used on more than one occasion to win a fight.

"Ready?" asked Thompsel in full flex.

Arthur sprang forward, faster than Thompsel expected, especially with how heavy that shield looked. Arthur's first swing was overhead, sweeping down, which Thompsel blocked just in time, only to be smashed with the shield in the shoulder, which pushed him back a couple of steps.

"Excellent!" screamed Thompsel.

It was his turn to attack, which he did with a powerful horizontal swing.

All Arthur could do was take the full power with his shield, burying his body behind it, and it was as potent as the rumors he heard. Arthur and his shield were flung some six feet and then slammed on the ground. His sword was still in hand, however.

Huffing and clearly favoring his left side, which he held the shield with a second earlier, Arthur stood back up.

"Your reputation is well-earned, Crown Prince. Power like yours is seldom seen."

Thompsel signaled for him to steady himself and to make his next attack.

Arthur sprang forward, and at the moment when he was in Thompsel's range, he cut to the left, avoiding the vertical slash by mere inches, and slammed his shield into the clinched fists holding the giant sword, in hopes that it was enough to force a drop.

Unfortunately, at the moment of impact, Thompsel took a few steps back, significantly reducing the force received.

"You are not only quick in step but also in wit, Captain Arthur, a worthy opponent indeed."

"I thank the Crown Prince for his praise, and I must return with saying that your stepping back at the perfect moment could only occur with much experience and knowledge."

After a quick smile from Thompsel, the prince lifted his greatsword, both arms fully extended in front, with the hilt slightly below his eyes, where he looked through the sword at Arthur.

Arthur thought at that moment that the crown prince resembled a ferocious beast.

"It is now time for this great contest to come to a close."

Thompsel sprang forward, and as he began to swing downward, he expected Arthur to break to his left, which he did, and at that moment, Arthur realized it was a feint, too late.

Thompsel collapsed his right elbow, allowing the blade to fall to Arthur's left. All Arthur could do was take the blow with his shield, not in the optimal place, which threw him off balance.

Thompsel spun his blade, sweeping down towards Arthur's exposed neck.

Arthur knew he was dead.

Just at that moment, Thompsel slammed his foot into the ground, allowing himself to slow the momentum down enough to stop his blade, less than an inch from Arthur's collarbone.

Instead of hearing the welcoming sounds of the heavens, Arthur heard, "Do you yield?"

Arthur opened his eyes and then kneeled.

"I admit my defeat."

Thompsel reached down and helped Arthur up. "Well fought, Captain Arthur. King Drune has an excellent soldier in his service."

As Arthur made his way towards where King Drune was spectating, he was unsure how his king would react.

"Captain Arthur, I really wanted that sword."

"I have failed you, my king, I accept any punishment." Arthur kneeled in front of his king.

"Watching your fight, I could see that you were giving your all, and you wanted to bring honor to me. I also noticed that Thompsel is a man amongst boys, both in stature and power. Also, Thomascus has not lost his title of the strongest warrior to his son yet, which makes me think that I had no chance at all."

At that last comment, King Drune started to laugh, and then he looked at Thompsel and nodded to him as if he realized why Thompsel wanted to step in and fight in his father's stead.

After that eventful experience, it seemed almost strange that there was still one important task left before the conference could end. After everyone took their respective seats, Thompsel bade the servants pour wine for all of the guests and toast to Captain Arthur for making the challenge worth his effort.

"I am tempted to try and persuade you to join my elite guard."

This seemed half-jest, half-truth, but Arthur answered quickly, "Please forgive my answer, Crown Prince. I was born on the capital island of Jasker, and I have served His Majesty for twenty years. I have to respectfully refuse."

After the toast was finished, Thompsel made his way to the middle of the aisle, in front of King Marxus IX.

"The last point of interest is what concessions and conditions would allow Rahm to willingly become a vassal state of the Arrdussian Empire."

"I have not been king long, with my father dying last year, but he left behind a sturdy economic structure and an even sturdier fortress. You should be well aware that the influence of Rahm is nothing to scoff at, and I have little interest in becoming your puppet."

King Marxus IX, even though he knew he could not win a fight against Culver, was resolute and showed no signs of fear.

"King Marxus, you use the word puppet, but I think you should put yourself in the shoes of each of your citizens. Their day-to-day lives will not change by much, even after becoming a vassal state. A slightly higher tax on each citizen gains them protection from the greater empire, both from the looming invasion and the future. If you make a choice, today, to go against all of the other vassal states who already pledged fealty, it will not be an easy road for Rahm."

"You have given the other states what they needed most, but my kingdom and I have all we need, and, as we always have, will rely upon ourselves for any future problems."

At this last statement, King Marxus IX stood up and stepped up, only a foot away from Thompsel. Marxus was almost a half-head shorter.

"I will be leaving now. Go play your games at ruling the world somewhere else."

Thompsel laughed for a few seconds… long enough to annoy Marxus even more.

"You are brave to speak to me with such contempt. I accept your withdrawal."

"I will allow free passage to Rahm, for you and your retainers. After you leave Culver's borders, you will not be allowed to return unless upon request. Suppose an armed soldier of Rahm ever steps onto Arrdussian soil, be it here or any vassal state. In that case, it will be deemed a war declaration. Rahm will receive no aid if Zarrek makes it that far, and I hope for your people's sake your indifference does not come back to bite you, King Marxus."

"My liege, you've made a brave choice, although one that leaves this minister uneasy," said the Minister of Defense that made the trip with King Marxus IX.

"I have a foreboding feeling that those Decklers have many hidden agendas, and I knew that any questions I had would only be met with their annoyingly smug smiles. I will have our own scouts travel south and check how far along this Grexle person's fleet is truly coming."

At that moment, King Marxus and his retinue were in front of the fountains, as a very anxious soldier came clamoring by. He was sweating profusely and had clearly been traveling at top speed, likely for days.

"I have news from the southern scouts, my lord!" said the scout as he made his way into the hall. King Marxus decided to stay where he was to hear better.

"Scout, what's the urgent news?" asked Thompsel.

"My lord." As he bowed to Thompsel, he moved to the side and did the same to King Thomascus; he then looked at the other lords and hesitated.

"No need to falter; you can share the news with all of the vassal states of our newly formed empire, as this concerns them also."

"Yes, Your Highness. Our scouts in the south have reported that construction of the last one hundred ships of Grexle's armada is underway. He counted them himself, at no small risk to his personal well-being. The good news is that Grexle decided to build them quite far inland to avoid detection, so it will take some months to move all 1,000 of those huge ships to the shore."

"It seems that Culver's information was spot-on, my king."

"Minister Rhodes, it's time for us to head home. We have many preparations to make. It seems we have only a few months to solidify our defenses and adjust to life adjacent to an empire. It might be time to contact Blackbow and the other Jarls."

XI

There was a hazy mist that filled every inch of the meadow that Silla was walking in. There were voices that she did not recognize, in languages that she had no business understanding.

Still, every word was as recognizable as if she said them herself. Soon, after noticing she was all alone, she realized quite lucidly that she was dreaming.

It was not the first time she had such dreams, but they were happening more frequently. It all began when her father died.

"Please help us" was one of the most repeated lines in these dreams, but there was no clear face to go with the voice, and there were always many voices overlapped.

However, this dream was different as Silla heard a new voice, saying in Silla's native language, "Please, do not blame him, please help him. He is desperate and damned. He is desperate and damned."

Before, when trying to communicate with the voices, Silla felt that they could speak to her but could not hear her words. Perhaps they did not know she was there and were simply expressing the concerns and worries that weighed on their trapped souls.

Although she could not clearly make it out, this time, Silla thought she saw a shadowy figure wearing a crown very similar to her own, so Silla ran towards the apparition. Unfortunately, at that time, she woke up in a cold sweat.

Omega was on watch duty near the dying fire when he noticed some stirring in one of the tents.

Silla made her way out and sat across from him, poking at the fire with a nearby branch.

"That woman is not using you as a pillow for once, I see," said Silla in a tired voice.

"She was shivering, so I forced her to bundle up in the tent. She seemed unwilling."

Omega had no idea that this answer made Silla even more annoyed.

"Couldn't sleep?" asked Omega.

"You care about my sleeping habits now?" snapped Silla.

"I do. It's been getting colder the farther we head north, and a good rest might help keep you from getting sick. I don't want to see you ill."

"I have never been sick; even as a child when others got colds and drippy noses, I was always healthy."

Omega stood up and grabbed the throw that was next to him. He walked to where Silla was sitting and kneeled in front of her. He stretched out the throw and wrapped it around her shoulders, like a cape, and tied it under her neck.

"Even so."

Silla's heart began pounding, and she was quite sure that Omega could hear it beating.

"I have something I have meant to tell you for the last few days. We will reach Broken Bridge by tomorrow night, so I think it is time," said Silla, trying to ignore and push aside her still-pounding heart.

"Okay. I have noticed you acting a little strange since about the time Kita started traveling with us."

"I don't think you should get too attached to that woman. We don't know anything about her, other than the name she's given and some stories she's shared over the past few days. Also, she has her own life, and she is not beholden to our arduous journey. I know you have had bad relationships with other people for most of your life. When she decides to go back to her normal life, I fear you might not know how to handle the situation with your limited experience in such matters."

Omega was now sitting next to Silla, close enough to make her feel both happy and anxious.

"You are right that my expertise in personal relationships is lacking, especially at my age. I don't fully understand the nuances of the different types of close relationships that people have. When I talk to Rose, I think of her as a friend. When I talk to you and interact with you, it is different than with Rose."

Silla was having a hard time keeping her heart in her chest, especially after that comment.

"With you, I feel like I should be protecting you from any danger, regardless of the peril it puts me in. You have a unique personality, being very frank. With Kita, I feel different, still. I understand my feelings towards her the least of all. When she is around, I feel what I think is called happiness. When she is not around, I feel an unending anxiousness for which I have no precedent."

"Omega, I think it's time you got some sleep. I'll take the next watch."

Silla did not know how, or perhaps did not want to continue talking about these things.

"You should go lie down next to her tent and rest before we start traveling again."

Silla decided that night, after Omega fell asleep, that it was best for her and her mission to put these feelings she had been having towards Omega in the back of her mind. Perhaps after Kita left and they got closer to accomplishing their tasks, she might have the right to think such fanciful thoughts.

Early afternoon the next day, Silla, Rose, Omega, and Kita were all awake and packed. They were ready to make the last leg of the trip to Broken Bridge, which was the last stop before the Freewoods.

So far, it had been an easygoing journey, with little danger, as one of the main roads coming out of Culver led very near to the Freewoods. It tapered off only a few miles away from the woods' entrance, and Silla heard that one could see the trees in the distance where the road ends.

"We have been traveling together for a few days, Kita, and I just had a thought," said Rose.

Kita was always willing to enter any conversation. "Please, go ahead."

"Do you have a sister, perhaps a few years younger?"

"I have three younger sisters, a younger brother, and my older brother," answered Kita.

"Your distinguishing features are unique, and I frequent the History of Culver Library. I often see a girl there, who looks strikingly similar to you, and since we've been traveling, I have been wondering where I thought I knew you from."

"That would be my sister, Karah. She has shorter hair, hers only going down to her lower back, usually braided, and her eyes are a darker hue of blue, right?"

"Yes, I have not actually spoken to her, but that description is spot on."

"Karah is such a kind, curious woman. People often forget about her as part of the family because she always has her head in the books and seldom interacts with other living, breathing people. She much more prefers her heroes, villains, and other fictional characters. I think before long she will have finished every book in that library."

"If I am ever back in Culver, and we happen upon each other, would you be willing to introduce me to Karah?"

"Absolutely, Karah would do well to have some interactions with other people, and I think she would enjoy someone that has similar interests. Speaking of meeting people, I've wondered, since we've been traveling, how did the three of you meet and start traveling together?"

Kita looked at Omega, who was looking at Silla.

"I hope you don't take offense, but I don't really know you enough to share details about our past."

Since they had met, Silla had been abrupt the few times that she actually directed any words towards Kita. There was an exact distance between them that Silla wanted to maintain. Kita had noticed this throughout their time together.

"I understand when people want to maintain their privacy, but I am willing to travel with you three, and I will be helpful. I don't have any plans on separating, as I owe Omega a life debt and an innocence debt. I have a strong sense of pride when it comes to repaying what I owe, and even more than that, I really enjoy his company."

At that, Kita gave Omega one of her big smiles, which Omega did not know how to react to, making Kita smile even more.

Rose had been increasingly injecting herself in Silla and Kita's interactions to maintain a less awkward environment, and it had become second nature to her by then.

"Well, I first met Silla when she was about nine. I was seventeen, and I had been spending all of my time studying various subjects at the higher learning institutions in Rahm. Although he was not a full-time professor, Silla's father would show up at different facilities once or twice a year to lecture about many subjects, from ancient languages to contemporary art."

Rose started to reminisce.

A young Rose was running down the higher learning center hall; she was late for the class on ancient history and bumped into a young man in his early thirties.

"Oy, watch out! I'm late for my lecture. I'm sorry, but I can't stay to apologize properly."

"What class are you running to?" asked a young, handsome Dr. Gladen.

"Ancient history!" said Rose as she started to run.

"Stop!"

Rose stopped and turned around. "What, I'm really late?"

"If you could do me a favor, I can ask the lecturer for ancient history to wait for you."

"Wow, you know Dr. Gladen? I heard he only shows up maybe once a year, so it's a big deal to get this opportunity!" exclaimed an excited Rose.

"I do know him quite well. He has a daughter waiting in the auditorium, but he forgot some of his material in his office. Could you go keep an eye on his daughter while he runs to the office?"

"Sure, I can do that. What's her name?"

"It's Silla," said Dr. Gladen as he ran the opposite way towards his office.

Rose made her way towards the auditorium. As she stepped in, there were probably fifty people waiting, some seated with writing materials ready for note-taking, while others were in small groups of peers, chatting.

Finally, a little girl with long brown hair in one single braid draped over her right shoulder was near the podium up on stage.

"That must be Silla," said Rose as she made her way up the steps onto the stage to introduce herself.

"Hello, my name is Rose; are you Silla?" The little girl was a bit hesitant, but even more amazed by how beautiful Rose was.

"Yes, I'm Silla; do I know you?" Silla held her hand out to shake.

Rose reciprocated. "I ran into somebody that told me that Dr. Gladen needed to grab some materials, and he asked me to come to watch after you until he returns."

Since only her father would know who she was, Silla was confused.

About ten minutes later, the man showed up, with a big box of various ancient items. As he approached the podium area, Rose began to realize who he was.

"Hey, thanks for watching Silla. I'm Dr. Octavius Gladen."

He shook Rose's hand and grabbed Silla's hand to lead her to a seat off to the side of the stage. "Okay, Silla, sit here, and after Dad finishes with this lecture, we can go home." Silla nodded.

Rose began to walk towards the steps to join her fellow peers.

"Excuse me, I forgot to get your name," said Dr. Gladen.

"It's Rose, Rose Sauveterre."

"Hello Rose, are you interested in ancient history?"

"Very much so. I love all kinds of subjects, but ancient history, languages, and cultures are my favorite." Dr. Gladen smiled at her.

"Excellent. Would you like to be my assistant for this lecture?"

Rose excitedly agreed. Then Dr. Gladen spent the next hour pulling ancient literature and items out of his box and explained what each one was and how some of them might have been used in that time's culture. Rose was the one pulling out the items and holding them up, and sometimes she would look over and do something funny to make Silla laugh.

After the lecture, Dr. Gladen thanked Rose and was planning to take Silla home for lunch.

"Dad, can Rose come home with us for lunch?" Silla had become attached to Rose in that hour of lecturing.

"That's fine with me, but she might have something important to do."

Dr. Gladen and Silla both looked at Rose with innocent eyes, clearly planned out.

"Hmm, I am hungry." They all three laughed and made their way to Dr. Gladen's house.

Now back on the road to Broken Bridge.

"And later, Silla's father asked me if I could look after Silla whenever possible, as his life's work often did not allow him to stay in Rahm for more than a few days a year. From then until about ten years later, Silla and I spent most days together, studying, growing, and maturing together. A few years ago, after Silla became an adult and some other things started to happen, we grew apart a bit. Before we started this adventure about a week ago, we hadn't seen each other for a couple of years."

Kita was very appreciative of Rose's candidness, as she was used to the cold shoulder that Silla was fluent in.

"That's a great experience, Rose. How long have you and Omega known each other?"

Rose looked at Omega and then back at Kita.

"Actually, I only met Omega one day before meeting you, Kita. I had heard about him about a year ago when I bumped into Dr. Gladen in Culver. Dr. Gladen told me that he had saved him from—"

Silla cut off Rose before she could finish her sentence.

"Rose, that's not something outsiders need to know."

Rose looked at Silla and thought about keeping quiet but decided against it.

"Silla, you have to know that with what your responsibilities might be in the future, this way of not trusting and not wishing to be civil with anybody but Omega and I will lead to a very lonely life."

Silla wasn't used to being admonished by people, as Omega rarely talked much, and he was usually her only company.

Omega was busy looking ahead as Broken Bridge was coming into view. Broken Bridge was a town built butted up against the Yue River, whose source was Moon Lake, which was in what used to be the Ruseberg Kingdom. An ancient-looking broken bridge still stood not far from the town, although the bridge people used was much more modern.

As Silla and Rose continued to go back and forth, Omega finally spoke up.

"There is something wrong."

Right at that time, they heard a scream in the distance from inside the town. That scream made Rose and Silla stop arguing.

"What was that?" asked Rose.

"Let's go see if we can help."

Although Silla was hesitant about trusting others with her private matters, she was always willing to help others in need. The four of them made their way into town, only to find a body splayed out near a well and the likely owner of the scream they heard earlier.

A young girl, maybe ten, was sitting beside the corpse of a man—her father.

"Daddy, get up!" said the girl as she sobbed and shook the body that had an apparent stab wound to its back as it lay face down.

Rose got off her horse first and kneeled next to the girl.

"Hi, my name is Rose. Is your mommy around?"

The girl looked up, wiping her eyes. She shook her head.

"Those bandits stole Mommy after they stabbed Daddy." She began sobbing again.

"I'll take her and try to find her house; you guys should figure out what happened here," said Rose as she helped up the girl.

The three of them noticed a large house near the bank of the river. "Maybe that's an elder's house; they might have information," said Kita. As they were making their way to the large house, it was easy to feel a palpable disparity in the air. With that girl screaming, there was nobody out to check on her, and they heard doors being locked and windows slammed closed as they passed.

The three went there and knocked on the door.

"Excuse me, is anyone there?"

An older lady opened the door, just enough to look out.

"Who are you? It's not safe right now."

"I'm Kita; this is Silla and Omega. We are traveling to the Freewoods, and we heard a scream, so we came to help." The lady opened the door wider.

"Please come in. I would be very grateful if young, able travelers would help us."

The inside of the house was quaint with its scented candles, and a fat cat was yawning on the floor. This cat walked up to Omega and started to rub against his legs.

"That's strange; Bats doesn't usually take to strangers," said the older lady. "My name is Pauline, by the way."

Omega bent down and started scratching behind the cat's ears, which Bats seemed to enjoy very much. "Animals tend to be friendly to me and seek my company," said Omega as he picked up Bats and continued to pet him. Kita smiled and reached out and patted Bats.

"Can you tell us what happened to that man outside?" asked Silla, and she seemed a little irked at how casual those two were being.

Pauline began to tell them that very near to Broken Bridge, there are outlaws and bandits in an area known as Safe Harbor. This Safe Harbor was a tentatively put-together community that resided in an area that was not part of any kingdom. Right outside the borders of each.

"Most of the time when they come, it is just to pillage some of our provisions, which we allow, because we don't have very many citizens and even fewer with the vigor to fight. However, this time, they wanted to take some of our pretty girls for what they called peace offerings, much like how some kingdoms offer marriages between each other to maintain peace. The problem was that we didn't agree to that, as they wanted girls that were already married, and we wouldn't give away our young women to those fiends anyway."

Omega and Kita were now listening intently, having put down Bats.

"So, all I have to do is go to this Safe Harbor and teach some bandits a much-needed lesson?" asked Omega earnestly.

"I don't know what you are thinking by saying you have to go alone," said Silla, now looking deep into Omega's eyes, which did not look as soft as usual but looked fierce.

"I just figure, these animals are looking for beautiful women, and I have three beautiful women traveling with me. There is no option where any of you are coming with me to Safe Harbor."

Omega's resolute tone made Silla both happy and concerned.

"I couldn't ask just one guy to go there to help complete strangers. There are probably thirty bandits there."

Pauline was torn between concern for those girls and feeling guilty for being elated that someone was willing to help save them.

Pauline pointed them in the direction of Safe Harbor. It was only about five miles north of the town, west of the old Ruseberg border, and north of Rahm's border.

"Okay, Safe Harbor is just a few miles away, so I should be back in a couple of hours."

Kita wasn't one to sit back at home and wait like a proper lady.

"Omega, I am skilled with weaponry, and I can help more than you think." Omega looked at her and Silla.

"I'll be most effective if I go by myself. If some danger befell either of you, I fear what my reaction might be."

Silla had some understanding of his words, but Kita, having just met Omega, knew nothing of his past traumas.

"I don't know what that means, but—" Kita was cut off by Silla.

"Omega, you already know what I want to warn you about, but in this case, if you have no other options, I won't blame you for using that last resort on those scum that bully and treat women in those ways."

Kita realized that there were hidden secrets between Silla and Omega, and she was jealous.

"I'm not happy about being left alone, but make sure you come back safely with those scared women."

Kita said this while looking deep into Omega's eyes, without her usual big smile.

This sudden seriousness of Kita's surprisingly left Omega with a smile of his own.

"Another new side of you makes me want to return even quicker." Kita tried to remain resolute, but she could feel herself starting to blush. Silla felt invisible.

As Omega got on Coal, his horse, Pauline noticed he had no weapon. "Excuse me, did you forget your sword?"

Omega turned around and looked down at Pauline, Silla, and Kita. "I prefer to do these types of things with my own hands." As he looked at his palm, he spoke in a low voice, perhaps to himself, "They are capable of terrible things."

Omega urged Coal and sped towards the north of town and would arrive at Safe Harbor in no more than fifteen minutes. Silla made her way back to see if she could help Rose calm everyone down and offer whatever help she could. On the other hand, Kita was pacing back and forth where she said farewell to Omega. She had an internal struggle with her next choice.

Omega found himself coming up to a little village with some small cliffs surrounding it on all sides. There was a mouth where the main gate was, with tall walls that went from either side of the entrance to the cliffs, making it look like a big misshaped bowl. Safe Harbor was both suitably named and ironically named.

Omega decided to tie up the horse a few hundred feet away, and he walked up to the front gate, which only had one guard.

"Hey, stranger, do you realize where this place is? We don't welcome newcomers here, especially those that are unannounced and don't have tits."

Omega walked up to the guard, getting maybe two feet away before stopping. The guard took this as aggressive and reached for his sword. Before he could draw it, Omega reached around and grabbed the back of the guard's head and slammed his elbow, with great force, into the guard's nose, which wholly shattered. He fell unconscious without so much as a scream.

"That's one down," said Omega as he opened the gate and slid in.

Inside, the town was smaller than he thought from looking on the outside. Omega's first thought, strangely enough, was how it didn't flood when there was heavy rain in this bowl-like town. As he made his way around the east wall, he noticed a large, grated hole in the ground with little trenches running to it, which made him smile.

"Ah, that's why it doesn't flood."

Omega was not seeing other people, which made him a bit worried about those women. Then he heard a commotion towards the other side of the village.

"Hey, bring those two bitches into the royal chamber; with the other three we took, they are all supposed to be part of the harem," said one of the kidnappers.

"The king don't know how many we took; how about we keep these two in our house on the other side of town?" said another kidnapper. There were six residents of Safe Harbor and two girls from Broken Bridge in front of Omega.

"Looks like six more are added to the list," said Omega as he approached the six kidnappers without much stealth. Omega was seldom interested in sneaking or observing first, especially if he was alone.

"Oy, what's Mac doing out there, letting some unknown bastard in 'ere? Must be sleeping on the job again."

Omega approached the six men, all of whom were in their thirties and looked dirty and dangerous. All six had swords on their side. Two grabbed for their whips while the other four drew iron.

"You must have a death wish, bastard. Walking up to us in this way, you must be new to the area." Omega was ignoring the man speaking.

He thought for a second and figured he would have little chance to win and keep the women safe with just his gloved hands... not without going into that scary place.

"Both of you from Broken Bridge; I would appreciate it if you could close your eyes until I finish with these six scoundrels. You will be back home within the next hour." Omega gave them a soft smile with his gentle eyes. The two scared women looked at each other and then closed their eyes.

"Okay, how about we get started?" said Omega as he took off his gloves for the first time in a long time.

"This guy must be crazy. Let's kill him and go have some fun with these two before we go to the king's marriage party later," said one of the kidnappers that was holding a whip.

What happened next was quite interesting.

Omega charged the guy closest to him as the kidnapper furthest from him snapped his whip and grabbed Omega around the neck, which stopped Omega in his tracks. Omega turned and looked at him with a scary smile. "I guess you want to be first."

Omega rushed him, and as he got close, he touched the whip, making it vanish, which completely astonished the six men. "What?" was all he could say as Omega grabbed his throat; he disappeared, leaving only his clothes. "That's one."

This impossible occurrence made four of the remaining five fall to the ground. The fifth kidnapper reached for one of the women, presumably to use her as a hostage, but before he could get a good hold on her, a massive elbow connected with his eye, forcing him to the ground.

Omega ran towards the group of kidnappers still on the ground, dumbfounded. "No, please don't kill me!" said one of them, but as he saw Omega get close and the look in his eyes, he knew that it was hopeless. The kidnapper barely had time to ponder his life's choices.

Omega touched one and then another, and as he reached out and touched the third, he heard a scream. As he turned and looked, the kidnapper he punched earlier, with one swollen eye shut, held one of the women, knife to the throat.

Omega was not quite sure how to handle a situation like this as he was used to only having to worry about himself in a fight.

"Don't worry, just keep your eyes closed."

"Hey, Jake, get up and go get the boys out of the king's cavern. I don't know what he is, but with enough numbers, we should be okay," said the swollen-eyed kidnapper.

Omega didn't mind if everyone came out at once, as it would make his task even more manageable. Still, he didn't want anything to happen to the women.

"What a drag" was all he could say, but just then, he got some unexpected aid.

One arrow hit Jake in the center of his back, and as soon as the hostage-holder noticed, a second arrow found him this time, right between the eyes. Omega looked behind him and saw a familiar face.

"Hi, I told you I could help," said Kita with her bow in hand. Omega immediately looked at his hands, and then he looked on the ground where he was earlier, searching for his gloves.

He was afraid of Kita's reaction and had been wondering how to broach this magic of his since they first met.

He spotted them and picked them up, putting them on his hands.

"Okay, both of you can open your eyes now." The two girls looked around and saw a few pairs of clothes on the ground and were confused, concerned, and terrified at the same time.

"Don't worry too much about what happened to these bastards. You are safe now and can return to Broken Bridge. I'll take care of your friends that are still here, don't worry."

The abrupt switch from terrifying to gentle was very Omega.

The two women thanked Omega and ran towards the gate. They also thanked Kita as they passed her.

"I appreciate the assist, but you should head back with them."

Kita gave Omega a frown. Another new look he hadn't experienced from her.

"I'm not going anywhere except to get the rest of those girls out of here. I let you stop me once, earlier, but that went against my will, and I won't let it happen again."

Kita said this with a rugged look. She valued her freedom and free will more than anything else.

Omega had so many thoughts and feelings that he didn't know how to order them or deal with them. He could only sighed and walked up to her and did something that Kita was shocked by.

Omega walked up to her and gave her a hug. "I'm sorry I forced you to do something against your will. Freedom is still new to me, but I also really value it after getting a taste of it. I'll never force you to do anything again."

Kita was standing there in Omega's embrace, her arms at her sides, probably due to the shock of the surprise.

Omega released his embrace. "I have some things to say before we go looking for the king's cavern." Kita was still in shock, and Omega had to wave his hand in front of her eyes to snap her out of her bewitchment.

"What?" was all she could stammer out.

"I have a secret that I have been hiding from you. I won't be able to get out of this upcoming fight without revealing my true self, so all I can do is warn you in advance that it's terrifying."

Kita looked at Omega and then at his hands. "Does it have something to do with your hands?"

Omega must have had an incredulous look on his face because Kita smiled.

"I have noticed throughout the time that we have been together, you have never taken off your gloves, not once. Also, when you first saw me a few minutes ago, you were in a panic to find your gloves and put them back on."

"Yes, it is my hands. Silla had advised me not to reveal my secret to people, but at this point, I don't want to lie to you anymore. We don't have time to go into all the details, but I have lived more than twenty years of my life in Irkdale, in one of the Ascension Integration Centers as they are known. Those places' purpose is to use any means necessary to draw out a slave's magic and break their minds to create a perfect soldier... He's made thousands from what I've heard. I'll tell you in full detail another day, but if things get bad in there, there's a chance I'll lose full control of myself. If that happens, I can't guarantee your safety."

Kita's facial expressions were not what Omega had expected.

"So, it's true that people used to have magic, and perhaps still do, locked deep inside?" asked Kita with a look of wonderment.

"My sister, Karah, read in an ancient tome found in Culver that something happened hundreds of years ago that sealed everyone's magical acupoints, but the innate, unique magical properties of each person were still inside, waiting to be unlocked. I have often heard that only those officials from the church were ordained by the gods and goddesses to be worthy of possessing magic."

"You're amazing," was all Omega could say, and he thought how foolish he was for worrying about Kita's reaction.

Although she was excited at hearing what Omega had to say, Kita remembered their original purpose. "Let's go save these women and go back to Broken Bridge."

The two of them made their way towards the back of town, where there was a large cave in the cliff. The self-proclaimed king used this as his residence. The other three women from Broken Bridge were supposed to be in there and possibly already in danger.

Inside the cavern, Omega and Kita could see a series of trails leading to different size caves.

"Which way do you think we should check first, Omega?" Omega walked to each of the three entrances and listened.

The first two were silent, and then suddenly, from the one in the middle, a distant muffled voice could be heard.

"Today is my wedding and the official beginning of my harem. Where are those worthless idiots? You said I have more wives coming, right? You two, go check and see what the hold-up is."

Omega motioned to Kita to hide in the entrance behind her, and he would hide in the other one. Omega took off his gloves and dropped them in the cave entrance he was standing in.

The three men the king sent all came out of the middle entrance. "I wonder how much fun those bastards had with the king's wives. I knew I should have stayed with the second group," said the frontman.

Right when the third guy was clear of the entrance, Omega swept out of his hiding spot. He placed his hand on the third and second man's necks before they could make a sound, and the first guy began to pull out his sword, but before he could, Omega grabbed his face, poof. Omega decided to touch their clothes as well.

Omega then looked over to where Kita was to see her reaction.

Kita had seen the whole situation, and to his surprise, she was not terrified by Omega.

"I never imagined something like that existed." Kita went and picked up Omega's gloves. "Do you have control over what you can destroy? Are these gloves impervious?"

"They were soaked in Silla's blood. I won't go into detail because, one: It's not my story to tell, and two: I don't fully understand her destiny, myself."

Kita was becoming more intrigued by Omega every second but had to remind herself again of their mission.

"Let's go; judging from the time the king told those three to come to the time they arrived, this tunnel is not very long," said Kita as they both made their way through the tunnel.

Upon finding the exit of the tunnel, Omega and Kita saw a big opening, more prominent than they expected. The king was sitting at his throne in the middle of the cavern. It was probably two hundred feet from end to end. There were more people there than the two of them had estimated. They had heard maybe thirty people stayed in Safe Harbor, but it looked closer to fifty from their perspective.

"Okay, it looks like everyone is close together, which makes my job a lot easier," said Omega in a whispered voice. The two of them were very close to each other, which they both noticed.

"I'm going to rush them, and while I am drawing attention, you go around and come up from behind the throne to grab the women."

Omega was resolute, but Kita wasn't sure.

"There are too many for you to handle on your own. You saw how fast I am with the bow. I have ten arrows left, so I could take down a few to help."

"These guys are not against taking hostages, so what do we do once one of them grabs a girl, and there is nobody to make a stealth attack this time?" asked Omega.

Kita had no right answer, so they decided on Omega's rush plan.

Omega was very good at drawing attention. He walked straight in the hollow and up the path that led to the seating area and throne where everybody was gathered.

"Hey, you, kidnapping bastards! I'm here to take back those three women you stole from Broken Bridge."

This sudden outburst stunned everyone as they got up and looked around, expecting to see a large group of soldiers. To their amazement, it was just one man with no weapon to boot.

The king was likely made king because he was larger than the rest and probably the nastiest. He had a few scars and scabs on his face. He had at least one disease. The king stood up and walked towards where everyone was sitting, leaving the three women unguarded, precisely what Omega had wanted.

"Who the hell are you, pal? Today is my wedding day and the opening of my official harem. These women are a strategic move that I took, and they will bring a sense of long-lasting peace to Broken Bridge. I even killed their husbands, so they wouldn't have any other options as used goods. I'm doing them a service, allowing them to join my harem."

There were cheers and affirmations from the king's subjects. Omega was becoming more angered by each word of nonsense the king spewed.

"You should know, Your Highness, that I have already saved those two girls outside and killed ten of your citizens. What would make for an even longer-lasting peace would be that all of you die, right here, right now," said Omega with vitriol that would make anybody shudder.

All of those that were sitting now stood up, and they all grabbed their various weapons. Some had clubs, while most had swords, and two men had crossbows.

Omega took inventory of their weaponry as he made his way, slowly, closer to where everyone was gathered. He knew that he had to take out the two bowmen first, as they would be the most annoying.

"I will give you one opportunity to join my kingdom and swear fealty to me," said the king. "I am impressed that you killed so many of my men outside, and although I am angry that I lost two of my wives, I can always return to Broken Bridge to retrieve them whenever I feel like it."

Omega noticed in his peripheral that Kita had finally made her way behind the throne area and was in place to save the women. "Okay, Your Highness, if any of your men can defeat me, whether in groups or by themselves, I will join your kingdom and swear allegiance."

This made the king happy. "You hear that, my loyal subjects. Whoever defeats him for me will be handsomely rewarded with one of my wives."

As the king said this, he and his subjects turned to look at the three women, and to their surprise and ire, they saw Kita luring all three away from the area, towards the way she had come from.

"It looks like I just found the fourth wife, and she's gorgeous!" exclaimed the king, now salivating. Omega regretted that everyone spotted Kita already, but he was already right behind the first bowman, who he touched on the arm. *Poof.*

Much to Omega's dismay, however, most of the king's subjects took chase after Kita, with only a handful trying to block his path. Those few that stayed behind died very quickly.

"Block off the exit. I will have that redhead as my queen! She will warm my bed tonight!" shouted the king, who was full of passion and energy.

As everyone was running, Omega could pick off a few stragglers. Still, before he could catch up, Kita exhausted her arrows and was surrounded by the twenty or so remaining subjects and the king.

"Ah, my queen, you are the most beautiful woman that has ever existed in this world. I will gladly give up these three dogs if you come warm my bed this very moment!" The king was licking his lips as he was speaking to Kita.

"I will kill myself long before I allow you to do anything to me," said Kita as she reached for a small dagger on her hip.

She grabbed it and at first put it up to her neck, but it was a feint. She lunged towards the king as he tried to calm her down, but one of his subjects sacrificed himself, which allowed the king to grab Kita from behind.

As the king was holding on tight, his remaining followers were closing in their circle.

"Stop!" Omega shouted, but at the same time, he was feeling light-headed, and he was having chest pains, blood on fire. He dropped to one knee and looked up and made eye contact with Kita, who was struggling desperately to get free. "Not now ..."

Just then, painful memories completely enveloped Omega's senses.

"Fifty-four, you have a new cellblock neighbor," said the guard. Fifty-four was around twenty-seven at this point and had already gone through all the usual stages, with only the lost love stage remaining.

"This is 128, a transfer from one of the other facilities. As the longest-lasting, most defunct slave, use your experiences to get along with her."

Fifty-four didn't say anything in response, but a gruff could be taken as a *yes*. Subject 128 was a woman close to the same age as 54, and it was the first time he had seen a female prisoner. Fifty-four always assumed the female test subjects were kept in separate facilities.

"Hey, you. The number they gave me is 128, but I call myself Lucy," said the newcomer in a whispered voice. "What's your name?"

Fifty-four took a few seconds and then said, "I don't remember my name from before coming here, so 54 is fine."

From what 54 could see, as the lighting was not significant in those facilities, Lucy was skinny and had short black hair, and she appeared to be tanner than he was. This made 54 think she was newly captured.

"Did they just capture you, Lucy?"

"Nope, I've been here for almost ten years. I used to live in southern Faruqh near the Ardian Sea. My name used to be Riley, but after being here so long, I figured it was better for my mental state to forget about ever returning to my past life."

As a few weeks passed, 54 had no experiments ran on him, and neither did Lucy, which was odd, but a welcome reprieve. The two of them rarely saw any guards or researchers, usually only at mealtimes.

The two became fast friends, and they began to find themselves having feelings of love for each other. Lucy had many stories to share, from before she got captured, as she was old enough to remember many things, unlike 54. The two were in cells that were just close enough to where they could touch each other's hands at full stretch.

About one month after the two met, 54 realized a pain far worse than any that left the scars that covered his body.

Early in the morning, 54 woke up and looked towards Lucy's cage. "Good morning, Lucy, how'd you sleep?"

Lucy gave a big yawn. "As good as can be expected on a stone floor."

Fifty-four only knew stone-floor beds, so he was quite used to it.

Three big men Omega did not recognize opened and went into Lucy's cell, which was not very big, and seemed even smaller with four people in it.

"What's going on? Is it time for breakfast?" asked Lucy in a voice that showed she didn't believe the question she asked.

"It's going to be an experiment for one of you, a chance for freedom for us three, and terrible tragedy for the other," said the man in the front.

Fifty-four knew that something was different. "Hey! I don't know what you guys are doing, but I swear if you touch her, I'll make you regret it!" The three started laughing.

The guy furthest from Lucy chimed in, "That's what they are hoping happens, and what we are betting against."

Just then, the three guys lunged forward and started to grab at Lucy's clothes, and while she was fierce and giving great effort, she was far too weak to defend herself. First, they ripped off her shirt, then her pants and underclothes.

All the time, 54 was screaming at them, "Stop it! I'll kill you all!" Fifty-four was pleading in his mind for whatever magic that they thought he had in him to come out and help her.

Lucy was crying and reaching through her cage, towards 54. "Please don't look!"

Fifty-four was hysterical at this point, trying to rip apart the bars with his brute strength, to no avail, and his innate magic was nowhere to be found. The three men continued to assault Lucy, both physically and sexually, for what seemed like an eternity. By the time they finished, 54's voice was completely gone from screaming and cursing his uselessness. Lucy was lying lifelessly on the ground.

The three men got up and made their way out of the cell. They turned, and one of them spoke to 54.

"We want to be free, and they promised that if we raped her in front of you, and you didn't unlock your magic, that we could leave this hellhole."

Another one spoke up, "I'm sorry, but I don't want to die in this dark, depressing place."

Fifty-four looked at them with a blank look full of despair and hopelessness. He was breathing so heavily and sweating profusely. Just then, one of the researchers walked into Lucy's cell.

"One Twenty-eight is useless now," he said as he grabbed her by the leg and dragged her out of the cell. Fifty-four could only press his head against the gap between bars and try his strength again, which of course, was worthless.

The researcher returned a few minutes later with a spear in hand, and 54 figured he was about to receive another round of pain, presumably because he failed to unlock his potential. When the spear came through the cage, 54 had an idea that had never crossed his mind before. He reached and grabbed the spear and torqued it to where it was jammed sideways in the gap of the bars.

"Hey! What the hell do you think you're up to?" asked the researcher. Fifty-four had decided that his life was no longer worth preserving. As he held the spear, he placed the tip where his heart was and backed up as far as his arms would stretch.

"Shit!" said the researcher as he desperately tried to pry the spear free.

"Hurry, 54 is going to kill himself! Faulk will kill us all if we let him die!"

Just as 54 began his forward lunge, something happened in his body that felt like the opening of a great dam, with raging waters behind it. Suddenly, when the spear tip touched his chest, it disappeared, which caused Omega to fall forward, grabbing the cell bars, which also disappeared.

As soon as Omega recalled grabbing the researcher, he returned to reality, and some terrifying force unleashed from his body. It seemed like only a few seconds passed in the real world because Kita was almost in the same spot, with the king behind her, grabbing both breasts and licking her neck.

A shockwave emanated from Omega's body, causing the cavern to shake, as he let out a shockingly loud, thunderous roar, "AAAHHH!!!!" and Kita was quite sure that she saw Omega begin to float off the ground, as his body bent backward, but what happened next forced Kita to worry about other matters.

As Omega was screaming, parts of different people were disintegrating without being touched. Both of the king's hands disappeared to about halfway up his forearms, causing him to scream in agony. One subject lost half of his right arm to the elbow, and another lost both legs. Parts of the cave floor beneath Omega were also cracking and vanishing. Blood was spraying from every direction, with another subject losing half his skull, and yet another getting a large hole in the middle of his chest.

Omega was still hovering off the ground, body contorted, howling a blood-curdling scream, but somehow, as fate deemed it, Kita was left entirely unscathed. She looked around, and it seemed that the three girls had long since run out of the cave, and all the subjects were either dead or bleeding out, soon to be finished.

Just then, Omega stopped screaming and landed on his feet, hunched forward. He picked up his head and looked ahead at Kita with eyes that were as red as her hair, much like what many would assume a demon's eyes resembled.

"Omega, it's me, Kita." Kita was in shock from what she had witnessed seconds ago and couldn't produce any other words.

Omega did not have any acknowledgment on his face. Kita thought it was somebody else standing there because Omega looked at her as if she wasn't even there, or as if his eyes didn't work the way everyone else's did. Just at that moment, though, Omega closed his eyes and fell backward, unconscious.

Kita was in a panic because it was now nighttime, and it was getting cold. Unfortunately, Omega, who had been passed out for the last ten minutes, had been shivering more violently at each passing minute, with his body being colder than it should have, even in that dark, cold cavern.

"What do I do, Omega!? Please wake up. You are going to die if your body temperature keeps dropping at this rate." Kita decided that her best chance of helping Omega overcome his ordeal was to use her body heat to insulate him.

She couldn't move Omega's massive body, so she ripped open his shirt, exposing his bare, scarred chest. She then did the same to her own shirt, exposing her breasts. She went flat, chest to chest on top of Omega, and then draped her sable fur overcoat that she had been wearing over them both.

"Please be okay, Omega," spoke Kita in a soft voice right by Omega's ear, as he was still shivering, though slightly less violently.

At about the same time Omega was almost finishing his flashback, back in Broken Bridge, Silla was sitting up against the wall, eyes closed, and to look at her, people would think she was meditating. In fact, she was experiencing what Omega was going through, along with him.

"Omega, these events I'm seeing, I'm so sorry. I will surely help you understand that there is happiness waiting for you."

Rose was right beside her in wonderment, as this was the first time she had seen such an event. Dr. Gladen had told her about binding magic in the past but seeing it first-hand was different.

"Can you really see and hear what Omega is experiencing?" asked Rose.

"It's more vivid when he's emotionally charged or distressed, so right now, if I was there, in person, it would not seem any more real," answered Silla, with tears running down her cheeks.

"Is something happening to the girls?" asked Rose. Silla shook her head.

"He seems to be having a flashback, much like he did during his fight in the arena. I'm not sure what triggered it, but as soon as it started, all of my senses were immediately dragged into his memory recall."

Just at about the time that Omega broke the memory, returning to himself and releasing the shockwave, Silla screamed in pain and fell to her side, blood seeping out of her nose and ears. She opened her tearful eyes.

"Something horrendous just happened that forced me out of his consciousness." Rose was helping her up and walking her to the bed.

Back in the cavern, Kita had fallen asleep on top of Omega, and a few hours had passed since Omega's outburst.

Just then, Omega opened his eyes, which were now back to normal. He could feel the weight of someone on him, and he looked down to see the top of Kita's very red-haired head, which was cupped right under his chin. She was sleeping ever so soundly.

Omega was confused about what happened, and he realized that his memory between the flashback and waking up was blank.

Although he was anxious, he also didn't want to wake her up. As he tried to reposition his arms, he realized that his gloves were not on, and he thought how lucky she was not to have accidentally touched his hands.

Even though he was trying to be quiet, he stifled a sneeze, which shook Kita awake. She put her hands down on both shoulders of Omega to raise herself up, and their eyes met.

"You're back!" Omega suddenly realized that she had her shirt wide open and tried not to look.

"Sorry," was all he could muster.

Kita also realized her breasts were showing still and grabbed her shirt and re-buttoned it. "You were shivering so fiercely after you passed out that this was the only way I could think of to warm you up," said a slightly embarrassed Kita.

"Are you okay, Omega? Has that ever happened before? You mentioned losing yourself before, but I didn't realize it would be so drastic." Kita said all of these quite quickly as she climbed off of Omega and sat next to him.

"I don't remember what happened after returning from my flashback. I've lost myself before, but only partially, and I could recall what happened afterward. I guess I lost full control of my consciousness this time. Did I hurt you?" asked Omega.

Kita smiled.

"No, you were literally floating while screaming, and if you look at that man-gled pile of rapists over there," she said as she pointed to the mound, "you did all of that without moving, but not one hair on my body was touched. I think fate has other things in store for us."

Omega looked at the gruesome site of bodies. He did not feel remorse, only more anxiety when thinking about this close call.

"Someone that desires her freedom as much as you... I'm surprised you believe in fate."

"Before this incident, I didn't, but after what just happened, and the way you looked at me with those red eyes, as if I didn't exist. If it wasn't Desitine that spared me, I don't know what else it could be."

"Have you seen my gloves?" asked Omega.

"I grabbed them after you passed out." She pulled them out of her pocket.

Omega and Kita decided to drag what was left of the bodies of denizens of Safe Harbor outside and burn them, which was the custom in the north. After that, they decided to make their way back to Broken Bridge, even though it was still a few hours before dawn.

As they got on the horses, Omega was still deep in thought about what just happened and was even more quiet than usual. Kita noticed this and decided to bring up different topics for discussion.

"Hey, I wonder what magic I have welled up inside of me."

Omega thought for a second. "Whatever it is, I hope it's more manageable than my destruction. Also, hopefully, there are ways to unlock it that are less severe than my experience. I have only ever seen my magic and some of the researchers and other experiments, and also Silla's father's curse magic."

Omega realized right away that he brought up something that Silla would disapprove of.

"Forget I said that last part. Please don't bring it up to Silla."

"I have been wondering what kind of relationship the two of you have." Omega wasn't sure how to answer.

"I don't understand, fully, the labels and ideas associated with relationships. I do know that our souls are connected as one, and I'm obligated to protect her at all costs."

Kita was a little downtrodden. "Souls connected as one... No wonder she looks at you that way." Omega was confused.

"What way?" asked Omega, but Kita was silent for most of the trip back to Broken Bridge.

Now back in town, there was still a couple of hours until sunup, so the two decided to rest until morning. Omega expected Kita to follow him. He moved towards what looked like a comfortable spot behind the well house under an awning. Still, she instead made her way towards where Silla and Rose were supposed to be lodging for the night.

"Omega, I'll see you tomorrow; stay out of the wind."

"Okay," was all he could say as he made himself comfortable.

After entering the room, both Silla and Rose were still awake.

"You're finally back! Is Omega okay? I could sense that something difficult happened to him."

Kita thought to herself that these two did have a connection, one she could only dream about.

"He's fine now, out resting not far from here. Did all five women make it back safely?" asked Kita, who was hoping that none of them were traumatized by what they may have seen.

"Yes, two came back first, speaking of some brave man and woman that saved them, which was when I realized you were gone," said Rose, now leading Kita over to a cushy chair.

"The strange thing is that the other three showed up not long after, but with a vastly different reaction. The second set went straight into their respective homes with looks of despair and disbelief. Were they attacked before you could help them?"

Kita was unsure how much she should say or even find suitable words to explain what she saw.

"They weren't attacked. Some things happened, and I was attacked by the self-proclaimed king and probably twenty of his rapist friends." Kita stopped and closed her eyes.

"Oh my. Where was Omega?" asked Silla in a caring way, which was the first time she had shown such emotion towards Kita.

"I'm not sure what Omega went through, and I think whenever he can, he should explain what happened next, but in the end, he saved me again, before anything severe happened. There were probably fifty people in Safe Harbor. Now there are zero." Kita said these last words as she made her way to the bed and fell in it, sleeping before she hit the pillow.

A few hours after returning, Silla, Rose, and Kita all awoke to loud yelling and cursing. They ran outside.

"Demon! Demon!" said one of the women that Omega saved. Omega was now in the middle of the small village, all alone with about twenty-five residents surrounding him, throwing old vegetables, and cursing his presence.

"I saw it with my own eyes. The demon in front of us began to float, and then people all around started to lose parts of their bodies; blood was everywhere! We are so lucky that the demon did not notice us near the exit of the inner cave!" said one of the girls.

Then another chimed in, "After he fell back to the ground, his eyes were as red as those in the demon tales we heard as children!"

Another tomato hit Omega in the head. However, he wasn't aggressive or angry, and he was standing there, taking all of their insults and accepting them.

"I don't blame you for fearing me. As long as you three are safe, it's okay," said Omega as he looked at the blonde girl that he saved.

"Don't look at me! I will be cursed for all eternity."

Then the three companions of Omega showed up.

"What's going on, why the hostility?" inquired Rose as she stood in front of Omega. She only came up to his chest, so someone still threw an old head of cabbage, which hit Omega on the side of his head.

"This man saved your village's women from a terrible fate." The villagers were not much interested in logic at the moment, full of emotion.

"I see no man, only a demon, might even be the king of demons," said an elderly man.

"You three should go pack up; I can handle the ire," said Omega, who was still not the least bit aggressive. Next, someone from the crowd threw a rock, slightly smaller than a fist. It struck Omega in the temple, which made him stagger.

Just when Silla stepped forward to yell at the villagers, Omega grabbed her and buried her into his embrace, completely concealing her slight frame, as another rock hit him in the back.

Omega led Silla from behind, through the throng of villagers, to the outskirts of town, and finished encapsulating her only after it was safe to do so. Kita and Rose were right behind them.

"You okay?" asked Omega as he lightly checked Silla's head and arms for wounds.

"Idiot, you're bleeding and asking me if I'm okay. How can you protect me if you don't protect yourself?" asked Silla as she took out her handkerchief and dabbed Omega's temple.

"Something like this, I can't even feel it."

The four decided their time in Broken Bridge was over, and they had overstayed their welcome. After retrieving their horses, Kita went back by herself and gathered what few supplies she could from those willing to aid her. They set off towards the goal of the Freewoods, which was only about a day and a half away at an average pace.

XII

A man, slight in build and fair in what you could see of his pale face, was sitting, not very kingly, on his throne. This man had a metal covering that went from the middle of the bridge in his nose and ended towards the bottom of his neck, and it was contoured around his collarbone.

There were plenty of theories of why he wore this and even more ongoing bets about whether or not he ever ate anything.

The metal mask had a dark sheen to it. He had jet-black hair, pale skin, and jet-black eyes, although if one looked long and hard enough into those eyes, they would swear that they could see the slightest deep purple hue.

"Your Majesty, all of our preparations for completing the last block of ships are progressing well. If everything stays on schedule, within the year, we will be in Arrdus," said General Pike, who was Emperor Grexle's top commander.

General Pike was in his early forties, and he was completely bald, with a small scar under his right eye.

"Good, how are the provisions procurement coming?" asked the emperor as he was sitting on his throne, which was simply made.

Grexle was not interested in anything luxurious or fancy. Even his palace, if one could call it, was no bigger than a large single-family home. Only Grexle and his harem stayed in that palace. If there was a need for a large meeting with all ministers and courtiers, the nearby restaurant, The Folly's Fowl, was commissioned. Grexle also disliked large conferences and gatherings and usually passed and received needed intel via a few close officials or generals.

"As you know, Zarrek is covered in a large desert; probably 40 percent of your land is desert. This is the main reason for our invasion," explained Pike.

Zarrek was actually bowl-shaped around its desert, Alco. The Alco desert in the center of Zarrek took up about 40 percent of the landmass, with the various Zarrekian allied kingdoms being around that bowl. Zarrek had very few fertile soils left to them, and they used up a large portion of their forestry to make their warships.

Zarrek had been trading, peacefully, with the Barnette kingdom, to the southeast, for food and other needs. However, Barnette has had its own civil wars. Each time a new king took the throne, either renegotiation or complete canceling of the treaties would occur. It was no longer reasonable or efficient to rely on those trade agreements.

"I know all of these, Pike. That arrogant man, Thomascus, refused to listen to our proposal of a trade treaty that could aid both nations. He won't give me what I need peacefully, so I will have to go and take what I need. Now, as to the answer to my original question?"

"Sorry, Your Excellency. From reviewing all of the ministers' figures, it looks like we will have sufficient provisions for a short war. I would say maybe three months of fighting, and after that, we would have to procure more food."

Grexle was in deep thought, eyes closed, and he had a habit of putting his feet up, sitting cross-legged in his throne. Some of the ministers secretly thought that Grexle did not fully respect his own position. Still, anyone that knew Grexle knew that he was full of perplexing behaviors, and he was quite eclectic.

"So, you are saying that I should go in the first battle," said Grexle as he opened his eyes.

"I wouldn't dare to dictate your role, my lord."

Even though Pike was a full head taller than Grexle and probably had fifty pounds on the weight advantage, he personally saw Grexle kill so many warring clans, singlehandedly claiming the throne. Grexle also had unpredictable mood swings.

"I prefer to go with the vanguard, so there's no need to hold your tongue, Pike. If we are in such dire need of food for the troops, perhaps we should invade, via Braske Bay, instead of conquering Gradon Islands first, and then coming up through Faruqh as we first planned," explained Grexle.

"I think if we can come up through Braske and then make our way straight to the communal harvesting area, which our scouts say is more extensive than we can imagine, then holding that area might decimate the divided states. Arrdus's biggest weakness is that all of the nations are reluctant to reach out for help with each other, and even less likely to put their neck on the line for others," answered Pike.

"What's the latest from our spies in Irkdale?" asked Emperor Grexle as he pushed his unkempt hair out of his eyes.

"We only have two spies left in Irkdale's inner-regulatory governing body. News can't come out very often, but the last report received was two days ago, and much of what you predicted was in the report," said Pike. Grexle showed some sympathy in his eyes …

"That fool Thomascus has no idea that he is falling victim to a grander plot than he could imagine," said Grexle as Pike shook his head in disbelief.

"He really believes that Irkdale's Grandmaster and Supreme Leader Faulk is relaying information on other kingdoms, wanting nothing in return," said Pike as Grexle stopped him.

"Thomascus is not naïve, but I fear his desire for a worthy opponent and a memorable battle is clouding his judgment. Everyone has a demon in his or her heart; it's just unfortunate when a person with supreme authority puts others in danger to satiate their greed. An old friend that helped me find information on my past warned me years ago that something like this might happen."

"It's the sword, is what he told me."

"What sword?"

"That's not important for now."

Although Pike was probably the closest of any official to Grexle, even he knew nothing of Grexle's life before he appeared in Zarrek's multi-family war for power. Pike had also never seen his emperor without that strange metal covering on his face. But he dare not ask its purpose.

"Irkdale has been focusing on its militarization more in the last year than possibly the last one hundred years. Before, our spies always reported, even before you took command, Emperor, on the fascination with experimenting and opening the prisoners' magical acupoints. Now Faulk seems to be focused on strategy, and he is going over methods to either help Arrdus or Zarrek," explained Pike.

Grexle had his eyes closed again, as he liked to picture what people were saying.

"That means that he won't make a move, possibly at all, but it would be at least a year before we know decisively which side is coming out on top. Faulk has been passing information to both Thomascus and me. Unfortunately, he has been corrupting Thomascus and who knows how many others with his manipulation magic. He has long hated me because his magic has zero effect on me."

Just at that time, the two of them heard a hawk screech. It flew in the open door of the unspectacular palace and landed on Pike's outstretched arm. He clicked his teeth a couple of times, patted the hawk on the neck, and withdrew the note from its leg. He handed the note of Grexle.

Conference finished at Culver. All but Rahm agree, tentatively, to become Arrdussian Empire, with Thomascus as the first emperor. His son, Thompsel, the Crown Prince, had extensive knowledge of our war preparations.

"Looks like we have a leak, or their spies are more skilled than we thought," said a clearly unhappy Grexle as he handed the note over to Pike. Pike seemed less surprised and more anxious than his emperor.

"Thomascus is shrewder than I had perceived. He used our war-building effort with precise timing to unite Arrdus. Their fear of the tales of Your Majesty's conquering abilities, plus the less than exquisite circumstances that some of the royal families are in, were used pristinely by the new Emperor of Arrdus," said Pike, in reverence.

"Our biggest advantage was their divisiveness, but we've come too far and put in much too grand an effort to turn back now," said Grexle as he closed his eyes again.

"What do you think, Pike?"

"I have a few different ideas, but one that could catch them off guard, and has a better chance of succeeding than some of the others involves speeding up all activities, at least two-fold, and invading directly into Culver. We could use the Culver mountain range as a natural cover on both sides to flank the castle. I don't think all of the different soldiers would have time to join together in Culver."

"Hmm, while that plan does have some merit, mine is much more interesting. I've had ulterior motives this entire time, but with this news, I will be going on some excursions very soon."

Just then, though, Grexle's harem all came into the throne room. Consorts Mary, Elizabeth, Jill, Rosalinda, and Grace all called to their husband, "Grexle, it's time." Grexle looked at Pike.

"We will have to discuss this a little later. Please shut the door on your way out." Grexle walked to the five consorts, and they all went into the room behind the throne.

Pike made his way out of the palace. He always was amazed that the emperor had five consorts that still went to bed together.

None of them argued or fought with each other, like what was commonplace in other harems. Pike knew that Grexle wouldn't summon him again for at least a whole day, so he made his way to Bolden's center city area, which was the Zarrekian Empire's capital.

Each family or clan that took power would move the resources and the capital to their respective family's cities. Even though Pike didn't know Grexle's background, he assumed that Bolden had some significance to his emperor.

Bolden was to the northwest of the Alco desert. It was only a couple of hours away from where the warships were built, so perhaps Grexle had set all of these events in motion with the purpose of efficacy in mind. Bolden's center was now bustling as merchants and traders from the different kingdoms in the empire and even some neighboring sovereign states had traveled to set up shop where the emperor lived. Pike knew in his heart, however, that hard times were coming for everyone, not just the soldiers or his emperor.

XIII

The day and a half ride from Broken Bridge to the lush entrance of the Freewoods was coming to an end as the group was maybe a hundred feet from the first thicket.

"Welcome to the Freewoods. Although it's thick in many places, I have found various paths that are traversable, and we should be able to comb the forest," said Kita, who was mostly back to her free-spirited self.

Silla was in front. "Rose, do you have any leads as to where in the Freewoods the text references point to?"

Rose thought for a moment.

"No, there were never specific landmarks mentioned, but it was clear that there was a heavily-visited hub here, but again some of the text is from hundreds, possibly thousands of years ago."

Kita added some thoughts from her own experiences in the woods.

"I don't know what you are looking for, but there has always been a strange occurrence, without fail, when I head to the center of the Freewoods." Silla seemed very interested in strange occurrences as she took out her notepad.

"Please share with us, Kita," said Silla, and it seemed like their collective experiences in Broken Bridge helped bring the two closer together.

"I have tried to enter the center of the forest, a handful of times, and each time I had to turn back or go around. When getting to what I guessed was the center, a thick mist, which was not their seconds before, would permeate every inch of space, so dense that I could not catch a breath. It felt magical. Up until seeing Omega's magic first-hand, I hardly believed magic existed. Still, now I'm almost certain that the center of the forest is guarded by a magical ward."

Silla and Rose looked at each other and nodded.

"If any place in the Freewoods would house remnants of an ancient, secret society like the Velantosse, a magical ward is a good place to start," said Rose.

Omega half-expected Silla to get annoyed with Rose's slip of the tongue, but much to his surprise, Silla held it in.

"I see you finally accept our friend Kita as being trustable," said Rose, with a smug face.

Silla scoffed and rode a little faster, which made Kita and Rose laugh.

"It's too dark to enter the woods now, so let's set up camp right at the edge and wait for the morning," said Silla, still in a huff.

As they set up camp and got ready to sleep, Omega was responsible for watch duties. He was outside anyway, and he preferred to let them all rest well.

Omega had noticed the last few times that Kita was no longer using him as a pillow, as Silla liked to put it.

However, he still wondered if this time would be different. Kita made her way directly into her tent, merely saying, "Have a nice rest, everyone." She didn't look at Omega, which made him sad.

A few hours passed, and it was the dead of night, with everyone sound asleep; just then, Silla found herself in another of her dreams… although they felt like a separate reality. The now very familiar thick mist was present. Women's voices in languages that she somehow could understand were giving out what felt like warnings.

"*Be careful of them!*" said one voice.

"*They aren't what you think!*" said another specter.

The problem with the visions was that these voices belonged to women that Silla could never fully see. They never gave comprehensive reasonings, only one-line warnings. This time was much different, as it was the first time she heard a familiar male voice.

"*Silla, I'll help you,*" said a very visible Omega, as he looked at her and then turned and started walking away from her.

Silla started running, chasing after Omega, until she finally caught up to him, grabbing his shoulder, and he turned.

"Omega, how are you here?" asked Silla, who was quite happy to see a face that she knew. Unfortunately, when Omega turned around, his eyes were clearly a very dark gray, almost black, and he reached out his ungloved hand and grabbed Silla's face, completely covering it from hair to chin.

Just then, Silla woke up in a cold sweat, short of breath. Silla made her way outside and noticed that Omega was asleep. She didn't want to wake him up, but she also wanted to share her dream with him.

As she contemplated waking him up, an owl in the nearby thicket hooted a couple of times, which, combined with Silla walking around, made the decision for her. Omega opened his eyes.

"Another dream?" asked Omega as he noticed her frightened look. He got up and went and helped her take a seat next to him.

"Yeah, this one was similar in most aspects to the rest, but there was one significant difference," said Silla as she fixed her eyes to his.

This was perhaps the first time that Omega noticed how beautiful Silla was. Even though it was the dead of night, Silla's green eyes were reflecting almost unnaturally bright in the light of the moon.

"You were in my dream this time, Omega. You told me that you would help me, and then when I caught up to you, your eyes had gone almost black, and you reached out and grabbed my face, with so much force, shaking me awake."

Omega didn't know how to respond.

Silla noticed Omega's confusion and guilt.

"Even though you seemed to want to kill me, there was concern in those dark gray eyes and no malice. I felt like in your own way, you thought you were helping me."

Omega broke eye contact with her, reached over her left shoulder, brought his face quite close to hers, and grabbed an extra blanket, throwing it over her and covering her head. He then flicked her head in an attempt to add some levity to the situation.

Silla started to laugh, almost uncontrollably, like she had wanted to lower her guard. When she finally pulled the blanket off of her head, her hair was all splayed out and unkempt, with the moon reflecting her face; Omega couldn't take his eyes off of her, although he also felt many other feelings, like guilt and betrayal, mixed with a sense thinking forbidden thoughts.

All of this was also experienced by a third person, Kita, inside her tent. She had woken up when Silla had woken in a fright, as their two tent walls were touching.

She could see how they looked at each other through the tent, which generated a single tear, but she decided it was best to go back to sleep.

Silla eventually went back into her tent and went back to sleep as daylight approached.

Now a new day started, and after everything was packed and ready, the foursome made their way into the forest.

The Freewoods were mostly evergreens, yew, and pine, with various other types here and there. The Freewoods sprawled quite a considerable distance, with almost as much land mass as Rahm's kingdom. It was mostly unbothered by people other than hunters.

As they made their way in, they could see paths, some more traveled and clear, and some not so clearly visible. Kita, being the only one with any experience, led the way.

"If we use the paths that keep the various creeks to our right, then we should reach where that fog pops up before nightfall. Where the main road from Culver took us is a benefit, as the Freewoods where we entered is much closer to the center than if we came from the west."

About three hours into their march, the four came across their first encounter with other people in the forest. There were two people, coming from the west carrying a few prey—rabbits and pheasants. The two hunters, one man, and one woman spotted them almost at the same time.

Everyone from both sides stopped.

Kita spoke up first, "Hello, I'm Kita." The two hunters were clearly not used to running into unknown people in their daily lives, as they did not reply.

Silla walked forward a little bit, which caused the two hunters to take a step back.

"We aren't here with any malicious intent; we only want to go to the center, where there is supposed to be a mysterious fog."

At that time, the two groups were about twenty feet apart. Silla noticed a familiar marking right under the woman's right collarbone, which was slightly exposed.

"Velantosse?" asked Silla as she pointed to the woman's marking. The marking was an ornate V, which Silla had seen on some of the papers in the trunk back at her father's house, which felt like ages ago, even though it had been less than a month.

At Silla's comment, both hunters dropped their prey and pulled taught their bows, both aiming at Silla.

"We mean you no harm; I have been looking for you guys—" but before Silla could finish, the male hunter, who was in his early thirties, interjected.

"He has been seeking for a way in for years... Are you his spies?" Silla took another step forward, but at that time, the female hunter spoke up.

"Be careful, Ben; Irkdale spies are always cunning. That one has the stink of Irkdale on him," she said as she pointed at Omega.

Ben looked at his fellow hunter. "Sarah, go get reinforcements. Captain should be nearby."

Sarah hesitated for a second, not wanting to leave him alone, but agreed, nevertheless. At about the same time the two talked, Omega made his way in front of Silla to block her from the bow's path.

Ben noticed after Sarah headed deeper into the forest.

"Hey, don't move! Just because I haven't shot yet, doesn't mean I will hesitate to kill you." Omega, who was very calm, gave a small smile.

"If you release that arrow, it will be the last thing you'll ever do in this life."

Ben could see in his eyes and hear in his voice that Omega was not bluffing but did not falter. "I'd be interested in seeing how you pull off that feat," said Ben. When it seemed like the tension between the two was at its breaking point, Silla found her way on the side of Omega, grabbing his arm.

"Omega, he will be an ally soon, be nice."

Omega backed up a step, which also lessened the tension on Ben's side as he lowered the bow. After a few moments of silence, Sarah came back with reinforcements.

"Ben, I'm back with Captain Cross," said Sarah as she and Captain Cross appeared. Sarah was in her late twenties, and Cross was around forty, with almost as many scars on his arms as Omega.

"What's the situation, Ben?" asked Cross as he and Sarah made their way to Ben's side.

"These people recognized our mark and said they have been searching for Velantosse."

Cross looked mostly at Omega, seeing all of his scars. "What's your number?"

Omega looked at him for a moment, "Fifty-four."

"I'm number 19 from facility three. I escaped about ten years ago."

There was some silence for a moment, then Silla spoke up, "We are in the same boat, and my goal for coming here was to meet Velantosse who could help me with my quest." Silla said this in a very resolute way that maybe didn't match her small stature.

"I can see that he has a similar background as me, and I can also assume that he has unclogged his magic channel, so I have to be on my guard," said Cross.

Silla thought for a moment, then reached into her backpack, which she always had on her, grabbing the crown for the first time since putting it in there. Silla took out the crown, which was more majestic and mysterious than she remembered, and she held it up above her head.

Cross immediately dropped to his knees upon seeing the crown, crossing his arms and kowtowing to Silla. Although the other two hunters were unsure of what that crown was, they soon followed the captain's lead.

"Please rise," said Silla as she put the crown back in her backpack. At the same time, Kita was thinking to herself how that crown looked very familiar.

Cross, Ben, and Sarah stood up. Cross stepped forward. "Guardian?" Silla shook her head.

"My mother was a Guardian. Iris Darcius was my mother," she said proudly.

"I've heard about her from some of the elders," said Cross.

"I'd like to meet these elders before I say anymore," explained Silla. Cross bid them to all follow him back to their base. As they were walking, Cross explained a little of their current plight.

"We have a self-sustaining model that offers the food and water we need, and we only rarely come out to hunt, as sometimes we really want meat. Spies from Irkdale are sometimes spotted in the woods; they are forever interested in our movements."

At that time, Sarah spoke up, "I'm sorry about how agitated we were, but the few times I have come across other people this deep in the woods, it has been spies from Irkdale or bandits."

"I understand; we have had our own bandit troubles in the past," replied Rose.

The group of Velantosse and the four travelers were still a couple of hours away from the center. They were going at a comfortable pace, with Cross acting as a tour guide.

"If you were to go farther northwest, along the edge of the deadlands, it can be quite dangerous. There seems to be an evil air about the place, with beasts being more aggressive and even larger than their usual kind."

Silla wrote down some of what Cross was saying—what she found pertinent or interesting.

"I've never heard much about the deadlands, only the name. What is north of Arrdus, Cross?"

Cross looked at Silla and smiled.

"There is mostly snow, mountains, forest, and more snow north of the Freewoods. The northern tip of the Freewoods is the natural border that ends the continent of Arrdus. I have explored north into the dead lands a few times, wondering what was up there, but the farther I go, the less I find. Perhaps it is an endless expanse of unlivable frost. I have heard tales of Faulk traveling into the deadlands from time to time, but I know not what he seeks there."

As they were edging closer to the center, Cross bid them continue with the nearby creek staying to the right, as he made his way to the back of the group, where Omega was.

"Omega, right?" Omega nodded.

"What stage did you have your breakthrough on?" asked Cross. Omega had very little interaction with the other experiments during his time in Irkdale, so seeing someone else survive was inspiring.

"I cleared all the stages without my ascension. I guess I could claim the creation of a final stage."

Cross was very interested in this final stage. "I ascended on the wrath stage. Certain events took place that led me into such an extreme chagrin that my ascension occurred, and mere minutes later, I used my new power to escape the facility. What's your final stage?"

"I finished the love-lost stage and entered the surrender stage. I decided to end my suffering, and when I attempted to kill myself, my ascension finally occurred, which saved my life. Fate has a sense of humor."

"I'm always thankful to Desitine that I didn't have to experience that love-lost stage. Although my wrath did come because of someone I love, but I don't talk about that."

The group was now passing a large, moss-covered hill. Cross spoke up, "This is a barrow," as he pointed to the mound. "Some of the order's more prestigious elders and guardians rest in there. Just ahead is our home."

Just then, a dense fog appeared, just as Kita described. Cross bid them stay close, and the fog would dissipate, recognizing the Velantosse as friendly.

Seconds later, when the fog cleared, what they saw was truly unbelievable. There was a large castle, similar in size to Rahm's. Around the castle was a clear freshwater moat fed in from the small lake directly behind the palace. The group was getting close to a draw bridge, which was currently down. The thickets of bramble and evergreens that permeated the forest before the fog was now all but gone. Mostly grass and small hills made up the landscape. There were also flowers scattered everywhere.

From inside, they could see the trees' clear outlines, far behind the castle, where the forest began again. There appeared to be no wildlife, save birds, which perhaps were able to fly above the fog that shielded this utopia.

Rose and the rest of the group were dumbfounded. "Is this another world? How is it possible?"

Cross gave a chuckle. "This paradise is a gift from an extraordinary lady, a very long time ago. The elders will be able to tell you more. I'm sure they will be quite interested in meeting Iris's daughter and seeing that crown again after such a long time."

As they made their way across the bridge, Omega looked down, and even though it was at least twenty feet deep, he could see the bottom and even saw some fish, which Sarah noticed. "Sometimes, we will catch fish outside and bring them back in hopes that they can spawn and create a self-sustained source of food."

Now inside the gate, Sarah and Ben bid farewell as they made their way to the kitchens with their prey hunted earlier.

"Such a large castle, there must be hundreds of people that live here," said Kita.

Cross sighed. "Perhaps when the great goddess created this place, it was for hundreds of devout, loyal protectors, but right now, only thirty of us live in this castle. Six elders, some hunters, and some historians, with me as the captain of the guards. In fairness, though, there are but three official guards."

Upon walking into the castle, it was quite unique, being so wide open that they could see all the way to the bottom of the top floor when they looked up. The layout was unique in that it resembled the inside of an enormous, misshapen silo. As the group looked around while following Cross, they could perceive how ancient this place was, but it also gave off an air that it would never crumble, not because of time, at the least.

Cross had led the foursome to a large ornate door east of the castle's entrance.

"Inside here is the housing and gathering area for our six elders," explained Cross.

The symbol for Velantosse was displayed on those ten-foot-tall doors, and it took up almost that entire space.

"As a Guardian's heir, they will very much want to speak to you."

Silla was beginning to feel a sense of accomplishment, like getting results for something she had been longing for. At least a few of her questions would be answered, and hopefully, some concerns alleviated.

As the group made their way through the door, they could see many halls leading off the main hall they were in, all going here and there. The end of the main entrance, which was probably one hundred feet long, led to a raised stage with six seats. This was where the six elders listened to concerns, made decisions, and discussed all manner of topics. There were three of the six elders up there currently debating a matter on composting and soil.

As Cross led the group closer, the elders noticed.

The one in the center, a man in his early sixties, not very tall, with a graying, long unkempt beard, spoke up.

"Captain Cross, welcome back. I see you brought some interesting strangers to our castle." As he was scanning, the elder's eyes stayed fixed on Kita more than the rest combined, making her feel uncomfortable.

After a bow, Cross introduced the elders. "This is Elder Jacobs," he said, pointing to the tall, slim man in his sixties, with no beard at all, making it all the more contrast, as he stood next to the elder that spoke earlier. "This is Elder Ross, and this is Elder Darcius," he said as he pointed to the woman on the right. Elder Darcius was the same height as Silla, and even though she had just had her seventieth birthday, her hair was brown without a speck of gray in it. Her eyes were a beautiful shade of green.

Silla, upon hearing the last elder's name, began to approach her. "Darcius? What relation did you have to Iris?" Silla inched ever closer.

"She was my daughter. How do you know that name?" Silla found herself welling up.

"She was my mother." Elder Darcius did something that startled everyone in the room; she dropped to her knees upon hearing Silla's answer; she kowtowed and spoke sincerely.

"Forgive my rudeness, Goddess!"

The other two elders realized almost as soon as Darcius hit the ground what Silla was, and they both dropped into a similar position. "Welcome back, Goddess."

Omega, at this monumental occasion, found himself somewhat distanced from the group. He was perusing some of the tapestries that were along the walls. Omega's proclivity for not being as enthralled on such occasions was usually received with ire from Silla. Still, luckily for Omega, she was too preoccupied to notice.

Rose simply looked at Silla and chuckled. Kita did not know what was happening, but she thought it must be important because it was rare to see elders show such deep resounding respect for such a young lady. Kita looked to see what Omega's reaction was and noticed him on the outskirts, in his own world, which made her smile.

"Please rise, Grandmother." Ross, Jacobs, and Darcius all got up and bid Silla come up on the stage. Silla went up and hugged her grandmother, who did not know how to react. It was the first time a goddess reincarnation had ever hugged her, but she eventually gave in and hugged back.

"Goddess, I saw you only one time, right after you were born. Your mother took you here to meet everyone, so I guess that was over twenty years ago," said Elder Jacobs.

After the three elders began to reminisce about those times, Silla interrupted them. "Grandmother, elders, I am very much interested in learning about the Velantosse while I am here, but I have one question which is at the crux of my quest, that I hope you can answer."

The three elders were waiting with bated breath for her inquiry.

Silla reached into her backpack and pulled out the Goddess Crown, holding it in both palms. The three elders gave a bow to the crown.

"I have the task of finding all of the remaining Goddess items, and we have zero clues to go on, and it is the main reason I wanted to find this place." Silla almost lost her breath, saying these things, which made her grandmother smile and laugh.

"That is not a problem at all for us, Goddess. As Velantosse, we are not only charged with protecting each iteration of the Goddess but also over the last fifteen thousand years, we Velantosse have guarded and kept track of the Goddess set," explained Elder Ross.

"We keep track of each Guardian, so we know which item is in each region, and we know the Guardian charged with its protection. We also know how you can get in contact with a Guardian once you get to their respective kingdom. There is a secret phrase that we have used for thousands of years, although the translations likely altered the original."

Ross stopped here and became much more severe.

"After learning who you were, Goddess, I did not want to bring up a certain matter, but I now realize that far too much sensitive information will soon come to light, and you have a member that is unwelcome, and I cannot condone further connection."

Silla was perplexed.

"I don't know who you are talking about, Elder Ross. I can't see how any of my fellow travelers have had any negative interactions with you."

Ross began to explain about one of the items.

"There is a sword in Culver that very much resembles your crown, Goddess. Someone in your group has seen this sword before." Ross started moving slowly towards Kita as he was speaking.

"Your father, King Thomascus, is a murderer that killed the Guardian charged with protecting that sword many years ago." Kita had never known where, how, or when her father got that sword, but she could remember having seen it multiple times since she was a young girl.

"My father isn't perfect, and he loves to fight strong opponents, but he wouldn't murder someone in cold blood, just for a fancy sword."

Ross slammed down the walking stick he had been carrying. "A fancy sword?! That sword is the rightful property of the reincarnation of the Goddess of Creation. The Guardian charged with its protection refused to bargain with it or give it up, and the then prince used his guards to corner the Guardian and killed him. To this day, I do not know how your father knew the location of the sword's protector."

Kita wasn't sure of how to process this information.

"I can't just take your word for it. I'd have to ask my father. Are you sure this was information from a reliable source?" Kita was beginning to feel like she was somewhere she didn't belong.

"I was the one to discover him. He was still alive, barely, gaping sword wounds covering his body. That was my son. As soon as you walked in, I knew by your unique family characteristics that you were one of his children. It was due to my great mercy that I didn't kill you as soon as I saw your face."

At that point, some knarled, sharp vines were beginning to *grow* from underneath Ross's feet, inching closer to Kita.

The other elders knew what Ross was referring to and decided to observe. Silla and Rose were contemplating their choices and next moves. Just when Kita felt the lowest she had felt in a while and definitely the loneliest, someone stepped in front of her, blocking the path between her and Ross.

"I don't know about these events in the past that happened when she was a child, but I do know that it's a bad idea to threaten Kita in front of me."

The vines stopped moving forward.

"How dare you! A common Irkdale magic slave has no bearing on speaking such strong words in this castle," steamed Ross, who at this point must have been near the peak of his anger capacity.

"I AM an experiment; 54 was my name for over two decades. I have experienced hells that most people would dare not imagine, so at this point, I fear nothing. Whether you want to make her leave, or you want to kill her… with me standing here, this entire castle would crumble to its foundation before a hair on her head was ever touched."

Omega, who was aloof earlier, was very much in attention now. Cross, who had been near the elders, was agitated at this last comment but chose not to speak out of turn.

Finally, Silla spoke up.

"Omega, you cannot talk to our benefactors like that, and definitely not my grandmother. I do agree that blaming a child for her parent's crime is unreasonable and killing her for it is unacceptable."

Omega had not taken his eyes off Elder Ross. The two appeared to be battling inside each other's glare.

"Elder Ross, do you take me, the so-called Goddess, as someone whose order you must follow?" asked Silla, now trying to defuse this tenuous situation.

"Of course, your worship."

"Okay, then my first edict as Goddess is for you to put this matter aside for now. Kita cannot be charged for her father's actions—even more so that they happened when she was a young child. I don't know the story, but I am sorry that your son died."

Ross, who had always been stubborn, was not easily convinced.

"You are saying that you don't allow me to punish her, but I will not let her stay here to learn about magic or your predecessors or any of our hidden knowledge. For all we know, she is a spy for her father, sent to follow you to this place. Don't think that I haven't seen the Culver spies eyeing the Freewoods. There are few even in this vast forest that escapes my far-seeing vision."

Silla sighed.

"Kita, I am sorry for what's happening. I know we don't know each other well, and we aren't exactly best friends, but I would never blame children for their parent's actions. If you had just told us who you were, I think things could have gone smoother."

Kita was aware that it was a gamble to not reveal her identity, so she didn't blame Silla for her thoughts.

"I honestly had no idea about the origins of that sword, and I have never cared about my title of princess, not even a little. I don't tell people because I just want them to know me and not the pressures people put on what it means to be a princess. I wanted to learn and figure out what magic I have in me to help you guys. Omega saved my life twice in less than ten days. I don't want to leave this place without you guys, but I understand that I would be the first to get kicked out of the group. I don't want to put you guys in an awkward position." Kita was near to admitting defeat.

"Silla, there has to be some compromise, right?" asked Rose, who had grown fond of Kita.

"Grandmother?" asked Silla as she made herself look less like a Goddess and more like a child in need of her grandmother.

"Elder Ross, I know about your pain, having lost a child myself. If one day Thomascus shows himself to you, then exact whatever revenge you can muster. If I were to call elders Flowers, Sharp, and Frost in here and we voted, you would lose. The benevolent thing to do, and you are that—today's actions notwithstanding—is to let her stay."

Ross, who had finished his internal struggle with Omega, closed his eyes and sighed.

"You are right, Darcius. I am going into solitude for some personal reflection." Before leaving, Ross looked at Kita without an ounce of hate in his eyes. "Forgive an old man's pain."

After being shown their lodgings, which were to the west of the main entrance, opposite the elders, Silla was not very happy with Omega.

"I am satisfied that everything worked out and Kita can stay, but why do you always have to try and make enemies of people? Just because you received so much hatred growing up doesn't mean you should immediately attack others. If anything, you should use your past experiences to become more benevolent and forgiving."

Omega and Silla were in the room by themselves. Kita and Rose were in the kitchens helping with the welcome banquet that the elders had announced earlier.

"I have my own thoughts on how to handle situations. It's apparent that many people are not deserving of forgiveness, and my benevolence is selective."

Silla was usually unsatisfied with Omega's answers. This time was no different.

"So, what would have happened earlier if my grandmother didn't resolve that conflict?"

"I noticed that Cross was losing his patience as I was speaking, so my guess is that I would have gotten to learn what magic he has, first-hand."

Omega said that with a smile and wondering look, almost disappointed that it didn't get to that point.

"Kita never explained what happened in that cavern. She said when you could, you should give the details." Silla was getting nowhere with her scolding, so she decided to change tact and satiate one of her curiosities.

"I still have no recollection of what I did. It is a complete blank, but I can tell you what Kita told me." Omega retold what Kita had said happened, and Silla was quite astonished.

"You were floating? Destroying without having to directly touch?"

Omega shrugged. "Perhaps I was in a state of desperation and used a more advanced version of my ability. I had heard some of the researchers talk about magic and different tiers, but always in passing, and I never got much of the whole story."

"Hopefully, Grandmother and the other elders and historians have extensive knowledge of magic. Let's go get ready for the welcoming party, Omega."

XIV

The welcoming feast was now in full swing, with a small section of the grand hall to entertain all the castle's residents. Elder Ross was still in seclusion for self-reflection, and it was unclear how long it would take before enlightenment.

The castle didn't have extravagant clothes, but they did offer Kita, Rose, and Goddess Silla, as they started calling her, gowns. The gowns were light blue, black, and white, respectively. Kita's gown's shade matched her eyes perfectly, which left quite the impression. Omega was offered a new outfit for the occasion. It was gray and black.

All the different people were coming to offer welcome toasts and respectful gestures to the newest Goddess. The four guests of honor were sitting together with Kita on the left, then Rose, Silla, and Omega to her right. Omega noticed that Kita was still avoiding him throughout most of each day. It was no different at the party.

The group finally met the other three elders, Flowers, Frost, and Sharp. Sharp was the youngest at forty-nine, and she was chubby but had a comely face and long black hair. Frost and Flowers were both in their late fifties. Frost had a black beard with many flecks of white. Flowers had long, light brown hair, almost as long as Kita's, and she had a face that no matter what tone she used, her look was kind and benevolent.

Next, the group met the five magical experts. Each of them had a specialty area of expertise in different types of magic.

"Excuse me, Goddess, I was wondering if I could have the honor of seeing you create something?" asked one of the teachers.

"Ah, sorry, but when I was a baby, my mother and father sealed my powers to protect me, so I cannot create anything, yet."

There was a disappointment on the teacher's face, but another teacher chimed in.

"I think I understand the seal you speak of, and I have peculiar magic that might be of help to you. I would like to speak more about it when it is less noisy, perhaps tomorrow."

The maidservants of each elder, minus Ross's as she was with her master, and the butlers that kept the castle clean also came and introduced themselves.

Finally, Cross, Sarah, and Ben came to say hello, and Rose bid them sit and join them.

"Cross, Sarah, and Ben, thank you for the welcome. Please join us and help us enjoy all of this wine and food," said Rose. The three of them could not dare decline the Goddess's request, although they were also happy to enjoy some wine.

As people were toasting and chatting, Omega noticed that Kita had gotten up and excused herself, wanting some fresh air. He decided that now was a good time to tackle his concerns and hopefully help her solve her noticeable predicament.

It was a cloudless night, with a full moon shining in the sky. The moon was closer than any Omega had ever seen, and he almost thought he could pick up a stone and hit the moon, although he didn't actually try it.

Omega, after leaving through one of the castle's rear exits, noticed that Kita was heading towards the lake that sat behind the fortress. There were multiple, small islands scattered in the lake, with most having only some shrubbery.

One of the islands had a little cottage, and Omega could see smoke coming from the chimney, and he wondered who was skipping the party.

Omega noticed that Kita sat at the end of one of the docks, her feet dangling off, a few feet above the flat, reflective water. It was cold out there, their breadth visible, so Omega took off his coat, and as he sat down, he draped it over her shoulders.

"Hi."

Kita didn't respond but instead made to get up, but before she could take a step, a gloved hand grabbed her forearm.

"Please stay," said Omega. Kita turned and looked at him, with a single tear running down her cheek. Upon seeing it drip, he let go of her arm.

"What's wrong? Did I hurt you?" asked a concerned Omega as he stood up, now a couple of feet away from Kita, the moon reflecting so vibrantly in her wet eyes.

"Not my arm. You have saved me so many times in such a short amount of time, I find myself falling further in love with you, Omega. I know I might be selfish, but I can't stay here anymore." Kita was clearly saying things that had been building up inside of her for a while.

"I'm not sure what I did, but please don't leave before I try to fix my mistakes. You say you are falling in love with me, but that you also have to leave. I know I'm selfish now, but please explain further."

Kita was still trying to organize all of her thoughts. Her heart was racing, her stomach in knots, and her thoughts were dancing between wanting to jump into Omega's arms and walking away and never looking back.

"I can't share someone's heart, Omega. I know you and Silla have, what you call connected souls, and I have heard you two laughing and noticed you two sharing closeness in our camp when everyone is asleep."

Omega was hearing and remembering these things that he said and did, and he started to laugh.

Kita was dumbfounded at his reaction.

"How could you laugh at my anguish?" As Kita stepped closer and began to swing and slap Omega, he grabbed her swinging right hand with his left, and he slid his right hand behind her lower back and gave her his very first kiss.

Simultaneously, as the two connected, Silla dropped her wine glass back in the hall and sat back in her chair, eyes closed. Two tears fell, one down each cheek. Those who noticed were quick to go to their Goddess's aid, but she opened her eyes and relieved them of their concerns.

"Sorry, I just had a shock. I didn't mean to scare everyone." Rose was the only one who knew about Silla's connection with Omega. She was experienced enough to guess what happened.

As they embraced, both of their eyes were open, gazing into the other's. Kita's heart was pounding as if she just circled the entire castle. They finally finished after a few seconds.

"Omega, that was …" Kita was absent-minded for a moment, reliving what just happened, but then shook her head.

"I need you to clear up the misunderstandings, and I don't think Silla would appreciate you going behind her back and doing that," said Kita, who regained her resolve.

"Kita, I was laughing because your concerns are very fixable, and I realized at that moment that I wouldn't lose you."

That phrase gave Kita hope.

"A happiness that I haven't felt before took over my mind. I do have a connection with Silla. She does have my soul. Well, we share a soul, I guess… It's hard for me to explain because I don't fully understand it. The other things you saw at night are perhaps akin to a close friendship or maybe what one would do to their little sister. I can't lie and say that she isn't beautiful, but my feelings towards her are different …"

"She has been having very vivid, lucid visions in her sleep that have caused her pain. In those moments, I could only help by making her laugh, but even if she has my soul in the literal sense… I think you've taken everything else."

Kita's heart started to race again.

"Since the first time I opened my eyes and saw you there trying to touch my scar, I knew that there was something different about how I felt about you. Although, at the time, I didn't realize what it was. Even now, I'm not sure what these feelings welling up inside me are."

Kita and Omega shared a long silence, just looking at each other.

Finally, Omega opened his arms, gesturing for her to enter his embrace. Kita was the perfect height when she hugged him. Her head fit snuggly under his chin as if the gods created them specifically for each other.

The two just stood there, moonlight reflecting their silhouette off the still, black lake.

"How was my kissing earlier? It was my first time kissing someone," said a now nervous Omega.

"That was also my first kiss. I think the person it's with carries more weight than if it was done well. I thought it was amazing, and my heart is still racing."

Omega was happy to hear that he was her first and that it wasn't disappointing.

Just at that moment of bliss, the two heard a blood-curdling howling coming from the island with the cottage, although it sounded slightly hollowed and echoed.

What the hell was that? Wondered Omega as he looked around to see if anyone else was nearby, but it was just the two of them.

"There's a boat right over there," he said, pointing a few yards to the right. "I'll go check it out and see who's in trouble while you go back in and get some help."

Kita wasn't convinced.

"Definitely not. I'm going with you whether it's somewhere joyous or somewhere dangerous." As Omega looked at her, he wanted to hold his ground, but she brought up a point that always worked.

"You promised to never make me do anything I didn't want to do." She said that and smiled.

Omega lightly tapped his mouth as if to remind himself not to impulsively say things in the future.

"It's unfair to always use that against me… Okay, together then, but if something dangerous is in there, please be safe."

The two of them made their way over to the little wooden boat that was just big enough to seat two comfortably. The vessel had one oar, which Omega took after helping Kita to sit in the boat. It only took three minutes to get to the island with the cottage at only about a hundred feet and such still water.

A loud yelling came out again, definitely from underground, due to its hollow tone.

"There must be a basement or underground chamber," said Kita.

The two made their way down the small path from the boat to the cottage's front door. The door was not locked, so they walked inside.

Inside the hut was one large room with the kitchen area, bedroom, and fireplace all nestled together. Even though it wasn't spotless, it was still quaint, and the two could tell that someone likely lived here and wasn't merely staying to avoid the party.

"Let's look for the entrance to get under this place. It could also be outside, Kita, so I'll look in here, and you go check around the back of the hut." Kita nodded and headed out the door.

Omega had a feeling that the entrance was indeed inside the hut, so he was hoping that he could find it and check if it was safe before Kita figured out what happened. He gave a little smile, as he thought *I didn't break my promise.*

Omega saw what looked like a door to a small closet, and when he opened it, he could feel a draft, and he saw a hatch on the floor. His instincts were spot on, so he hurriedly opened the hatch, turned around, and shut the door, then made his way down the steps into the underground space.

About fifteen steps went down quite steeply before coming to flat ground. It was pitch black down there, and Omega didn't have any flares or other light sources, so he used his instincts.

Luckily for Omega, the tunnel was not very long, maybe thirty feet, sloping downward. Also, there were no forks, so he ended up finding a door with his outstretched hands as he started to walk forward.

Upon getting to the door, Kita still hadn't opened the door on the floor, so he knew he had time to see what was behind this door in front of him. Just when he reached for the knob, a raspy, very strained voice called out to Omega.

"Please stop! Don't open the door! You don't smell familiar. Who are you?" Omega stopped reaching for the knob.

"I'm Omega. I was by the docks, and I heard a painful yell, and I thought to come and help."

"It's not something you can help with. I have a curse that activates with the light of a full moon. Usually, being down here in this pitch-black space allows me to maintain my sanity, but something is different this time. I can… feel my mutation being forcefully pulled out," said the man behind the door.

Omega thought perhaps his mutation was worse because of the size of the full moon outside.

"Curse? I have some experience with curses. How did you get yours?" asked Omega, who seemed genuinely interested.

"Sorry, I forgot to introduce myself. My name is Foster Franklin. You are interesting, Omega. You don't seem to be afraid of me, even though I told you about my curse."

"I've been noticing since gaining my freedom that many people have their own problems, and maybe I'm not so unique. I was an experiment at one of Irkdale's facilities most of my life, only being rescued a little over a year ago. I don't know how you were cursed, but I do have experience with feeling like you have no control and possibly not liking yourself too much in those moments."

Foster started to laugh as Omega could hear him sit down and lean up against the door, so Omega did the same on his end.

"Omega, I also was an experiment... in Irkdale. I'm guessing you... were one of the magic ascension slaves. I... was one of the... curse experimental projects conducted by Faulk himself. Perhaps if... we can meet another day, we can share our tragic upbringings."

Foster was straining very hard now, although he said that last part with a bit of laughter.

Just when Omega was wondering if Kita had noticed his trick yet, he heard the door to the closet open. Then before he could say anything, she opened the trapdoor. If the closet door was left ajar, the room's position allowed for a little moonlight to shine down the steps, and that was all it took.

Right when that faintest of light hit the bottom of the steps, it caught Foster's eyes via the gaps in the frame of the door. As he stood up, he let out a ferocious roar, and with the last of his sanity, he gave Omega a tip, "RUN!"

Omega didn't hesitate to heed Foster's advice, and he was at the base of the steps in three seconds. At the top, he picked up Kita. With her across his shoulder, Omega shut the trapdoor, then the closet door, and made his way to the boat. He set Kita in the boat, grabbed the coat he put on her earlier, and proceeded to kick the boat into the water, separating the two of them.

"Something is coming, and I'm hoping it is not much of a swimmer." Omega smiled when he said that.

He made his way to the right of the hut entrance, hoping to have an opportunity to ambush the mutated Foster.

Kita was in the boat, but only ten feet or so away from the island. "I could easily row back and help you if I want."

Omega looked at her and mouthed some words, inaudibly, that looked in the moonlight to be *I love you*. This flustered Kita, driving out the thought of rowing back to shore.

At that time, Foster made his way to the trapdoor, completely ripping it from its hinges. Next was the closet door, which he broke with a swing of his arm. Although Foster was not able to form words anymore, he at least wasn't fully mutated. Still, after exiting the closet, much more ambient moonlight was in the hut, causing further transformation.

Foster began changing into a ferocious beast. His jaws were extending, teeth growing. His cranium became more jagged and denser. About half of his body was now covered in bloody fur.

Foster, as he was still transforming, was walking towards the front door, hunched forward, smelling for his prey. As he was about to exit, Kita realized that Foster was smelling Omega and yelled out, "Hey, ugly! Come and get me if you dare!"

Foster locked eyes with her and let out a vicious howl as if to say that he did indeed dare.

As the monster moved forward out of the house, Omega seized his chance before Foster could look directly at the moon behind the hut. Omega jumped on Foster's back, wrapping the coat around his head.

He hoped that by completely blocking out the moonlight, it would reverse the situation. Unfortunately, it was only a spur-of-the-moment idea, with no grounds for efficacy.

After wrapping the coat around Foster's head, he twisted the remainder around his own arm to create a very tight hold. He also wrapped his legs around Foster's body to better control the beast.

It seemed like the darkness helped because Foster stopped and just stood there, which gave Omega optimism.

Unfortunately, it was only a momentary relief as even a partially mutated Foster was far too powerful, even for Omega. Foster reached his now longer arms above his head and seized Omega by the neck and shoulder. Foster's fingers were now much denser, and his fingernails resembled claws.

Omega screamed like he hadn't done since he was a child, but in that instant, he had a moment of clarity. Omega used his positioning to turn Foster back facing the entrance.

"Go get Cross! Hurry! If I'm right, he's the one that brought Foster here!"

Kita thought about going to help Omega, but he had thought of that also. "You can punish me later, but go now!"

As Kita rowed back to the docks as fast as she could, Silla found herself being pulled into Omega's consciousness around the time that Foster grabbed him.

She made her way to get Cross, who was sitting about thirty feet away.

"I don't know where he is, but Omega is fighting some fierce beast, and he is in great pain, yelling for your aid!"

"Shit, Foster!" was all Cross said as he started running towards the back of the castle.

When Kita got to the docks, Cross was exiting the castle with everyone else way behind but following.

As Cross got to the docks, he jumped with enough force to crack the nearby pier and collapse the ground around him.

A few seconds before Cross made his jump, Omega was thrown into the hut, to the back wall, almost landing in the hole where the trap door had been.

Omega didn't want to take his gloves off because he mostly felt pity for Foster, with no animosity. He thought that he and Foster were kindred spirits.

"Come on, Foster, you can do better than that!"

Omega was now bleeding profusely from his shoulder, and he was feeling light-headed and wobbly. As Omega was ready to make his last stand, he heard and felt a loud crash outside the hut.

Cross had jumped the entirety of the gap, some one hundred feet, between the shore and the island.

Upon landing, Cross ran into the hut, shouting.

"FOSTER!"

As the mutated Foster turned, coat still tied around his head, Cross rammed him, launching him into the wall next to Omega with enough force to knock Foster unconscious.

"Quickly, before he wakes! There are chains in the cabinet over there. We need to chain him and then bring him back down to the darkness below."

As Omega made his way to the cabinet, quite awkwardly, Cross could hear the splashing of blood as it erupted from Omega's body.

"That wound is nasty. I can handle Foster myself." Omega waved him off.

"It's too dangerous here to worry about myself yet. Help me get Foster down the stairs."

The two of them chained and carried Foster down to the room underground. After barricading the door down there and going back up the steps, Kita, Rose, and Silla were getting off the boat.

As soon as Kita's eyes met Omega's, he smiled.

"Everything's okay now …"

Omega fell forward, crashing through the table in front of him.

XV

Thompsel found himself in his most challenging position since becoming crown prince. He could hear a girl screaming at him and refusing to open the door he was standing in front of. Kansel, his youngest sister, was none too pleased to get the news that she was being married off and sent away from her family and friends to the vassal state of Faruqh.

"Claudia, can you persuade her to open up?" asked Thompsel to Kansel's maidservant.

"I've tried, Your Highness, but she is very stubborn today." Thompsel was at a loss.

"I wish my sister Kitannica was here. She is always able to calm Kansel down." Thompsel looked around and spotted his personal guard, Nico.

"Hey, Nico. Have we received any news from Joe on Kitannica's current whereabouts?"

Nico approached his ruler. "Last note from his hawk, two days ago, stated that Kita was in the Freewoods. As you know, she was trying to fulfill an oath to the person that saved her life in Briaridge." Thompsel was very anxious when he first received the news of Kita's attack.

"She wanted to get her saviors safely to the Freewoods, so hopefully, she is on her way back now," said Thompsel as he heard what sounded like a table being leaned up against Kansel's door.

"The latest note said that Joe had lost Kita's trail in the center of the forest where an oddly thick fog sprouts up past a certain point," explained Nico.

Thompsel, for the time being, had given up hope on reasoning with Kansel.

"You win, for now, sis, but this is something that you cannot avoid, so it will be best for you to accept it sooner."

"I hate you!" was all that Thompsel heard as he walked away with Nico, towards his own palace.

Thompsel's palace was on the opposite side of the main throne hall, so as he looked around, he remembered that his wife, Jennifer, was likely at the Sacred Sevens Tower, which was about a thousand feet away from where he stood.

The Culver Tower had stood for about three thousand years. Not far from it, one could see what was left of an earlier Sacred Sevens Tower of Bastion, one of the nation's former names. It was mostly rubble that only stood some thirty feet high. However, it was believed to have been some five-hundred feet tall at its completion, housing all of the True Pious as they are known.

As Thompsel made his way towards the tower, he turned to Nico,

"Please send your swiftest hawk to Joe, telling him to bring Kitannica back as soon as possible. The last thing I want to do is force my way into Kansel's room and make her hate me even more."

Nico nodded. "Right away, Crown Prince."

Now alone, Thompsel was near some stalls that stood in the inner market. One was selling linens and other fabrics, and another had all sorts of different spices. As he was going to each stall and greeting the merchants, he was picturing the diverse marketplace that would be there after Culver's capital fully converted to the Arrdussian Empire's capital, and merchants from every vassal state set up their respective shops.

Just then, one street seller passed him. "Candy-coated Haws!"

Thompsel did not eat many sweet things, but his guilty pleasure was candied haws.

"My bad luck that you passed at this time. I cannot resist. How much for one stick?"

Each stick had four haws skewed, much like a kebab.

"Your Highness, I dare not charge you," said the seller as he tried to bow while holding his goods, but Thompsel stopped him.

"Nonsense. You are an honest merchant making an honest living, and you happen to be selling my favorite sweet, so I'll be paying full price." After the transaction, the merchant thanked the crown prince, and Thompsel made his way closer to the tower.

As Thompsel got within shouting distance of the tower, he spotted his wife. She enjoyed spending time with the orphans that lived in the tower. The Sacred

Towers throughout Arrdus were usually the main housing for the orphans of each respective nation.

Most citizens, especially the women, found the crown princess's appearance very average. They wondered why Thompsel, whom every woman in Culver thought was too handsome to be mortal, would choose her as his wife. Jennifer was not unattractive but had no striking features and rarely even wore makeup.

As he approached her, he passed a statue of the God of War, Melchior. He stopped to ask for a blessing to win the upcoming war against Zarrek with as little loss of life as possible.

Because it was a sunny day, Jennifer was reading to some of the orphans outside.

"Jen, no luck with Kansel," said Thompsel, obviously distressed but also not surprised as it's been the same for the last couple of days.

The orphans stood up to bow and greet their crown prince.

"Honey, I know it's a tough task to get a young girl to willingly leave all of her friends and family, go somewhere foreign, and marry someone she's never met. All for the sake of some war that she has no interest in or knowledge about."

Thompsel looked at her with joy and love as he always did.

"Do you think I was unreasonable to force her and Thomo to marry into the vassal states and leave home?"

Thompsel had been weighing that very question since he made the decision back at the conference.

"Without marriage alliances, would the other nations have agreed, willingly?" Jennifer was good at helping her husband find the answer he needed, even if it was not always the one he wanted.

"I fear Father would have chosen invasion, perhaps right there at the conference, but there is no time for that, and I did what I thought was best to avoid Arrdussian bloodshed."

Jennifer knew the choice of shipping his siblings off to foreign lands weighed heavier on his mind than he ever let on.

"Thomo left without much argument, but I guess it's different for a boy. He sees this as an adventure, and he has always wanted to be like his sister Kitannica and travel here or there at his whim. Kansel might always hate me, but I hope when she gets older, she accepts and understands."

At that time, a scout was running towards the emperor's palace and spotted the crown prince.

"Report!"

Thompsel turned and made his way to meet the messenger halfway.

"What's the matter?" asked Thompsel as he saw the wide-eyed scout that looked like he held grave news.

"Here, Your Majesty," said the scout as he handed a rolled-up note that he would have got from a messenger hawk.

As Thompsel unraveled the note and read it, he began to lose his usual relaxed demeanor. He was downright seething by the end of the message. Jennifer knew something devastating happened.

Thompsel took a deep breath and composed himself.

"Scout, I need you to go to the hawkery and send a message to Kitannica, directly. Tell her that there is a family emergency, and Thomo has been abducted. I order her, as the crown prince, to return immediately."

The scout bowed and ran back the way he came towards the hawkery. Jennifer looked scared.

"Abducted. What actually happened, dear?"

"The letter says that the caravan taking Thomo to Gradon was attacked while they were in Cricket's Thicket. There are a few strange things in the note. From the writer's perspective, it seems like they were attacked only after passing into Faruqh's side of the thicket."

Cricket's Thicket was a small forest a few miles north of the Ardian Sea, and it sat on both Culver and Faruqh land.

"That means ..." started Jennifer.

"I don't think Queen Regent Felicia would plan such a thing, but I have to keep that possibility in mind," explained Thompsel, who was now walking with Jennifer back towards his palace after saying farewell to the children.

"What else did the letter say?" Thompsel handed it to her and began explaining the peculiarities.

"The note says that only the men of the caravan were killed, while the six women that were there, and even the ones that fought back, were unharmed. The women only had their hands tied together and were blindfolded." Jennifer found this sequence strange.

"One would think that you might leave a single witness in a kidnapping for ransom purposes, but to leave all six women alive and unharmed is indeed strange."

Thompsel urged her to keep reading.

"The writer swears that she heard one of the masked assailants say that they were explicitly ordered to never harm the women in any way. One man warned another that if any woman was even bruised, terrible things would happen. They both mentioned the fear that came with looking at that man's eyes."

As Jennifer finished reading, she asked the question on Thompsel's mind since reading the note.

"Do you tell Father? I'm concerned about the fact that it happened on Faruqh land."

Thompsel gave a big sigh.

"If I tell the emperor that his son was kidnapped on Faruqh's land, I have to assume that within a fortnight, he would be at Faruqh's palace. There to take both the Queen Regent and her son's head."

Jennifer observed her father, slightly different than Thompsel.

"Father is impulsive and loves a good fight, but he also adores his children, even if he acts stern towards them. The mere fact that he never tries to control or corral Kita indicates his desire to spoil his children."

"Since they were blindfolded, the writer said that they don't know which direction they went towards after leaving. I will tell Father and then personally go to Cricket's Thicket to investigate the tracks left," said a resolute Thompsel as he made his way towards his father's palace.

After leading his wife back to their palace, Thompsel made his way to report to his father. Upon entering the emperor's palace, Thompsel saw his father practicing his swordsmanship with his usual two-sword style.

The emperor used the special ruby-gold sword and a slightly larger broadsword, which he had in his dominant hand. Thompsel knew better than to interrupt his father's practice, so he waited until he finished.

"Father, I have something important to report." Thomascus was breathing heavily, but he was also in a good mood, which was often the case after using his favorite sword.

"Go ahead."

"Report from the caravan that was transporting Thomo has some upsetting news." Thomascus didn't respond, so his son continued.

"There was an attack on the caravan in Cricket's Thicket, and from the report, it appears that Thomo was kidnapped, but one strange thing is that all of the males were slain, but the females were purposely left unharmed."

Thompsel omitted the information about the attack occurring on Faruqh's side of the thicket and hoped his father wouldn't inquire.

Thomascus had lost his smile but was calmer than most parents would have been upon hearing this sort of news.

"What's your plan for fixing this? If I had done things my way, not marrying off my children to foreign lands, would this have happened?" Thompsel took a deep breath.

"For the first question, I plan to personally go to the location of the incident to investigate and hopefully find tracks or clues as to who was involved and which direction they might have traveled after. Also, I find it interesting that these people were able to kill the guards and overpower Thomo. Even though he's young, you and I both know that he is powerful and has trained under both of us in swordsmanship and the arts and strategies of battles."

Thomascus was thinking back to his youngest son's training, and he knew even at fifteen, few people in Arrdus would beat him in a fair fight.

"As for the second question, All I can do is reiterate my original take on that situation. Even though my option leads to my two youngest siblings leaving home forever, it would lead to the least aggressive outcome. Everyone involved, besides our immediate family, would find the results acceptable. We don't have the time for infighting. Even though we didn't tell the others, we both know how monstrous Grexle is. I'm not convinced he's even human."

Thomascus was unhappy at that last comment. "That's not something that you should say out loud... even in the confines of this palace. As for your request to go to the scene of the crime to personally investigate, I approve. I would also like to remind you that although I seem calm right now, I am not. If you cannot find my baby boy… I suggest *not* coming back empty-handed."

Thompsel would rather not find out how angry his father can become.

"Ah, I almost forgot. I sent a couple of letters to Kitannica, so hopefully, at least one finds her hands. I gave her a direct order to return to Culver. I'm not as good at dealing with Kansel as Kitannica is, so once she returns, Kansel will hopefully, willingly, go to Faruqh."

Thomascus agreed that it was time for Kita to return, so after a few hours of preparing, Thompsel set off for Cricket's Thicket, which was pretty far, maybe seven days' ride at an exhausting pace, so there was no time to waste. Thompsel decided not to tell any of his siblings about Thomo and simply told them that he had to go check on some imperial matters in Faruqh.

About three days after Thompsel left, a hawk arrived at the palace of the Crown Prince. One of the servants took the note and brought it to the emperor.

Thomascus had some wine in the late afternoon with his wife, Empress Karmellia. Karmellia was two years younger than her husband, and she had the same striking features as her daughters. Karmellia looked closest in appearance to Karah. At Karah's age, the empress and her third daughter looked almost like twins. Often the portrait in the palace of Karmellia in her early twenties is believed to be Karah to those that do not know any better.

Karmellia was not in the public eye much, and she spent the majority of her time in the palace. She was adored by the servants and maids as she always helped with their tasks and only scolded them on rare occasions.

Upon unrolling the letter, Thomascus turned to his wife.

"Good news, Karmy, Kitannica says that she is leaving immediately to return home. She says she also has some of her own news that she wishes to relay to us in person."

Karmellia gave a huge smile, another characteristic she shared with her daughters.

"I miss Kita every time she goes off, and after hearing the news of her attack in Briaridge, I was so scared for my baby girl."

Thomascus almost rushed to Briaridge to personally punish the person that attacked his daughter. Unfortunately for the fat man, his sister promised that she would deal with him with extreme prejudice.

"While Thompsel is gone, I was wondering if you would go try your hand at trying to convince Kansel to come out of her room and accept her pivotal role in keeping the peace of the empire."

Karmellia looked at her husband and chuckled. "You sounded just like your son when you said that."

"Even though it wasn't my first thought, Thompsel's suggestions all made great sense, and I think he has grown to possess all of my good features without my bad ones. Having him as the crown prince is a great thing for the future of the empire."

Karmellia looked a little worried suddenly.

"I know that Thompsel feels responsible for what happened to Thomo, and there is nobody more capable than him to find my baby boy, but the thicket is so close to the Ardian Sea and Zarrek."

"That's precisely why Thompsel needs to go. There is nobody outside of Irkdale that could challenge your eldest son and live. Only if Grexle himself were there waiting would I be worried."

Just then, a messenger came in, very panicked.

"Report! Report!"

"What's the panic, scout?" asked the emperor.

"Your Majesty," said the scout as he bowed. "News from the north… Black Garden and Ruseberg have joined forces in direct defiance of Your Majesty's edict. They are moving south to take advantage of our armies having moved to Orcasium…"

Thomascus slammed his fist down on the table, cracking the corner.

"What!?"

XVI

All around Arrdus, there were various hawks and falcons bringing letters to specific individuals. News travels fastest via birds of prey, and those of import received notice of the existence of the newest Goddess. Some rejoiced while others began to put into motion their sinister plans.

In Braske, a certain tall, slender man received a message from Velantosse castle that shared the secret phrase that all Guardians understood to mean that the Goddess of Creation was found: *The rising sun knows no bounds.* "Ah, things are finally about to get interesting around here," said the slender man with a smile that looked both innocent and ominous.

On a tiny island in Southwest Gradon Archipelago named Goji, a woman with thick, nappy dreadlocks and tanned skin received her own letter with the same phrase. This letter also had a question: *Have you found it yet?* The woman, who was currently knee-deep in quite murky water, was now anxious.

"I'm happy she's finally here, but I haven't found it yet. What do I do?"

Right outside the Sacred Seven Tower in Irkdale, which was no longer used for its original purpose but used as Faulk's palace—Faulk received a letter different from those others. This one also came from someone inside Velantosse castle, but it was clearly from someone planted there to leak such vital news bits.

The Goddess of Creation has shown herself. Her name is Silla. She has a strange companion who came from one of your labs. His name is Omega, but I heard that his number was 54, if that rings any bells. I will keep you informed of their next destination, but knowing Your Excellency, you likely already know which item she will go after first.

Faulk showed a malicious grin.

"Fifty-four, how have you been? I was unable to fully break you, even in the twenty-two years that you were here. Octavius used every ounce of his willpower, even in his sleep, to hide your exact location from me. While I laud his abilities, it was quite unnecessary. I never planned to recapture you, or I wouldn't have let you escape in the first place. To think, as smart as Octavius was, he truly thought that every single action that transpires in Irkdale is not under my ever-watchful eye. My son must be happy now that he can have his fun."

In Faruqh, there was a town far to the northeast, on the border with Irkdale, called Yewce. A man with long brown and gray hair with a large scar that traveled down his left temple, past his jawline, received a note like the other Guardians.

"I was wondering when she would show herself. Octavius was very secretive about his daughter's location. Not even sharing it with the Guardians. I've been keeping watch over this item and keeping watch over all the movements from Irkdale and that psycho Faulk for half of my life. I'm glad that she will be around while I'm still young enough to use my full potential as the third strongest fighter in Arrdus."

Inside the Tower of Faruqh resided the spiritual leader of those who worshiped the Sacred Seven and was known as Piatous 191. As was the case for the 190 Piatous before him, his birth name was forgotten after the coronation.

The role of Piatous was to lead all of those that see the Seven Gods and Goddesses, as expressed by the holy scriptures found in the Sacred Towers, as the real and only religious and spiritual beings acceptable to worship. The other role of Piatous was to condemn all magic worship, acceptance, or usage outside of those that work directly under Piatous. Magic is a gift, fit only for those most pious and righteous. The title and responsibilities of the person chosen to be Piatous have existed at least as long as the Goddesses of Creation. They have always been at odds for quite obvious reasons.

Piatous 191 also received a letter from someone inside Velantosse castle, and it did not make his morning any better.

"So, the blasphemous one has finally shown herself. My predecessor told me that I would be the leader during a fascinating time in our history. My coronation took place twenty-five years ago when I was still a young man. Piatous 190 told me that night that soon, the true terror would be reincarnated into this world. It would be my task to find her and destroy her before she had the opportunity to use her heretical powers."

Another slightly older member of the tower was standing next to Piatous.

"Your Worship, the histories in our private library talk of this heretic's powers, and if half of them are to be believed, we will have our hands full dealing with her."

Piatous looked at his underling and touched his shoulder.

"Not to worry, Grand Cleric Ignatius, we have many devout followers in many high and powerful places. When the time comes, and we call upon all our true believers, no matter what she can do, that monster will fall prey to our overwhelming righteousness!"

At that time, Piatous was looking around for someone and spotted a maid walking by.

"You, maid, come over here and take this message and give it to brother Tallis and tell him to send it to Irkdale." As she made her way over and reached out for the message, she saw a hand swinging out and hitting her across the cheek and eye.

"Have you forgotten your place, maid? At the very least, you will bow and offer praise to both Grand Cleric and me."

Piatous was wearing his signet ring, and that slap was far more painful than the maid let on. "Please spare me, Your Worship!" cried the maid as she dropped to her knees. Her accent was not of Arrdus.

"I will spare you this time. You are lucky I allowed a Zarrekian to live here. Take the letter and make haste to your destination." The maid grabbed the letter and scurried off.

Piatous could tell that Ignatius was intrigued about the letter to Irkdale.

"The letter gives Faulk an ultimatum. He is either with us or against us as it pertains to this heathen that has finally shown herself. Faulk is not a religious man, but I overlook it because we see eye to eye in most situations. In this case, though, there can be no doubts or dissension. I will destroy what the beast stands for, and I can't allow him to get in my way."

Ignatius was awestruck at the sight of his leader's confidence and devotion to their faith.

"There's also some information in there about a certain Guardian's whereabouts that Grandmaster Faulk has been probing about for, for the last few years. It's important to remember that information is power, especially when dealing with people as cunning as Faulk."

Piatous was very cunning himself. Unfortunately, he was also not kind to those he saw as insignificant.

A few rooms away from Piatous and Ignatius, the maid was there with a fellow servant, and she was crying as her friend tried to apply some salve to her wound.

"Jasmine, why did His Worship strike you so?" asked the other maid, Roan.

Stifling her tears and trying to gain her composure, Jasmine was none too pleased.

"That weak old man can only hit us maids and those he feels are too plain to deserve his respect. I wonder how he will react when his precious letter doesn't reach its destination."

Before Roan could talk her out of it, Jasmine put the letter on top of the flame of a candle on the nearby table and watched with mirth as the paper began to blacken and curl.

"Jasmine, His Worship will surely punish you with torture for doing that! Do you remember what the letter said? You could rewrite and hope nobody notices." Jasmine was not deterred.

"I will be gone from this tower before that bastard knows that his letter never went out. Make sure that you say you were never here, or he will surely punish you for not turning me in right away."

This was the first time that Roan had heard her friend's plans to leave the tower.

"Where are you going to go? We've been in this tower together for the last five years."

Jasmine regretted leaving her only friend in the tower, but she had always known this day was going to come. "I will miss you, Roan. Please take care of yourself, and I promise that one day I will come back and take you outside and give you freedom. I came here for a reason, and I've tarried here... far too long."

It was common knowledge that the servants, maids, and or slaves of the Sacred Towers were bound to its walls.

However, it was explained to the masses as being willingly accepted by those maids and servants. In contrast, the slaves had no say, regardless. It was believed that their being in the towers would save their souls, and it was their penance towards regaining purity.

"To answer your question, I saw that in the letter there was mention of a location of a Guardian, and although I am unsure of the connotation, I think I will head to that location and tell this person that they are no longer hidden. It's the least I can do."

Jasmine was in her early twenties, and she had shown up to the tower of her own accord, which was uncommon. Parents usually willingly sacrificed their children to the towers. Those most devout saw it as their most tremendous honor—giving their children to the faith.

Jasmine was a bit of a tomboy with her short hair, not even shoulder length, and her habit of preferring pants over dresses. She did have beautiful, hazel eyes and a button nose but had little interest in prettying herself up.

As Jasmine was making her preparations for escape, Piatous was making his way down to one of the tower's many basements. The Tower of Faruqh had basement levels underground that stretched further down than most citizens were aware. Mostly it was home to nasty criminals that the local government either didn't want to deal with or couldn't deal with. It was often left to the tower to straighten and reform these miscreants, by any means necessary.

Piatous was currently walking down spiral steps that seemed to go down and down for ages, with each floor having exits that went to various rooms. The stairs were well-built of stone, and there were magical lanterns on the walls, every twenty feet or so, although it seemed to get darker and darker the farther down one traveled.

After going down about ten minutes, Piatous exited in the door marked *Those that cannot be forgiven,* which meant that torture for information or efficacy purposes would occur there. There were multiple rooms with iron doors, quite sturdy and quite useful for keeping order.

Piatous chose the third iron door on the right. After opening it, there was a man chained to a vertical rack. He was haggard and skinny. To look at him, one would guess he had been there for years.

"You still alive?" asked Piatous. The man opened his eyes and smiled.

"I will not die before you do, Essien. I've told you that many times." Piatous did not react to this name the man called him, but one would assume it was his birth name.

"I doubt you get much news down here, Mercurius, but I've come to inform you that the blasphemous one, your so-called Creationist, has finally surfaced. My faithful eyes and ears in Velantosse castle have sent me this excellent news." Mercurius's reaction was elation for a moment, but then anxiety took over him.

"Silla, you have finally grown up and are beginning the undertaking of your destiny. As your uncle, I wish that I was in a position to aid you in your dangerous endeavors. Alas, Desitine has me on a different, no less dangerous path."

Piatous walked up close to Mercurius, who had the same green eyes and sharp nose as Silla.

"I know from my informant that your sister sealed your niece's magic at the cost of her life, but I was never able to get a bead on where Octavius was keeping her, or I would have killed her many years ago."

Mercurius was none too pleased when he heard Piatous threatening his niece.

"You have tortured me for decades, trying to pry that information from my lips. Ha, now that my knowledge is no longer sought, I wonder if it's my turn to meet Hespa at the gates of the eternal."

"Hmm, honestly, even though you are an enemy of the righteous, I have grown fond of your wit and banter," said Piatous, who was internally weighing the pros and cons of killing Mercurius.

"I might allow you a reunion with your niece, Mercurius. If you do me a small favor."

At that last sentence, Piatous showed a huge grin, showing all his teeth, one of which was gold.

"I'm listening," answered Mercurius, ready to meet his niece.

XVII

It was the third afternoon since Omega had collapsed in the hut in the middle of the lake, and he was still unconscious. Kita and Silla had spent each night sleeping in the same room as Omega.

He stayed in one of the many spare rooms, this one on the second-highest floor. Cross had carried him up there with little effort.

The first night, right after it happened, was very hectic as the elders and teachers did all they could to staunch the bleeding. Still, nobody there was a legitimate doctor, and they thought it was a miracle that he even survived the first night. They thought that perhaps the hell he was raised in played a significant role in building up his body's ability to survive.

Coming into Omega's room, Silla saw Kita placing a folded letter on the mahogany table next to his bed. Silla didn't say anything as Kita bent down and kissed right between his eyes, touched his forehead scar, and said, "Goodbye, Omega. I'm sorry I can't be here when you awaken."

Turning to leave, she spotted Silla standing by the door and stopped, their eyes meeting.

"You are leaving the castle?" asked Silla, with a less than somber tone.

"Yes, I got a letter from Culver that told me of a couple of different family emergencies and a direct order from the crown prince to return. To be honest, I would normally ignore such an order, but the emergencies cannot be overlooked."

Silla understood that royal orders were not to be taken lightly and even less so in family emergencies.

"Please have Omega read the letter when he wakes up. I don't know when we will see each other again. I know your quests will take you all around Arrdus. We started off not too friendly, but I hope you can take good care of Omega. I don't know if I'm immodest, but I don't know if he'll be able to handle my disappearing." Kita was obviously holding back tears.

Silla walked up to her and gave her a big hug.

"Don't worry, I will always take good care of him. I know that he has you in his heart; even if I can't accept my fate, I can respect his heart."

Those words lifted a great weight off both of their shoulders. Kita made to leave the castle after bidding farewell to those few that she made contact with within the castle, and then Rose walked her to where the exit was.

The entrance was simply walking through the fog with a recognized Velantosse castle member, but the exits were a little different. There were doors throughout the fortress that acted as portals to different parts of the forest. One such portal was in the kitchens, and it opened into the woods, near the eastern edge of the Freewoods.

Near the exit, the two said farewell.

"Kita, I hope you can solve whatever your family emergency is, and we can meet one day again. Omega has had a unique upbringing, compared to us, and he found the most beautiful thing a person can experience." Kita looked at her and wondered.

"He found true, requited love. People search for their whole lives, coming up short."

Kita bid farewell to Rose and walked out the door, which on the other end simply disappeared when closed by Kita.

After walking only a few minutes, Kita spotted Joe and some of her personal guards. They began the long journey back to Culver.

During the days since Omega has been comatose, Silla and Rose have been spending the vast majority of their non-visitation time in magic classes with the five experts.

Each expert had their own area of interest. Victoria Washmire was the elemental expert. Jackson Pouldron was the expert on healing and did most of the extensive work on Omega. Regilia Mutton was the magic historian expert and the teacher that Rose spent most of her time with. Stuart Willerton was the mind control and other augmentations expert. Finally, the curse expert was Malory Masters. She offered some help to Silla during the welcoming feast.

Silla found herself always excited to go see Malory, who was in her early forties. She had significantly magnified glasses with long brown hair and black eyes.

"Professor Masters, could you explain the help that you offered during the welcoming feast?" asked Silla, who had not had the time or concentration to dive into anything significant after Omega's crisis.

"Of course, Goddess. Although I am an expert in explaining curse magic, my own magic is perhaps more interesting and useful to Your Grace." Silla interrupted her.

"Please, call me Silla. I do not even have any magical abilities yet, and I think it would be hard to stay humble and grounded with people calling me Goddess." Malory agreed on one condition.

"You must call me Malory in return. Many interesting occurrences will occur while you are here, and I can help with one of those right now. My magic allows me to see not only those that are cursed but also, I can see connected curses between individuals and between individuals and objects. Pretty much anything course-related can be seen by my eyes."

Silla was very intrigued. "So, you can see that I am cursed. What does it look like?"

Malory smiled, pleased by Silla's enthusiasm. Even though she was happy to be part of the Velantosse sect, there were very few people there, mainly because the elders had been afraid of opening the doors to the world. There were many enemies, some hidden and some brazen. Malory had very few opportunities to exercise her abilities in a practical setting. She was as enthusiastic as Silla.

"It's hard to explain how it looks. If I had to help you illustrate it in your mind, I would say it resembles a thin, fluid cloud, specifically for those curses that connect two or more people or things. As far as the curse that your parents put on you, as both conduits are no longer here, the remaining curse lies around your heart. However, at this point, it is becoming more and more transparent. I would have expected it to be quite opaque if you still had almost a year left."

"So, you are saying that I might be able to create something soon!" Silla was getting excited.

"Before answering that, I have been noticing a curse between you and many objects. This one has a solid, blood-red-colored connection with something in your pack on your back. Is that the crown?"

Silla was taken aback by this information. She pulled out the Goddess Crown, holding it in her hand for only the third time. Malory had an expression on her face that made Silla both worried and a little excited. Malory was tracing things with her eyes in all directions, moving her head in this direction and that.

"I've never seen a curse connection so strong, thick, and solid... not cloud-like at all, but closer to metallic. From what I can see, there are a total of six connections between you and the ends. Those other five, excluding the crown, should coincide with the other pieces of the Goddess armament. There are two going east, one southeast, one south, and one southwest."

Silla was so excited to understand that the other items were real and somewhere in the world. But she was concerned about the idea that these items were the result and conduits of a curse. Perhaps Malory noticed the concern on Silla's face.

"The term curse does not only signify negative events, although that is the common connotation. A curse is basically any magically induced connection, whether willing or unwilling, to the participants. It would make sense that there is a curse on the items as they are believed to have been created by Glyndyl herself after obtaining her powers from the Goddess Hespa."

Silla was much relieved to hear the expert's advice about curses, and she wondered what kind of woman Glyndyl was. Like many of her predecessors, she wondered how Glyndyl gained such favor from the Goddess Hespa.

"Is there any history that has survived that speaks about how Glyndyl received such favor from a Goddess?"

Malory first recommended she join Rose in Regilia Mutton's room for history lessons. Still, she told what she knew or hoped.

"There is only one object believed to be from Glyndyl's time, here in this castle. It is, however, only a small, wholly rusted sword. It is nestled in one of the deepest chambers under the castle. We have always ignored it because we dare not risk destroying it. I like to think that she used that sword to help people and eventually moved Hespa's heart.

"I'm no historian; I find the subject quite tedious, but I have studied it for scholarly reasons. The world around Glyndyl's time was quite different from ours. Very chaotic, without established laws or systems and constructs of society as we know them."

Silla was leaning over her desk, giving Malory her absolute attention.

"Perhaps Glyndyl put herself in constant danger, trying to help everyone survive the harsh times, always getting injured but never stopping. It moved Hespa's heart to give Glyndyl a gift that could truly change and make the world a better place."

Silla was wholly enthralled in Malory's words, and she was thinking that this encounter was precisely what she had hoped for since starting her adventure. Although she loved traveling and exploring, she also sincerely enjoyed learning.

"I think for now we can put aside the Goddess objects and that curse and talk about the curse between you and Omega. I use the word curse here, but you possibly think of it as a blessing, right?"

Malory had noticed, before Omega's incident, how Silla had looked at him.

Silla nodded her head.

"Yes, I wouldn't consider it a curse in a negative aspect, but my greatest blessing and protection. Even though there are some things that I wish happened differently, I know that Omega will always protect me during my journey to recover all the items, and whatever comes after that."

"The connection between you two is quite strong and opaque. I think I can explain the expedited expiration of your parent's curse."

Silla had a thought.

"You mean it has something to do with Omega's destruction?" Malory was impressed.

"Yes, even though Omega's magic is not a curse, I can see a foreign presence or shadow slowly eating away and destroying that specific curse, quite autonomously. I would imagine that Omega has no waking idea that he is doing that, but it is quite controlled, not harming you at all."

"Actually, Omega's destruction magic has no effect on me. When he touches something, it instantly dematerializes. Those gloves he has on were made by my father, soaked in my blood, and he cannot destroy them."

Silla was secretly proud, momentarily, for knowing something that Malory did not …

"I don't think that is accurate. In fact, I would be willing to bet on the fact that Omega's magic has not been awakened fully to even the first stage yet. You will learn that the easiest application of many magics comes from our palms, which is done unconsciously in Omega's case. That in and of itself is unique. I have to want to see your curses, and I can turn it off, for lack of a better phrase, when I want to rest my mind."

All this was still brand new to Silla, so she did not know how to further the conversation.

"You will notice when you unlock your creation magic that you will not randomly create things but have to visualize in your mind and desire in your heart an object before you can create it."

Silla was silently hoping that the autonomous destruction coming from Omega on her curse would speed up so she could test out Malory's theory.

"So, you are saying that Omega will be able to gain further levels or ascensions of his magic and be able to destroy at his will, thus having no further need for his gloves?"

"If I'm honest, I do not believe that his power is negated by your gloves or your blood, but perhaps in your blood, there is an unconscious presence of creation that is constantly and concurrently recreating the gloves as Omega is doing the opposite."

Silla was amazed by this theory and perhaps scared of the thought also.

"Of course, this is 100 percent conjecture on my part, but it's worth experimentation once Omega regains consciousness, and we get into the depths of the castle. In the magical resonance cavern. Actually, if you go there, it might rid you of the remaining opposition to the awakening of your magic."

"So, am I immortal then?" asked Silla, that summation popping in her mind.

"Actually, that is a topic that has been debated for decades if not centuries. Again, I would refer you to Mutton for such inquiries. I think the magical resonance cavern will provide some answers also."

Not knowing what or where this resonance cavern was, Silla simply exclaimed, "What are we waiting for!" as she hurriedly got up from her seat.

Malory was both pleased with Silla's enthusiasm and disappointed that she had not thought of that sooner.

As the two made their way out of the room, they began to descend into the bowels of the castle, going farther and farther downward. Under Velantosse castle, much like under the Sacred Tower in Faruqh, stairs and more stairs were going downward. As the two went lower, it was getting colder and darker. Silla was beginning to wonder how far down they would go when Malory stopped at a grated metal door that led to what Silla could see as a natural walkway, quite slim in width.

"After passing this gate, you will be in the resonance chamber. You likely are unaware of this, but there are multiple springs of magic throughout Arrdus. Even though we don't know for sure, there is some literature that the elders have passed from one to the next for thousands of years that imply that Glyndyl created these springs to help with magic training and understanding."

Silla was amazed by her predecessor and even more excited about going into the room.

"Inside is a long, very tight walkway with unknown depths on either side and, at the end, is the spring of raw magicka. It can rid people of the blocks in their magic acupoints and increase our understanding of the subtleties of controlling magic and comprehending potency. This ascension method only exists past the gate, and we like to use them to help us train out magics, being able to grasp how our magic should feel and how we can interact with them."

Silla could tell by how Malory spoke rapidly and comprehensively; she was very interested in such topics. She knew that she would get along well with her teacher for years to come.

"Will you go in with me?" asked Silla, who wasn't scared but preferred a senior's company.

"Sorry, everyone must enter the chamber of their own accord and experience whatever comes to pass, with their own ability."

Silla reached out and grabbed the old iron gate, which had no knob or latch but was held firmly closed, as if by magic. After pulling open the gate, entering, and closing the gate behind her, she could immediately feel a surge of energy that she would have a hard time explaining.

It was a sensation that felt like goosebumps mixed with almost breathlessness.

She turned to look at Malory, but through the gate was nothing. There was no Malory, no light, perhaps no... anything. She now understood what her teacher meant earlier.

Silla took a deep breath and walked towards the end of the path, which jettied out about fifty feet.

Every step Silla took increased that sense of energy and power. It was welling up at such a rate that made her heart start pounding. She stopped about ten feet into the gate. She thought if she took too many more steps, she might burst from the welling of magic.

"I guess this is my current level. Maybe I should try creating something …" She could hardly contain her excitement.

Silla thought for a few seconds, closed her eyes, and pictured the pair of shoes that she had seen when she and Omega first got into Culver. She held out both hands, palms up, and thought, *I want these shoes to appear in my hands.*

Right after that thought, Silla felt weight suddenly fill both hands. She was almost afraid to open her eyes because perhaps she imagined that weight and everything Silla thought she *was* might have been a very lucid dream.

Silla opened her eyes and saw the exact pretty shoes that she wanted Omega to buy for her back in Culver. She let out a loud scream and a long laugh that seemed to link so many different feelings into place.

She put the shoes down, and they were a perfect size, and they were very well made. They were leather and dark brown in color with red and black stitching and a slightly raised heel.

She now understood what the feeling of creating something was, and she thought that Malory had explained everything very well. After going out, she would be able to practice efficiently.

Silla decided to create an entire outfit to go with the shoes but dared not take another step farther down the walkway. After completing the matching dress, Silla chose to take a deep breath and walk back out of the gate.

As she approached the gate, she was still very aware of the nothingness beyond it. Much to her relief, when she pulled it open, Malory was standing there waiting.

Malory looked and realized she didn't have to ask if it was a success.

"Nice dress… I see my theory of the last of your curse disappearing was correct."

"I don't think so. I couldn't get farther than ten steps. I don't know if it was a foolish thought, but it crossed my mind that I might be in danger if I continued forward."

"It wasn't foolish. Few ever get to the end of the walkway and look down and interact directly with the dense magicka. I've theorized that each person that could get to that point would see something different, as each person's journey is different. It seems like your parents' curse is exceptionally strong."

"I can't wait to tell Rose about this. You said that if Rose stepped in there, her blocked acupoints would clear, and she would obtain her magic abilities?" Silla was excited to have her friend experience something so unique.

"Yes, every person in the world has magic in them, but it was all blocked by your closest predecessor, Rocilyn. There are surviving records from Velantosse of that time, but her reasons for doing this are not explicit. Fortunately for Rose, she is not cursed, so her magic should spring forward with less complication."

Silla was curious about her closest predecessor, and it led her to recall her visions that happen almost nightly.

"Are there records of previous Creationists having nightly visions, showing women, whom I have perceived to be my predecessors usually talking ambiguously and in languages I have no business understanding, although I do?" This was something that weighed heavily on Silla's mind.

"There are so few surviving records, but the elders might have information that I'm not privy to. Elders pass on information via spoken word and written exerts to their own predecessors."

Silla thought that she might ask her grandmother later, but for now, she wanted to go back and tell Omega the excellent news, even if he couldn't hear it.

"I would be remiss if I didn't recommend you keep your first creation a secret."

Silla figured Malory meant once she left Velantosse castle ...

"I have reasons to believe that there are leaks inside the castle, and as long as they believe your parents' curse is still in effect for another year, you are more likely to have less heat on you, at least for some time."

Silla was sad and a little angry to hear Malory's worries, but agreed nonetheless.

XVIII

It was now the tenth day that Omega had been comatose in his room. Silla had spent each day sneaking off to the cavern of magicka resonance to practice. Each night she would go back and talk to Omega while he slept. Every time that she went into his room, her eyes always found the note that Kita had left for him still there, folded and waiting for his awakening. Those few days since Kita left, Silla had been feeling greedier in what her heart wanted. Although it was not her intention when going to his room, Silla grabbed the letter and unfolded it.

She read the first line: *Omega, I have so many things that I want to experience with you, but right now, I have to …*

Just as Silla finished the first line, she heard a groan from the bed, and again, contrary to her better judgment, she folded the letter and put it in her pocket, turning to see Omega looking at her.

"Omega! You've come back to me," said Silla as she fell on him and gave him a hug.

"Uh, water …," spoke Omega in a raspy voice. He was haggard, and he hadn't eaten more than some very thin porridge a few times in the last ten days—probably losing ten pounds.

There was water on the table near the door, which Silla ran to, and Omega tried to lean up and noticed a stiffness from his wound.

"Please be patient; I think, although your wound has been healing at a ridiculous rate, it will likely be some time before you can move again like normal."

Omega, lying back down, waited for Silla to bring the water, which he quickly gulped down.

"Delicious."

"Help me sit up and pull this bandage off. Tell me how it looks." Silla tried to reason with him, but she decided to help when he started to pull it off himself.

After sitting up, Silla pulled off the dressing, which she had helped change every night. The stitches that Jackson had put in were to be removed the next day.

"Jackson said that there should be no damage to your ability to move your arm, which he said was a small miracle."

"Jackson?" wondered Omega.

"Ah, I forget how much you've missed. Jackson is one of the experts in magic here in the castle. I have been spending most of my time with Malory, the curse expert."

"How long was I asleep?"

"This is the tenth night. I was so worried because of how much blood you lost. You were so pale when Jackson started to operate on you."

Omega was thinking for a few seconds. "Ten days... What have I missed? Did you discover any information about the other pieces?"

Silla was both confused and secretly happy that Omega hadn't mentioned Kita yet.

"Should I go tell *her* that you're finally awake?" slipped in Silla to give him an in.

"You mean Rose? Sure, we have traveled for a time, so I'm sure she'd be relieved."

As Silla made her way out the door, she felt the note in her pocket and was perplexed by Omega's lack of immediacy.

Rose, at this time, was in Victoria Washmire, the elemental expert's room. A few days earlier, right after Silla unlocked her magic, she encouraged Rose to go to that chamber and free her magic from its proverbial cage.

When Rose closed the gate, she immediately felt a similar sensation to that of Silla. Rose's was much colder in nature. The moisture in the air and on the rocks, and even on her skin began to freeze. Rose only took two steps before stopping because her feet felt like they would freeze to the ground had she gone any farther.

After turning around and exiting the gate, Silla was a little surprised by how fast she had returned.

"Done already?"

Rose was shivering and dripping from her extremities.

"I think I can freeze things. As soon as I closed the gate, I felt this sensation wash through my body, then all around me, freezing began to occur. I got a little scared and left."

Rose was laughing a little bit, mostly because she now had magic, even if she couldn't yet control it.

Since then, Rose had spent her time almost equally between elemental magic training and Velantosse history.

Right now, it was still early evening, and Rose was beginning to get the hang of how to control her ice-making magic.

"Perfect, Rose. Remember that ice magic is one of the rarer types of elemental magic, with only lightning magic being more uncommon," explained Ms. Washmire.

Rose was trying to listen while also trying to freeze the water in the glass without freezing the glass or table or floor, which was usually what happened.

"Fire magic is the most common, which is what I have, then earth manipulation, then wind, water, ice, and lightning. As I understand it, Piatous can use what he calls light-magic, but without seeing it myself, I cannot classify it."

At that time, Victoria placed her hand on the table.

After laying her hand down, palm up, she poured a little water, making a small pool.

"Okay, now freeze this pool of water without freezing my hand."

Rose was hesitant, as it was the first practice that involved another person and the prospect of hurting that person.

"Remember to focus on what you can see, for now. You will get to the point, through enlightenment, where you can pinpoint your magic even with your eyes closed. For now, though, if you focus that feeling and sensation that comes when forming ice, directly and solely on the little pool, everything should work fine."

Rose was encouraged by Ms. Washmire's explanations and trust. She was successful in freezing only the pool, at least until someone rushed into the room.

"Rose, guess what!" shouted Silla as she barged into the room.

At that exact time, Rose lost concentration, and the ice began to spread over Victoria's arm, which caused her to screech and jump back. She then used her magic to heat up and melt the ice.

"Oh no, I'm so sorry," said Silla as she moved to help Victoria.

"There's no harm, Your Worship. Elemental magic training relies heavily on concentration and can be quite dangerous to the user and anybody close by, so please use a less boisterous voice next time, and perhaps knock."

Silla could tell that Ms. Washmire took elemental magic seriously, and she did feel guilty about the disturbance.

"Rose, I have big news. Please come outside with me."

Silla was saying this calmly while bobbing up and down on her toes.

Chuckling, Rose followed her outside.

"What's the news."

"Omega is finally awake!"

"That's great! I was worried about how long he was out and how much blood he lost. How sad is he that Kita left?"

"That's the strange part. For a few minutes, I talked to him, helped him check his wound, and even got some water. He never asked about her. I even gave an ambiguous comment about letting a woman know he's awake, and he thought I meant you."

"Amnesia?"

"Maybe, but I have a feeling that it's my doing …"

Silla's words tapered off, and Rose could tell that she was feeling guilty about something.

"What did you *do*?" Silla looked around and thought for a second.

"Malory told me a few days ago that she believed that because of the curse linking me and Omega together, my magic, which is already extensive, perhaps beyond our imaginations, might, in theory, be even more potent towards him."

"Okay, but what does that have to do with him forgetting Kita, but nothing else... You didn't."

Rose realized what Silla had likely done.

"I honestly didn't think that it might work, but I did have a desire, which is the key, according to Malory. After unlocking my magic, I had been thinking. I never said it out loud, that I hoped, for his sake, and selfishly for mine, that Omega would forget Kita since she left anyway."

"You didn't want him to be sad. And perhaps... you didn't want to be sad yourself."

Silla was sometimes pleased and sometimes annoyed by how well Rose knew her.

"So, with your connected souls, even thinking anything about Omega can force it into existence. That is very dangerous, Silla. He feels a responsibility, because of your father, to protect you at any cost. I think he also has come to desire to protect you of his own accord. With this revelation, if it's true, you have to be very careful with how you approach him in the future."

Silla was conflicted, internally, and hated herself a little for hoping both that it was *not* what Rose thought and that it *was* what Rose thought.

"What about the note?" asked Rose. Silla scrunched up her nose, hoping Rose forgot about it.

"It's in my pocket." She looked at Rose, hoping that she wouldn't hate her too much.

Rose sighed.

"What am I going to do with you? Ultimately, I am on your side, and I know you are a good person, even though you can be childish and selfish. I won't butt into the business of you, him, Kita, and that note, but I hope that you will eventually figure out what is best for all parties and act on it."

Rose had to often remind herself that Silla is still a young woman with no practical experience in love and those similar emotions. Often young people make mistakes in love, and they must go through those hardships and trials on their own.

As Rose and Silla made their way up to Omega's room, they opened the door, and Omega was shirtless, and he had his hands on his pants, pulling them down to get changed.

"Sorry!"

Silla closed the door and looked at Rose. Rose had a fascinating look on her face.

"I can see why you like him. Even with all the scars, he has a very nice, hard body. If we had arrived a few seconds later, we would have gotten the real show."

Rose decided to stop there after looking at Silla and seeing that she was blushing so hard that someone might mistake her cheeks for cherries.

A couple of minutes later, Omega bid them come in.

"Sorry, I should have locked the door."

"Oh no, it is okay; we didn't mind, did we, Silla?" Rose elbowed her in the side, but Silla was still trying to calm down.

"It's good to see that you are finally awake and that you have the strength to get up and change. We were worried about you, battling Foster, even if he wasn't fully transformed."

"You've been able to talk to Foster?" Omega was wondering how he was.

"Yeah, he's quite normal, all things considered, on every day other than that of the full moon. He's come to visit a couple times," explained Rose.

"Oh yeah, was I hallucinating from blood loss, or did Cross jump the distance from shore to shack?"

Omega knew what he saw, and he had a feeling that Cross had an ability that allowed for muscle manipulation.

He thought he noticed Cross's arms getting bigger during the altercation with Elder Ross. Suddenly, though, he couldn't remember the reason for the conflict. He put that out of his mind for now.

"It was a sight to see, for sure!" exclaimed Silla. "I haven't talked much to him since then as he goes out to hunt and patrol often, but he did mention that he wanted to talk to you when you finally woke up."

As the three of them talked for a while, Silla finally remembered to mention her awakening.

"Omega, there is cavernous space deep under the castle that houses an extremely dense magicka, and after stepping into that space, the blockage holding our magic in check comes undone. Well, mine isn't fully useable. I think the chamber opened the door, perhaps equivalent to the amount of time since my curse started to dissipate."

Silla stood up and held out her hand, palm out as if she was pushing the air. After about two seconds, a pillow identical to the one on the bed appeared on the nightstand next to the bed.

"You've finally become a full-fledged Goddess of Creation. I'm not sure if you should use that too much, though." Silla was impressed by Omega's understanding of the larger situation.

"Malory also warned me not to use it around anybody else, but I know that you two are safe and would never betray me to our enemies."

"This Malory person is prudent. What do you think would happen if I went into that chamber?"

"You could at least ask if I have unlocked my magic yet," said Rose in a huff, which was not her usual tone at all. This caught both Silla and Omega off guard for a second.

"Sorry, Rose, I got ahead of myself. I can guess that you did unlock yours, but I would love to see it first-hand." Most people would have reacted sarcastically, but Omega was always sincere.

Rose moved to the center, bidding Omega to follow her. She then took two cups of water, placing one in each of his gloved hands. After concentrating for a few seconds, Rose held out both hands. Then from both cups, a stream of ice formed and exited the cups, reaching each other in midair and creating one arching stream connecting both cups. It resembled an icy rainbow.

Omega placed both cups down, carefully as to not break the arch, and then clapped.

"You can conjure ice? That's cool ..." Omega knew it wasn't the best joke, so he didn't expect much reaction... Rose laughed quite loudly, punching his arm playfully.

"What's wrong with you tonight?" asked Silla, furrowing her brow.

"Nothing, I'm a bit muddle-headed. I think I should go before I do something I regret."

After walking out the door, Rose spoke to herself.

"Control your urges, Rose. I know it has been months, but he's not yours. You can't do that to her."

About an hour after getting the stitches removed, Omega, Silla, and Malory made for the resonance chamber. Omega was quite interested in what results the chamber would produce, and Malory was perhaps just as intrigued.

"Okay, Omega. I'm glad that you are feeling better, and now that your stitches are out, I think it should be safe for you to enter the chamber."

"Silla told me that the chamber can unblock the channels of our acupoints, but what happens to someone that already has magic?"

"Your magic is unique, Omega. I've been conversing with the other experts and elders, and none of us have any knowledge of your magic ever having existed. That shouldn't be taken as absolute, as records are scarce, past about two thousand years ago."

"Didn't you mention a couple of days ago that there is a shadow around me that you think is Omega's destruction magic, constantly protecting me?" asked Silla.

"The fact that I can see it is unnatural, but yes, and I have to admit something to you, Goddess."

This was the first time that Malory had called her by that moniker since their first meeting.

"What is it?"

"To test my theory, the night before last, when Omega was still unconscious, I snuck in your room, and I attacked you by throwing a knife at you while you were sleeping. I threw it at your leg, just in case my theory didn't pan out."

"I trust you, Malory, and I can tell your theory worked out."

Silla was touching her legs.

"Thank you, Silla. Yes, when I threw the knife, about six inches before it hit you, it vanished. From my eyes, the shadow enveloped it, and it was gone. My theory of his autonomous protection seems to be accurate."

"I don't take well to people trying to hurt her. Please don't decide on your own to test any dangerous theories on Silla in the future." Omega, even with his kind eyes, was quite serious.

Malory could only nod her head in accordance.

"Omega, don't be too hard on her. She helped me tremendously when you were comatose."

Now at the gate to the chamber, Malory explained what she thought might happen when Omega entered.

"My guess, as it concerns your magic, Omega, is that you have not, officially, awakened your magic. Silla explained what she saw from your memories on how you first unlocked your magic, and even what she saw before she was forcefully ejected back in Safe Harbor. My guess is that each time your magic has manifested itself, it has been without your direct command to do so. I also have a theory about the gloves you're wearing, but if I get into that now, you might not enter the chamber for another hour."

Malory smiled as if to say sorry for prodding into your memories, Omega.

"When you enter the chamber, I think your power will officially enter stage one, and you should no longer have any need for those gloves. I need you to focus on the feelings and sensations that occur when you are destroying in that space. By doing so, you should be able to control this destruction after exiting the gate. That's the best-case scenario."

"And the worst-case scenario?" asked Omega.

"Worst-case, as far as I can hypothesize, is that you go into a state of uncontrollable destruction, completely challenging the very fabric of reality itself. You must remember that the inside of that chamber is pure, dense magic, created and polished by Glyndyl herself."

That thought didn't make Omega or Silla or Malory feel very excited.

"Okay, I'm going in. Wish me luck."

Before entering, Silla came up and hugged him from behind. He just stood there.

"Please try and be careful." After she released him, Omega opened the gate, entered the chamber, and closed the gate.

Omega took one step, then another, and so far, there was nothing that felt abnormal. After about ten more steps, Omega felt a rush of sensation flowing from his chest, through his legs, and through his arms.

"This feels new."

He looked at his hands, and he had what felt like an awakening.

"That must be the feeling I'm looking for. Time to test it out."

He stopped moving forward and looked over across the drop and looked at the rock wall, maybe thirty feet away. He decided to focus on that feeling he had, and it worked! The rock he was looking at was destroyed, but nothing next to it, nor the glove he was wearing.

"Amazing! I wonder what happens if I keep going forward."

Omega knew almost immediately that it was a mistake to go forward.

He started to have trouble breathing. His entire body tensed up so much that he thought his muscles might constrict to the point of no return. He began to float, but he couldn't scream due to the lack of air.

He thought for a second that he might be destroying the force that keeps everything grounded, and even the air people breathe, but that was a matter for later if he could survive.

He looked up, with great effort, as his body was beginning to contort, and he felt himself going in and out of consciousness.

He was still under the overhang of rock. With the most effort he's ever used, he focused on that feeling of concentration and destroyed some stone in a way that allowed another piece to break off and fall, crashing into his outstretched chest, knocking him back a few feet, which much to his relief caused the stoppage of that ultimate destruction. He was confused but glad that the stone didn't disappear when it made contact.

Omega, after catching his breath and standing up, realized that both his gloves and all his clothes were gone. After making his way back to the gate, he opened it, entirely naked, closing it behind him.

Silla and Malory were there, of course, but right before the gate opened; Rose came around down the hall.

"How's it going—" Before she could finish, Omega exited. Rose looked. "You're really testing me, huh, Marse?"

Malory looked away,

"I thought that might happen."

Silla closed her eyes unnecessarily, as she had front-row seats.

"Omega, are you okay?"

As she asked that, he collapsed forward onto her, now entirely naked and unconscious.

XIX

Thompsel was now at the scene of the kidnapping of his brother, and he could see that the guards' bodies were all but picked clean by the local wildlife who indeed enjoyed the free meal.

Thompsel thought to bury the bones and say a prayer to Sulce after his investigation. Unfortunately, a series of monumental events would soon unfold, forcing those thoughts out of his mind.

As Thompsel was investigating the different tracks, searching for anything that might show him which direction Thomo went, he found a promising lead.

There were hoof tracks, quite clear, leading southwest back into Culver. After following the tracks in that direction for about an hour, Thompsel realized he would be at the beach soon, getting close to the Ardian Sea. He also realized that these tracks were too perfect and likely staged by someone.

Anyone that was cunning and experienced enough to overpower Thomo and his guards would not leave such a blatant marker.

As Thompsel was approaching the shore, the tracks were no longer necessary because he could see a figure standing at the beach, indeed the one that left the tracks. Surely, he was waiting for the crown prince.

The man, slight in figure, was standing, facing the sea with no shoes on, toes buried in the sand. The tide was pulling in and going back out, quite indifferent to the plights of people. At its highest, the water level was mid-shin to the man enjoying the late afternoon, near-dusk scene.

As Thompsel got about thirty feet away, he realized abruptly who this person was and reached for his sword. The crown prince's breath started to hasten. Anxiety, possibly fear, began running through his veins.

The slight-framed man in the sea raised up one hand, fingers fully extended.

"You are right to fear me, Crown Prince Thompsel. I can smell your blood pumping from here."

As the man turned and looked at Thompsel, he could confirm that it was Grexle, Emperor of Zarrek.

Back in Culver, Thomascus was finishing reading the scouting report of the movements of Black Garden and Ruseberg.

"The timing of their movements is suspect, Your Majesty," said Palace Guard Captain Henderson.

"I agree. For this type of gathering of most of the two nation's soldiers in unison towards our borders is not possible so soon after the conference," explained the captain of the capital city guard, Bison.

Thomascus only had about one thousand soldiers and guards left in the capital. The bulk of the soldiers had already traveled to Orcasium. Orcasium was the massive fortress built into the southern expanse of the Culver Mountains. It was about four days away from the capital if one made full haste. The southern border of Ruseberg was only two and a half days at the same pace.

"So, it seems as though the two nations have had these thoughts for a while but had not the chance to implement their desires. This also means that someone inside Culver has been leaking our strategical movements, giving them the chance to get ahead of me."

The two captains could feel their emperor's anger.

"We have maybe five thousand soldiers north of the capital in all of Culver, but the majority are near the Faruqh border and would not get here in time to help," explained Captain Bison.

"We can assume that these false kings' goal is to get to the palace and attempt a takeover before any reinforcements could get here," stated Captain Henderson.

"Indeed, if they can get here and take me and my family prisoner, no matter our numbers outside, there would be little our immense power could do to counterattack."

"Your Majesty, how many soldiers are coming to attack the palace?" asked Henderson.

"Counting every man, not just the trained soldiers, there is some 14,000 heading this way now. I have already sent out a hawk to let Thompsel know that if he receives word of this, to stay there and continue to look for my son. He couldn't get here in time to help, anyway."

"The crown prince has been building and implementing strategic, unique changes to the capital's defenses, and they should prove useful. Unfortunately, he kept much of their inner workings a secret to us," stated Bison, who was both proud and worried.

Thomascus began to walk out of their staging area, with the two captains following.

"We can at least use Thompsel's moat mechanism, which should allow for a bottleneck situation. Get ready to send out the orders to raise the chains around the entire capital!"

"Right away, Your Majesty!" shouted both Bison and Henderson as they went their separate ways.

Back at the beach, Grexle and Thompsel were staring at each other. Grexle was enjoying the sea breeze and wet sand, with Thompsel not enjoying the moment much at all. If they were closer, one would see that Thompsel was more than a foot taller and close to a hundred pounds heavier.

"I've heard about that metal face-covering of yours, but now that I see it, I can't see any hinges in the back, so I'm guessing you never take it off."

Thompsel was still holding his sword, it now resting on his shoulder.

"You can put your sword away. There's no need for it today. If the worst happened, and we had to fight, it would do little to change your fate, anyway."

Thompsel could tell by his eyes that Grexle had smiled at that last comment. Even though he had heard the stories about Grexle, now being so close was different. Judging by their sizes, Thompsel has no reason to fear this adversary. Still, even if he needed to, he doubted he could even take a step forward. Grexle's eyes were indeed mesmerizing and dangerous.

Thompsel decided to strap his sword on his back again.

"Some intriguing things are occurring right this second in Arrdus and in other continents. Some world-changing, and some much more local. You will likely soon receive a hawk stating that Black Garden and Ruseberg have decided to ignore your edict, join forces, and invade northern Culver in hopes of reaching the palace unaware and unobstructed."

Thompsel started to contemplate the possibilities of what Grexle was saying. For an unknown reason, he felt that Grexle was not the lying sort.

"You should know that I have never lied, in my very, very long life. You are likely wondering how I know this, but that is unimportant. What is important is that I had no hand in orchestrating those false kings' dissensions. Still, I do like to take advantage of an efficient opportunity."

The sun was beginning to set with reds, oranges, and yellows sprinkling behind Grexle's silhouette.

"I can venture a guess that because of what might happen between our empires, there are not very many soldiers to take up arms inside the capital."

Thompsel was calculating the numbers, and he was not very optimistic.

"I won't divulge squadron information to an eminent enemy, but yes, the capital is scarcely defended, especially if up against an armored assault."

"From my scouts, there's probably over 12,000 total soldiers and militia heading towards the capital right now. You can run the numbers in your head and decide how dire that show of force sounds for yourself. My purpose for kidnapping your brother, in Faruqh territory, was to get you here, on this beach, face to face."

Thompsel was impressed by Grexle's calmness and foresight, even if he dared not admit it.

"So, you do not plan to hurt Thomo?" asked Thompsel, whose focus shifted again.

"I have no immediate plans to hurt, help, or release him. All of those depend on your decisions in the next few minutes."

Grexle's eyes had never left Thompsel's, and the crown prince was convinced that he had not even blinked, but Thompsel met his stare, full force.

"I have two requests, which will either lead to your brother's death or his release. Also, one of the requests would allow you to return to the capital, in time, to help your family."

Thompsel did not think it possible as he was many days away from his home.

"My first offer... is something that I would call a gift. This gift would allow you to get back in time to help your family while also giving you the capability to protect those important to you in the future. Events are approaching that will shake your resolve to its core... and I am getting so very tired."

Thompsel was, of course, lost as to these ambiguous events, but the immediate threat did make him want to accept this gift.

"Before I agree to the first, I would hear the second."

Grexle laughed. "Smart man. The second thing is simply a request and a piece of information that you likely did not know before coming here. The giving of the first is not contingent on the second's outcome. I simply need your word that you will make an attempt on that request."

Thompsel felt that no matter the request or gift, getting back to Culver was worth any risk.

"Okay, what is this gift?"

About two hours after Thompsel and Grexle were making deals, Thomascus had his soldiers and guards working tirelessly to yank each chain on the defensive moat mechanism, as Thompsel called it.

Culver's capital city was itself quite ordinary looking, with its high, stone walls going around the entirety of its oval shape, but what Thompsel had been working on for years was the unique defensive structure that was put in place to guarantee bottlenecks if attacked.

There were large metal plates that extended on the exterior of the capital's tall walls, along the ground, covering every inch of the city. Each plate budded up against both the one to its left and right, and they were about forty feet tall and twenty feet wide. Every blacksmith in Culver was commissioned and worked on these plates for six years straight. Each plate had three large loops near the far end, which were typically ignored, maybe even thought of as aesthetics to the unknowing.

Still, huge ropes and chains on the ramparts could connect to those loops, and the enormous plates could be lifted and fitted to the city walls. What was under the plates was key... there was a man-made moat-like structure that spanned around the capital. There was no water in that thirty-foot-deep moat, but wooden spikes, caltrops, and other impediments.

The other key to this defensive structure was that any of the four gates, be it east, west, north, or south, could be the solo opening for the entire capital, forcing a bottleneck. The gates also had the same giant plates in front of them, and any or all of these could be hoisted, all but eliminating the gate, hiding it behind the plate.

Thomascus knew that his son had implemented other hidden defensive gems. However, he was not aware of their locations, so he hoped that the bottleneck would be enough to even out the numbers disparity.

As the rebelling allied forces were about thirty-six hours away from the capital, Thomascus had ordered all citizens inside the capital's walls to stay in their homes and all able-bodied men to take up arms and head to the north gate area. Thomascus also sent a few of his free scouts to search for the citizens outside the capital's walls, maybe working or hunting.

The emperor also sent his fastest hawks to the settlements that were in the direct path, north of the capital. He told those magisters or lords that were in charge not to retaliate or impede the rebel's movement. He hoped that if those settlements' citizens remained hidden, the encroaching army would simply pass them by as they were making haste to get to the capital ahead of reinforcements.

The Black Garden/Ruseberg conjoined forces were now only twenty-four hours away. Thomascus had scarcely slept and was only in his nap for a few minutes when he was jolted awake by the slamming of the door to his inner chamber.

Thomascus stirred, annoyed but also wondering if something happened ...

"Hi, Father, I'm back," said Thompsel as Thomascus got up, speechless.

"How did you get back so fast? I commanded that you were not to know what had happened."

"Not to worry, Father, nobody ignored your edict. I will explain fully after we make sure the capital survives this attack. How much time do we have?"

"Their army should be here by this time tomorrow. Did they open the gate for you?"

Thompsel smiled.

"No, but I had my way of getting in." Upon seeing his father's worried look, he reiterated that it was safe. "The rebel forces won't be able to get in the same way I did."

"How many soldiers and able-bodied citizens did we have?"

"The last count was 1781." This number made Thompsel unexpectedly happy, given the situation.

"That's very close. As you know, I have been working on a new, repeating crossbow that would allow even someone with no training the ability to defend their home. We have about 1500, and I have been considering their potential the entire way here. Do I have your trust to give me the authority to act on my plan?"

Thomascus walked to his son and put his hand on his shoulder.

"You are the crown prince. I would have been disappointed if you didn't want the authority to command and position all of our soldiers."

After another eighteen hours of getting all of the weapons in place and people in their armor, then putting them in their positions along the ramparts of the northern walls of the capital, it was almost time.

The only two people that were outside of the sole-remaining opened gate were Thompsel and Thomascus. Thompsel was in his favorite black heavy armor with which he never wore a helmet. The armor was jet black with the crest of House Deckler, which was a golden tree with many branches but no leaves. There were not many Houses in Arrdus. It was more of a traditional system that mostly died out centuries ago. Still, the Decklers were proud of their crest. Thompsel had his giant two-handed sword strapped to his back, ready to fight for his home.

Thomascus had a light, studded leather armor of the highest quality. He had his usual dual swords, one of which was, of course, his precious treasure, Death's Flame.

"Aren't we a bit exposed, out here on this bridge, exactly where the bottleneck needs to take place?" asked Thomascus as he looked around, seeing smoke on the horizon to the north.

Thompsel laughed. "If everything goes according to my plan, not one enemy will make it to this bridge. Also, I have mechanisms built under our feet, so if it comes to that, we have protections in place."

Thomascus was impressed and proud of his son and crown prince. He felt confident they would win and hoped that his son's defenses weren't so perfect that he wouldn't get his fighting share.

As the last few hours were coming to a close, and the emperor and crown prince could now see the rebel army, just the two of them were standing on the only remaining bridge.

Thompsel turned and looked up at the high walls of his capital, and dotted from left to right, shoulder to shoulder, were all of the citizens, ready to defend their pride and home.

Almost all of them had one of the new repeating crossbows, created by Thompsel. There were also twenty enormously oversized crossbows hoisted to the ramparts a few hours earlier via hard work and many pullies.

From end to end, these larger crossbows were about ten feet wide, and it took four or five people to load and pull back the bolt to set it. Calling it a bolt was subjective because the ammunition for the enormous crossbow was naught more than a medium-sized tree trunk, smoothed out and pointed. Its primary purpose was to induce fear and decimate cavalry.

As the approaching armies were now in plain sight, all of the soldiers could make out the lifted walls and the two brave warriors in front of the gate.

The two kings were at the rear, both in their crowns without weapons, which made both father and son smirk.

"These fools; false kings had only to submit to the greater cause, and they could have kept high positions and a comfortable life," said Thomascus as he surveyed the encroaching army that had halted about three hundred feet away.

"They were clearly communicating with each other for longer than we know, for such a concerted effort to take place, so efficiently," spoke Thompsel in a low voice.

Thompsel proceeded to walk up some twenty paces and spoke in a booming voice.

"All of you fine soldiers are in direct defiance of your emperor, and I'm sure the false kings behind you have coerced you with fear, emotion, and pride to get you here so fast!"

Some of the captains and lieutenants in the front line interrupted Thompsel… "You have no right to swallow up the pride and traditions that we in Black Garden have, and we will always stand with our true king!" One of the captains pointed back to the former king, Julius Scectore.

"We are here today to prove that we are worthy of fear and respect, and although we don't want to slaughter your family, you have left us little choice!"

Thompsel looked back at his father, who was clearly seething at that last comment, but he held up his hands as if to say, *give me one chance, Father.*

After turning back around, he proceeded to give everyone there that one chance.

"Please hear what I have to say and make a decision that will shape the future of both Ruseberg and Black Garden! I respect all your pride as citizens and your desire to protect your homes. However, this aggression is misplaced! You all could have lived your lives, with your families and friends, knowing that you were under the protection of the empire, and enjoyed all of the benefits that come with that!"

Some scoffed, but none interrupted him again.

"The only people that stood to lose anything significant, at least in their eyes, was the royal families of the two nations! They would have become ordinary citizens, albeit nobles! They could not bring themselves to lose their power, so they likely told you that my father and I would destroy your states and take your resources! It might be too late at this juncture for your collective feelings of pride to turn back, but I implore you to make the logical decision!"

There was even more murmuring now as some of the infantry and cavalry were starting to doubt the reasons they were there.

"Only two people have to die here today! If you bring me the heads of those two former kings, everyone else can leave and return to their wives and children! If you choose to fight against me, I will have no choice but kill you quite ruthlessly!"

For most of his plea, Thompsel was using a voice full of empathy, but for that last breath, his voice turned to one that instilled certain doom to those hearing his words.

There was no immediate answer or action, and then former King Julius spoke up.

"That false crown prince wishes to divide us because he fears our numbers, right on his doorstep! I say to ye now, fierce citizens of Black Garden and Ruseberg, whoever kills those two will be made a Marquis and given more land than they could ever use!"

Julius's idea of playing on lowly soldiers' desire for glory and stability worked. The rallying cries could be felt in the ground.

The armies began to slowly march forward to get within a good bow range.

Thompsel sighed and turned, walking to join his father.

"Your message fell on deaf ears, son. That's often the case when fear and ignorance are abundant. Take note of that for future negotiations."

"Yes, Father."

As the armies got to within one hundred feet, Thompsel found himself towards the far end of the bridge and placed his right foot near a large pressure plate. Thomascus did not know what that plate did, but he was, admittedly, curious to find out.

Thompsel raised his left hand in the air, fingers spread open, which told all of the soldiers on the ramparts to take aim. There were many thousands of soldiers in front of them, and they felt fear... not for themselves, but for their two most respected leaders. They were, after all, outside the closed gate.

The advancing troops, now one hundred feet away from the emperor and his son, stopped and, behind the cavalry, which was about 500 strong, was the bowmen, numbering about one thousand.

Even though there were approximately 14,000 people in this rebelling group of fighters, only some three hundred had dependable heavy armor. The rest were made up of men wearing jerkins and tunics or extra-padded gambesons.

Thompsel knew that his repeating crossbows could easily shred the lesser-armed fighters at their current range and armor. In contrast, the heavy armored one's calvary would be the prey of the massive crossbows.

Just then, one of the captains, part of the calvary, gave an order that set an exciting day in motion.

"Archers! Center formation!"

The calvary from the middle went left and right to clear a path, which the archers entered into, now dead center, looking straight at the two men on the bridge.

This formation was exactly what Thompsel wanted, and it told him that they planned not to attack those on the rampart. Archers enjoyed land and titles, also.

As the archers lined up in five long rows, about a hundred in each, slightly staggered as to not impede the aim of the archers behind them, the captain gave out another order.

"Ready... Aim... Fire!"

As soon as the archers let loose their grip. The arrows whistled towards the bridge; Thompsel slammed his foot down on that pressure plate, which triggered a metal wall. It was as wide as the bridge and only a few inches taller than Thompsel, shooting up to block the arrows.

This wall was not sturdy or strong enough to stop a battering ram or even charging cavalry. Still, it was designed to prevent arrows or be reinforced from the rear to impede foot soldiers.

Only one second after the plate rose, arrows started to ting off it, creating a melody, quite pleasing to the ear.

During this cacophony of arrow collisions, Thompsel's hand never went down, which created a target for the arrows, as his hand was less than half a foot above the wall. This also seemed to be part of Thompsel's strategy as it created a distraction for both the commanders and the bowmen.

During this distraction, those crossbow wielders on the ramparts were aiming at their pre-ordered targets. The others were making sure that each soldier had a substantial amount of extra ammunition close at hand. The massive crossbows had now been turned and adjusted to point at their intended targets, and everyone awaited the signal.

As the arrows got less and less, none of them hit Thompsel's hand. When there were two seconds of no arrow tings, Thompsel closed his hand into a fist.

From here, all hell broke loose. The massive crossbows, upon impact, had an even more significant effect than Thompsel guessed they might. It was the first time that he had used them in a real-life scenario. The thunderous sound from impact, alone, induced fear and confusion.

Each massive crossbow was aimed at a calvary grouping or heavily armored group of infantrymen. Upon release, these tree-like bolts completely decimated the horses. After hitting one horse, chopping it almost in half, the bolt kept bouncing and rolling, breaking limbs and smashing in the soldiers' heads around its landing. These bolts would bounce and roll for a hundred feet.

Thompsel felt guilty the night before as he knew the horses were innocent, but it was another regret he was willing to live with.

It only took the maiming of forty horses before the remaining more than four hundred bucked their riders off and bolted away from the battlefield to safety.

Unfortunately for the riders, most of them had thick armor and were now the massive crossbows' sole target.

The men on the ramparts were doing an excellent job of quickly reloading those gigantic crossbows. Each of the twenty massive bows had ten tree bolts each, which meant as many as two hundred sharpened trees were available.

Amid the screams, confusion, and hysteria, the repeating crossbows were working brilliantly.

They could shoot bolts as fast as the wielder could cock the lever, with ten bolts being loaded at one time. With enough remaining power to kill, their range was only two hundred feet, so once the army had made it into that range, Thompsel knew things would go as planned.

There were 1500 repeating crossbows and some 100 bolts for each.

The former kings from the north had not had Culver's resources. Culver had plenty of forestry south of Lake Arrdus and west of the Culver Mountains. Thompsel had been ordering the logging and replanting of trees since he was a young teenager. He felt that in many aspects, wood was just as important as iron.

After ten rounds of the repeater and big bow attacks, Thompsel opened his hand again. The shooting stopped, each soldier on the rampart now focusing on having ammunition ready and aiming all setup.

"I'm going to release the plate, Father. We don't know how many are left ..."

"Ha, I hope some are left, or this will be a very boring siege!" said an excited Thomascus, getting into his stance.

As Thompsel released the pressure plate and the wall dropped back down, the site was both glamorous and horrendous. Demolished horse carcasses, thousands of dead soldiers, many missing limbs, or entire halves of their bodies.

As the two looked around, zero of the heavy armors remained, which was the strategy's focal point. There were zero bowmen left and only some 2,500 of the 14,000 that marched there.

Against a well-funded and well-trained enemy, this strategy would not have been even half as effective. Still, a good crown prince should strategize for many different types of enemies, which Thomascus always drilled into his son.

Now Thompsel spoke up to the remaining enemies.

"That was but a taste! The opportunity... The last opportunity to bring the heads of those two kings is given again! Take this last chance to end this suicide mission, go home to your families, and rebuild your pride as citizens of Culver! I do not wish to wipe out so many new members of my home! You have five seconds!"

Upon counting down on his still-extended hand, before one finger went down, and before the two kings could try to negotiate, the remaining soldiers, almost in unison, rushed towards their former kings.

King Julius was the first to get caught by a spearman's spear that pierced his shoulder, throwing him off his horse. They crowded him fast, lobbing his head off.

King Derek of Ruseberg made a break for it and had some distance on his pursuers.

After killing Julius, there was now a horse to ride, which one of the soldiers hopped on, and the chase ensued.

After less than a minute, the soldier, Albert Oswain, the only survivor from the first line of regular infantry, sped King Derek down, leaping from his horse, tackling the king, and taking him to the ground. He likely felt it was easier to behead Derek, as Albert was from Black Garden and had no ties to the King of Ruseberg.

Now that the battle was over, Thompsel, after receiving both heads, kept his word and did not kill those remaining soldiers.

"I think it's best if we all just put this unfortunate business behind us! Please return to your homes! There will be some administration changes occurring in Northern Culver, where you live! As citizens of Northern Culver, I hope that you can help protect your eastern border against any Irkdale movements and unwanted advances from the deadlands and freelands to the north and west, respectively."

After a couple of hours, all the former rebels, now full-fledged Northern Culver citizens, were in the capital's walls receiving treatment, food, and lodging for the night.

Thompsel, now back in his own home, knew that he would have to explain how he got home so quickly and fulfill the request of Grexle, both of which related to his father.

Just then, Emperor Thomascus walked in, still in his battle attire.

"I think we have some things to discuss, son."

XX

The night after exiting the magical chamber and passing out, Omega found himself roaming the castle grounds. He had realized that almost the entirety of his time at Velantosse Castle was spent comatose. Now that he was awake, he felt his usual anxieties related to being inside walls too often. It made him chuckle to think how many days he had been sleeping inside the castle.

Omega was now near the docks, and as he walked closer, he noticed the spot where Cross had likely jumped from the shore to the hut. The ground was smashed in, and three of the planks of the nearby dock were cracked.

Omega wondered what Cross's magic was, exactly. However, he had an idea that it must be related to changing the structure of his muscles, tendons, and bones. He had heard that they would be leaving very soon, so he figured it was time to talk to Cross and satiate his curiosities.

As Omega took a few steps to the left of Cross's takeoff spot, he suddenly stopped and was staring at a seemingly inauspicious section of the dock, but his feet wouldn't move. He knew that something significant happened, but he had a confusing memory recall, as this spot was precisely where he had kissed Kita for the first and only time.

Recalling his memories, he could remember standing there. There was extreme joy and passion, but everything else was strange. He could see a shadowy figure in front of him with no discernable features. Much like a dream, as he tried harder to fill in that haze, it became less opaque to the point that it was almost transparent.

As the visage was getting less noticeable, Omega reached up and touched his cheek, where a tear was running down. He had no idea why he was sad, which made him feel strange, and it also helped him understand that this disappearance was meaningful and sincere.

Omega figured staying there would do naught but make him sadder, so he decided to go find Cross. Omega had heard that Cross had a room near the castle's front entrance, so Omega hoped that he would still be awake.

Cross's room had flickering candlelight emanating through the crease between door and frame, which gave Omega some hope.

Upon knocking, a few seconds later, Cross opened the door.

"Hey, Omega. Finally awake for more than a few minutes, I see."

"Yeah, we've been here for about two weeks, and I've been awake for less than a day. I would say it's a waste, but the trip here wasn't for me, from the start anyway."

"Come in; I assume you have something to discuss," said Cross as he motioned Omega to sit in the green chair that was near the center of the room.

Cross's room was quite large but did not have much in it, making it appear shockingly empty. Omega knew that Cross had been there for years, so he was surprised that his room was so minimal. There was a bed in one corner, three chairs near the center of the room, a chimney in the opposite corner of his bed, and a few necessities like his tea kettle and cups.

Omega took a seat and then asked his questions.

"So, does your magic have something to do with the state of your muscles and bones?"

"Ha, that's an excellent observation. In fact, I can freely change and control the density of my bones, muscles, and tendons, while also being able to change the elasticity of my muscles and tendons, as needed."

"Jumping across the lake likely took a lot of control and subtle adjustments to avoid injury."

Cross was impressed with Omega's observations, even during such a stressful situation.

"Yep, for jumping large distances, I usually adjust during the run-up, for extra speed, then again during the jumping process so as not to shred my muscles, and then again right when I land. Any laziness or lack of concentration would likely cause me to die from the impact."

"That's an interesting magic, although I'm not sure if it is magic at all."

"Right. Malory told me that it's not explicitly part of any class of magic. Still, she also said that there are many magical abilities that they do not have experience in or even comprehensive knowledge of. Yours is a prime example."

After speaking for a few minutes, Cross brought up the Kita topic, as he did not know why Kita left, being gone himself when she did, so he was curious.

"So, do you mind me asking why Kita left so soon after getting here? I could tell the two of you were very close, so it was a surprise when I came back from checking our defenses to find her gone."

Omega looked at Cross for a moment. He clearly saw Cross's lips move when saying that name, but it was not audible. As if Omega went completely deaf only for that word.

"It seems that something terrible happened to my memories. I assume you said a name …"

Omega was feeling strange inside. He was dizzy while also feeling hot and cold at the same time. His chest was tight. As he closed his eyes and started to breathe in and out at a fast, quick interval, Cross stood up and took a jump backward. Omega was having trouble controlling himself, and in a couple of seconds, Cross lost one of his cups and one of his chairs, *poof.*

Omega seemed to be somewhere else. Although he was distressed seconds earlier, he seemed calm now, albeit unresponsive to Cross's concerns.

Omega had flashes, too fast to fully distinguish, slicing through his mind. He saw red… *was that hair?* He saw two blue dots… *eyes?* He saw a flash of curved white… *a smile.*

Without being conscious of it, Omega was challenging the blockade that Silla had put on his memories of Kita. When it came to memories, it was challenging to eliminate them entirely. In most cases, simple hiding of the memory occurs, with barriers being put in the mind.

Unfortunately for Omega, a combination of intervention and the fact that Silla's power is not ordinary led to him not fully recovering his hidden memories.

Instead, he now had glimpses of someone with very red hair with large blue eyes and a huge smile. However, with the interruption, all feelings of love or other emotional angles were very muddled and confusing.

From Cross's perspective, something didn't seem right, so after no response to his pleas, he decided to power up his arm and knock Omega towards the bed. The thought was that some force, not enough to kill, would knock Omega back to reality.

"Uh, my head… A sliver of my lost memory perhaps returned …"

"What was that? You were destroying… but without intention, Omega," explained Cross as he walked towards Omega, looking perplexed.

"It has happened before in Safe Harbor. Up until I entered the chamber, I usually had to touch things to destroy them. Malory told me that I likely hadn't unlocked my magic yet and that it activated, initially, as a survival mechanism. Now with this upgrade, I'll need to practice control. Thanks."

"That's a beneficial and dangerous power, Omega. Make sure you are the one in control."

"Ah, I heard that Foster wanted to talk to me, but I won't be here much longer. If I miss the chance, tell him not to worry about my injuries, and try to seal up the cracks around that door."

After wishing Cross a good night, Omega decided to go up to Silla's room and see if she could fill in the blanks of who it was swimming in his mind. At that time, he still had no notion of how his memory became so foggy.

Silla's room was on the third floor, and it was nothing spectacular. It was not very big and not well-furnished. Her beloved followers offered her bigger spaces, with the elders gladly vacating their rooms, but Silla was happy with her small room, close by to Rose's.

At this time, Omega was just entering the castle, and Silla was sitting on her bed, Kita's letter in her hands. She still had not read the letter, destroyed it, or given it to Omega and explained what she had done. Silla found herself unable to decide, fearing each's consequences.

Silla unfolded the letter then folded it back, Rose's words echoing in her mind: *You must tell him about the message and her and what you did. If he finds out before you reveal it… he will likely feel betrayed by someone he cares for.*

As she was busy being stubborn with herself, a knock came on her door. The timing felt like the work of Desitine.

Silla raised up from the bed, placing the now unfolded letter on the table near the center of the room, which had a deformed candle burning on it, wax half melted. When she opened the door, Omega met her with a look of intrigue.

"Hi, were you asleep?"

"Nope, I was just pondering some things."

"I have a series of questions that have sprouted recently. I'm hoping you can answer some."

Silla, even though she had no idea, guessed the nature of these inquiries.

"Okay, shoot."

"I have heard from multiple people that there was somebody else with us when we arrived here. Someone who is gone now, but I've been told that this lady and I had a close relationship."

The mere mention of this topic made Silla's heartbeat increase as if she felt both guilt and relief towards the coming moments.

Silla found her tongue glued, so Omega continued.

"Earlier, there were flashes... of characteristics. Hair, eyes, and a smile, but there might be something foreign, consistently driving these images back into obscurity. I thought I could work out a general idea of appearance, but even walking to your room has driven that back out of my mind... As we are talking, this person is gone again. I know not her name or even those characteristics."

Silla turned and looked at the letter next to the flickering candlelight and was still hesitant.

Omega noticed her gaze and approached the table. As he got closer, Silla walked over and grabbed the note.

"Is that a note you've been writing to someone?" asked Omega, now standing only a step away from Silla.

Just at that time, Rose opened the door, ready to treat Silla to their nightly tea, which had become a habit since being in the castle.

As she walked in, she commented on what she thought was happening.

"So, you finally decided to come clean about her letter to Omega ..."

Silla's eyes became huge for a moment, and Rose realized what she had done, a step too late.

"Is that mine? It's from the person I have no memory of?" asked Omega, a little less calm than before.

"Um, yes. There was someone else traveling with us when we arrived here, and she left for one reason or another after you went into that coma," answered Rose.

Silla was still quiet, holding the letter in her hands.

Rose continued, but it turned out that Silla's power was nothing to be trifled with.

"This person's name is Kita, and I don't know your relationship, but it seemed special."

Omega was confused. "What's her name? I didn't hear you say anything."

Rose repeated the name.

Omega looked at Rose's mouth, and nothing came out, only the movement of her lips, same as back in Cross's room. Omega had hoped that Cross simply didn't know the pronunciation.

"Is this a joke? There are no sounds when you get to the name."

Rose and Silla looked at each other, sharing the same fearful thought.

Silla spoke up, finally. "Is it because of that?" Rose had no more answers than her friend, but she could feel the tension starting to grow in the room.

"Because of what?" asked Omega, becoming slightly more annoyed but still not angry.

"I don't know how to explain what happened… While you were unconscious, after my breakthrough, I had a terribly selfish desire… I didn't know it would come to fruition… Please understand."

"Understand what? Are you the cause of my eviscerated memories?" demanded Omega, now very much needing some answers.

"I am. When you woke up, I wondered why you didn't bring Kita up, and I realized that perhaps what I had conjured in my mind became a reality."

Before Silla could continue, Omega interrupted her, voice shaking.

"Please don't use her name. It's sadder than I hoped, having no sound every time you say that *name*. Why can't I hear it? Even when Cross said it earlier, I didn't catch it, but I convinced myself that I missed it."

Silla was panicking a little now, finally realizing that she crossed the line, invading her friend's mind.

"I didn't know how to tell you about her. I didn't know if I wanted to tell you about her. She left after all, even though you saved her from Foster."

Rose could see Silla drifting off course; deriding Kita was not going to make things better.

"She had her reasons for leaving how she did. Family emergencies and other issues."

Omega was finding himself inundated with questions and fears.

"So, you can go into my mind, at will, and block or erase memories?" Silla didn't know how to answer or didn't want to answer that question.

"I'm sorry, but I don't know how to take it back either."

"You are sorry? Sorry for *which* part? Stealing my private thoughts, or not revealing that you did so, perhaps hoping I never bring up the subject!? The coma would create a perfect scenario, right!?" asked a growingly frustrated Omega, voice getting louder.

"Calm down, Omega. It was not malicious," said Rose, trying to stem the rising tide.

"You have your own fault in this. From what I gather, you also knew all of these things from the beginning and didn't deem me worthy of my own truth."

Rose knew that she could have been more forceful in having Silla some clean and felt guilty.

"This is not the first time that you have overstepped yourself into matters of my mind," said Omega, now turning back to Silla.

"You might have a notion in your head that I am yours to control as you see fit. Please rid that foolishness from your thoughts."

Silla was now tearing up, but her pride and hardheadedness were also bubbling.

"That other time, you needed to be controlled, corralled. You can't simply do whatever you want and have no consequences, Omega!" shouted Silla.

At the mention of consequences, Omega slammed his hand down onto the table, making half of it disappear. The candle, along with the other half toppled over, onto the floor. Rose grabbed the candle and placed it on the nightstand.

"There's your anger again! Can't you accept that it was an accident and be nice?" Even in her own mind, as she was arguing with Omega, Silla knew that she had no right to quarrel, and Omega's slight anger was less than she deserved.

"Give me the note, Goddess," said Omega in a low, serious tone.

"I haven't read it, just so you know." Silla handed the note to Omega.

As Omega flipped it over, he touched the paper, then flipped it repeatedly and touched both sides.

Silla and Rose were looking at the note in Omega's hand. They could see the words, but Omega was acting strange.

"Why is nothing written on it?" asked Omega as he looked at Silla.

"What? I can see the words from here." Silla stepped next to Omega.

"Look, it says *Dear Omega.*" But Omega dropped the letter, putting his head in his hands.

"I can't see anything on that paper… You allow not even words to reach my eyes?"

"I… I don't know," was all Silla could muster. "I didn't mean it to be that absolute …"

Omega reached down and grabbed the blank paper, folded it, and put it in his pocket.

"I'm beginning to regret …"

"Regret what? Being connected?" asked Silla in her bossiest tone.

"I have only one recourse. I'm leaving the castle," said Omega as he turned to exit.

Silla darted past him in front of the door.

"Where are you going?" asked a stunned and anxious Silla.

"Anywhere but here. I have this feeling that I will never regain my recollection if I am near you. The little details I was able to hold earlier all disappeared as soon as I entered your room. Perhaps you are emanating your desires, and the closer I am, the more powerful. Could you at least tell me which nation she lives in?"

Silla was silent, staring into Omega's eyes, and his gaze looked away, for perhaps the first time ever.

"You can't even give me that? Am I less than a person to you?"

"She was going back home to Culver, but you cannot leave us alone, Omega. Who will protect Silla on her journey?" asked Rose, Silla still quiet.

"I know that I owe Silla lasting protection. It's the least I can do for her father's sake. Still, I do not need to be present to protect her... I've asked Malory for clarification. She believes that my destruction properties have created a protective ring around Silla because our souls are one. It's there now."

"You can see it now?" asked Silla, finally chiming in.

"Yes, there's nothing that could hurt you, so my task is fulfilled." Omega was still not looking at Silla.

"Even if that's the case, Silla will need you on her journey to become a full-fledged Goddess," said Rose, trying to salvage this deteriorating situation.

"I won't be gone forever. Just until I find the answers I seek. I hope that if I can get far enough away, some memories will show themselves again. There's no point convincing me... I've never felt as strongly about one of my decisions."

"Please look after Silla, Rose. If you find yourself in trouble, simply get close to her, and my protection will help you as well."

"Wait. I don't want you to leave. I won't allow it!" said a hysteric Silla.

Omega finally looked her in the eyes.

"Please don't destroy my mind any further." Omega had a look of despair in his eyes.

Silla dropped to her knees at his words, having given up her vain struggles.

As Omega walked out the door, shutting it behind him, Silla began bawling as if her worst fear had been realized.

All Rose could do was sit next to her, offering a shoulder.

"It's okay... It's okay. He will be safe. I doubt anything in this world could harm him. He said we will meet again, which means that he is willing to forgive you."

"What was... I thought to hide... such things from him?" asked Silla, trying to staunch the tears.

"Silly girl. You have this unimaginable power and a shared soul with the man you love, and you are still so young. I'm sure he will come to understand your struggles and efforts. I will make sure to tell him that we are going to Braske next. That way, he can come to find us when he's ready."

Silla stood up. "Go tell him *now*... please. I need some rest."

XXI

While Omega and Silla were having their falling out, one man was putting into motion his long-cultivated plans over a thousand miles away.

The Tower of Irkdale, which was at least four hundred feet tall, and over one hundred more feet subterranean, lived but only a few people.

The Magical Grandmaster and Supreme Commander of Irkdale, known by all only as Faulk, lived there. Also, Faulk's wives, their servants, and the Three Immortal Generals, as they were known, lived inside the tower.

Faulk and his wives lived in the top ten floors, with each of the three generals having a few floors to do with as they pleased.

Whether inside those ever-spiraling halls or outside in greater Irkdale, Faulk was revered and acknowledged as a living god. Faulk enjoyed being treated and looked at as a higher being. Although he did not demand it, he often looked forward to his citizens worshipping and treating him like the eighth god.

Outside of Irkdale, Faulk was only a whisper on the tongue for most, being a name that carried some unknown fear.

The entirety of Irkdale's border, which spanned over a thousand miles, was contained in a massive wall. Outsiders assumed, rightly so, that the wall was put there with magic as it was far too perfect to be the work of laborers and craftsmen. Although outsiders feared Irkdale, they did appreciate that colossal wall.

Those inside Irkdale's borders loved Faulk, although he did not often come out of his tower. When he did, there were banquets held, and many wished to catch a glimpse of a living god.

Being in the frigid, northeastern section of Arrdus, there were few farmable lands. This... *geography* prompted the capture of eastern Faruqh.

About twelve years ago, Faulk was nice enough to ask then King Astile for farming lands but was met with little collective negotiations.

After only a few weeks of battle, Astile conceded a large stretch of fertile lands east of the capital, stretching almost to the Ardian Sea. It turns out fighting a war with Faulk is frightening indeed, but that's a story for another time.

Faulk insisted that all experimental laboratories and workshops be in northwest Irkdale near the wall opposite former Black Garden, where no civilians lived. Also, Faulk never used Irkdale citizens in his magic slave machinations.

Citizens in Irkdale were all too happy to forget about what took place in the northwest, and a famous saying in Irkdale was *out of sight, out of mind.*

On this night, not a cloud in the sky, Faulk was standing on top of the tower, looking over the edge. One could see very far, in all directions, when standing on that high tower.

"Ah, such a pleasant night. A chilly breeze blowing in from the mountains. I think it's about time to start the plan that puts this world as it should be."

Faulk was tall, and his build was on the slim side. To look at him, one would guess he was in his early thirties. The names Faulk and Irkdale were synonymous, as a Faulk had been in charge for at least the last 500 years. He had long, black hair, halfway down his back, which was almost always disheveled, and he had dark green eyes, like grass on a moonless night. Even his gaunt cheekbones didn't detract from his reverence.

Faulk walked to the hatch that led to the roof of the tower. Upon descending, he met his personal servant, Savoy, Faulk's most fervent worshipper and a hard worker himself.

"Perfect timing, Savoy. It's time to unleash some havoc on this unchanging, boring world."

Savoy knew of most of his god's plans and was happy to help.

"Send word to labs one, two, and three to release all experimental animal test subjects into the wilds, outside the walls," said Faulk as he and Savoy made their way down a spiraling staircase lit by floating lights.

"The failed ones as well, my lord?"

"Absolutely! Those will likely be the greatest entertainment for me. Go now, and on your way down, send word to the Three Immortals that I have some measures to discuss tonight. They are to meet me in my throne room as soon as possible. Ah, and don't forget that we are delaying the release of the miasma."

"Yes, my lord," said Savoy as he ran down the stairs, out of sight.

The experiments ran in the listed labs were different from Omega's. They were the magic-animal test subjects that Faulk had been tinkering with for many years. Their purpose was to conjure real, tangible fear and get people's thoughts and focus back on Irkdale.

Even though Faulk's three generals also lived in the tower, they rarely interacted with each other or Faulk. One could think of each person's section of the tower as their private abode. From the ground floor to the top, the tower itself had a spiraling staircase on the east side only. All exits from the stairs were on the west side, so a person like Savoy could travel freely without disturbing the few residents.

The three generals were prideful and headstrong, so it was best that they did not meet often. Faulk would only convene a meeting when something of a certain level of importance came up or wanted to do some sparring.

About half an hour after Savoy went down, General Mac'Vor showed up and entered the throne room.

"The general of the lowest section shows up first. Are your sworn brothers lazing about?" asked Faulk as he approached Mac'Vor, and they embraced by firmly shaking hands.

"I'm not sure about their effort level, but I've been bored, so I was hoping some sparring was in order."

Even though he lived in the tower, Mac'Vor knew to come in full armor, weapons at the ready, when Faulk summoned. The first general had his helmet on, which resembled an eagle's head. The entire suit was shiny silver, made shinier by the magical light sconces.

His weapon of choice was dual axes, which resembled woodcutting hatchets, but with slightly longer shafts and more massive heads.

"There might be some sparring after we discuss something significant," said Faulk as he heard someone else approaching.

General Gul'Sar walked into the throne room, and he was less flashy than Mac'Vor.

Upon approaching Faulk, Gul'Sar did not look at nor acknowledge his sworn brother.

Gul'Sar was in full armor, even more massive than Mac'Vor's, and it was a dark gray color, with evident wear and tear from years of use. His helmet resembled a lizard or dragon. Gul'Sar's weapon of choice was a peculiar pair of perfectly round metal orbs, one in each hand. Each was about the size of a cantaloupe.

"So, Brek'Lin will be last, as usual," said Faulk as he embraced the second general with another firm handshake.

A few moments later, the final general and the self-appointed leader of the three, Brek'Lin, showed up, with Savoy behind him.

"I have a report about Piatous, Your Worship," announced Savoy.

"Any letters?" asked Faulk as he approached Brek'Lin.

"No, sir, as of now, there is still zero correspondence with Piatous."

As Savoy made his way out, Faulk was annoyed and probably pleased about the lack of news.

"I knew that 191 was cockier than many of his predecessors, but he's making an unacceptable mistake by shunning Irkdale. I guess he feels his faithful flock will shield him from my wrath. He's more *foolish* than his predecessors as well."

Brek'Lin was wearing the full armor of a dark green hue with a helmet that resembled, quite realistically, a human skull. His weapon of choice was a long, curved sword, but he also had a steel whip at his waist. This whip had huge spikes, or fangs as he called them.

Although none of the generals were overly chatty, Brek'Lin spoke the least of the three.

"Now that my generals are here, we can discuss plans for the future... and yes, we can have a beautiful, bloody fight afterward."

The three generals were now keen on getting the boring stuff out of the way.

Less than two hundred miles west, southwest of the Irkdale Tower, in the small, border town of Yewce, the Guardian and third strongest fighter in Arrdus, Brock was mending a fence outside his little hut. The village of Yewce was right next to the giant wall that marked the border of Irkdale. Brock's cabin was less than one hundred feet from the wall, and he felt that being so close to Irkdale would keep his trail cold.

Over the last day or so, Brock had been feeling like he was being watched.

Brock feared nobody, and he knew he would only meet a challenge in a fair fight to a handful of people for two thousand miles in any direction.

But, seeing as how his Goddess had revealed herself, it was best to take extra precautions.

Brock was mumbling under his breath, walking around to the back of the hut. "Hmm, I better make sure it's still there... been a few days since I looked."

Upon reaching the hut's back, there was a patch of very ordinary-looking grass and leaves that was, in reality, a covering for a secret hatch. The hatch opened to a shallow hole with what looked like ordinary dirt. Brock pushed the earth around and revealed something that was gold.

As he was leaning down, he smiled and mumbled to himself again, "Finally showed yourself."

Brock stood up, grasped his sword from his hip, and slid backward around the edge of the hut, all in a single motion, placing the blade at a young woman's neck.

"Who are you? You have the stink of the towers on you."

Brock did not let the sword move.

"I am from the tower, but that's not important. I've been trying to find a Guardian that's supposed to be here—" Before she could finish her plea, Brock grabbed her shoulder and pressed her against the wall of the hut, leaning in close.

"How do you know that title? A spy... neigh, a distraction?"

At this point, the lady was scared, but there were more pressing matters.

"If you are that Guardian, I've escaped from Piatous and the tower to warn you. I burned a letter that was meant for Irkdale, revealing your location. I'm Jasmine, by the way."

Brock loosened his grip a bit, as this woman did not seem to be lying, nor was she a threat.

"Why would you leave the safety of the Sacred Towers to help a complete stranger?"

Jasmine reached up and touched her temple, still tender and red from the slap she took.

"That man made a poor decision that must be paid for ..."

All Brock could do was snicker. "One Ninety-one is an ass, after all."

Unfortunately, their bashing of Piatous was cut short as Brock smelled something.

Brock cupped his hand over Jasmine's mouth. "Go inside the hut and bar the door."

"Why, what happened?" muffled Jasmine through his grip, which made him falter and drop his hand.

"I smell junipers… The Faithful are here. Go now!" exclaimed Brock as he shoved her inside, grabbed and slammed the door, and leaped back just in time to avoid the ax swing of a man in dark blue robes.

As soon as Brock raised his sword, he caught a glimpse in his peripheral and rolled to his left side, barely avoiding an arrow. Brock was walking backward, not only to get an idea of his enemies' positions but to also lead them away from the hut.

Brock counted five of The Faithful, which were the personal soldiers, very devout, of Piatous.

The Faithful take vowels of silence towards all except Piatous, so there was no reasoning or pleading with them, but Brock wasn't a meek individual.

"One Ninety-one sends only five of you silent fools for me? For me!?" Brock started to laugh as he continued to back farther away from the hut, parrying arrows when necessary.

Luckily, the village of Yewce had become more sparsely populated in recent years, so innocents were not around.

"I suppose your leader had no way of knowing who I was when he sent you here… You guys are so boring. Fight me!" shouted Brock as he lunged towards the closest enemy.

Brock used a single-handed curved sword but no shield. He was a masterclass in dexterity, having full control and strength in both arms, meaning his attacks and stance could change at any time to fit any situation.

Brock was in his mid-forties, so he was not as agile or strong as twenty years ago, but he was more seasoned and tactical.

Brock easily slid past the sword swing of the warrior, tossing his sword from his left to his right hand and then spinning and slashing the man's neck, making quick work of him.

With Brock now getting farther away, Jasmine found herself in the hut, looking around for something to defend herself with. The house was cleaner than she expected, and it seemed like Brock was orderly, even if his outward expressions were aloof.

Jasmine spotted a small knife on the table, next to a tea kettle and figured it was used for meals.

Jasmine had this curiosity spring up in her mind… *What was that in the ground?*

Thinking that those robed people were here for her, she wanted to make sure that Brock's secrets remained.

As Jasmine made her way behind the hut, she had intended to close the hatch and cover it. While everyone was distracted, it was the perfect opportunity, but as she peeked down there and caught a glimpse of the gold and red, her curiosity won.

Brock was now working on the second to last robed warrior, none of which proved a challenge, further giving evidence that they did not know who was in Yewce.

As Brock was dealing with his closest adversary, the loan bowman remaining was not far away on a small hillock. The nearby warrior swung his halberd towards Brock, forcing him to turn his back to the bowmen, who launched his arrow.

When Brock knocked the halberd away and stuck his sword in the man's gullet, he saw a flash of light and felt the heat of fire directly behind him.

Jasmine was standing there in a stunning set of head-to-toe armor. Mostly gold with ruby accents here and there. Jasmine was smiling,

"Did you see me protect you?" she asked as her eyes met Brock's.

Brock looked like he saw the most terrifying creature in the world.

Brock said in a strained whisper, "That armor… We will be knee-deep in hell very soon. Find my horse near the south exit of the town and ride as fast as you can. He knows where to go. I'll find you."

Jasmine didn't know what was happening, and she was frozen, almost literally, as a wave of frost began filling the air, making it hard to breathe.

At that moment, Brock pushed her towards the south of town. "GO!"

Brock ran towards the hillock, throwing his blade and striking it right in the stomach of the last warrior. Upon running up the hillock to retrieve his sword, he had trouble due to the hillock now being frozen solid.

"I guess we lucked out, it being him that came ..."

As Jasmine got to the other edge of the village, she jumped on the only horse there and looked back. It was snowing heavily at the far edge, near the hut, and Brock was on top of the Hillock. She thought she saw someone on the wall, but the horse took off, south.

As Brock was standing, shivering on the hillock, he saw the general, Gul'Sar, jumping from the top of the wall. The border wall of Irkdale was no less than seventy feet tall at its shortest points, and this section was closer to one hundred feet high.

Gul'Sar, like his sworn brothers, was proficient in many different magics, but he preferred elemental in most scenarios. The orbs that he carried were used for the unique magic that he possessed. He could freely exploit the magnetic push and pull of them and other metals, which was a dreadful enemy to deal with in battle.

It wasn't the first time Brock had engaged with the general.

Gul'Sar landed near the hut, with a thunderous bang, causing it to collapse.

Brock slid down the hillock, greeting the uninvited guest.

"I liked that house," said Brock, trying to sound like his usual, confident self.

"So, you haven't died yet... pity. Where is it?" asked the general as he approached Brock.

Brock, taking a few steps back, noticed that the hatch was still open.

"It's right in there—I accidentally slid my hand in trying to move it," said the Guardian as he pointed towards the hatch.

The armor had been in there so long that some of its radiance must still permeate there, or so Brock hoped. It seemed accurate, as Gul'Sar was entranced by the energy radiating from the area. The general took in such deep breaths through his nose, like smelling a scrumptious roast.

Brock was near a tree stump, with an ax embedded in it, less than ten feet from the hatch. As the general approached the hatch, he stopped one step away from the hatch and looked around the ground surrounding it. Brock was uncharacteristically quiet, and much to his delight, Gul'Sar's curiosity won out over his reluctance.

Upon kneeling down to reach into the hatch, Brock grabbed the ax handle, which was, in fact, a lever, and pulled it towards him, triggering the more massive trap door that encompassed the hatch to open it, swallowing the general.

As soon as Brock pulled the lever, he bolted to the south as fast as his legs would carry him, leaving everything in the hut behind.

"I… know that… won't hold him long… I have to get out of here while I can." Brock was panting as he ran.

Getting to the edge of Yewce, he stopped near the entrance of a small forest known as the Piney Woods.

"Okay, I'm getting too old for this. Lamb would have taken her to the cavern."

The Piney Woods was not a large forest, but it was dense, and it offered protection for those seeking to stay hidden.

Near the center of the forest was a cavern whose entrance was well-hidden between a thicket of large pines and underbrush. Brock caught the tracks of his horse, Lamb, near the entrance and grabbed some pine needles and leaves to cover all the tracks near the cave.

The cavern went less than fifty feet into the ground, and it was so shallow Brock could barely stand with his back straight. He had prepared for the eventuality that his location would leak, so he had been stockpiling supplies, including cured meats and other long-lasting foodstuffs, in case he had to hole up and wait out his enemies.

Towards the back of the cavern, there was a lady, still wearing that golden armor.

As Brock approached, she ran up to him.

"Are you okay? Who was that man in the armor?"

Brock did not hear her questions… Instead, he looked at her, scanning up and down.

"What are you leering at!?" shrieked Jasmine as she covered the chest portion of her armor with her hands.

Brock grabbed both of her wrists, gently but firm enough to prove his intention.

"How are you wearing that armor!?" asked Brock in amazement.

XXII

Omega had been on the road for five days, and it was the sixth night. Having used an exit from the castle that led him to the southern tip of the Freewoods, Omega was much farther west than when he and his former traveling companions first reached the forest.

Omega was now almost in Culver territory, near the border of Rahm and Culver. There was a small town called Homestead, which he was just outside, and based on the delicious smell, he took it as a suitable place to rest for the night.

Now, well past halfway to the capital of Culver, Omega realized that his memory was not getting any more straightforward. He was now coming to the realization that perhaps, much like his power affects her, hers would likely affect him, regardless of physical distance.

"I guess if she doesn't sincerely desire for me to know this hidden truth, there is little I can do other than hoping fate intervenes," muttered Omega as he was entering the town.

Now alone, Omega realized that he was uncomfortable around people and usually let Silla or Rose do much of the talking.

"The only way you can get anything done will be to interact with people... Such is this world."

There was a tavern near the town's entrance, which is where the smell was coming from.

Homestead was a small border town, which in the past didn't mean much.

However, with Rahm not accepting vassalhood, there would eventually be guards in strategic border areas to ensure order was maintained. Not that he would care much, but as everything was still new, these guardhouses and watchtowers were not yet under construction.

Upon walking into Sam's Tavern, aptly named after its proprietor, there were only three people inside, plus Sam, behind the bar.

As Omega approached the bar, Sam greeted him: "Good evening, stranger, be closing soon. What can I do for you?"

Three other patrons, two men and a woman, were staring at Omega's right arm, which was revealed.

The farther south Omega traveled, the warmer it was getting, causing him to alternately raise his sleeves. He forgot to lower that one before entering the town. Before he left, Rose had warned him that people might stare at those scars and even have hostile or aggressive reactions to them.

"I smelled something delicious in the air, and I was hoping to taste it. I'd be happy to eat it outside if you are closing up."

The man walked into the door behind him and, a few minutes later, came back with a big bowl of beef stew, which had potatoes and carrots in it and two chunks of slightly stale bread on a big platter. Omega started to drool.

"No need to eat outside. I can just as easily close up after you get your fill."

Omega grabbed the platter and barely sat at the nearest table before grabbing a taste.

"Delicious!"

As he was eating, he heard the lady at the bar speak in a clear voice, not being shy: "Letting vagrants in here now, Sam?"

"Don't know his background, but he enjoys my food, and he's not rude, so he's welcome," replied Sam.

Omega pretended not to hear her and decided to focus his full attention on his scrumptious meal. As he was eating, the three at the bar continued to make rude remarks, but Omega never reacted.

It was clear to him that the three had been enjoying Sam's peach wine, which was offered to Omega, but he decided it best he stay levelheaded.

Upon finishing his stew, Omega went to pay the tavern master and pulled out some Rahminian Marks.

"So, where in Rahm are you from, friend?" asked Sam as he handed Omega a couple of coins as change.

Without giving it any thought, Omega answered honestly.

"I'm not sure where I was born, but I have spent most of my life in Irkdale."

Until that moment, Omega had not fully understood or respected the taboo that is—Irkdale.

Sam suddenly changed from friendly to cold.

"Leave here at once, and don't return! Homestead is a humble village that respects the Sacred Seven, and we won't harbor any magical fanatics."

Suddenly, Omega acknowledged that he was all alone in an unfriendly world. He also realized why Silla had always warned him about his past and his magic.

As Sam came around the counter, he pointed at the door and held a small kitchen knife.

Omega pulled his hood over his head and walked towards the door.

"Thank you for the meal, and sorry for the trouble."

In Velantosse castle, two days after Omega left, Rose and Silla were in the main hall, all ready to depart.

"Not to worry, Ms. Rose, your horses and supplies are already waiting near where your exit will take you," said one of the servants.

Silla was putting on her best act of normalcy, although her thoughts were increasingly elsewhere.

Her grandmother pulled her to one of the nearby rooms to give her something.

"I'm sure you have heard this, and as sad as it makes me, there are likely spies in the castle—for Irkdale and Piatous, no doubt. I have something important to give you."

Silla was sad to leave her grandmother after only a short time together, but she made peace with it.

"Your father, about eighteen months ago, came and visited me for the last time. I didn't know it at the time, but I think he had an idea of what was coming, and he handed over to me something to give to you."

At that moment, Elder Darcius pulled out a strange key, if it could be called that.

It was the length of a standard key, the bow was regular, the shoulder stop average, but it had no millings. The tip was a perpendicular piece of metal about half as long as the shoulder stop.

"Your father asked me to keep this safe and never show it to anybody, under any circumstances, except for you. He dared to suggest that its remaining a secret was as important as my own life." Silla thought she was joking, but it didn't seem the case.

"I don't know what this is for, but he said, verbatim, '*When all hope seems lost, in that most terrible of places, this key will bring her back.*'"

Silla thought that his foreshadowing was too ominous but didn't interrupt her grandmother.

"He also told me to make sure that you understand that no other person should be apprised of the key's existence. Nobody. On an even more depressing note, if you wish to visit and pay your respects, your mother's grave is on the island of Maysle, where she was born."

"Maysle? I've never heard of it."

"It is a small island on the northeastern edge of the Gradon Archipelago. Your late grandfather and I were there on official Velantosse business when I went into labor."

Silla grabbed the key and put it inside the same pouch that the crown was in, and the two of them made their way back to the main hall.

"Last-minute goodbyes for your grandmother?" asked Elder Frost, walking towards Silla.

"Yes, I didn't know I had a grandmother, and I got a short amount of time with her, not knowing when I'll be able to return …"

"Well, we will all still be here when you can come to visit again," said Elder Jacobs, walking towards the fray.

"We have our own tasks to begin now, as elders and those loyal to the Goddess. You have more supporters in the world than you realize. Many understand and accept the existence of the Goddess reincarnations. The pressure put on citizens by the Sacred Seven's devout and others, especially during the long gaps between Goddesses, forces those faithful to our cause to hide their loyalties."

Silla was feeling more comfortable knowing that there was support in the world.

"Because of the large gaps, I won't be able to know who supports me, meaning I shouldn't use my powers after my year is over?" asked Silla contemplating her choices.

"That's where we come in. With our full effort, we will let out the secret to all the kingdoms of Arrdus and in our surrounding continents, letting them know of the resurrection. If you don't brandish the power, heedlessly, then there is no way of knowing who the new Goddess is," explained Elder Jacobs.

At this point, everything was ready, and the departure was imminent.

Near the closet door where they would be exiting, Cross was there to say farewell, and someone else was walking towards them.

"Goddess, originally, I wanted to send Ben with you upon your departure, but seeing as how Omega left, I was unsure of your comfortableness with a mostly unfamiliar man accompanying you."

Silla was considering Cross's words when the other hunter they met back in the forest, Sarah, came to greet them, gear strapped to her back.

"Hi, um, should I address you as Goddess?" asked Sarah, a little shy, perhaps because of their light contact or because of the quarreling when they first met.

Silla smiled and reached out to shake her hand.

"Please, call me Silla."

Sarah shook Silla's hand, then Rose's.

"I'm Sarah. I will be accompanying you for the rest of your journey. I'm good with a bow and tracking, and I can cook anything you might like to eat."

"Great, we haven't had a cook before. When Omega rejoins us, he will be happy. He has genuine appreciation for delicious food," said Rose.

"I remember him, he's not here anymore?" asked Sarah.

"He had his own temporary concerns he needed to handle by himself," answered Silla, nonchalantly.

Sarah was twenty-seven, and she was tall for a girl, a bit boyish, with blonde hair and green eyes. She also had a few freckles around her nose and cheeks. She had her bow but also carried a short sword.

As Silla, Rose, and Sarah were saying their final goodbyes, they were standing near the closet door, which was to be their exit.

"How do these exit doors work?" asked Rose, who had been curious about them since arriving at the castle. To that, Elder Jacobs chimed in.

"We think it was Silla's most recent predecessor, Rocilyn, that made them as they are, although details are limited. We know that something terrible happened here during Rocilyn's time. The castle was attacked, so perhaps she augmented these doors to prevent her people's deaths. Willerton just recently figured out how to change their exit locations, and they appear, for the time being, to be limited to the forest's border."

Silla was fascinated but also disappointed. "So we can't open a door directly to Braske?"

"Sorry, Your Worship, we do not have that capability yet. I wouldn't be surprised if when your powers unlock, you could travel in this same way... instantaneously."

The door's opening was always intriguing to Rose and Silla because even though they were standing in the castle, they could see their horses nibbling on nearby shrubberies upon looking into the closet.

After they exited, the door disappeared behind them, always a one-way trip.

"First things first," said Rose, as she walked to her horse, reached into the saddlebag, and pulled out a map of Arrdus.

"Your grandmother told us that if we went due south of the exit, we would reach the Nugle, where the mining town of Opulence is. We would be able to purchase a small river vessel."

The flow of the Nugle, west of Culver, was relatively subtle and easy to travel with few rapids and only short cascades.

Silla walked up to her horse, Lily, and patted her on the head.

"That would mean we have to get rid of Lily, Biscuit, and ...," Sarah walked over, "and Pride."

"We have to decide today because one path leads due south while the other leads southwest, diagonally covering the nation of Rahm," explained Rose, motioning with her fingers on the map.

Silla walked Lily to the edge of the forest and turned to face her companions.

"Let's put it to a vote. The majority wins."

Sarah was the first to speak up.

"Being a hunter, I don't know much about the important occurrences in Velantosse castle, but they told me you were a reincarnation of a Goddess. My vote
can't count the same as a Goddess's, right?"

Silla laughed sweetly. "The only way I think I can stay humble is if your vote
does indeed count the same as mine. I'll vote last, so there is no swaying or pressure
on you two."

Rose voted for the river route, due south, while Sarah voted for the southwest
horse-keeping route.

"Even though it will take probably two days longer to get to Braske, my vote is
for the southwest," said Silla as they all three got on their horses.

Having been on the path for two full days, the three women were making good
time, now getting deep into Rahm. Even with her protection, Silla worried about
possible ambushes since she was warned about probable information leaks from
inside the castle.

For the past few hours, the travelers had seen some smoke plumes in the direction they were heading, and they had been bantering about possible causes. They
were now close enough to understand the source.

The small town of Freedmarch was being quarantined from what they could
tell. There were black robes and rags strung up across the town's main entrance
with a few watchmen wearing black face coverings.

One of the men walked forward as the travelers got closer.

"Halt! Freedmarch is currently under quarantine due to an outbreak of some
disease. It's unsafe for travelers. If you are heading southwest, I suggest going north
past the cliffs then back south."

Silla hopped down from her horse and walked closer to the man.

"Do you have doctors here? Have they found the source of the disease, or how
it spreads?"

The watchmen were put at ease.

"Are you a physician? We have none here. Word was sent to Bluerun, the nearest town with physicians, but we have heard nothing back yet. All we can do is
isolate those that have no symptoms and burn those that have died," said the
watchman as he pointed towards the plumes.

Silla turned towards her comrades, who were within whispering distance. "I'm going in there. I'm wondering if what little of the abilities that are available to me can help these people."

Rose was none too happy.

"I know that he's protecting you, but we don't know if that works on the disease the same as physical trauma." Silla was undeterred and had been realizing something.

"After knowing who I am, I looked back at my youth and realized that I have never been sick. I haven't coughed, sneezed, or had a headache, other than during my visions, in my life. I think this power protects me from sickness, even without Omega's added layer."

Before Rose could continue her disagreements, Silla firmly stood her ground.

"How could a goddess ignore people in need? I was chosen by fate to have this incredible gift; for what? Personal gain... ease of life?" She just shook her head and headed towards the entrance.

"Miss, please cover your face ..." But she waved off the watchman and walked through the barrier.

Inside the town, Silla noticed the smells of burning flesh and the unmistakable stench that is death. She covered her nose from the overwhelming array of pungent aromas. Nearby, she saw houses with a big X drawn on doors, marking those that had been infected.

Towards the center of town, not far from the pyre, Silla noticed a man, face covered, trying to give aid to those that seemed sick.

"Hi, are you the physician from Bluerun?" asked Silla.

He was in his early forties, chubby, with short brown hair. He turned towards Silla.

"No, ma'am, I am the local baker... My father was a doctor, so I know a little bit of medicine," said the man as he pinched his fingers together to indicate how little that knowledge was.

"My name is Silla. My father was also a doctor, so I figured I could try to help the residents."

The man waved at Silla. "I'm Sten." Silla walked closer and saw that the woman Sten was helping was not looking too well.

"I have an idea of how to help, but I have to ask you to not overreact or become hysterical."

I was hoping that only sick people would be in here, but I have no choice, was what Silla was thinking.

Sten was just looking at Silla blankly.

"I'm going to use magic …"

Sten's reaction was beyond Silla's imagination.

"I'm intrigued to see what magic looks like."

Sten figured his reaction was unexpected, so he gave a soft smile.

"My father always told me that healing people was most important, no matter the means. He always wished he knew some of the ancient healing magics that were in the old books found at the medical academy in Rahm's capital."

Silla didn't know how to use her power, other than picturing what she wanted in her mind and having the desire to will it into existence.

Silla kneeled next to the lady, who was barely breathing. She placed her hands an inch above her chest and closed her eyes. Silla's desire was for the woman to no longer be sick. Silla felt something warm emanating from her entire body. It was not a terrifying heat but was a comforting warmth akin to a mother hugging her child.

Silla opened her eyes, and there was a bright, pure-white light encapsulating the woman on the ground. A few seconds later, the light faded, and the woman opened her eyes, blinking a few times.

"What?" was all the lady could muster as she sat up and looked around.

"I think it's best if you leave town as soon as possible, so you don't get infected again," said Sten as he helped the lady up. The lady looked at Sten and noticed he had a tear running down his cheek.

"I had no idea you cared so much, Sten," said the woman.

Actually, Sten had been moved to tears by the warmth and light that Silla created.

"Please make your way to Bluerun, Ms. Jane, at least until the epidemic is cleared."

After one patient, Silla felt drained, which she thought had to do with her powers only being partially unlocked. She was anxious since she wanted to save everyone.

Changing her tactic, Silla decided to try ridding the town of disease instead of finding and treating each person separately.

Silla, standing in what she figured was the center of town, closed her eyes and pictured the city without the disease. All of her thoughts went to that desire. She felt that same warmth beginning to billow out of her... Suddenly, though, it was as if that warmth ran into an unyielding, air-tight wall...

"Is this all I am capable of at the moment?" asked Silla, still standing there.

From Sten's perspective, there was that white light in the form of a perfectly spherical shape extending out from Silla's body. It only grew to about twenty feet in diameter before halting abruptly.

Just when Silla was beginning to lose hope, her straining caused her nose to bleed, and then something... unexpected happened.

Silla, her eyes still closed, felt something from inside herself pushing that wall. There was a hand, albeit not connected to an arm or body, that was pushing that wall, and Silla knew that it was Omega, even if not being done consciously.

His aid allowed the healing warmth to extend out farther and farther until the small town of Freedmarch was enveloped.

During the first pop of light that saved Jane, Rose and Sarah noticed that absolute whiteness and thought that Silla decided to use her magic.

The watchmen didn't see it the first time around, but it was impossible not to notice when the town itself was gone, and in its place, white, opaque light.

"What's happening to the town!?" asked one of the watchmen, walking towards the entrance. Rose stopped him, not knowing what his reaction might be.

"We have no way of knowing what that light is... maybe it's something good for the village, and we would be disturbing it."

After thinking about it, the watchman understood that he couldn't risk interrupting it if it was a miracle.

After about twenty seconds of envelopment, the cloud of white dispersed, and that smell of death was gone, and the rot that permeated the air was gone. Silla dropped to her knees, blood dripping out of her nose and ears, eyes bloodshot.

Sten went to help her, but Silla held up her hand.

"Please stay back!"

In her current state of pain and exhaustion of stamina, Silla was afraid that perhaps Omega's protection would blame someone.

Holding up her hand, she said, "Please find my friend Rose... outside the town. Make sure nobody gets close to me except for her ..." Silla laid down and took a well-deserved rest.

XXIII

Omega, after being run out of the tavern and then the town, decided to avoid answering personal questions in the future. The taboo and fear of Irkdale were what Faulk had been cultivating for a long time, and he would be happy to see how widespread it had become.

Being on his own allowed Omega to cover as much distance as he desired, and often, it was his horse, Coal, that needed a rest.

Now the second evening after being asked to leave Homestead, Omega was within sight of Culver's castle-town. He began to wonder if he would be able to enter as smoothly as the first time he came here when Silla did the talking.

The west gate was lightly guarded, and Omega made sure his sleeves were down, and he took his hood off, hoping to not arouse suspicion.

"Oy, what's your business in the castle-town tonight?" asked a guard with the flame of a torch dancing behind him.

"I got here earlier than expected... I was hoping to do some shopping for my family tomorrow... maybe stay at the New Attic tonight."

Omega tried to sound natural, but he was often a little clanky when talking to people.

The guard looked at him, focusing on the scar on his forehead for a few seconds.

"Okay, you are in luck. There was a big battle just a few days ago, and the capital just opened back up to nonresidents."

"A battle? In the capital?" asked Omega, genuinely curious.

"I know, right. Fools from the northern kingdoms didn't want to accept vassalhood and rebelled, only to be decimated by the crown prince."

The other guard that was farther back, near the gate's entrance, spoke up.

"Enough chatter, Blake!"

"Yes, sir!"

"Go ahead in, stranger."

The sun had only gone down an hour ago, so Omega knew he had at least eight hours before morning. Having no real angle to go after and having no personal relationships with anybody in town, he decided to leave it up to fate.

Even without a plan, he had such a resolute thought in his mind that he had to come back to Culver.

Still early, the capital's denizens were only beginning to make their way off the streets, leading to a bustling, nighttime traverse for Omega.

He remembered that the Library of Culver History was a landmark they used for locating the New Attic, so in the sporadically lit, torch-filled streets, Omega began his trek. Much faster this time, Omega was drawing near the library when he heard a screech coming from his right side, although he couldn't see the creator.

It was dark in this area. Omega could only hear abnormal huffing and puffing of air from someone in distress, seeing not being much of an option.

"Help …!" A cry for help, muffled halfway through, then a different voice letting out a deep howl. *Whoever asked for assistance must have counterattacked,* thought Omega.

He didn't usually care about people's plights. But the first screamer was a woman. Since Lucy, Omega promised himself and her memory that he would never allow such heinous actions again.

After going down the dark alley behind one large building, Omega knew he had to be close… Just then, someone ran into him, luckily, she let out a high-pitched shriek, or he might have finished her.

Before he could say anything or try to help, she kicked, blindly, and connected, hard, between his legs. Omega toppled over. "Wait."

It was a pain different from any he had felt during his torture-filled youth.

During the few seconds on his knees, Omega heard no less than three people rustle past him, which spurred his resolve.

The tall building mixed with a cloudy sky made it darker than expected, with no light from the moon to help, either.

Omega, now back on his feet, was getting annoyed at the situation.

"Where did they go?" he asked as he scampered in the direction those people went.

Now remembering that the lady was more important than his annoyance, Omega calmed his mind, and he heard them talking, maybe twenty feet away.

"Do you know who my father is? If you touch me—" The lady was cut off mid-sentence.

"Our task isn't touching you but killing you. Your father's arrogance will be his family's undoing."

Since the woman stopped to talk, Omega figured she must have gone down a dead-end, and right he was.

The path of the alley stopped where two buildings met, only a few inches gap between them. Too thin even for her slight frame.

Omega was afraid that using his powers in such a dark place might be disastrous, so he had to go in blindly and get close.

Omega knew that his prey was in front of him, but he didn't realize their weaponry or skill. Most people in that situation would have reservations, but once he decided on something, hesitancy never got in his way.

One of the assassins heard Omega kick a piece of wood as he walked.

"Someone's behind us!" shouted one assassin. "Her guard?"

"One is dead, I have no doubt," said another.

Before they could surmise the interloper, Omega had in his hand a wooden plank he found on the ground and swung it with all his might… To his surprise, it connected with the chest of the assassin farthest to the right, throwing him into the one next to him.

"Ah!"

"No more bullshit; kill her now!"

Omega lunged forward, hoping to bypass them and get to the woman in time. As he was bolting, his leg clipped the leg of the assassin, causing them both to stumble.

Unfortunately, as the cutthroat fell, he sliced his sword in Omega's direction, hitting Omega's left forearm, leaving a deep gash, but it was all Omega needed.

Before he could get another swing in, Omega found his shirt, grabbed it, and used his other hand to destroy him… one less problem.

Now, he knew that there could only be a few feet between him and the dead end, and just at that time, the clouds parted, releasing the moon from their grasp. Just enough light found the woman, cowering near where the two buildings met, and Omega saw hope.

He had covered more distance than the other assassin. Still, the angle was such that he wouldn't get to him in time, so he ran to her, getting in the way, just in time to take the dagger meant for her, directly in his left shoulder blade.

Before anything else could transpire, Omega spun around and tried to grab the assassin, but this one was skilled, and the light was also an aid to him. He stepped back in time, and the one that Omega hit with the plank met up with his partner.

"I don't know who you are, but our target is the princess. We didn't get paid for you, so you can walk away," said the skilled assassin that escaped Omega's grasp.

Omega smiled.

"Please don't open your eyes until I say it's safe, princess." She nodded fiercely, her hands still covering her head.

"You should focus on yourself, stranger. We are part of the Berserkers. You don't want to make an enemy of us," said the assassin whose chest was still throbbing.

Omega chortled, "If you tell me who paid for the contract, I will make sure you die without pain. If you continue this folly, you will suffer beyond your imagination."

Both assassins, to their profession's credit, did not hesitate. One raised his dagger, flipping it in his hand, ready to launch it, while the other separated, trying to force Omega to choose a focus.

Of course, they didn't know Omega or his unique attributes. Omega, deciding to handle the assassin that he hit earlier, flashed his eyes at the man's left ankle.

"I wonder how precise I can be now." His foot, from halfway up his shin, down, disappeared in a bloody mess.

That assassin hit the ground, screaming and clutching at where his leg used to be.

The other assassin was busy trying to decipher the attack method. *Razor wire? When would he have planted it? No, the foot's gone... maybe a trap of some kind.*

Now that one was incapacitated, Omega could get a good look at the more skilled assassin. Omega couldn't make out his appearance. Dressed in all black, the assassin was in his element in that dark alleyway.

"I don't know how you dropped my associate, but you should know that for such a high-profile target, those in charge would send one of the elites."

Omega simply motioned his hand, calling the assassin forward.

"Don't be so eager. Your left arm has been gashed, and your shoulder stabbed."

Omega was not looking good. The gash from earlier was the real problem. It was deep, and blood was pouring down his arm, pooling next to the girl. She must have felt its encroachment because she reached up and touched Omega's hand, eyes still closed.

"Please, be careful."

"Not to worry… I've been through much worse than this."

Omega reached with his other hand and patted the lady's hand. He would realize later that it was the first person, other than Silla, that he had touched with his bare hand.

Omega and the assassin were inching closer to each other, while the other assassin had passed out from blood loss. The cutthroat wanted to know Omega's secret, so he threw one of his daggers towards Omega's chest. When it got close, it simply vanished.

The assassin was confused, but he didn't let it deter him. He backed his way to the deepest shadows along the wall, void of any moonlight. The entire alleyway was less than twenty feet wide.

Omega could no longer see him, so he waited. An object came from Omega's right. As he looked at it, it vanished, which gave the assassin the information he desired. That object was a feint, but when Omega realized it, it was already too late.

Omega looked forward only to see something hit him right between the eyes. A blinding powder substance. With the moonlight, Omega could make out objects and movement. However, this powder made his vision worse even than before the clouds parted.

The assassin knew he had won, Omega's eyes being the key to what ability he was using.

Omega was clearly agitated with the situation, backing up for the first time since the standoff. The assassin took advantage with no hesitancy; dashing out of the shadows, dagger in hand, he lunged at Omega, aiming for his chest.

The assassin noticed that Omega was grinning as he was about to make contact, and his intuition saved him.

As soon as he noticed that smirk, he stopped and leapt back. Omega reached out, not needing to see to know he was close, grabbing the side of his hood.

As he reached his other hand forward to finish the job, the assassin wiggled out of the robe and jumped back into the shadows. He looked at his dagger, and more than half the blade was gone.

"Your intuition and reflexes are amazing, assassin," said Omega, still unable to see but smiling.

Having been alerted a few minutes earlier, the guards arrived, near the opening, torches and swords drawn.

The assassin knew it was time to escape. He got a more detailed look at Omega. "I'll remember your face. Hopefully, we will meet again."

The assassin used the close-knit buildings to stagger-jump up until he got to the roof. He was gone, just like that.

Now, Omega still couldn't see, but he kneeled near the lady.

"You can open your eyes now. The danger has passed."

When she opened her eyes, Omega had his eyes closed; they were red and swollen, the torches getting closer, guards shouting and calling from maybe forty feet away.

The princess reached up and touched Omega's swollen eyes, her hand covering both eyes.

"Are you okay?" asked the princess in a high-pitched voice.

Omega thought that she had the softest hands of anyone he had ever met.

Omega gave her a smile.

"I'm very resilient, even if I look a little haggard. Did I get here in time? I can't see you to check if you're okay."

At that point, Omega, adrenaline no longer keeping him going, realized that his left arm and shoulder were near worthless, and he couldn't lift that arm.

When the princess realized it and moved to check was when the guards caught up. They tackled Omega, restraining his arms and legs. He felt it might be troublesome, later on, if he killed them all. Omega didn't want to traumatize the one he just saved... so he accepted being arrested.

"Stop, he's not the one that tried to kill me. He's the one that saved me from certain death. He's my hero!" screamed a now frantic princess.

"Sorry, Princess Karah, but whether or not he lives is not something any of us can make a decision on... After all, you are the daughter of the emperor."

After a few more appeals, Omega decided to help her out.

"Is there any chance I could get a doctor to look at my eyes while in prison? I'd rather not be blind forever."

"No talking, prisoner!" said one of the guards as he punched Omega in the gut, which didn't hurt much, but Omega felt it necessary to act his part, so he hunched over in pain.

Karah's other personal guards, who were drawn away earlier, finally showed up, heavily wounded. She helped them make it to the infirmary. Omega found out later that more assassins and the princess's personal guards split up, leading to the whole situation.

Omega was sitting in his cell about an hour after being arrested. The guards haphazardly wrapped his arm up. As he looked around his cell, he, of course, saw nothing but was still none too happy about being back inside one.

Omega heard a familiar voice, clear as day, but she wasn't anywhere around. *Are you okay, Omega? I could sense distress from your end.*

"Silla? I guess we can communicate through the curse as well."
I think it's only during extreme times, much like before.

"I'm fine. I just need a physician to bandage up my arm. Don't get distracted because of me. You know I'm resilient."

Omega knew how to get Silla in a huff, even if it wasn't his aim, and she left him alone after that. She figured if he could talk like that, then it couldn't be too bad.

Over in the palace in a room filled with books, books, and a bed with a few more books on it, was Princess Karah, talking to her mother and father.

Empress Karmellia was still checking her daughter for injuries even after the head physician examined her.

"Are you sure you're not hurt, honey?" Karah was trying to discuss other matters.

"I'm fine, Mother. That man saved my life. Please send head physician Lee to check his eyes."

Her father was standing near a pile of books, almost his height, while his daughter and wife were on the bed. "I know that you favor that library, but I've made it clear that you shouldn't be out after dark, Karah. Especially after the attack on the capital. Your disregard for my rules played no small part in Morris's death."

Thomascus's wife was one of the few people in Arrdus who dared talk back to the emperor.

"Dear, that's unfair to word it in that way. This was clearly a well-orchestrated attempt on our daughter's life. The Berserkers are known throughout all of the continents as the top brotherhood of assassins."

"They don't come cheap, either. Whoever it was had to be nobility or a top merchant, but that's something for me to deal with later," answered Thomascus.

"If Thompsel hadn't already left for Braske, things might have ended on a better note... Perhaps they never would have made a move. From now on, you are not allowed to step foot out of my sight without a full guard service... no less than ten." Karah saw an opportunity.

"Mother, Father... I want that man to be my guard. He risked his life to save mine when he could have just ignored my call for help. Even blind, he fought valiantly against multiple assassins."

Karah was excellent at acting cute and charming to get what she wanted, especially from her father. She had long, characteristically red hair that she usually wore in two braids tied together near her scalp. This resembled a rabbit's ears that were laying down flat. She was twenty-one, but people often thought she looked younger. Even though she was younger than Kita, she was more shapely. She was the only child of the emperor and empress that wore spectacles.

"Impossible," said her mother.

"I don't know who he is or where he came from. One of the guards informed me that he showed up less than half an hour before you were attacked. The timing is too coincidental, which leads me to wonder if there is a larger scheme in the works," said the emperor.

"That's unlikely, Father. You didn't hear the sincerity in his voice, or when he was clearly in great pain, how he put on a smile to make me calm. He's either unrelated, or he's part of a traveling troupe that does plays."

Thomascus wasn't interested in arguing with any more of his daughters.

"It took me a few days to finally convince your sister Kitannica to coax Kansel out of her room and convince her to head to Faruqh. I'd like at least one of my daughters to not add more stress to my already full plate."

"Forcing her to marry and move to a foreign place was your idea, so don't put the blame on me."

"Karah! Don't speak to your father that way," said her mother in her stern voice. Karah was now pouting.

"Apologize to your father."

Karah looked at her mother as if to object but then gave in. "Sorry, Father. I know you did what you thought best for the people."

Thomascus sighed. He didn't like what happened to his youngest children any more than Karah, but such was the sacrifices of a royal family.

"Did Kita already depart? I heard that she wanted to go with Thompsel to Braske, but I didn't know why."

"She did. Two days ago. Honestly, I don't know either. She didn't give a firm reason, but it felt like she had some expectation for going there," answered Thomascus.

"Be a good girl and go to bed now. Your father will determine what happens next for that man."

As the two left the room, Karah got out of bed and walked over to a pile of books. As she was rummaging through them, she was muttering, "Won't help him… then I will."

"Found it!" The book was about remedies for a vast array of maladies. She skimmed through a few pages and found what she was after, took some notes, and then, knowing her guards were outside the door, she snuck out the window and headed for the apothecary's shop, not far away.

Back in Omega's cell with his poorly wrapped bandages and still swollen eyes, about an hour had passed since Karah and her parents' chat.

There were no other prisoners around. Due to the incident, they didn't take Omega to the regular prison near the capital's southeasternmost point. Instead, they put him in the nearest guardhouse's cells, which were mainly for holding until transportation to the jail.

Omega heard light steps approaching. More delicate than any guards that had come since he had been in there. He then smelled perhaps flowers or oils. It was a pleasing smell, unlike the stink of sweat that the guards carried.

"Hey," whispered Karah, having snuck into the cell to help Omega with his wounds.

"Could you come to my voice? I made some medicine and brought some bandages. I don't think the guards are in a hurry to help you."

Omega inched his way towards her voice as she guided him, ever so quietly, until they were face to face, iron bars between them.

"It won't be easy to help you through the bars. Especially the dressing and bandaging of your arm," said Karah with an anxious voice.

Omega couldn't see it, but his bandages, at that point, were worthless, saturated, and matted with stale blood in places, still wet in others.

"You smell nice," was what Omega said first, catching Karah off guard.

She smiled. "You have a unique personality to notice my scent in such a situation."

Omega took a deep breath in through his nose. "It would be impossible to not notice such a pleasant scent."

After a light, high-pitched chuckle, Karah gained her composure. "I made an ointment, which should help your eyes."

She sounded frustrated, from Omega's perspective. He heard the container tapping and scraping against the bars, which were only a few inches apart.

Omega decided to help her. "If you promise to close your eyes, I can make it easier for you to treat my wounds." Karah was curious as to what Omega could do, so she agreed.

"Please back up about a foot, making sure no part of you is touching the bars."

After a few seconds, Omega reached in front of him and grabbed two of the bars. Then two more, and after ten bars, he figured that it should be enough space for her to work.

"Okay, you can open them." Karah looked and saw a large space with no trace of the iron bars.

"How did you do that?"

Omega grinned. "I like you …"

But before he could continue his sentence, Karah felt her face getting hot, and she stammered, "Th-th-that's… We sh-sh-should focus on the wounds."

Karah applied the ointment to Omega's eyes, nice and thick.

At that point, she figured it most comfortable to climb in the cell with him. Kneeling in front of him, she wrapped a bandage around his head. Then it was time to work on the stab wound in his back and the nasty gash on his arm.

"Could you take your top off? I need better access."

Omega hesitated because of his scars.

"I can, but please don't react too loudly to what you see."

Omega took off his bloodstained tunic and revealed his many, many scars. Karah found herself engrossed with his body and was suddenly aware that it was the first time she had been alone with a shirtless man in a dimly lit room.

After what seemed an eternity of silence, Omega spoke up, "Did you faint from the sight of my scars?" Karah was selfishly glad that Omega was temporarily blind because she was feeling embarrassed by the whole situation.

After dressing his arm and his back, Karah helped Omega put on one of Thompsel's tunics, which she nicked from a maid.

"I have to go now, but I'll come back tomorrow to redress your wounds."

"My wounds will likely be fine by tomorrow. My body is unlike most other people's. I'm sure you noticed. I did enjoy your company, but I don't think you will be able to see me here again. When they notice the bars, I will likely be transported, or beaten, probably both."

Karah didn't detect any fear or anxiety from Omega, even given the circumstances he was in.

"If you had already thought of the aftermath, why get rid of the bars?"

"You sounded frustrated, and I wanted to help. It was the most efficient method."

Omega's unique way of thinking and how he spoke in that nonchalant tone made it all the more impossible for Karah to get him out of her thoughts.

After Karah left, Omega acknowledged something important. "I hoped that space would aid my memory... now that it seems impossible; I guess it's time to move forward with the other reason that I came here.

XXIV

A couple of days ago, Silla, having fully recovered from her draining heroics, now found herself and her companions drawing near the Lake of Hope.

The Lake of Hope was the only lake in the kingdom of Rahm. They had heard in Freedmarch of its location. Upon checking their route, they decided that it was a suitable location for respite before the second half of their journey to Braske. The lake was near exactly half the distance from Freedmarch to the Braske border.

"Look, Silla, we are finally at the lake," said Rose as she hopped off Biscuit.

It was only a little past midday, and it was muggy. They had been noticing, the closer they got to Braske, the more saturated the moisture in the air became. Upon getting to the edge of the lake, they saw a sign, written in the common tongue: *Beware! Heavy Fog Rolls in at Both Dusk and Dawn! Kidnappings and Banditry are Known to Take Place!*

"I appreciate the honest warning …," mumbled Sarah as the three walked along the edge.

There were cabins here and there surrounding the lake. Being the only lake in the kingdom, it was a popular place for tourists, especially in spring and summer.

Silla wasn't saying much and hadn't been herself after her efforts in Freedmarch.

"Silla?" asked Rose as she noticed her friend looking out into the middle of the lake, falling behind as Rose and Sarah kept walking.

Silla snapped out of her lull and met Rose's gaze.

"What happened?"

"Silla, you have been muddleheaded since we left Freedmarch. Did using so much of your power before it was unsealed have such a transformational effect?"

Silla shrugged her shoulders, with droopy eyes.

"I feel exhausted. And worse still are my visions."

"They've changed again?" asked a growingly concerned Rose.

"The last two nights, my visions have been much more draining. Both physically and mentally. It started when I fell asleep after helping the town. When I wake up... instead of feeling refreshed and rested, it's as if I have been in a mental battle for hours."

"If there is a correlation between power usage and vision intensity, then what will we do when your seal disappears, and you gain full control?"

Silla shrugged again.

"I was pondering on that earlier, and my hope is that once the seal is lifted, I will no longer have to strain. According to the rule of the sealing curse my parents placed on me, I should have no access to my magic ..."

Rose sighed. "So, it is a backlash? A sort of punishment to rebalance the scales?"

Silla smiled. "Perhaps."

Silla looked at a lost Sarah and smiled.

"Sorry, Sarah. You have no idea what we are referring to, huh?"

"No, but as I am part of this adventure now, as we travel, I would want to hear these problems. Maybe I can offer some aid or even a different viewpoint." Sarah looked at Silla and felt a desire to help.

"I know we want to get to Braske as soon as possible, but I feel it's best if we stay at this lake, in that cabin," Sarah pointed to the nearest one, "and Silla gets one whole day of good rest."

"I like the thought, but those visions don't take days off, do they?" asked Rose.

Silla smiled. "Not once. Since the first night after my father died and the seal began to dissolve, I have not had one night's sleep without those visions."

"I might have a solution if you are willing," said Sarah.

Silla nodded.

After making their way to the nearest cabin, they found that it had a vacancy they could fill for the night, so step one was complete. After the manager showed them their room, which was the closest door to the manager's counter, the three were surprised by how small their space was.

One bed, made for two people, for the three of them, and the only other thing in the room was a small table and one chair. There was a second door, other than the entrance that opened out to the lake, so the view offered a serene feeling on that still lake.

Sarah proceeded to pull out from her sack some white flowers with hints of pink, and underneath that were the roots of the same plant. Silla and Rose were interested in the pretty flowers, but it was the root that Sarah was focusing on.

"This is Valerian root, and if we steep it for a while in hot water, it creates a soothing tea that is excellent for helping people sleep."

Silla and Rose were impressed, and Silla was excited at the thought of being well-rested.

"Spending the bulk of my time in nature, I picked up some knowledge about different plants, flowers, and herbs that might be useful for us in the future. But I learned about Valerian tea from my mother ..."

Silla and Rose had heard that Sarah joined the Velantosse after her family was massacred by the church for being unfaithful. Still, they never felt right to ask about it.

Instead of diving into those painful memories, Sarah went outside to get some water and start a fire.

"So, while we are waiting for Sarah, care to talk in more detail about your visions?" asked Rose. She knew that Silla was suffering alone and had no Omega around to distract her.

Silla was sitting on the bed, looking quite exhausted.

"Before Freedmarch, the visions were there, but they did not impede on my sleep. I would find myself in that dense mist with many unknown faces, barely distinguishable. They would call out to me, mostly in foreign speech, but I could somehow translate it, inherently. Their words are never complete, and they don't make sense."

Rose found herself blaming Omega, internally, for leaving. Even if he didn't realize it, his presence was a calming factor for Silla that was now far, far away.

"In the past, I would awake in the vision, go through that process of trying to help them, to no avail, then wake up, feeling sad but also somewhat rested. Now..."

"Now, what?"

Silla sighed.

"It's almost as if I am still awake, even in my dreams. I find myself in that same mist, but it's more vibrant, tangible, and actual. When I fall asleep here, I awake there, and for hours I am walking around. Oddly, last night I kept walking for hours, and those other people did not follow me. Perhaps they are chained to that one location?"

Rose was understanding that something peculiar was happening, and perhaps something that she would not be able to comprehend, but she had a thought and decided to share it.

"This might sound strange, but perhaps you could try laying down and going to sleep inside of that dream world. Supposing you are teetering between two real worlds simultaneously. In that case, doing in one might have a lasting effect on the other."

Silla was not pleased with the thought of living in two worlds, and she was scared, even if she didn't admit it.

"I don't know if I believe in multiple realities existing simultaneously, but if that is happening and we look at your being exhausted in this world, from walking in that dreamworld all night, then perhaps the opposite is also true."

Silla stood up and gave Rose a hug, which startled her, but she then reciprocated.

"Thank you for always staying rational, Rose. Without you, I would likely lose my way."

Just when they were having their emotional bonding, Sarah walked in with the steaming cup of Valerian tea.

"I know it's still early, a couple hours from dusk, but you look like you could sleep at least an entire day."

Silla was happy to take the cup and down it, climbing under the blanket and hoping for a nice rest. She thought that Rose's idea was worth exploring, as well.

It didn't take long for Silla to start drifting, eyes becoming heavier, breath steadying with each passing second. At the exact moment she fell asleep at the Lake of Hope, Silla awoke in her familiar, hazy dreamworld.

"I can see all of you, and you can clearly see me. You talk to me, but you cannot respond to my questions." Silla was trying to reason with the specters, but they did not directly respond to her... as always.

As if on an endless loop, the phantom faces said snippets of dialogue, none of which meant anything to Silla. One thing she had noticed was that Omega was not always present in her dream world. He seemed to be the only thing that changed from one night to the next, there sometimes, and not there at others. This sleep, Omega was not in the crowd of faces.

"Since you won't help me or say anything useful, I'm going to lay down right here and get some sleep."

The ground felt similar to sand, but with the thick fog and lack of light, Silla was blindly lying down.

Much to her surprise, the voices stopped as she lay herself down, almost as if they were willing to let her rest in peace. Even with no pillow roll, blanket, or bedding, she found it easy to get comfortable in that deafening silence. Unfortunately, fate had more exciting things in store for her that night.

Not knowing how long she was asleep in that world, Silla was shocked awake by the ear-piercing screams

of all the phantom faces, which shot her up off the ground.

As she looked at them, hair disheveled, and eyes wide, one of them stepped forward, which they had never done before, and pushed Silla backward.

As Silla fell on her back, she awoke back at the lake, with people clamoring about, and she realized she couldn't see well.

The fog mentioned on that warning sign did not disappoint. It had permeated the room and was so dense she could not see her hand in front of her face. Silla then heard Sarah and Rose calling to her from outside the cabin.

"Silla! Wake up and get out here! This fog is ridiculous."

Silla could tell that she was asleep for hours, as it was dark, and she felt rested for the first time in a while. The two outside seemed not to be in a panic but were in amazement, so she thought to join them.

As Silla sat up in the bed, she adjusted the backpack, which she always flipped to the front when she slept. She realized it was light, far too light... The crown was gone! She felt around, and the mysterious key, thankfully, at least, was still there.

Silla's heart immediately sank to the floor. She felt around the bed, in vain. Then she checked under the bed, then crawled to the table, bumping her head into one of its legs.

"ROSE! ROSE!" cried Silla as she was already creating scenarios in her mind of what would happen if she never found the crown.

Rose knew from her tone that Silla was in trouble, so she slowly edged her way back towards the direction of the voice. As she approached, she bumped into someone moving in the opposite direction, someone bigger than Silla.

"Sarah? Is that you?"

Sarah answered from a few paces behind, "What?"

"Someone just passed me, Sarah. I'm going to check on Silla; try to catch whoever that is, please!"

It was a tall task in that impenetrable fog, but Sarah tried her best to follow Rose's order.

As Rose finally made it to the cabin door and went in, she ran into Silla this time.

"Are you okay?"

Silla was panicking at this point.

"The crown is gone, Rose! When I woke up, it was not in my backpack. Please tell me you took it." Rose looked back, realizing that the person she bumped into was likely the one responsible.

"I would never touch the crown without your permission, Silla. I bumped into someone on the way to the cabin, and I sent Sarah after them. It's possible it was a bandit."

"How do we follow in this crazy fog!?" asked Silla, sincerely.

As Silla was walking out of the room, she wondered if that phantom pushed her to let her know that the crown was gone, and she needed to hurry.

Although Sarah was an excellent tracker, she was at a significant disadvantage, not seeing the ground with both the heavy fog and it being late at night. She decided to go to the cabin and grab a candle that was in the manager's office.

Sarah could see the ground with light, and although it was a chore, she picked up on that other person's tracks, leading away from their cabin. The footprints were broader and longer than hers, so she knew that it was a man.

As she followed them, they went along the edge of the water for about two hundred feet before turning east. Less than a hundred paces away, she could make out a hut, and there were candles lit on the inside.

Deciding to put hers out, she crept up close to the hut, hoping to hear an admission of the crime.

There were three different voices.

"Bring it closer to the candle, Ericson."

"Ay, can you believe the size of the rubies on this thing?" remarked Ericson, now holding the crown close to the flame.

"That's the purest gold I've ever seen," hissed another of the thieves.

"Oy! Don't get so close, Chase! This be my treasure. I nicked it off that sleeping lady all by meself."

"Did you get a handful as well, Ericson?" asked the third man as he started laughing perversely.

"Of course I did, Jensen. There weren't much there, but they sure were perky."

Sarah was getting agitated, listening to their indecent conversation. Still, she was unsure of her success if she attacked all three of them together.

"I wonder if'n she is still asleep? I could go get me a handful, or even more," said Jensen as his focus shifted from the treasure to more base desires.

"There's someone much better than her, staying in the same cabin."

Both Jensen and Chase were now all ears.

"I bumped into 'er friend as I were fleein in the fog, and she had some of the best tits I ever felt. It took all my willpower not to stop right then and jump on 'er. Easily more than a handful."

Now, all the treasure thoughts were gone from the other two, which was precisely what Ericson wanted.

"So, what are we standin' round here for? We could have some real fun tonight."

As the three were inside getting ready to head back to Rose and Silla's location, Sarah was at her anger's peak and decided to attack, long before those bastards could get close to her friends.

Sarah had grabbed her bow and quiver when she snatched the candle. She hoped that when they opened the door, the candle still flickering, she would get a clear shot on one and deal with the others in the ensuing mayhem.

Jensen, the most randy of the three, opened the door before Ericson was even done grabbing his dagger. As the door opened, Sarah could see Jensen clear enough to take a shot even through the fog.

Jensen stopped at the threshold, pants revealing his appetite.

"Jensen, least let me grab the dagger, you horny bastard."

Just as Jensen turned to respond, an arrow went in the center of his back and came halfway out his chest. Jensen fell forward back into the hut.

"FUCK! Jansen! Quick, put out the candles! Someone's huntin' us," said Ericson as he put out the candle closest to himself. Chase did the same, and there was silence for what seemed forever.

While Chase was watching the door and Sarah was contemplating her next move, Ericson, quiet as a mouse, exited the back door of the hut, crown in tow. *Sorry, Chase, but all's fair in banditry.*

As Ericson was making his way north, he assumed to freedom, a familiar pair of siblings were heading south from their own cabin.

"I sort of understand the desire to come to the Lake of Hope—ten years since our last visit, but we came from the south, and you wanted to stay in one of the cabins on the north side."

Kita smiled, which also worked like magic against Thompsel.

"Hmm, I just figured the weather would be nicer on the north side."

Thompsel figured she was lying, but the weather was, in fact, fairer. The north side of the lake did not get as dense a fog as the middle or south, and as they were walking farther south, it was easy to see the line of demarcation.

"Kitannica, this fog is getting dense, and it's dark; why did you want to investigate the south part of the lake at this hour?"

Thompsel was trying to get his sister to reveal her hidden agenda.

Kita was holding a torch that she made herself. Its fire was more prominent than a candle, and so far, it was useful in that thick fog.

"I'll be honest with you, brother. I am hopeful that some friends of mine might be here. Although I wasn't apprised of their schedule before I left, I did hear that their next destination was Braske, and their route would likely take them towards this lake."

"I didn't know you had friends this far from home. They must mean a lot to you, to come this far with only a possibility of meeting."

Kita was silent for a moment. "One of them is the man that saved my life... on more than one occasion. I wanted to reunite with him, and I wanted you to meet him."

Thompsel had never heard his sister talk about a guy like that, and it sounded like he was meeting his future brother.

"I have a feeling where this is headed, but you have to know that Mother and Father will have the final say on anything related to marriage."

Kita looked at her brother with the eyes of a little sister.

"They will accept my heartfelt desire, won't they?"

Right when Thompsel sighed and thought to answer, a man, blindly running through the fog, slammed into him. Thompsel was bigger than most men and as sturdy as they come. It was similar to a dog running into a grizzly.

"Ah!" said the man as he fell to the ground, dropping something.

"Did I run into a tree? Shouldn't be no tree in this clearin'."

The thief, Ericson, looked up and saw Thompsel looking down at him, his large stature, black hair, and honey eyes dancing in the torchlight.

"Sorry, milord, didn't see ya there."

As Thompsel reached down, the man cowered, covering his head. Thompsel grabbed his wrist and helped him up.

"It's thick out here, sir. You shouldn't run without light or at least announcing yourself."

Thompsel reached down again to grab the thing the man dropped, the crown.

As he reached to hand it back to him, he said, "Here, you dropped this… crown. Normally, I would question how a common man like you got his hands on a crown of such quality."

Thompsel knew that he wasn't supposed to be in Rahm, not after the conference, and he didn't want the attention that this crown might bring, so he handed it back to Ericson.

Thompsel could see that Ericson was clearly anxious to get it before but dare not forcefully take it… a thief indeed.

Just in time, though, the torchlight gave Kita a clear view of that crown.

"Stop, brother! That's her crown! Grab him!"

Thompsel didn't know what was going on, but he knew when his sister was serious about something. Thompsel, clenching the crown, reached forward to grab Ericson by his collar. Ericson dropped down into the fog in classic slippery form and rolled out of sight of the torchlight.

As Thompsel made to give chase, Kita stopped him.

"He's not important, brother; let's find Silla and give back her property. I'm sure she's full-anxiety mode over it."

Ericson, having barely escaped capture, decided that Desitine smiled on him that night, and he best not test his luck. He chose to flee northwest out of Rahm, never planning to return again.

Still not knowing that Ericson fled, Chase and Sarah were having their silent standoff.

"Oy, Ericson, what should we do? Ericson?" Sarah could hear shuffling inside.

As Chase found his way to the back door, still open, he guessed his luck.

"That bastard fled with the treasure! Hey, whoever's out there, he left wit' the crown, so leave me be!" Chase's voice was wavering as he tried to sound standoffish.

Sarah realized her folly and wanted to move farther north, but it had been minutes since the arrow, and Ericson was likely long gone. Moving around the left side of the hut, Sarah noticed a torchlight approaching from that direction.

"Rose? Is that you?"

Sarah readied another arrow with no response and the torchlight getting closer, aiming at the center of the glow.

As the figures came into focus, Sarah spotted the sparkling of light, jittering on the crown's rubies, which was being held by a large man.

As Sarah released the arrow, aimed at Thompsel's gut, she was knocked to the ground almost immediately, and a large man had disarmed and mounted her.

When she released the arrow, Thompsel caught it and shot forward, much like an arrow... faster than any average person.

"Who are you, woman? Shooting arrows, arbitrarily, is not very nice."

Sarah was ashamed of her defeat.

"You have the crown and got the better of me. What are you waiting for? Finish me off, and you can sell the treasure somewhere."

Just then, Kita bent down to get a good look at the shooter.

"Sarah!? Thompsel, let her up; she's a friend."

"A friend that tried to kill me."

Kita reached down and grabbed him, although without his wanting to, she couldn't lift him up off Sarah.

After helping Sarah up, Kita was quite curious and hopeful about a certain someone.

"Sarah, what happened? How did the crown end up in that thief's hands? Omega would never let that happen."

"Omega... is not with us. He went on his own, somewhere else."

Kita's heart sank a little, but there was time for that later. Thompsel handed the crown to Sarah, and the three of them slowly made their way back to the cabin.

Silla and Rose knew that going out blind in that fog would do little good, so they could only wait and believe in Sarah's ability as a hunter. As Silla was still breathing heavy, short breaths, hyperventilating, Rose was sitting behind her, massaging her shoulders, trying to calm her down.

"Sarah is an excellent hunter, and she realizes the importance of the crown. Let's believe in her and wait for the good news."

Knock, knock, knock. Both women looked at the back door, waiting for a familiar voice.

"Silla, Rose, unlock the door. I have the crown." Silla shot up and opened the door, giving Sarah a big hug before she could even enter the room.

After releasing the embrace, Sarah handed the crown to Silla, who promptly put it in her backpack, hugging it in the process.

They all three sat on the bed; multiple candles alight on the table gave the room better visibility.

"What happened out there, Sarah? You were gone for a while, and honestly, I wasn't sure I'd ever see the crown again."

"I didn't do much, but I did kill one of the thieves, but it was because I heard their more perverse plans... They were coming back to the cabin, and I wouldn't let that happen."

Silla was pleased that Sarah caught wind of their plans but had other thoughts.

"Even if they came, Omega's protection would have stopped them."

Sarah, deciding not to tell them about the molestation, was thinking about the crown.

"I had heard about that protection you have, but I am curious as to why it didn't activate when the crown was stolen. Maybe it's only a physical threat to you and doesn't work with your belongings?"

Honestly, Silla had the same question, but she had also felt some distress on Omega's end after waking up. Hence, she figured that he was going through something dangerous, and perhaps that shifted his soul's focus.

"Silla, Rose. The person that found the crown wasn't me... it was a friend and her brother."

At that mention, Kita opened the door and walked in, with Thompsel right behind her. Thompsel had to lean down, slightly, to fit through the door.

"Kita, you're here!" exclaimed Rose when Kita's image was clear enough to make out, and she got up and gave her a hug. With all the drama between Silla and Omega, Silla did not immediately react to seeing her; instead, she focused on Thompsel, who just came into view.

Thompsel was even taller than Omega and a little more muscular as well. He was also very handsome.

That room full of women, all looking at him, excluding Kita, made him a little uncomfortable.

"Perhaps it's not appropriate for me to be in such a small dark room with three beautiful women."

Kita, not hearing her brother, wanted an answer to her most burning question.

"Where's Omega? Why would he let three women go unaided on a perilous adventure?"

Silla didn't like Kita's tone or line of questioning, but she was also sensitive to everything Kita and Omega related.

"He has his own reasons for going where he went, none of your concern, I'd say."

Kita had grown accustomed to Silla's way of speaking, but it was novel to Thompsel.

"My sister tells me there is love between her and this Omega, so I'd say it is of her concern. Wouldn't you agree, miss?"

As Silla met his eyes, he gave her a handsome smile, which was hard to argue with.

Rose, the ever-present tension killer, decided introductions were in order.

"Hi, my name is Rose, and this is Silla. She's young and headstrong, but please don't be too hard on her. She has a very demanding fate." Silla looked at Rose as if to tell her to shush, but Rose laughed.

"Look at him. He would be a great ally."

"This is my older brother, Thompsel. He is the Crown Prince of the Arrdussian Empire."

They didn't know if they were supposed to bow. Seeing their confusion, Thompsel made them feel at ease.

"Don't worry, Rahm is a sovereign nation, not accepting vassalhood, so no bows are needed." Just then, Kita elbowed her brother in the ribs.

"You never force anyone's bow, even at home."

"I've meant to ask… That crown looks very familiar," said Thompsel as he was looking at Silla.

Silla backed up, pressing the crown against the wall.

"You will not have it… even try to force it, and you will pay dearly."

Even though she was comparatively small, Thompsel appreciated her protective nature, much like a mamma bear to her cubs.

"I mean no offense. I had a sense of familiarity, is all."

Rose, still having the desire to make Thompsel an ally, spoke some truths.

"That crown is part of the same set that your father's sword belongs to. It's something that may put us at odds down the road."

Thompsel's eyes widened, and his expression was akin to his knowledge and understanding of something, ascending to a higher level.

Silla took that look like one of greed and desire, but it couldn't be further from the truth.

"So that's what he meant... I think I understand now," muttered Thompsel, barely audible.

Thompsel kneeled to make it easier for Silla.

"Would you mind placing your hand flat against my temple? I just want to check something."

Silla was hesitant, but the look in his eyes at that moment was similar to Omega's, and she could not resist.

After getting up and stepping closer, she placed her hand flat against his temple, as he requested. A ribbon of light poured out of her hand and into the crown prince's mind, his eyes rolling backward, showing only whites. Silla had no idea what was happening, but it did not feel like an evil thing, but one, strangely, of reunion.

After a few seconds, Thompsel pulled away reluctantly and looked up at Silla, a tear rolling down his face. "You are the one... My lady." Thompsel gave her a respectful bow.

XXV

Omega, having decided to leave the cell and start on his secret mission, was now walking towards the center of the capital. Omega had been asked by Elder Sharp to embark on what might be a suicide mission, right up Omega's alley.

Omega left a note on one of the bandages that Karah had put on him the night before.

Omega, when he woke up, could see just fine, and the wound on his forearm was sealed up and scabbed. He had what many would consider unnatural healing abilities.

He wasn't sure if Karah would go check on him in the morning. Still, he figured when he saw that one of the guards had dropped his charcoal pencil, he might as well try writing the first meaningful letter in his life… His penmanship was admittedly terrible.

Omega made his way towards a particular house, having slipped past the guard, who was fast asleep, even though it was midmorning. The home of Elder Ross's son, Placidius, was still there, uninhabited as far as the Velantosse knew.

After Prince Thomascus killed Placidius; he never raided the home but didn't let it go up for sale either.

Elder Sharp thought Omega would have his best chance of being accepted in the latter part of his quest if he got a signifier, showing he was friendly.

Omega's mission was to meet up with Guardian Brock in Faruqh. Still, Brock would likely see Omega as a spy of Irkdale, given his appearance. There should be a pin, given to all Velantosse faithful, in the house. Elder Sharp said that Ross didn't see the signifier on his son's dying body, so it must be in the house.

Omega, not knowing the capital's layout, was focusing on the landmarks mentioned by Sharp.

"Okay, when I see the crumbled tower, I need to go east, thirty paces, and there should be a tavern called From the Froth to the Back."

Omega continued for about twenty minutes, finally spotting the crumbling tower. He found himself excited. He realized that he enjoyed scavenger hunts.

"Ah, there's the tavern... I like the name... no time to drink, though. It's twenty paces north of the tavern. It should be easy to spot, being overgrown with shrubbery."

Upon walking a few paces north of the tavern, Omega spotted a small house, tucked in between two larger, more exquisite dwellings, and it seemed to disappear if one wasn't looking for it. The vegetation was slightly unkempt, but Omega figured the neighbors took care of it when they couldn't stand it anymore.

Upon entering the house, the door was quite jammed, and Omega had to put his shoulder into it. He heard the rats and other varmints scurrying into hiding as he opened the door.

"Don't worry, I'm not here to exterminate you. The place is yours. I only need one little pin."

Omega decided to leave the door cracked, letting in some light. He checked the chest on the floor first. Some papers and gloves, and a used, notched dagger, but no pin... Next was the large dresser near the collapsed bed.

It seemed that even thieves had not been in there. All the clothes, now moth-eaten, were still there, shoes and all. Omega could see a spear, and a sword and shield hung proudly on the discolored walls. The whole place reeked of animal droppings.

He was confused because the weapons should be gone, as they would fetch enough to eat for a month, for a beggar.

"This is strange, but perhaps there are no beggars in the area."

After about half an hour of searching under things and on top of things, and through every nook, Omega decided to go outside and explore behind the house.

When he walked up, he noticed enough space between the houses to slide through and a small lot behind the place that might hold another chest or storage.

When Omega walked outside, he saw some people that were not there before. Some people who were obviously waiting for him to finish searching.

"Come on out. The fact that you are empty-handed tells me that you likely came for this," said a man holding up a pin with the ornate V that is associated with the Velantosse.

"I did come for that. I'm guessing that you won't just hand it to me. We both go about our days as if we never met …"

Omega wasn't optimistic his request would work, but he thought it more prudent than simply killing all of them.

"Ha! I like your spunk," said the man who was quite dashing and had two swords strapped to his back.

"Your Majesty, who is that man coming out of the house we've been watching for years?" asked one of the five guards that were with His Majesty, Emperor Thomascus Deckler. It was the first time that Omega and Thomascus met.

"That is an unlucky soul, who trespassed in a forbidden residence. Even worse for him, he is looking for a symbol of a very secret entity that few have ever heard of and even fewer have seen in action."

During his answer, the emperor never took his eyes off Omega.

"You don't know the half of it, Your *Majesty*." Omega gave a half-hearted bow.

"My soul is blessed, cursed, unlucky, and fortuitous." Omega also never looked away.

"You are a cheeky one. Tell me why you want this pin and why you came to my capital?"

Omega, as was his habit, told the truth.

"I need the pin because I am to meet up with a Guardian in Faruqh. That Guardian was given the instructions on the mission after that, but all I know is Irkdale is the destination."

Thomascus was surprised at his forthright answer while the guards were dumbfounded.

"I'm sorry, my boy, but you may not know that as the emperor, Faruqh, a vassal-state, is under my protection. I do not know you or this Guardian; therefore, I cannot let you go to Faruqh without further interrogation. Irkdale is a whole other problem of its own."

Omega understood from the start that this man, the emperor, was very confident, and he had an aura that Omega could feel.

"You are the emperor? So that woman I saved last night… the one that said she was a princess… she is your daughter?"

"You're that man she was begging me to make her personal guard? We can add breaking out of jail to your list of crimes, I see."

"If you go look at that cell, there are multiple bars, just missing... who wouldn't walk out?"

Thomascus was getting noticeably irritated, which was what Omega was hoping for.

"Enough of this foolishness. I will investigate the cell, and you will go to the dungeon under the palace until I am satisfied with your answers. Guards! Arrest him now!"

Omega put up his hands.

"STOP!"

Omega took a step back. "Despite what some think of me, I really don't want to kill all of you. Keep the pin, I'll figure out another way... Just let me walk away... It is in your best interest."

Omega's plea fell on deaf ears. As the emperor's guards closed in on Omega, swords drawn, he contemplated the outcomes of each of his potential decisions.

Just as Omega made his choice, he heard a familiar, high-pitched voice.

"Stop, Father! Don't hurt him; he's already injured!" Karah came charging in and stood in front of Omega, facing her father.

"Step aside, Karah, this doesn't concern you. It is a matter of the realm." Karah didn't budge, but Omega could see her shaking.

Karah was shorter than Kita and only came midway up his sternum, so it was comical for her to be there protecting him.

"Whatever his crime is, he has redeemed himself by saving my life. His merits offset his demerits, or is my life worth less than whatever petty crime you are charging him with?"

Karah was usually very logical, being a bookworm, and there was little that her father could argue.

As Thomascus and Karah were going back and forth, Omega bent forward slightly and smelled a familiar aroma.

"You're the one that I saved," said Omega very close to her ear. "You have the same smell. My note was readable, after all. It's the first one I've ever written."

Karah was happy and sad when she saw the note. Still, she needed to focus on getting Omega out of this precarious situation.

As Karah turned to help Omega focus on the problem at hand, Omega saw her for the first time. Her features brought his original purpose back to the forefront.

Just as Omega met Karah's eyes, the emotion inside him hit that threshold, which dragged Silla into his perspective. Silla had just given that ribbon of light to Thompsel. She staggered back and sat in the lone chair. Rose was all too familiar with her reactions while in this trance.

"Is it Omega again? Good or bad?"

Kita looked around the foggy insides of the cabin. "Omega? He's back?" She was excited.

Rose spoke up. "No, Omega should be in Culver at this point. Without going into too much detail, Silla can experience Omega's senses and thoughts... his reality, in real time. It's not always, but during times of great pain or elation."

Silla was impressed by how much Rose paid attention, not putting it any better herself.

"Is he in great pain!?" asked a concerned Kita.

Silla shook her head. "No, it's so vivid and crystal clear. I can see someone in front of him, looking up at him, and he feels like the missing puzzle pieces have fallen into place. Honestly, she has the same vibrant hair and eyes as you, Kita, but she has glasses."

Kita and Thompsel both said, "Karah?"

Rose remembered.

"Oh yeah, your sister that loves reading and going to the library. I wonder how they know each other."

Now back in Culver, Omega didn't know how to proceed. He wanted to talk to Karah, alone and not while in jail or the dungeon, but he knew that he now couldn't hurt her father. As she stared up at him, she smiled because, from her perspective, he was looking like he saw a ghost.

"Hi, Karah... my name is Omega. We didn't have a chance to properly introduce ourselves before."

"Step away from my daughter, criminal," shouted Thomascus, but to his even further annoyance, Omega continued to talk to Karah, completely ignoring him.

"I don't know if you will understand, but I have had visions of someone that resembles you. Never as vivid as the real thing, which originally led me here… for some reason, the Goddess of Fate has chosen to intertwine our destinies."

Omega was beginning to understand the sad truth that he would have to abandon his heartfelt desire to spend more time with this beautiful woman in front of him. He wanted to say these small truths before it was too late.

Thomascus was done talking at that point; he walked up and grabbed his daughter under her arms and carried her back a few paces. She was struggling in his arms, but he was too strong to overtake.

Omega was actually grateful for the emperor's appearance and apprehension of his daughter because he was losing his will to resist those pretty blue eyes.

Just then, another appearance made a mess of Omega's just-figured-out next step.

"You two guards. Escort Princess Karah back to the palace. I'm done talking to this man." Thomascus drew the two swords from his back, one unspectacular and one that, although he had never seen it, Omega recognized right away.

Back at the lake, Silla could also see the sword.

"He's being confronted by a man and some guards. That lady called him father. That's… the sword! It must be! Omega, don't do anything stupid. We can get it later!"

"That sword does not belong to you. I know it's true owner," said Omega, not having heard Silla.

"I am its owner now. I killed the man that had it, years ago, in fair combat."

"That was not the sword's owner, only its ward… its Guardian. She's not ready to make herself known to the world, but now that I know where the sword is, there is no rush to take it. But know that one day… I will take it; one way or the other."

"Insolence! I am the number one warrior in all Arrdus! If my daughter had not interfered, I would have reached your heart long ago! You want this sword, then why wait?"

Omega knew that he had to leave soon… He could feel his grip on reality, his control, slipping, his anger seething. He found it curious how he could like the daughter and hate the father.

"After I leave here in a moment, you should praise your daughter. In my current state, she is the only reason this entire neighborhood still exists."

Omega could feel his breathing getting tighter, less steady, *damnit, you idiot... run away before you do something regrettable.*

As his rage let itself out, he was able to direct it to the hut where Placidius once lived. After an ear-splitting whipping sound filled the air, *CRACK!*

Half of it disappeared, rats and all, causing the other half to crash to the ground. *First time I've heard that sound from it.*

Omega was trying to get his breathing under control, to little avail.

Upon hearing a crack and seeing that disappearance, Karah kneed one of the guards in the groin and ran up to Omega. She had no idea what drove her, but she could tell that he was in great agony. She stepped forward, wrapping her arms around him.

As if her touch was the embodiment of calmness, he immediately regained his composure and took a deep inhale. He just stood there, embracing that serenity.

Thomascus knew there was nothing he could do while she was so close to him. Omega could easily strangle her at their current positioning.

Nobody has ever had that effect on me when I'm so close to losing myself... What an ill-timed fate, he thought.

Omega grabbed her by the shoulders and pushed her backward, hard enough to make her fall on her butt. He almost gave in to what he truly wanted at that look of sadness and surprise but knew it was the only way.

"Go to your father!" he yelled as he pointed towards Thomascus. "No good will come from trying to protect me. I need not your protection, Princess. You would only be... a burden."

Karah could see straight through his facade. The words didn't match the eyes.

"He's finally making sense. Come, daughter. You have had your fun."

Karah was not listening to her father. Perhaps she didn't hear him at all.

"Is it possible to know someone for less than a day and know for absolute certainty that this person is the hero that I've read about in so many stories? Could he be right in front of me?"

She said this while drowning Omega with her gaze.

Omega's plan had the opposite effect of what he needed, and he decided that there was only one prudent thing left to do.

"Karah. Thank you for your genuine care and for calming me down earlier. It had a bigger impact than you can even grasp. You saved your father's life. Giving who I am and what perilous obligations I will have in the future, I am not the hero you seek …We will never meet again …"

As he turned his gaze away from those welling eyes, he took off running as fast as he could.

Although the emperor ordered his men to chase, Omega could sneak here and there through the bustling capital. He knew once he reached the west gate and exited the capital, he would be able to escape both the capital and his own folly.

Ultimately needing to head east in search of Brock, Omega had little choice but to break west to get Coal. Once on horseback, he could easily ride past the south gate, north of Lake Arrdus, and make his way to Faruqh.

The search was intensifying, so he took a detour into the hayfields south of the capital walls. Coal could eat, while Omega waited for his pursuers to head in another direction.

No pin in hand was a disadvantage, but given the circumstances, he knew there was little he could do for one problem that would not cause irreparable harm to many others.

Back at the lake, Silla opened her eyes once Omega, having calmed down, drove her out. Even though it was still very foggy inside, she knew all eyes were on her.

"I don't know the context, having slipped in near the end, but from his own thoughts, there is genuine love towards Karah."

Silla was confused… another rival.

"This Omega is a womanizer?" asked Thompsel, worried about his sisters.

Kita and Silla had their own internal struggles with what had just happened, so Rose spoke.

"Things are complicated with Omega. More than most of us can guess."

It had been at least an hour since Omega took refuge in the hayfield, and he didn't see guards in any direction. However, he could hear a commotion and people shouting from inside the capital walls.

"Let's go, Coal. We are heading east to Lansing. It's just inside of Faruqh's border. Sharp said it was where Brock would meet us. Being so close to Irkdale, this Guardian stays on the move to keep his item safe."

Omega had wished Sharp would tell him who to look for, but the elder simply let Omega know that Brock would know his appearance and look for him instead.

When Omega had grabbed the reigns and hopped on Coal, he heard *her* voice. He froze, hidden behind a small barn, but she couldn't have been more than fifty feet away, clearly searching for him.

Karah was loudly whispering his name to not alert the guards if she found him, and she had no idea how close she was.

Please keep moving! Don't keep tempting me.

Omega wanted to call out to her, probably more than he's ever wanted anything else.

As if Coal could read Omega's mind, he let out a soft nicker. Now Omega was looking at the barn wall, hoping that she wouldn't come around... waiting, waiting.

"Found you!" yelled Karah from the other side, frightening Coal, which led to Omega falling on his back, knocking his wind out.

"Oh! I'm sorry. Are you okay?" Karah kneeled to help him as he was sitting up, which led to them almost butting heads and very close faces.

Omega, staying resolute, moved to the side and stood up while not helping her up. Unfortunately, she was far too smart for Omega to ever have any hope of outwitting her.

"I know that you are behaving crudely because you don't want to take me with you, but even more than that, you *do* want to take me with you. By being an ass, you hope that I will grow tired of you and go home."

Omega still hadn't looked at her... He knew that his resolve would crumble to dust if he looked in those eyes or saw that grin. Instead, he closed his eyes and turned to face her.

"Did you not hear that I was going to Irkdale? I'm sure in all your books, Irkdale has been mentioned. It's not a place that I even want to go back to, but my... *abilities* make it obligatory."

As Omega was talking, Karah wasn't responding. Instead, she had a quirky smile and stood right in front of him. As Omega continued to list reasons why he could not allow her to go, she did something that had a more destructive effect on his resolve than any ability he could muster.

Right in front of him, Karah bent her knees and jumped up, kissing him, flush on the lips, while in mid-sentence. Omega, of course, shut up upon contact.

Omega opened his eyes and saw that she was staring up at him, with a straight face, although he could see her chest's heaving motion. Omega was defeated, emphatically.

"Okay, you can go. I will protect you, but you have to listen to me without question any time a dangerous situation arises."

Karah was bouncing on her heels, agreeing to everything Omega said before he could finish his words. She then jumped up and wrapped her arms around his neck, kissing him on the cheek.

"Let's go!"

XXVI

In the cavern where Brock and Jasmine were hiding, it had been a few hours since their hasty escape of Yewce, and Brock had convinced Jasmine to take off the Goddess armor.

"You said that freak that froze everything could smell the armor?" she asked as she pointed to the beautiful, ornate set of armor.

"They all can. Faulk and his three generals. I don't know the real reason, but I have had run-ins with that Gul'Sar on a few occasions, and he's sniffed while searching for the armor every time."

"As far as I know, it is impossible for anybody other than the reincarnation to wear the items of the Goddess. A few years ago, while moving the armor, my hand slipped inside for only a moment, and look at what happened."

Brock showed his right hand, and from his fingertips to his wrist was discolored and rough. The clear signs of a nasty burn.

"The armor not only let you put it on, but it also activated its sequence to protect you."

Jasmine thought about it and remembered the arrow shot at Brock and how it burned to ash as it made contact with the armor.

"You said there were multiple items, right?"

"Yes, and each one has its own unique trait or sequence as I like to word it. The Armor of the Goddess, as you saw, becomes unimaginably hot in the exact spot it is needed to ward off danger, and I've read that it stays surprisingly cool and comfortable on the inside."

"It is very comfortable, and it's not heavy at all, similar to wearing light garb," said Jasmine.

"Being charged with protecting the Armor of the Goddess, I know very little about the others, save the types and the kingdoms they should reside in."

"Didn't you mention earlier that the king of Culver has had and used the Sword of the Goddess for years?" Jasmine was confused about why he could use the sword, but it was shocking for her to wear the armor.

"I had found that strange as well, but my guess is that the sword is, in fact, attacking him every time Thomascus holds it. Be it training, fighting, or cleaning, he's causing some damage, likely to his mind since nobody has noticed a physical reaction."

Brock decided that it was best if Jasmine went with him to meet this Omega person that Elder Sharp mentioned in the mission letter. He didn't know if there were hidden enemies during the action in Yewce, for if there were, her identity would have made its way to Piatous.

She would be a target for the rest of her life. Piatous did not accept being made a fool of.

Four days after Brock and Jasmine left the cavern, heading southwest for Lansing, a man in Faruqh's castle-town saw the sun for the first time in over twenty years.

After providing a particular promise to Piatous, Mercurius was freed from his imprisonment. As he basked in sunlight after so much darkness, he felt a few tears run down his cheeks.

"Will his magic be a problem for us in the future, Your Worship?" asked Grand Cleric Ignatius as the two of them watched Mercurius from a window halfway up the tower.

"Not to worry, my child. Although his magic is frightening, the condition for his being allowed to leave was that he could, under no circumstance, use his magic against any of the Faithful. He is a man of his word if nothing else. Also, he was correct in that I held him captive and tortured him to find his niece, but now she has shown herself."

"Ah, so there's no need to hold him captive anymore. He can see his niece but not help her when we call the wrath of the heavens upon her."

Piatous and Ignatius both chuckled.

Mercurius only had the clothes that he originally came to the tower with, which at this point were a right mess. Piatous instructed that Mercurius be given a few silver bits.

The currency changed since the last time Mercurius purchased goods, so he hoped that it was enough to get something to eat… maybe take a hot bath.

Mercurius looked, to the citizens of Faruqh's capital, like an old beggar. He was only fifty years old but already had a long gray beard, stretching to his stomach and disheveled gray hair, shoulder-length.

Having not walked for over twenty years, his legs looked and moved much like a newborn doe. People in the capital were quite generous, he thought, because he had received another three silver bits as a charity before he fully got his bearings.

"Thank you. Can you point me to the nearest place I can take a hot bath?"

One of the donators told him that there was an inn about half an hour north.

After his bath, Mercurius's next obstacle was getting some clothes. He figured the fashion had also changed since his last outing.

Feeling like a new man, both hair and beard clean and tied in a ponytail, Mercurius decided to go north to what he knew as Kender, known as Black Garden, until recently.

From Kender/Black Garden, he would head west and eventually make his way to Velantosse castle.

It was probably eight days on a horse from the capital to Kender, but Mercurius had no horse, so he knew it would be a long journey. His unwavering determination was one of Mercurius's best traits, so a month or more of drudging was no problem.

Having walked about five miles north of the capital, his stamina was shot. He was very optimistic when he set out, but Mercurius quickly accepted the cruel truth that he was getting old.

Off in the distance, he could see a town, Hemp. He hoped that he might get lucky, and someone would let him sleep and eat without having to pay. He did look more presentable now, he thought.

As Mercurius was dealing with his troubles, Brock and Jasmine had to make some decisions.

"We can't get too close to the capital. I've never taken the armor this close to Piatous's tower, and we can't risk them seeing you. But we could also use another horse as this arrangement is not the most appropriate."

Brock and Jasmine shared his horse, Lamb, and she felt most comfortable holding on tight to Brock.

"Sorry, but I have never been very comfortable on horseback, and I don't want to *fall*." She grabbed even tighter.

"He's going at a light trot… I say we stop at Hemp up ahead. I grabbed all my coins and bits in the cavern, just in case, so I hope they have a wagon."

The thought of relaxing in a wagon while Brock handled the horse sounded too good to be true for Jasmine.

Hemp was a sprawling town, having seen some growth in the last few years due to the nearby discovery of a large iron ore deposit. A few different blacksmiths and merchants from the capital and from other kingdoms moved there to take advantage of the discovery. The good thing about busy towns is that people are usually distracted.

Brock only needed to look for a few minutes before he found a general store that had a wagon for sale, for a bargain, nonetheless. His biggest problem now solved, it was time to put distance between them and Piatous. They were only two days out from Lansing, so no need to rest yet.

After outfitting Lamb with the necessary adjustments and connecting the wagon, a man walked up behind Brock. The latter was helping Jasmine take a seat.

"Excuse, kind people. If you are heading for Kender, could I tag along… it's an awfully long walk."

Brock was taken aback by that name, not having heard it for over ten years.

"Kender? There's a name I haven't—" As Brock turned and saw who was speaking, his jaw dropped.

"Mercurius?"

"Brock!?"

The two men hugged each other, laughing in the process.

"I thought you were dead," said Brock, not kidding.

"Captured. Piatous cornered me not long after we separated following the last conflict with Irkdale."

"Damn, you were injured after that skirmish. Wish I knew. I would have stayed and helped."

Jasmine coughed to get their attention from inside the wagon.

"I'm Jasmine, former tower resident and fellow Piatous hater." She held out her hand while Mercurius laughed and shook it.

"Nice to meet you, Jasmine. How did you two end up traveling together?"

"It's a bit of a tale; let's get on the road first," said Brock, remembering their need to keep moving.

"Gul'Sar, huh? I wonder if he still remembers me and that scar I gave him."

"Definitely. He still carries those orbs, you know. I was surprised he didn't ditch them after your last battle with him."

Brock and Mercurius were reminiscing for almost an hour, while Jasmine was stuck in the back. She didn't seem as happy about the wagon now that Brock wasn't as bored as she was.

"Are we not on the way to, what did you call it? Black Garden? Looks like we are going west."

"No, sorry. I have been given a mission from Elder Sharp."

At that, Mercurius laughed.

"Elder? She's younger than me… I guess I would be an Elder if I were still in the castle… Sorry, go ahead."

"Sharp sent me on a mission that she didn't tell the other elders about, save your mother, who's in good health, by the way. She's been full of spirit, as Sharp wrote, since her granddaughter reappeared."

Mercurius knew that his mother likely feared him dead as Brock did, but he hoped he would be able to see her again, in time.

"So, she's all but certain there is a leak amongst the Elders …," inferred Mercurius.

"Anyway, we are to meet a man named Omega. I don't know much about him other than he had traveled with your niece for quite a while. Something happened, and they separated. According to Sharp, he has unimaginable magic that should aid my mission."

"He a fellow Guardian?" asked Mercurius curiously.

"Actually, he's one of Faulk's captives. Sharp said that Silla's father helped Omega escape a little over a year ago. As you can guess, Octavius is dead now."

Mercurius nodded.

"When Piatous came down and informed me that the Goddess had finally appeared, I knew that Octavius must have died. He wouldn't tell Silla about her nature until he had everything in place. I never forgave him for my sister's death... a regret I can't atone for."

There was silence for a while; Jasmine was now snoring lightly, feeling comfort in the secure wagon.

"So why did you take her?" he asked, pointing to Jasmine. "I'm guessing this mission is not going to be easy or safe."

"Other than the fact that Piatous will want to kill her for helping me, there is something very queer about her." Mercurius was all ears.

"She can not only wear the armor without getting burned," he said as he held up his charred hand, "but it also activated its sequence and protected her."

Mercurius, brows furrowed, sat in thought for a few moments. "Perhaps it's the blood... ancestry, maybe?"

"Ah, might be. Do you recall reading about any of the more recent reincarnations, giving birth?"

XXVII

Omega and Karah were in Lansing, having just arrived the night before. It was the first time that Karah had ever experienced sleeping outside next to a stable. Much like Kita, Karah found Omega's unique proclivities charming.

Omega and Karah, unfortunately, could not get any peace, which they should have expected.

The emperor was none too pleased that his daughter was missing, and he guessed, based on her missing belongings—a few of her favorite books and all the money and expensive jewelry she had in her little chest under the bed—that Karah had run off with the thief that got away.

It didn't take long for the emperor's edict to spread as far as Lansing. The Imperial Order was plastered on every building in Lansing, and Omega assumed every township, city, or village after that.

After noticing the edict in the morning when they woke up, Omega made Karah put on her hood, hiding her vibrant, dead giveaway hair. The order talked about the reward for the princess's safe return and an even bigger prize for the man's head that kidnapped her.

Karah shrieked with anger the first time she read that part.

"Five thousand pounds of silver for my head… I guess I should be honored," remarked Omega.

With that kind of reward, Omega guessed the entire populace of Lansing would attack if given a chance.

"No matter what happens, you cannot leave my side, understand?"

Karah wrapped her arms around his left arm, pressing her body firmly against his, hood falling past her nose. "Like this?"

Omega, his arm buried between her breasts, was feeling a little hot. "Yes… that will work, although it might be hard to walk properly."

Luckily, the order did not have much to go on about Omega's description, other than his head scar, but that was easy enough to cover with his hood. Even if they were safe for the moment, Omega wished that Brock was very near, so they could leave.

Based on that notion, Omega decided to stay in the far eastern part of the town, keeping track of every person that rode in or out of town. Karah was more than happy to sit next to him, reading one of her books, not a care in the world.

Omega came to the realization, after being with Karah, that his power allowed those close to him to feel less burdened and be more carefree. *That's not so bad*, thought Omega as he leaned down and kissed the top of her hood.

As the day was getting late, Omega was getting more anxious, only a couple of hours away from dusk. He had been noticing hooded figures, here and there, going into town but none exiting. He thought he caught a few of them looking their way, only to have them sharply avert their eyes.

From Omega's perspective, Lansing was more prominent than average and seemed to be mostly farmers who lived there.

He had heard some of those that walked by talking about the good harvests they were having. Juniper was blessing them this year. The span between Lansing and Faruqh castle was farmland, mostly corn. Because it was so close to Culver's capital, Lansing had extensive passthrough traffic.

With so many people, houses, stores, and guards, Omega could only hope, silently, that nobody accosted them, looking for that reward.

Omega wasn't afraid of defending himself, but he was pessimistic about his ability to control his fury when situations got out of hand. He didn't want to scare Karah off.

Omega accepted, at this point, that his anxiety was warranted. There were, Omega counted, eight people in black robes with a red stripe going down the center.

They were all together, maybe fifty paces away, and they weren't trying to hide the fact that they were talking about Omega and Karah over there sitting next to a fur tree, pointing while talking.

Omega now gave them his full focus. Karah, oblivious, was leaning against a tree, her right foot linked with Omega's left, reading a book about a warrior who had to fight an entire kingdom to protect his love.

At that moment, Omega understood the meaning of irony.

"Karah... stand up, please. Things are about to happen, and I need your full attention."

Karah, her foot linked with Omega's, could feel his tension and anxiety, so she closed the book and stood up.

"Are they about to make their move?"

Omega was incredulous for a moment. "You've actually been paying attention this whole time?"

She smiled at him.

"Of course. I could tell from your foot that you were tense, so I wanted to make sure I didn't add to the burden."

Omega leaned forward and kissed her on the head.

"I'm about to have to leave for a little while to handle those in the black robes. I couldn't see them clearly last time, but my guess is that those over there are Berserkers, come to take revenge on me and collect the bounty on you."

"Okay, what should I do?" Karah didn't look scared in the least.

"You're not afraid?"

"I know that you would never let anything happen to me. Even my father didn't scare *you*, so why would some assassins scare *me*... You *are* my fabled hero, after all."

Omega led her a few paces behind the tree, away from the main road and innocent people.

"Do you trust me?" Omega asked, seriously but also with some anxiety concerning the answer.

Karah simply nodded.

Omega stood there and then took a deep breath and spread his hands. He molded his hands in an arch that encapsulated Karah's body.

Omega had been practicing a new ability, and now, with this inevitable battle, it was a prime opportunity to use it. He practiced putting his destruction power around something, protecting it.

He thought about how his soul was doing something similar for Silla and figured he could do it, at will, also.

Of his practice tries the night before, five out of six ended well.

He would cover a rock or tree during the first five attempts, and it worked. He would throw a rock or stick at the enveloped object, and his power would protect it, giving him hope for this new ability.

The sixth trial, the one that failed, was done on a living creature. A rabbit crept close to where he and Karah were camping, so Omega encapsulated it and threw a rock.

At first, it did work the same as before… Unfortunately, the rabbit saw the rock coming. When it tried to hop away, the same protective shell destroyed the rabbit, poof.

"Okay, it's finished. Now, this is important. More important than anything you've ever heard… No matter what happens, you cannot take a step forward or backward or move your arms or legs in any direction. Do you understand?"

"I do… What if they come at me instead of following your distractions?"

Omega pictured something, and the corner of his mouth grinned.

"They could drop a mountain on you, and your clothes wouldn't even get dirty."

Karah pictured that scenario and started laughing.

"Remember, no moving until I come back and give you a thumbs up… If one of them comes by and can grab you, then they got the better of me, and I died. I apologize in advance."

Omega took off in the direction of leaving Lansing before Karah could respond to his last comment.

Those in robes started to follow Omega, all of them. This confused Karah, thinking she was the target, but it could be a feint. Also, it didn't matter since she couldn't move.

As Omega had hoped, all eight followed him, east, outside of town. After about ten minutes of running, he figured it was enough distance for the innocents to be safe.

Upon stopping and catching his breath, he turned and saw the assassins were only ten paces away.

"Berserkers?" asked Omega as he observed them trying to discern strategies based on their weapons, but he didn't see any.

A familiar voice spoke.

"Yes, I am back for revenge for my failure to kill you last time."

The assassin that escaped that night removed his hood, and Omega saw a young man, younger than him with slicked-back, light brown hair and black eyes. A scar was on his left cheek, starting under his eye, down to his jaw.

"I see your eyes are back to normal. Never seen healing like that."

Omega started laughing, and his usual kind eyes were anything but.

"Walk away …," was all that he said.

All eight assassins, the other seven still having their faces mostly covered, started to laugh, which caused Omega to stop laughing.

"We are The Berserkers! We never forsake on a contract, and now we have two. One for your head from the emperor and then the other for that princess back there," said the assassin on the far right.

"The rewards are enough to turn the organization into a national power that the world will fear," said a different assassin.

Omega was planning to test out some strategies he'd invented… ones that were not fatal but could end a fight. However, his desire to show mercy was slowly waning.

"So, I would be doing the world a favor by ridding it of the eight of you? You are some of the elites or just the dregs?" The assassins got quiet.

"We are eight of the top twelve in the organization. Some of the others are obligated to be elsewhere. Still, with the bounty on your head, the second-highest we've ever seen, headquarters sent all available agents to make sure the job was completed."

Omega had a flash of inspiration.

"Here's a novel idea... live and join me. You want to be known around the world. My fate is taking me in a direction where everyone will know my name before the day I die."

"You aren't the first to request our betrayal of the brotherhood. The others didn't fare so well."

Omega sighed. He thought his idea would be best for everyone, but he understood that most people had pride and loyalty they would stick to even if it meant death.

"Okay, then. I suggest you all come at me together... maybe you can overwhelm me, though I doubt it." Omega was done negotiating.

"I have discussed with my brothers that strange ability of yours. My name is Henry, by the way. I accept you as worthy of my name."

"I accept you as a speck of dust on my boot, Henry."

Omega hoped that these assassins, like most prideful people, would get upset at such a comment.

One of the assassins jolted forward, clearly angry.

"WAIT!" shouted Henry, with no effect.

Not even getting halfway to Omega, everyone heard a loud cracking sound. A space of ground, the size of a small house and over twenty feet deep, disappeared, causing the assassin to fall into it. After the sounds of screaming, they could hear him groaning.

"You okay!? asked one of the assassins.

"Both legs are worthless! Some ribs shattered... arm broken ...," his voice trailed off, passing out from the pain.

"You can still surrender," said Omega.

Henry pulled out an intriguing weapon. It was a long reed, which was foreign to Omega, as far as weaponry went.

"Formation A! Break!" bellowed Henry.

The six assassins, excluding Henry, broke off, spreading out, but always creeping towards Omega. He looked at one, and right then, another released a small knife, weighted perfectly for throwing, *whoosh*.

Omega held up his hand, and the blade disappeared, which is what Henry thought would happen.

Omega wasn't advanced enough to concentrate on everything at once.

To be safe, he knew that he had to maintain most of his focus on Karah's shell. His long-range destruction appeared to be impossible while maintaining the shell, so it was back to the old way—more dangerous, but far less concentration.

Idiot, if you survive this, you have to focus on the next ascension.

Omega decided it best, with his limitations, to go on the offensive. He sprung forward, towards the nearest Berserker. Henry expected this as well because, during the commotion, he found himself on Omega's left flank.

He blew into the reed, which contained a dart, and Omega had no idea it was coming.

Omega felt a sharp pain in his neck, similar to a hornet sting. He reached up and pulled out the dart, dropping it, and as he looked left, he saw Henry getting ready for a second shot.

Before he could decide if he wanted to change course, the assassin furthest to his right pulled out and chucked a smile knife.

"Ahh!" Omega yelled as it embedded itself in his right bicep.

Omega decided to stop and reassess, backing up a few steps. All the assassins halted at the same time.

They weren't quite in reach, only four paces away, about five feet between each of them. Omega knew that hole was to his right, so left or back were his two options... or forward.

"It was dark, and you caught me off guard last time. You are now in a desperate situation, taking on so many Berserkers, with no help and nowhere to run. I know that the princess is back there. Someone is waiting to finish her after I signal your death."

Omega was wincing now. That knife in his bicep was deep, buried in the bone.

Omega noticed his sight get blurry for just a moment, so he shook his head, but that only made it worse. Noticeably dizzy, the Berserkers were like hyenas.

"That's the secret poison we sometimes use. Both that dart and the blade in your arm were slathered in it," said the assassin directly in front of Omega.

"That's not very fair, you know?" Omega was breathing shakily now, a heavy sweat on his brow. "Not now... I'm sorry, Karah. Please survive."

The shell around Karah disappeared. She only knew because she saw a butterfly heading her way, and she tried to tell it to stop, but it went through and landed on her nose.

"OMEGA!" Recalling his last words, Karah took off running faster than ever before towards his direction.

Back at the battle, Omega, who was hunched over, stood up straight and took a deep breath, steadying himself.

"I guess you guys are the first test subjects for my new ability." He started laughing, shakily, and quite like a lunatic. "Like you said to me earlier... you should be honored."

Omega started to scream as he motioned his arms as if he was pushing open a large double door. Upon opening that invisible door, he brought his hands back to his chest, palms out, and started pushing them forward. It looked like he was trying to push over a house or boulder.

"Be careful, everyone. I've never seen this technique," said Henry as he was ready to retreat.

And very shakily, maniacally, Omega retorted, "And none of you... will ever... see anything again!"

As he was pushing forward, the ground near his feet slowly started vanishing, about five feet deep, and it was spreading forward towards the assassins.

"Flee! It's slow, but you will die if that catches up!" shouted Henry as he retreated.

Omega knew he needed to release even more power. He recalled the sensation of when he would destroy everything and begin floating.

Channeling that feeling, Omega let out a fierce roar and a cracking shockwave.

The field of destruction started to expand at an alarming rate, now spherical, in all directions... even back towards Lansing, but Omega wasn't thinking clearly.

The assassins had no hope of survival, all except Henry, who was the farthest away to begin with.

At about the same time Henry was fleeing with all his might, away from the cone of destruction, Karah was plowing towards it, unaware.

As Karah was running, Omega finally came into view, and she could hardly believe her eyes. She thought it was someone else; even as it became evident, she didn't want to believe it—a man floating a few feet above the ground, unleashing a terrible, sinister laugh.

As that field of destruction got close, Karah realized what it was and stopped.

"OMEGA! PLEASE COME BACK TO ME!" Karah screamed her throat raw... but it worked.

Was it perfect timing, or did Karah's voice reach him? She never really knew, but Karah saw the destruction stop moving towards her, and then she saw Omega fall into the crater he had formed.

Upon trudging through the now unfamiliar terrain, Karah finally reached Omega, having tripped and fallen into the deepest part of the crater, where Omega was lifeless.

Karah, having read some medical books, checked Omega's pulse at the wrist... nothing. She then put her fingers in front of his nostrils... nothing.

Karah could feel panic coming, but she didn't have time for that. She had read that breathing into the mouth can sometimes resuscitate a person.

After each breath into Omega's mouth, Karah would scream for help. Breath, "HELP!" Breath, "HELP, PLEASE!" This went on for about ten breaths, then there was hope.

"Hey, out of the way, girl," said a man who slid down the crater, with another man and a lady not far behind.

"Do that thing you used to do, to bring people back," said the first man to the other.

The second man held up his hands, and electricity shot between them.

"It's been decades since I've tried that."

XXVIII

When Omega was beginning his final assault on the assassins, Silla, Kita, Rose, Sarah, and Thompsel were all traveling together. They were all traveling to Braske anyway, so going there together was the most common-sense solution.

Kita and Silla's minds were on that situation between Karah and Omega.

"So, you said that when Omega woke up, he had no memory of me... only I was omitted from his memory?" asked Kita as the group was traveling, now less than a day from Braske's border.

"It seems so," responded Silla, halfheartedly. She had no desire to open that particular can of worms.

"What about the letter I wrote to him? Wouldn't that jar his memory?" Kita wasn't satisfied with Silla's responses. More so, though, she was unhappy with Karah being alone with Omega.

"I don't know. Memory restoration *isn't* my specialty. He kept the letter, even though he said it didn't mean anything to him... if that makes you feel any better."

Rose had agreed long ago to not butt in and let Silla handle it herself, but she was torn.

Before she had to decide, though, another situation arose.

Silla pulled the reigns on Lily.

"Something's wrong." She dropped to the ground and collapsed to her butt.

Everyone stopped, and Rose was the first to reach her, followed closely by Thompsel.

"Omega again?" inquired Rose, putting her hand behind Silla's head and forcing her to lie down.

"Omega, stop it! That's too much strain! Even I can feel it!"

Silla was not with the others, like usual, but was pulled into Omega's side, completely this time. She started to convulse, but only sporadically at first.

"Omega! I command you to STOP! NOW!"

With the forceful commands not working, Silla went with tenderness.

"Omega, please. I feel your lifeforce dissipating… I need you in my life …"

At this point, back with the group, Silla's convulsions were getting far too aggravated. All they could do was try to hold her down, but it was unnecessary.

Silla stopped moving altogether.

Rose had been secretly pondering what happens if one of them dies, souls being connected and all.

Silla lay there, lifeless, blood dripping from her closed eyes and her ears.

Upon the cacophony of pleas and cries from the group, Silla heard nothing.

As Silla lay there in that same spot, she opened her eyes, but she wasn't in the same space. It was dark, like nighttime but different. No moon, no breeze. No stars, no sounds… nothing.

"Am I dead?" was all she asked, but then a figure appeared before her.

Silla saw a woman floating down to meet her. She was beautiful… no. Silla knew that words didn't exist that would do this woman's beauty justice.

She looked much like a human, but her body was taller than a human… even taller, much taller than Thompsel, and her eyes were slightly rounder than human proportion.

Her ears were also pointier than an average human's. Her hair, white gold… flowed as if it was in the water, and her eyes were different too. Almost no sclera existed; instead, the iris took up the majority of those round eyes. Silla thought them red at first, but those irises were a comfortable shade of lavender as this being got closer.

As this being approached, Silla found the energy to stand up.

"Do not worry, Silla… It is not the time for you to meet me yet." The being stared into Silla's eyes.

"Hespa?" was all that Silla could say, as she thought it must be a Goddess in front of her.

The being simply beamed such an awe-inspiring smile, and Silla, without even trying, smiled back.

"I knew it was you! I'm the reincarnation!" Silla was beside herself with joy.

"I know. You are connected with another... He died. This forced you to join him, but I could not sit by and watch you perish."

"I knew he died. Could you save him, like you are doing for me?"

The being looked down, clearly distressed.

"I cannot. Sulce and Desitine work together seamlessly and endlessly to mold humans' lifespans and other lifeforms. I cannot interfere with their wills. Because *you* have the piece of soul, I will observe and intercede on your behalf, in dire circumstances... until the time is right."

Silla's head was swimming from this information. She always had faith, but Hespa, herself, talked about the God of Death and the Goddess of Fate, so it all must be true.

"You said I have a piece of the soul? You mean your soul... so that's how the reincarnations happen? Why pick me?"

The being sighed.

"I am sorry, but you have to go now. This is Sulce's domain, and you cannot spend too much time here, or even I will not be able to send you back. All the answers you seek will be found. Just follow your heart... and try not to die again."

After the last part, the being gave a small chuckle, and Silla was overtaken with joy that Hespa had a sense of humor.

"But—" Before she could say anymore, the being touched Silla on the forehead.

Amid the seas of cries, Silla sat up, knocking over Rose and taking in the deepest, sharpest breath ever. The breath of life.

"Hespa? Don't leave so soon... I have so many questions."

"Silla!" they all shouted and hugged her, even Kita.

"You were dead, for quite some time. Too long to simply wake up and be fine," said Thompsel, quite amazed at what he had witnessed.

Silla was still breathing in deep pockets of air, trying to make up for lost time.

"She came to me and brought me back, Rose... I always knew she really existed." Silla was so excited that Rose was hesitant.

"Who existed?"

"Hespa. The Goddess of Creation, herself. She's such a beautiful, benevolent being... it almost seemed a crime to even look upon her."

"*The* Hespa? Hespa that created everything, even the other Gods and Goddesses?" Sarah was a believer in herself and what she could see, so this news opened another level of what she thought she knew.

"Yes! I wanted to talk more to her, but she told me that staying too long in Sulce's domain would force me to remain there. I had so many questions ..."

"I think we should set up camp," said Rose.

"Aye. You've had a harrowing experience, Silla. Some food and rest will do us all good," said Thompsel, and they all started to unpack their gear.

"One more time. Everyone back away. No touching." *Zap!*

Mercurius was a user of lightning magic. One of the rarest and most potent magics. He was busy trying to jumpstart Omega's heart. He had not done it in a very long time, so getting the shock's intensity at the correct level was critical.

Mercurius placed one hand on Omega's right peck, above the nipple, and the other on his left side, below the peck. Another zap of lightning, lasting less than a second.

Omega started to cough. Desitine wasn't done with him yet.

Brock and Mercurius fell on their backs and started laughing.

"Bringing somebody back to life sure is draining... and all I did was watch!" shouted Brock.

Karah, beside herself with joy, started to kiss Omega. The lips, nose, cheeks, forehead... every inch of his face got a kiss.

Omega didn't shoot up and take a deep breath like Silla. It took almost a minute of kisses before he opened his eyes.

"I'm sorry, Karah. I let the shell go... without making sure you were safe first."

Karah leaned in and gave him a long, deep kiss. So long that Jasmine cleared her throat. "Maybe we should give them some privacy."

Before they could get up, Karah finished.

"Idiot... No matter what happens in the future, you're not allowed to leave me alone, not even to die."

Omega smiled and sat up. "Okay, I promise."

Omega made to stand up, but Mercurius stopped him.

"Hold now... Omega, was it?" Omega thought this elderly gentleman looked familiar, so he sat back down.

"Yes, I am Omega. Might I ask who brought me back to life?"

"My name is Mercurius. This is Brock and Jasmine." They all greeted Omega with a nod and a small wave.

Omega eyed Brock for a moment.

"Velantosse?"

Brock stood up and pulled his jerkin up, revealing his abdomen, which had the V on it, with a long scar going through the middle of it.

"You remember when you got that scar? That was a hell of a battle," said Mercurius as the two looked likely to go on another trip down memory lane... Jasmine interrupted.

"Are you two also Velantosse?"

Jasmine found herself intrigued by the secret order and was ready to meet more of them.

"Not quite. I am not an official member, but I am traveling on official business. This is Karah, a princess of Culver, and my ..." Omega looked at Karah, not exactly sure of how one categorizes relationships.

"His wife-to-be." Karah had noticed that Jasmine was near her age and not bad to look at, so she felt it necessary to claim her territory. Karah grabbed Omega's arm and turned her nose up at Jasmine.

"Jasmine, your accent is?" wondered Omega.

"I'm from Zerrek. I ended up in the Tower in Faruqh, and now I'm here with Brock. My tale isn't fascinating."

"I like it." Karah looked at Omega sideways with a pout.

"It didn't say in the letter that your fiancé would be joining in on this adventure," said Brock as he wondered about the efficacy of bringing her along and not paying much attention.

"I didn't hear anything about an old man and a woman joining on your end either," replied Omega, still sitting.

"Ah, you must be fine now, with that kind of sass," said Mercurius, helping Omega stand up.

The five of them headed almost due north from Lansing.

"Our first goal is to reach Stenum. It is a logging village and mill, right on the Nugle. I have a safe house there. From Stenum, we just follow the Nugle until we reach Irkdale. From Stenum, the Nugle would take us very close to the laboratories, Omega. Also, we will have a choice to make by that point."

Omega had no desire to ever step foot in his childhood home again, but he knew from the jump, it was a possibility.

"Is that the plan then, destroy the laboratories?"

"We will speak about that once we are in the safe house. Stenum is more than a day's ride from here, so we shouldn't dally."

"Can I ask why you look so familiar, Mercurius?" Omega was now riding beside Mercurius and needed his curiosity satiated.

"If I'm honest, you also look familiar, Omega. It shouldn't be possible, as I've been held captive almost as long as you've been alive, but I know I've seen those eyes and those cheeks somewhere."

"Maybe you know my birth parents. I think I was taken to the labs as a small child. I could run and talk, so I must have been around five. I don't remember my childhood save a flash of a tall, all-white tree with gold leaves. That memory only comes when it wants to, though."

Mercurius, and Brock, who was on his other side, looked at each other, showing recognizing looks at Omega's comment about that white tree.

"I think you probably recognize me from the time you spent with my niece," said Mercurius, putting aside the tree for the time being.

"Yes! It's the eyes. You have the same green eyes as Silla. So that must make you her mother's brother, and not Octavius's."

"Right. You also met my mother, I presume."

"I did. Due to an unfortunate incident with a cursed test subject liberated from Irkdale, even though we were at the castle going on two weeks, I was only conscious for about two days. She did seem like a sweet lady from the few times I saw her."

"A cursed subject? One of the creatures that Faulk has been cultivating?" asked Brock.

"His name is Foster Franklin, and he had some strange curse put in his blood that forced him to transform into a mighty beast during a full moon. I happened to be near his home during such a moon ..."

Brock and Mercurius started to laugh. "I like you, Omega. I think we will get along like peas in a pod," said Brock.

"From what I've seen of your magic, albeit from far away, you could have killed that creature, right?" asked Mercurius, curious about Omega's power.

"I could have, but I don't like to use it against people that I don't feel... deserve it. I did all I could to stop him without my magic. It was Cross that ended up stopping him with his magic."

"If you had been around in our glory days, you would have seen some intense battles with the church and with Irkdale," said Mercurius.

"Speak for yourself, old man. I'm a few years younger than you, and I'm still the third strongest fighter in Arrdus."

"Ah, the rankings. It's been so long, I completely forgot about those tournaments. What would twenty-plus years of inactivity do to one's ranking, you think?"

"I'd guess since nobody below you defeated you, you would still be eighth," stated Brock.

"I haven't fought in the last three tournaments, and I'm still third."

"I've heard of Cross from some of my correspondence, but I've never had the opportunity to meet him."

"He's been at the castle for ten years, at least ...," said a confused Omega.

Brock smiled.

"The life of a Guardian is... isolated. I haven't stepped foot into the Freewoods, much less the castle, in over fifteen years... since I became a Guardian, in fact."

"The Guardian's life is the item that he or she is charged with watching. As you can guess, most Guardians watch a Goddess item for decades, never meeting a reincarnation. For Guardians like Brock, it is such a rare honor that he will meet face-to-face with a Creationist. He might not speak it, but he has been training his entire adult life to aid her when the time is right."

Mercurius was proud to call Brock a friend and knew that he would prove valuable to Silla in the future.

Back in Silla's group, Silla and Kita were now reluctant to move forward, wanting to go back and check if Omega was dead, for good.

"For once, we agree on something, Silla. We need to go back and find Omega. If he is dead, Thompsel, we don't know what might have happened to Karah."

Thompsel, of course, would do anything for his siblings, so going back to check on Karah was fine, but they didn't all have to leave. If he went by himself, it would be only a few hours. But there would be no one left there to protect them.

"You said you could communicate with him from anywhere?" asked Thompsel.

"That's not something I've been able to do on command, even though I've tried. Omega's mental state has to be in a specific place for me to be sucked in."

Just then, Rose had an idea that would alleviate everyone's worries.

"I got it! The protective barrier, Silla. If you still have it, then he has to be alive, right?"

Silla hadn't thought of that. "Yes! That might be the best way."

Silla walked up to Thompsel.

"Could you grab that stick over there and swing it at me with the intent to injure me?"

"I'm not sure where you're going with this, but I know I shouldn't hurt you."

Silla walked over and picked up a stick. It was almost as long as she was tall and thick enough to break a rib or two if hit with it.

"If he is alive, then this stick will never reach me, and you will see something interesting. If it does hit me, then we all head back to Culver and begin the search."

Thompsel, after looking around and seeing that everyone was agreeable to the plan, decided to give it a go. He grabbed the stick and aimed it at Silla's arm. He pulled back, waited a moment, and then swung it—hard but not full power.

Instead of making contact, he kept spinning, doing two full circles before losing his balance and falling to one knee.

"What?" Thompsel looked at the stick, and less than half of the original length was there.

The girls started shouting and hugging, even Sarah, who didn't know what the results meant.

"He's alive! That means Karah is most likely alive also. Even though I have some words for her when we meet again, taking advantage of a man's missing memories. She's still my sister," stated an elated Kita.

"I don't know your sister, but she can't have known about Omega's memory problems. I'm sure they met spontaneously, and maybe he was missing something in his heart, and she filled it. Good timing, if nothing else."

Kita picked up on something in Silla's response.

"What aren't you telling me, Silla?"

"Thompsel. How long until we get to Braske's capital? I want to get in contact with the Guardian as soon as possible."

"I haven't been to Braske in six years, but I'd say we are about a day out from the capital and two hours more than that to the bay itself."

One more day of avoiding this annoying woman's questions; you can do it, Silla.

Back on the way to Stenum, it was evening, and Omega had no idea of Silla's self-induced troubles... he had his own.

"Again ..." *Huff, huff.* Omega had been busy for the last hour trying to train his ability to control multiple forms of his magic simultaneously.

"Omega, you've been practicing for an hour. How about taking a break?" mentioned a concerned Karah.

Omega was taking on Mercurius and Brock simultaneously. He was trying to destroy their magic while protecting a nearby tree. It was dark, and they were not near any villages or settlements, so witnesses to the magic show were unlikely.

Mercurius was busy using his electricity to attack the tree and Omega alternatively. In contrast, Brock used his wind magic to aggressively onslaught Omega.

"I'm sorry, Karah, but I will not stop until after ascension. I know that the next tier is close; I could feel it back in the bowels of the castle, in the resonance chamber."

"Again!"

Karah was sitting in the wagon with Jasmine, who was enjoying the show.

"Do you know any magic, Karah?"

Karah shook her head. "I've read loads of ancient books and missives that talk about magic being commonplace a few hundred years ago. I never witnessed magic until just recently."

"I know that the upper echelon of the church have access to their magic. Also, the commanding officers of the Faithful have been allowed to awaken. Still, I've never seen any in action," said Jasmine.

Omega was focusing on the tree's protective shell, which was decisively destroying Mercurius's lightning magic. The problem was that only sporadically could Omega successfully, simultaneously, take and negate an attack from Brock while protecting the tree.

Brock could create wind gusts of absolutely catastrophic proportions, but he held back since it was only for training.

Mercurius was feeling his youth again, having not been able to stretch his proverbial legs for so many years.

"Tell me if you remember this technique, Brock. Proper techniques have names, after all."

Mercurius put his hands together with a clap. As he pulled them apart horizontally, with great strain, lightning was conducting between them. He then rotated his hand vertically, and the clicking, screeching sound became more intense. His right hand flipped and grabbed the lightning, which was now in the shape of a sword.

"My ever-faithful Blade of the Forgotten."

Mercurius was holding this lightning blade with both hands, like a Greatsword, and Omega found it fascinating.

"Attack the tree at full force!" shouted Brock, now fully immersed in his role.

Mercurius rushed towards the tree, sword at the ready.

"Don't get too close!" shouted Omega.

"Not to worry, kid. My blade can't be extinguished so arbitrarily."

Mercurius stopped a few paces from the tree and showed off a very useful sub-ability of the blade. As he swung forward, the edge extended over ten feet and slashed downwards at the tree. As the blade hit the shell, the section that made contact vanished, though the rest was still safely in his hand.

"Yes! I finally broke through!" shouted Omega in sweet relief.

When Mercurius made contact, Brock also hurled a miniature tornado at Omega, capable of launching him dozens of feet into the air. Omega successfully destroyed the blade strike and the wind magic at a distance. He could quickly destroy by touching, but by ethereal means, it had not been so simple.

"Did you see that, Karah!? With more training, I can protect you from any-where in the world."

As Omega was leaning up against the tree, taking a well-deserved break, Karah and Jasmine had a girl's talk in the wagon.

"How long have you two been together? The affection is palpable."

"Officially? Less than two full days."

Jasmine was stunned. "Is it normal for two people to fall so hard, so fast for each other? I've never been in love, but relationships *are* forbidden in the towers."

Karah reached into her pocket and pulled out a folded piece of parchment. She handed it to Jasmine. Karah had found the note, blank to Omega's eyes, but full of love to anyone else's when she was dressing his wounds back in the cell.

After reading it, Jasmine was perplexed.

"Who is Kita?"

"My oldest sister. I have the feeling that Omega originally came to Culver to meet her. When he first saw me, he made strange comments, like he couldn't re-member properly. After seeing his battles and how he injures himself, I can imag-ine that memory loss isn't impossible."

Karah had been carrying both the letter and the fear this whole time.

"You think his love for you is misdirected? If his memories come back, he will realize that you are simply a stopgap?"

"When he saved me from those assassins, blinded and gashed, my heart flut-tered. Then, when he didn't hesitate even in the face of my father, the emperor, I knew that he was special and worth fighting for. My sister's love for him feels genuine from that letter, but mine is no less so."

"One thing that's strange is that it says her name on the letter, and he knows your name ..."

"That's the one point that I can't come up with a logical solution for."

"Is it possible that he's playing the fool? His memory never left, but something unfortunate happened between them, and he chose to avoid her?"

Karah shook her head.

"He's either the most genuine, honest man, in Arrdus, or he's the greatest actor in the realm."

Now that Omega was done training for the night, it was time for rest. Karah folded up the note and put it in her pocket. Problems for another day.

XXIX

The morning after training, Omega was the first to awaken, and he was in a good mood. As was the norm, Omega and Karah slept next to each other, usually under a tree, and by the time morning came, Karah had used him as a pillow.

After the two of them got up, before they could fully stretch, a horse carrying a rider dressed all in black, face painted white and covered in strange markings, slowly approached the camp. Omega figured he would ride past, on his way to some unknown place, but he stopped in front of the tree they slept under and hopped off his horse.

He turned and rummaged through his saddlebag.

Omega, scratching his head then rubbing his eyes, looked and saw Karah half-way falling back asleep as she leaned against his chest.

The man with the painted face pulled out three exquisite maroon envelopes that had gold writing.

"Hello, Omega. Would you be a lad and go wake up Mercurius and Brock?"

Without reacting, Omega left, grabbing Karah, and taking her with him, then returned a few moments later, Mercurius and Brock behind, while Jasmine was still sleeping in the wagon.

Omega didn't think it possible for someone to know all three of them, as the identities were likely some of the most well-kept secrets or uncared about in his case, in Arrdus.

"Hey, haven't seen one of those faces in years. When's the tournament?" asked Brock.

The man held out the invitations to Mercurius and to Brock. The invitations had their name and their ranking in big, bold letters at the top.

MERCURIUS Darcius:

Currently ranked as the #16 Fighter in Arrdus

"So, I dropped from eighth to sixteenth in over twenty years of absence?"

"We took into account your being held prisoner by Piatous 191 and counted it as extenuating circumstances."

Omega had a lingering, questioning expression on his face, which Mercurius satiated.

"The Organizers, as those with the markings are known, have more secrets than even Faulk. I've always assumed that there is magic at the heart of their knowledge base. Still, they have never confirmed or denied my suspicions."

Next was Brock's invitation.

BROCK Sepatia:

Currently ranked as the #3 Fighter in Arrdus

"Look, Omega. They even put my surname on here, which I haven't heard spoken or seen written since I was a child."

As Omega was busy reading Mercurius's invitation, wondering what the tournament would be like, the Organizer tapped him on the shoulder.

"Omega, you also have an invitation."

"Do I? I've only fought in one official tournament."

Omega grabbed his invitation.

"Whenever someone kills a ranked person, that survivor automatically takes over the ranking of the deceased," explained the Organizer.

OMEGA:

Currently ranked as the #4 Fighter in Arrdus (Defeated Jaxius (Previous #4 Fighter)).

Omega was surprised but also found himself excited at the prospect of battling the best on the continent.

Omega showed his invitation to the others.

"Wow, number four. You killed Jaxius… he wasn't a bad guy, but I doubt the world will miss him much. The Coalition will be gunning for you, though," said Brock.

"The Coalition?"

"Jaxius was four, so I assume the others are not far behind. The Rahminian Coalition is made up of five fighters... well, now four fighters from Rahm that always stick together in and outside of the tournaments. They find it beneficial to hunt in packs, for lack of a better phrase."

"Yes. I am prohibited from revealing others' rankings. Still, those specific fighters will want to avenge their fallen member," explained the strange man.

"Well, I must be off now. Remember, in two months' time, the tournament starts. While it's not mandatory, we encourage all fighters to take part, and we provide exceptional incentive."

"Money?" asked Omega, with the tournament in Rahm being his only experience.

"Nay. Information. Everyone has a question. One that is burning in their very soul. We can and will answer any single question that the winner of the tournament has."

The man looked at each of them, including Karah and Jasmine, still asleep in the wagon. Omega noticed that the foreign characters on his face were changing quite autonomously.

"For you, Mercurius... Your question is the same as ever. Who is Piatous's spy amongst the elders that constantly puts your mother in danger? An answer we've known for decades."

The man looked at Brock next.

"Your question has changed a few times over the years, but right now, it is: how is it possible for that lady sleeping in the wagon to have worn the Goddess Armor? The answer is as easy as you think it is," said the mysterious man as he shrugged his shoulders.

"Even though you cannot participate in the tournament, young princess, I also could answer your question... I will, in fact, for no fee."

"What question? As a lover of literature, I always have many questions." Karah did not sound particularly convincing.

The man leered at her for a moment. Before Omega became upset, he answered:

"The answer is yes, he will remember, and yes, it will be soon. What comes after is not so easily obtainable and not for free."

Of course, nobody knew what the man was referencing, but Karah walked away without saying a word.

Omega was going to pursue, but the man interrupted his thoughts.

"Not to worry, Mr. Omega, you will know her question soon enough. I can tell you are a greedy man, having more than a few questions with utmost desire. It's up to you which one, but if I were you, I would ask who your parents are and where you come from. The answer can shape the fortune and misfortune of more than a few."

The man jumped into his saddle before Omega could continue.

"Remember, two months. The location details are in the invitation. Farewell, three ranked fighters. I trust you will survive your mission in Irkdale and make the tournament on time."

As the man rode off, Omega was still looking at his invitation, while the other two were getting ready to depart for Stenum and then Irkdale.

Around the same time as Omega got his invitation, a similar-looking, painted-face-man walked through Culver's throne room, towards the emperor.

"Your Majesty," said the painted-face man as he gave a respectful bow.

"Ah, it is time again. My fifth answered question in a row is a forgone conclusion."

Because of Omega, Thomascus had been beyond livid, but he finally received some good news.

"Your Majesty. Because you have been such an excellent participant in our fighting festivals, I will give you a piece of information that you have desired as of late."

"Yes? Out with it."

"The one you seek has received his invitation also. If Faulk doesn't kill him in Irkdale, you will have your chance at the tournament."

Thomascus was all smiles as the man exited the main hall.

On a small island, just east of the capital of Gradon, a very plain woman in her late twenties received an ornate envelope from a hawk.

Winfred Adrid:

Currently ranked as the #14 Fighter in Arrdus (Once again, the only Female Fighter on the List of Invitees).

She showed the letter to her brother, who was heaving a cast net.

"Think you can win this time? You've been training like mad since the last tournament. So much so that even old Drune said he had nothing left to teach you."

Winfred shrugged. "The emperor's son just arrived. He looks strong, even though he's young. Perhaps if I befriend him, I can get some valuable feedback from one trained by the first and second strongest."

At the Tower of Rahm, there were two of the Faithful that received their invitations. The Commander of the Eagle Battalion and tenth-ranked fighter, Landon Neer. Also, his number two and twelfth-ranked fighter, Arlen Samyn.

They were both known, even amongst the Faithful, for their brutality towards nonconformers. Because Landon was a commander, his position dictated speaking. The standard practice of silence did not apply to him.

"Finally, we will have another chance to spread the Seven's mercy upon the other fighters. I pray to Desitine that bastard Brock shows up this time. I will have my revenge."

Landon had a large scar going almost from ear to ear across his neck, which twitched anytime Brock's name was mentioned.

Arlen simply nodded and kneeled in front of a statue of Melchior to pray.

A familiar face, outside of Velantosse castle, received an invitation of his own, unexpectedly.

Captain Cross:

Currently ranked as the #15 Fighter in Arrdus (News of Your Abilities Have Spread and a Spot was Open).

Cross was out scouting and protecting the perimeter, per usual, when the hawk dropped his invitation.

"Hmm. I've heard of these tournaments, and while it would be an enjoyable experience, I cannot leave my post."

As Cross continued to read the invitation, it was as if those that had written perceived his refusal to leave.

To help you decide to participate, we would like to share one possible nugget of information. We can relay to you if you win and ask us to, the location of your sister, whom you have assumed to be dead since you escaped from Irkdale.

"She's alive? I've heard from the Elders that those who run the tournaments have a seemingly inexhaustible wealth of secrets... Riley! Your brother will find you."

Over in the Capital of Braske, Thompsel, Kita, Rose, Sarah, and Silla were observing the ebb and flow of the tide, on the beach looking out at the Bay of Braske.

Just then, another man dressed in black with painted markings on his face was standing behind Thompsel.

"Your Highness," said the man, bowing sincerely.

Thompsel had participated on more than one occasion, so his appearance didn't spook him. The dates and even the years when a tournament would be held were unknown beforehand, so it was always a surprise.

He handed the crown prince a formal envelope.

Thompsel Deckler:

Currently ranked as the #2 Fighter in Arrdus.

"When is it? I always enjoy the atmosphere, but as the crown prince, I do have my own obligations."

"It is in two months. The location is in the invitation letter. We think that you will be able to help Braske with its shipbuilding and help the newest Goddess with her mission while still being able to make the tournament on time."

Silla backed up a pace or two upon hearing this strange man mention her by that moniker.

The man smiled as she backed up.

"Not to worry, my Goddess. We do not interfere, and we only share secrets with those deserving. He gave her a full 90-degree bow. Her status demanded it.

"As penance for my startling you, I will reveal some useful information. The emperor is none too pleased with your... friend. The one you call Omega. He has placed extraordinarily high bounties on his head and rewards for the safe return of the one he so-called kidnapped. The princess, Karah. Emperor Thomascus will be at the tournament, and so too, we hope, will Omega."

Even as Silla sought more information, the man bid farewell and walked away as calmly as if he owned the world.

"Don't fret, my lady. The Organization never gives any information that they do not want to… no matter how many times you ask," said Thompsel.

"Why would Omega go to the tournament?"

"Only those invited have the option. If he was hesitant, they must have given Omega some information that he couldn't refuse. They are exceptionally convincing," responded Thompsel.

Even though Silla had her concerns about this tournament she had never heard of, now that they were in Braske, it was time to find the Guardian.

While they were alone, her grandmother told her that the Guardian should be living in the southeastern part of the capital, right near the beach. The Guardian knew that Silla was coming, and he had a rough idea of what to look for. Silla understood that *he* would have to make contact with her.

"Okay, this is as far as I can accompany you, my lady. I have some official business to attend to, but I would be honored to aid you in the quest that brought you here if my duties allow."

"Thank you very much, Your Highness." As Silla attempted to bow, Thompsel lightly grabbed her arms and helped her up.

"I am not worthy, my lady. Not from you."

"Why do you think so? What did you see when I touched your head?" asked Silla, who had been questioning the crown prince's behavior since that night.

"A tale for when we have more time, my lady."

"I'll hang out with the girls, brother. I'm not one for official duties, anyhow."

Thompsel gave his sister a stern look before leaving.

"Don't make things difficult for my lady while I'm gone."

As the crown prince departed towards the leadership hall, the girls decided to enjoy the beach for a while.

None of them had seen a beach, with white sand and the tides' ever-constant movement, other than Kita.

Looking around, there were many docks, sprawling the crescent inlet of the bay. The area was always busy, from before sunrise until deep into the evening. Braske was the international trade hub with ships from as far away as Drakeon, far to east.

Braske was also the most diversified in terms of race. There were always jobs with all the different ships and all that cargo, so many foreign nations' people came and stayed.

The Bank of International Currency Exchange was also in the capital of Braske. There were many underground vaults where some of the wealthiest, most successful people in the world kept their valuables.

Braske was popular amongst the elite of the elite because it was not a monarchy. Monarchs often took advantage of their position and cleared out banks during wartime or famine and would say that it was for the realm.

As the girls were walking around, always heading east along the beach, they could see the gulls and pelicans diving at the schools of baitfish. They could see different crabs building their homes in the hot, moist sand, not being bothered by tides that came in and continuously destroyed their hard work. They accepted that there are things beyond their control, unlike most people.

Kita had been quiet for the last half hour while the others commented on the new and exciting views, smells, and experiences.

Silla had noticed the worried look, and it was mostly a look of feeling useless. Kita knew that what she felt in her heart was right, but she began to blame Omega for even being able to forget her, no matter the reason.

This selfish feeling made her feel unworthy of his previous love, which made her resent him, Silla, and the whole situation.

Silla was beginning to understand how Kita must feel and how she would feel if their roles were switched. This also made her understand how Omega must have thought in the beginning.

You are very selfish, Silla. Shouldn't a Goddess be more benevolent and self-sacrificial?

When Silla was beginning to have an epiphany of how her thoughts and actions needed to be more magnanimous, she saw someone walking towards her.

A man with no top on, and only some shorts that went to the knee, walked towards her and the other girls. He was tall. At least as tall as Thompsel, but he was slenderer, having lean muscle instead of bulk. He had short black hair and handsome dark green eyes. He had a medium tan. Silla figured that he walked around with no shirt on the beach often.

As he got closer, Silla could see the very familiar ornate V tattoo that he had on his rock-hard abs.

"Goddess," was all he said as he reached down and grabbed Silla's hand and kissed the top of it. He looked up at her while he was smiling, which was almost always. Silla thought that he had a lovely smile and that he was very dashing.

As the other girls walked over and stood next to Silla, she quickly introduced them.

"This is Kita," Silla said, but as he reached for her hand, she pulled it away.

"That won't be happening."

The man smiled and nodded, next looking at Sarah.

"This is Sarah." The man reached down and kissed her hand, which made her feel strange.

Now the man was looking at Rose.

"This is my best friend, Rose."

"A fitting name for someone so beautiful."

As Rose waited for him to kiss her hand, he didn't move, just stared into her eyes. By far the most mature and experienced, even Rose found herself embarrassed after a moment, looking away.

"My name is Jack. I am the Guardian of the Goddess Ring."

"How did you know that I was the reincarnation?"

Jack looked into Silla's eyes for what seemed an eternity. "I'm very intuitive. As soon as I saw you, I knew. You have this... glow about you. It's unlike anything I have ever experienced... not of this world, one could say."

Kita noticed that Jack was very casual and personable.

"You don't seem like others from your group. Everyone can see your tattoo. You are as carefree as me, even with such an important task."

"Princess Kita. As the eldest daughter of the emperor, you, yourself, should have a plethora of important responsibilities, all of which you forgo for your... freedoms. Besides, those that know who I am wouldn't dare bother me."

Jack always said things, whether positive or negative, foreboding or magnanimous, with a confident, borderline arrogant smile. People either liked or disliked this, with few having a gray opinion.

"You know the members of the Imperial bloodline?" asked Silla.

"Ay. I'm much more interested in the movements of the important people, compared to other Velantosse members. I think that I will prove invaluable to you, my Goddess. I'm not sure if you know this, but as a Guardian, alive during the time of reincarnation, my main purpose is not to protect the item I've been charged with. It is to travel with and protect the Goddess herself. As we meet other Guardians, they will also join our cause, and we will start to build a small army."

"That's good, Silla. We were concerned about there being so few of us on this quest of ours," said Rose, looking at Jack.

"Not to worry, Rose. Even though there are many enemies of the Goddess, some known to you and some who will surface later, we of the Velantosse will always put the Goddess first."

"Can we go to your house, Jack? I'd like to see it."

"That's more forward than I expected, Goddess ..." After a pause, only Rose seemed to catch the joke, so Jack continued.

"Okay, I have something to share with you about the ring, anyway."

After walking for a few minutes, they came to a sizeable house, right on the beach. Other Velantosse Guardians lived off the beaten path, being very minimal, but Jack was the opposite. His house had a maidservant, and he had many trinkets. Being right on the beachfront, Jack had some small boats right outside his home. His house had multiple rooms, including a study, a midsized library, and an armory.

As they entered, Melissa, the maidservant, greeted them.

"Hello, Jack, and guests."

Melissa was quite beautiful. She had the blondest hair that the girls had ever seen, and mixed with her black eyes, it was a unique combination that forced you to stare.

"My lord, is this …?"

"That's right, it is the Goddess that I have been waiting for."

"I don't think you should be relaying such information. Isn't it safer for me to remain a secret for as long as possible?"

"Goddess, you don't quite understand. Very soon, you will be the most well-known person in the world. Everyone will either love you and worship you, or they will try endlessly to kill you for nothing more than existing. Thousands fear your existence and see it as a test from the Seven… a test of devoutness."

"They won't even give me a chance to prove that I will not do them any harm?"

Jack tilted his head slightly and nodded.

"It's a power struggle. Those that control others based on their standing in the church have no desire to share that control with a blasphemer, as it is. That's not even mentioning some of the kingdom's likely reactions. It's a shame, but it has been such for thousands of years. It's likely every reincarnation in history, except for the one that existed during the dissolution of the church, had to do battle with and survive or fall against their respective Piatous."

"Dissolution of the church?"

"It's a long story that I don't have the expertise to tell, but there was a period, about four thousand years ago, in which there were no Piatous, and the church was ran by the monarchies of the nations. There was a war in which the State Powers joined the Velantosse and annihilated the Faithful. The rest is a tale for another time."

"Okay. Can you bring the ring to me now? I'm very interested in seeing it."

Jack hesitated. "I would. But it's no longer in my possession."

"I doubt you know this, but Braske is not all that you see."

"Where is the ring, Jack?" Silla was not interested in sightseeing.

"I am sorry, Goddess. I lost the ring in a bet with the King of Underworld."

XXX

In the Breen area, which is about one hundred miles south of the Ardian Sea, Pike was observing the finishing of the building of the 1,000 warships of Emperor Grexle's Exodus Army. Grexle was not around. He had told Pike, whom he had promoted to Supreme Commander and given full power of the troops, that he would be traveling to Drakeon and would be gone for the next half year. He would be back before it was time to invade.

"Supreme Commander. We are at the final stage, and it is almost time to begin transport," said Captain Xavier, leader of the armada's central battalion and captain of the *Elizabeth.*

The ships were built uniformly in structure, but each captain could add their own heraldry or designs to distinguish amongst each other when at sea.

Their building took over one million trees, decimating almost 50 percent of the forestry in Zarrek. It was a steep price to pay, but Grexle knew that seedlings could be planted in their place. Food in Zarrek, however, was much more challenging to grow than trees.

As Supreme Commander Pike was chatting to the captains of various warships, it all started to become real. He knew that it would take months to move all the ships, but they had chosen Breen because from that location to the sea was very flat, firm land, perfect for building the wooden lanes in which the ships could traverse. It would take raw manpower from both soldiers and slaves and even captains to tug those ships to the shore.

In Faruqh, Piatous was having an audience with Queen Regent Felicia.

"Your Highness, it is paramount that I have your support against the blasphemous one. It is good for both of us, *especially* if you desire the continued backing of the church."

"Are you threatening the Queen Regent?" asked the Minister of the Interior, Jarrod Palmer.

"I don't answer questions from dogs. Be a good boy and take a hint from The Faithful," said Piatous as he pointed to his retinue. There were six Faithful that traveled with Piatous. They were silent and ominous in their blue robes.

"How dare you!?" reacted Minister Palmer, but the Queen Regent bid him exit the room.

"My apologies, Piatous. Minister Palmer was impulsive."

Piatous smiled, showing that gold tooth.

"It's okay. There are always those that behave as if they are above their station. It's simplest and most effective not to enable such behavior. I have been informed that you will have a guest very soon."

"Yes, Princess Kansel should be arriving today. She will stay here and marry my son, Mason, once they both become of age."

"After the death of the king, there are those that would take advantage of a child being king. You have done what is best for the future of your lineage. You've heard of the reincarnation of the blasphemous one that occurs every five hundred years, yes?"

"I've heard that rumor before, but it always sounded so farfetched."

"It is true, and she has finally shown herself. My spies have relayed that she will first go to Braske and then likely to either Culver or Gradon Archipelago. I guess Gradon because what she is looking for in Culver resides in Thomascus's possession. As you know, he is not to be trifled with."

"What is she after?"

"That is not important. They are trinkets made by a Devil and passed off as divine. Her existence is a test from Hespa herself. Some of my predecessors had claimed that the resurrected one's powers were fake or given to her by an evil being. Still, many of us know that Hespa, the creator of everything, puts these powers in a girl every 500 years to test our faith and belief. As if any true believer could accept that a mere mortal would be a Goddess. It is such an affront to Hespa that I cannot let it pass."

Before Felicia could retort, Eunuch Humbre came in.

"Queen Regent. Princess Kansel and her retinue are here to meet Your Highness."

"Ah, excellent. I have been looking forward to her arrival with great hope. Send her in."

Princess Kansel and the captain of her personal guard, Fradius, walked into the throne room.

The Queen Regent walked hurriedly to meet them halfway. She was quite elegant today in her olive-colored gown and emerald crown.

Kansel was the youngest daughter of the Deckler family, and she had the same characteristics as her sisters and mother. Kansel's eyes were unique in their shade of blue compared to her sisters. Her eyes were tourmaline in shade and quite unforgettable. Her red hair was the same shade as her sisters and mother. Her favorite person in the world was Kita, and she mirrored her hair, having never had it cut or styled, it was almost as long as Kita's.

"Queen Regent. I'm sorry about my delay. I was reluctant to travel to a foreign place, upending my life. My sister Kita finally convinced me that this was for the betterment of the world and that you would take good care in making me feel comfortable."

The Queen Regent, after getting close to Kansel, stopped and gave her a small bow.

"Of course. I will love you as a daughter and make sure that you get settled in as soon as possible."

Before they could continue, Piatous walked up, uninvited, as was his wont.

"Young Princess Kansel. This is our first time meeting. I am Piatous 191, the one responsible for all faithful and those who see the Sacred Seven Divines as the only entities worthy of worship. Are *you* a believer?"

Piatous asked that question in such a standoffish tone that only a fool wouldn't pick up on it.

Luckily, Thompsel had schooled her on dealing with figures in high places, and even Piatous specifically.

"Of course, Your Grace. Although my personal favorite is Desitine, I recognize all seven as those beings that create, shape, and control everything. Worshipping of others is an affront that must be punished."

Piatous knew that her words were not her own, but he also did not see the benefits of accosting her.

Piatous reached down and grabbed Kansel's hand and kissed it.

He then gave her a smile. "Good girl."

Kansel didn't much like Piatous's leering... making her feel like she might be eaten by him.

Queen Regent Felicia didn't appreciate it either. Before any more words could be batted back and forth, Piatous got a message and left the hall.

"I'm sorry about that, Princess. Piatous has always been very arrogant, and I've heard rumors that he has many wives, all of them quite young."

"It's okay, Godmother. My brother would skin him alive if he ever touched me."

In the beautiful throne room in Rahm's capital, the king, sitting alone, was seemingly waiting for some news to come.

A retainer, Mr. Baker, walked briskly into the room up the long aisle slanted ever so slightly upward.

"My King, I have brought the news you have been so patient in waiting for."

Mr. Baker had a scroll in his hand. It was clear that the scroll had been traveling from place to place. Scuff marks, folds, and creases didn't make the king any less enthusiastic.

"Excellent, Mr. Baker. When they put their minds to it, those Jarls in the free lands *can* be efficient. Let me check the signatures."

Upon unraveling the scroll, the King of Rahm was delighted to see every Jarl had signed.

"I expected Jarls Brodugan, Fise, and Hjolmer to sign, but I expected to have to negotiate more with Risen and especially with Blackbow."

There were five noteworthy holds between Balistine, the continent to the west of Arrdus, and the fertile communal lands west of Rahm. Although the holds were officially independent, they had long ago made an oath of fealty, if ever called upon to do so, to the kingdom of Rahm.

"Now that I have the support of the Jarls, the next step in my plan can finally commence. I'm not sure why the emperor and his son would play all their cards in such a cocky manner, but they have awakened a fire in me that I did not know existed. When Drune asked why it had to be Thomascus, I had an epiphany. Rahm is more than capable of ruling the world… and we will start with ruling the harvest."

Omega and his group were now in Stenum, at Brock's safe house. It was not really big enough for five people, and it seemed very ordinary, but there was more than met the eye.

A hidden tunnel ran along the river behind the safe house a few yards and opened into a small cavern. The cavern was larger than the house, and it had different supplies, weapons, and armor.

"The most important thing in here is the information that I've been collecting on Irkdale over the past few years," said Brock as he tidied up some papers that were haphazardly splayed on the table and floor.

"You used to be fairly neat… I guess when you live alone for long enough, you *do* stop caring," pointed out Mercurius as Brock was finding all the intelligence he had been gathering.

Brock was busy mumbling and was clearly upset.

"Damnit! Somebody has been down here."

"How long has this place been deserted?" asked Jasmine as she helped him clean up.

Brock had multiple safehouses in Faruqh, so it wasn't rare for one to go unused for years.

"Maybe three years. I scatter the most crucial information between all my safehouses, so if one falls, all is not lost. The only thing I always take with me is the armor." He pointed at Jasmine.

She had it strapped to her back, much like a knapsack. She had wanted to wear it, but Brock wouldn't allow it.

"Is the material still pertinent, being three years old?" asked Karah.

"I'm not sure… but we won't be coming back here for quite some time."

After looking through his belongings, Brock realized that nothing was missing.

"You said Piatous knew there was a Guardian in Yewce, but it was unlikely he knew it was you. Perhaps he got wind of this safehouse also," pointed out Mercurius.

"Maybe… he obviously didn't come, personally, and his agent certainly didn't know the difference between benign and detrimental information. They didn't touch the weapons or armor, so it wasn't a common thief."

Brock was convincing himself that all was well, despite the break-in.

Omega was sitting near the cavern entrance, eyes closed, clearly concentrating on something different from the group.

Karah sat in front of him and put her hands on his knees.

"What's on your mind?"

Omega gave no reaction. Omega had noticed minutes earlier that something was happening with his previously lost memories. Although not entirely back, the haze was lifting. The jumbled images now had a more linear and chronological sorting.

Is Silla finally giving back my memories?

Suddenly his eyes sprang open.

"The letter! Maybe it has words now …"

Omega began fumbling through his pockets—breast, and pants, but they were empty. Since getting to Culver, he had all but forgotten that letter.

"Have any of you seen a folded letter? Perhaps it fell out at camp."

Brock and Mercurius shook their heads. "Sorry, no."

Jasmine didn't respond, wanting to give Karah her chance to be honest with Omega.

Karah reached into her pocket and pulled out the folded letter. She handed it to him without reluctance. She was confident that he would ultimately choose her no matter what happened between Omega and her sister.

"Thank you, Karah. I can always count on you. Did it fall out while we were traveling?"

"No. I've had it since I dressed your wounds in the prison cell. It fell out when you got undressed."

Jasmine and the others felt a little awkward but knew that silence was their best friend.

"Ah, that makes sense. We have been on the run for days since then, so it slipped your mind also."

Omega was unknowingly giving her every chance to cover up and lie about the letter.

"No. I opened it that same night, after leaving. It is from my older sister, after all."

Omega had assumed, since the beginning, that Karah was not the one from his blocked memories; being able to hear her name was the main trigger. He quickly realized that something about her slowed down his anxiety about many things, including his memories.

"I don't know the relationship or what feelings you have for her, but I won't lose, and I won't lie."

Omega got up and stepped towards the tunnel entrance.

Karah thought for a moment that he was walking away from her, and panic snuck in.

Fortunately, at that moment, he turned and held out his hand.

"Are you coming?" he asked as he extended his tangible invitation.

Karah gave an audible acceptance, and the two made their way back out.

"Sorry, I was starting to feel too closed in down there."

Omega and Karah were sitting outside the safehouse, leaning under the shade of the roof and nearby lemon tree.

Omega unfolded the letter. An even mixture of hope and disappointment filled him. There was a total of six visible words on the letter, which was an improvement.

"Is this your first time reading the letter?"

"I can't read it, even now." Omega shifted to the left, where the letter was in plain view of Karah.

"You can see words, yes?"

Karah was confused by the question.

"Yes. My sister's handwriting isn't perfect, but I can see a letter full of sentiment."

Omega laughed, although it came out in a pessimistic tone.

"I only see six words. I see Omega, a, time, hands, blood, and Culver. Although to you, these have a specific order, to me, it's just dotted on a page."

"How is that possible?" Karah was both concerned and intrigued.

"It's a long story. When we meet Silla in the future, I will be able to explain it better."

"Silla?"

"Yes. Her father saved me from a life of endless torment. After specific events, she and I came to share our everlasting souls with one another."

Omega still didn't realize what that sort of comment would make a potential lover feel in their heart. Before it could be expounded upon, the others came out of the tunnel.

Omega folded the letter and put it in his pocket.

Brock and the others exited the tunnel. "Let's get some sleep, and then tomorrow we can depart for Irkdale."

"I almost forgot, Brock. What are we doing in Irkdale?" asked Omega, who found that he didn't like being in the dark about things.

"Well… our goal, crazy as it sounds, is to confront Faulk and steal something from him."

Mercurius chimed in: "So we are finally taking that back?"

"Aye, he's been wearing the Goddess Amulet for far too long," answered Brock.

A couple of hours earlier in Braske, Silla was confused and angry.

"How could a Guardian wager something as important as my ring!?"

Even under Silla's ire, Jack had his charismatic smile. "I thought I would win."

The group was dumbfounded.

"Are you sure you are a Guardian? What are the selection criteria?" asked Rose.

"It's a long-standing tradition that Guardians volunteer. It's not a problem, my Goddess. We can enter the underworld and explain the situation to the king."

"Would a beggar-king even listen!?" asked Silla, barely containing her anger.

"I wouldn't call him that once we get down there. He is very much a real king with real power. But, concerning monarchs, he is fairer than most."

Jack was looking at Kita when he said that.

"Are you implying my father is more short-sighted than a cave-dwelling king?"

Jack cocked his head to the side, just a touch, and leaned in closer to Kita. Just looking at her, long enough to make everyone uncomfortable.

"You already know the answer to that, Princess."

Jack backed off and chuckled. "I'm just joking with you."

"You're lucky Omega isn't here. He might not remember me now, but he wouldn't let you get so close to me."

Even though Jack was generally kind, he did enjoy annoying people to no end.

"Unless I've misheard, isn't he having some wonderful alone time with your sister?"

"Enough!" shouted Silla.

She wasn't interested in any of their nonsense. All that memory stuff was already troubling enough, so adding to it was not high on her list of priorities.

"Kita. I appreciate your company, and I know Rose likes you, but I need Jack, so if you cannot get along, then please go back to your brother."

Rose and Sarah were happy to stay silent, letting the immature ones finish their quarrels.

"So, you steal his memories of me, and now you want to kick me out. I must have annoyed you in a past life, *Goddess*."

There was apparent mocking in her tone.

After a deep breath, a sigh, and some ludicrous laughter, Silla finally let go.

She opened her eyes after a moment.

"There... I've given back those memories of you... as far as I can tell."

"Truly!?" asked Kita in a now anxiously excited tone.

"I think so. I genuinely wanted to return them just now, with no remorse in my heart. I think that's the criteria for creation... or reconstruction in this case."

"Once the seal wears off completely, Goddess, you will be able to create at will... at least that's how I perceive the magic to work, based on my studies," explained Jack.

"You seem to know a lot about me, Jack."

"I've told you that I am very interested in the important figures in the world. I have a knack for making people uncomfortable, so please don't take it to heart.

Anyway, it is still early, and we have a large underworld to explore... Shall we depart?"

Kita interrupted before Silla could answer.

"I'd like to send word to Thompsel before we head that way. He will find us after he finishes his business. Where is the entrance to this underworld?"

As Jack was walking towards the nearest wall, he grabbed a tall wooden staff, quite ornate in its design. Although it was wooden, there was some iron at the tip, in a quirky design. There were some etchings on it, in some foreign language.

"There are many entrances, Princess. I have already given instructions to inform your brother of our route. The crown prince is very intuitive and cunning... and he has a newly acquired *skill*, so I doubt he needs my instructions."

As the group was leaving Jack's home, they were all looking at the staff.

"That's quite the craftsmanship, Jack," said Sarah, who enjoyed weaponry of many different types.

"You have a good eye, Sarah. I never go anywhere without this staff. Although I have magic, I find that using it can bring more annoyances than it fixes as the world is now. This staff has saved me more times than I can remember."

"What's your magic preference, Jack? The resonance chamber brought out ice for me," said Rose as she formed a small ball of ice in her cupped hands.

"Ice can be beneficial in many diverse situations. It can also be dangerous to the user, so stick close to me."

As Jack said that, he put his hand around her waist and pulled her in closer.

"Many people prefer to tap into different fields and subfields of magic to give themselves options, no matter the troubles they find. My dream is to be the greatest fire-magic user that has ever existed."

As Rose was walking hip-to-hip with Jack, she found herself getting quite hot, sweat rolling down her shoulders and neck.

"Is that you putting off this insane heat?"

Jack winked at her.

It wasn't far to the nearest entrance of the underworld. There was a seemingly abandoned shack that actually had a descending staircase, just inside the door.

"We don't need a password or anything?" asked Silla, still not fully appreciating the possibilities of the underworld.

"Nope. Other entrances lead to more... private areas of the underworld. Those are often guarded, but this is one of the "free-entries" that anybody can use to come or go from His Majesty's kingdom."

As they descended, the staircase went downward for no less than ten minutes. There were some decline changes, spiraling, and forking. Eventually, it led to a broad set of iron doors with two guards posted.

"Welcome to the underworld. Behave and follow the king's laws, and you can have an amazing experience. The mayor of Blie's Avenue wanted me to convey to newcomers that there are homes available for purchase if you are interested."

Upon stepping through the doors, what they saw was jaw-dropping, to put it mildly.

Back in Stenum, Omega and Karah were sleeping right near the entrance of the safehouse.

Since the time Omega had left Karah in the protected shell back in Lansing, she had taken to sleeping, practically on top of Omega, which he didn't mind.

Jasmine had the bed inside the safehouse, while Brock and Mercurius were on the floor. It was the dead of night, still three hours or more from sunrise.

"HELP!!" came a screech from quite a distance, but it was audible enough to wake Karah. As she looked around, waiting to hear what woke her, she noticed that her body was slowly rising and falling with Omega's breathing.

She stuck both hands on his cheeks, her face only an inch away from his. She kissed him.

"Wake up, Omega." She tapped both of her hands on his cheeks, and his eyes opened.

"It's still some time from sunup. What's the matter?"

Omega couldn't sit up in this position, so he just laid there, looking at her. Her spectacles were inching down her nose. Omega found a desire to kiss her.

As he lifted his head to do so, they both heard the screech, albeit from far in the distance.

"HELP ME! Monster!"

Omega looked in the direction of the voice. His heart raced from this beautiful woman lying on top of him. *Should I continue with my desires, or should I help that person in distress?*

The decision, however, was taken out of his hands.

Karah got up and went inside the house to wake up everyone.

Omega felt a tinge of guilt, as he was intending on choosing desire. After a big yawn and stretch, he got up and heard some different voices, these much closer.

"What's all the commotion, Blake?"

"I heard that strange creatures are attacking the eastern side of town."

"So those queer rumors were accurate, then. We had heard about some beasts moving along the northside of the Nugle. Must be from Irkdale."

That was all Omega needed to hear to know that he had to go investigate.

Just then, Mercurius, Brock, Jasmine, and Karah came out of the safehouse.

"What's the ruckus this late at night?" asked a still closed-eyed Jasmine.

At this point, it seemed nobody in the town was still asleep. It was beginning to get chaotic—too many screams from near and far to distinguish fear and uncertainty from immediate threat and harm.

"Strange beasts from Irkdale have made it to the eastern edge of town if the locals are correct," said Omega as he was trying to look to the east.

There were fires here and there, but he couldn't make anything out past a hundred feet.

"Faulk seems to be going ahead with his plans. I knew he was creating fearsome beasts, but I assumed a more glorious release. He usually enjoys watching the show," explained Brock, who had finally shaken off the last remnants of sleep.

"Okay. Brock, Omega, and I will go handle the beasts. You two don't know how to fight, and you haven't unclogged your magic channels... so stay put in the safehouse," said Mercurius with heavy undereye bags.

"I prefer that she stays by my side," said Omega as he pulled her closer.

"We don't know what's over there. Knowing Faulk, it is terrible. They will be safer in the cavern than in the thick of danger," explained Brock.

"I wasn't asking," said Omega as he and Karah started walking towards the eastern side of town.

"If you two happen to fall, I can just put on the armor, and none of the beasties could hurt me, right?" asked Jasmine as she started following the other two.

Mercurius and Brock could only look at each other incredulously.

"Let's go, I guess."

As the group got closer to the eastern side of town, the screams became more tragic, and there were homes on fire. The east side of the city had a large row of closely-knit dwellings and shops, and behind that was a large clearing where the bulk of screams was coming from.

Upon squeezing between a blacksmith's shop and the shop's owner's house, they emerged in the clearing.

"What the fuck!?" was all that Brock could muster at what they saw.

Omega had his own awakening at just that moment.

"So, her name is Kita..."

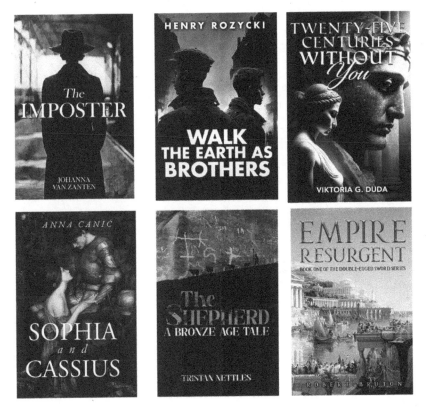